Alpha Queen

The Alphas think they need a Mate. What they really need is a Queen

USA TODAY BESTSELLING AUTHOR

REBEKAH R. GANIERE

Alpha Queen

Rebekah R. Ganiere

Alpha Queen © 2025 Rebekah R. Ganiere

All rights reserved. No part of this publication may be reproduced, distributed, or transmitted in any form or by any means, including photocopying, recording, or other electronic or mechanical methods, without the prior written permission of the publisher, except in the case of brief quotations embodied in critical reviews and certain other noncommercial uses permitted by copyright law. For permission requests, write to the publisher, addressed "Attention: Permissions Coordinator".

This book is a work of fiction. The names, characters, places and incidents are fictitious and are not to be construed as real in any way. Any resemblance to persons, living or dead, actual events, locales or organizations is entirely coincidental.

ISBN: 978-1-63300-086-5
ISBN: 978-1-63300-092-6

All ARTWORK by VWZDesigns.com

DEDICATION

For those who refuse to be ashamed of what they love to read!

CHAPTER ONE

ARES

A sharp set of fangs pierced Ares' shoulder. He roared, grabbed the rogue by his jaws, and pried them apart until they snapped. Then ripped the rogue's throat out.

Another rogue took the first's place, but Ares shoved his fist through the wolf's chest and yanked his heart out.

"Ares!"

He turned as a rogue slammed a chair on Apollo's head. Ares jumped over his brother and flung the rogue across the room.

"No one kills my brother but me," he roared.

Apollo bled profusely from several places, and his skin turned ashy. Another rogue raced at Ares, but Ares caught him by the throat and ripped his head clean off. Blood sprayed over Ares and rained down on Apollo.

He scanned the room for River and caught the hem of her pink gown as Titan disappeared with her into the hallway.

All around, Alphas and Betas battled rogues. Mates hurried from the room, but several had already been taken down.

There were too many rogues. They were outnumbered at least five to one.

Ares' gut clenched. He had no idea Titan had collected so many.

Apollo dragged himself next to Ares. "What the hell are you doing? Where is she?"

Ares pointed.

"What the fuck are you waiting for?"

Ares looked at his glassy-eyed brother, who could not even sit up.

Less poison coursed through Ares' veins, slowing and weakening him. It wouldn't be long before he himself lost consciousness. He couldn't imagine how Apollo wasn't already blacked out and convulsing.

Ares' vision clouded as he inspected Apollo. No. He was not going to lose them both. Apollo may be an asshole. But he was Ares' asshole.

Suddenly, shots rang out as Theo took down three more rogues. More men rushed into the room. Bloodied and ripped apart, both his and Apollo's men tore into the room like a tidal wave. They cut their way to the front of the room, taking out rogues as they went. Theo and Santiago grabbed Ares.

"We need to get you out of here."

Ares shook his head. "We need to save as many Alphas and mates as we can. And to keep as many rogues alive as possible."

Santiago scanned the melee. "Where's your Princess?"

"Titan."

A rogue rushed them, but Santiago pulled the trigger, and the wolf dropped.

Lachlan limped forward. "You're hurt."

"Not for long." Ares leaned on Theo and took a deep breath before digging a talon into a bullet wound and yanking the metal free. He did the same with the second bullet in his knee. Damn. That one was going to take time to heal.

With the bullets free, his wolf roared and clawed to be let out. Ares wasn't sure taking out the bullets would be enough, but he had to try. He'd heal faster in Lycan form.

"Silas, Thomas, pull Apollo out now! Santiago, Theo, and the rest of you save the Alphas," Ares called. "Don't kill all the traitors. I want answers. I am going after my mate."

"I should go with you," said Santiago.

"No." Ares stripped off his shirt. "I need you to take charge here. This is something I need to do myself."

"But what if-"

"You have Apollo. So make sure he lives."

Santiago wanted to say more, but Ares growled. He didn't have time for this.

"Go!" A ripple pulsed through Ares, and his Alpha command could not be ignored.

Santiago burst from his suit, fur sprouting all over his body as he leapt to the middle of the floor.

Ares shifted and raced for the door.

"Find her!" Apollo's words echoed down the hallway as he headed for the front entrance.

He had a single goal. Find River and rip Titan apart in the process.

CHAPTER TWO

A Week Later

TITAN

Titan strode down the stairs to the basement holding a tray of food. With each step, he moved closer to the door that held his mate, the more conflicted he became. Before he'd met her, it had been simple. Gather the rogues. Plan an attack. Take the throne. However, things had become infinitely more complicated.

Mine. Not theirs. Mine.

Titan fought his wolf with everything he had. His wolf had done this. Had ruined everything. It was because of his wolf that River rejected and hated him. He wouldn't let that happen again.

Titan approached the door, and the rogue outside bowed.

"Austin."

"Highness."

"Has she asked for anything?"

Austin shook his head. "She hasn't made a sound."

Titan sighed and nodded. It had been the same answer from every rogue who had stood guard over the last week. Titan wasn't sure how much longer he could take the silence.

Austin handed him the key to the door.

Titan balanced the tray in one hand and unlocked the door with the other. He pushed the door inward and waited.

She curled up on the floor in the same place she had been every time he'd come to check on her in the last seven days. If he hadn't heard her heart beating, he would have thought she was dead.

His wolf growled and sniffed the air, even though River's scent had been muted by the blockers he supplied in her water. No change.

Titan crossed to the table in the corner and set the tray down.

He waited. Her breathing was even but not deep. She was awake and aware of his presence.

Her refusal to acknowledge him had his wolf growling louder.

Shut it.

Titan swallowed and drew in a breath, forcing himself to relax. The room swam with the scents of unwashed clothing and stale air. At least the scents of the twins were mostly faded from her, leaving her scent of cherries and vanilla behind. That was a relief. It had been obvious she'd been with both of them before he'd taken her, and that alone had him wanting to kill his half-brothers. But he'd promised her he wouldn't. He still wasn't sure if the rogues had though.

After five minutes, he crouched next to her. "I assure you the bed is more than comfortable, but if it isn't to your liking, tell me what you want, and I'll buy a different one."

She kept her eyes shut, but her heartbeat kicked up.

He reached out to brush her hair from her eyes. "River-"

She caught his hand and shoved it away without looking at him.

His wolf snarled.

"You haven't eaten."

Silence.

He fought to keep his voice even. "Surely you would be more comfortable if you showered and put on some clean clothes."

"I would be more comfortable at home with my mates." They were the first words she'd spoken since being taken, and they slapped him so hard he almost fell over.

"You are home. I am your mate."

Her eyes flew open, and she bared her teeth. "I will never, ever, be your mate."

"You already are."

"You took from me what was never yours to take. That doesn't make me your mate."

"And I have apologized for that. It was-" What? Weakness? Desperation? Desire that had made him do what he did? How could he tell her that?

She eyed him intently.

He stood. "You should shower and eat. I have a surprise for you."

He turned and walked toward the door.

"I don't want a surprise."

His anger rose, and he swiped a vase of flowers from a dresser to the floor. "Why? Why can't you give me a chance?"

She leapt to her feet and rushed him. "Why didn't you give me one? A chance to find out for myself if you were to be my mate."

Her fierceness enflamed him. He wanted to touch her. To feel that passion for himself. He almost couldn't bear the fact that Ares and Apollo had felt what should have been his.

She stared at him. He opened and closed his mouth. His gut clenched.

His wolf growled and paced.

"I… wish more than anything I had," he whispered before he could stop himself.

His wolf growled. *Weak.*

Her gaze flickered with something he couldn't read, and his chest tightened. It was the same look she'd given him right before she'd rejected him, and again right after she'd kissed him to save Ares and Apollo.

He reached for her, but her palm slammed into him.

"Don't touch me." Her eyes went Omega golden but only for a second, probably because of the suppressant he was feeding her.

When she did that, it was the only time his wolf backed down. Truly backed down. He couldn't explain what happened to him when she looked at him like that, except to say that he wanted to comply. Wanted to give in to her. Wanted to please her.

"I have a surprise. I'll be back in a few hours. Shower. Eat."

"Is the surprise a police escort home?"

Titan's gut squeezed. "No."

"Is it a cellphone so I can call my mates to bring me home?"

Titan growled, and his wolf snarled. "This is your home."

"No," she said. "It's your home. It'll never be my home."

"Well then, if you are so set on going back, when I take the throne, we'll move back."

Her upper lip curled, and the fire in her eyes made a shiver run through him.

"Take the throne, don't take the throne, I don't care. All I care about is getting back to my family."

Titan clenched his fists as a string of curse words flew through his mind. He wanted to make her submit. Force her to her knees and have her obey him. But he couldn't, not with River. She would never do that. He needed to show her that their connection was real, not force her into it.

Without a word, Titan strode from the room.

He leaned on it and gulped down a breath. He'd never known pain like he had since finding and then being rejected by River. And every word she spoke was a further rejection. He wasn't sure how much more he could take.

Watching from afar for four and a half agonizing years. Seeing but never touching. Never tasting. Never having her with him. It had been what had started his desire to gather the rogues. To unite them under his rule. To have something to offer her. To give her. To make her want to stay.

Then Ares had found her, and Titan's heart had shattered all over again. She'd shown Ares her work. Had gone with him to his hotel. Had smiled and dressed up to go to the Opera with him.

Things she should have done with him. Not Ares. Him.

And then Apollo...

"How did it go?"

Titan's head whipped up. Vanessa watched him from the stairwell.

Titan growled and locked River's door before he strode up the stairs past her.

"What do you want?"

She shrugged. "Honestly? I want to know what it is about her that has all you Wolvenguard boys so happy and mushy. She doesn't seem to be anything special. If anything, I think she's rather-"

Titan pinned Vanessa to the wall by the throat.

His wolf sneered, and Titan's nails lengthened.

"If you want to keep breathing, I suggest you not finish that sentence."

Fear flashed in Vanessa's eyes, and then she smiled. "I simply meant to suggest that you seem to deserve a mate... better suited to your needs and status."

She went to touch him, but he swatted her hand away.

"She is everything I want as well as need, and as such, she is very much of my status. I am the first-born son of the Lycan king, and she is an Omega. Together we were meant to rule."

"She doesn't want you."

"Not yet. But given time, she will forget about Ares and Apollo, and the bond that I began will supersede anything she feels for them."

"She rejected you-"

"I will make her accept me. Now tell me, why did you come to find me? I told you to stay out of this area. Surely it can't be just petty jealousy. You can't be that stupid."

Something crossed her face, telling him it was jealousy that had sent her.

She rolled her eyes. "I came to tell you that the last of the rogues has returned."

"Last?"

"Yes. He says the others are... not likely to come back."

Titan growled. "Where is he?"

RIVER

RIVER WAITED UNTIL THE DOOR SHUT AND THEN SAGGED AGAINST the footboard of the bed and clutched her stomach. The food Titan brought made it roil for the millionth time. Man, sometimes she hated her shifter's super sense of smell. And being pregnant has made them even more acute.

He wanted her to eat. She scoffed. Hell, she wanted her to eat, but her body had other ideas. It had been having those other ideas the entire week. Luckily, Titan hadn't spent more than a few minutes with her at a time, so he'd only noticed that she hadn't eaten much. Not that she wasn't eating at all.

She'd taken small pieces of the food and flushed them down the toilet every day. She drank the ice water he brought, but even water was something her body had decided it no longer liked. Not that she could blame it. She had hated drinking water before getting pregnant. Still, she at least had to stay hydrated at the very least. She had wondered if she'd become dehydrated, if he would take her to a real hospital, but she doubted it. He probably had someone he'd call to give her an IV. She didn't want to take the chance.

She pressed her hand to her belly. A slight bulge in the front and an inch or so of widening in her waist were the only signs- aside from the constant vomiting, of course.

When her stomach calmed and the room stopped spinning, she sat on the bed. The bed didn't make a sound as she smooshed onto it. It took only a second, and then she sank into the foam mattress. It cocooned every curve until she felt as though she floated weightlessly. Her body involuntarily relaxed, and she sighed. She allowed herself to breathe as the mattress hugged every inch of her. For the first time in a week, everything floated away, and she just lay in complete silence, pushing all thoughts from her mind. No fear for her unborn baby. No sadness from missing her mates. No calculating how she would escape. Nothing, just… nothing.

Minutes drifted by, and she found herself falling asleep until her wolf grumbled, bringing everything back to the forefront of her mind.

Thanks a lot.

Her wolf whined.

Her wolf was right, though. River couldn't afford to let her guard down. Not for a single minute.

She reluctantly sat up and prodded the mattress. She loved it more than any bed she'd ever slept in. Too bad it had been a gift from Titan. If she'd had scissors, she'd cut it up inch by inch and left it in a pile for him. She'd have cut up or destroyed everything in the room if she'd had the energy.

The first moment she'd awakened in the room had completely confused her. It was a replica of her loft at her studio in New York. She'd thought everything she'd been through was a dream, but then she'd smelled him. And it had all flooded back.

New York. Ares. Apollo. The mating ceremony. Titan shooting both of them. The rogues. So many rogues. She'd had no idea there were so many out there.

She looked at the tray of food longingly and noticed a red can peeking out from behind a glass of ice.

Soda!

River got to her feet and hurried to the table. She snatched up the can and ripped the top open. She poured it over the ice and chugged it. For a moment, she wasn't sure her stomach would agree with her decision, but when nothing happened, she poured the rest of the soda in the glass and chugged it as well.

The taste was sweeter than she remembered; she hadn't gone without at least a soda a day for so long that it tasted different somehow.

She tossed the can in the trash and looked over the plate. Chips, a sandwich, fruit, and chocolate. A variety, as usual, but the array only seemed to punch her in the gut harder. It reminded her of the basket lunch Apollo had brought her, and of the meal she and Ares and Apollo had shared on her bed after her heat.

Those moments felt a lifetime ago, and her heart ached. Her wolf remained unusually quiet. She had been that way since River had awakened. She assumed that Titan had put her on blockers. If she figured it out how, though, she sure as hell was going to stop that.

In the almost two months she'd been off the blockers, she'd come to realize how much of a comfort her wolf was to her. Now she felt more alone than she had before she'd met her wolf.

The smell of the food soured in River's nostrils, and she turned away, but stopped and looked at the plate again… the food.

She hadn't taken a pill or been given a shot since arriving. So, the only way they could have been feeding her controlled doses of blockers was through her food.

Did that mean if she didn't eat long enough, the blockers would wear off? If so… how long could she go without eating and not harm her baby?

River threw her hands into her hair and screamed.

Stupid Titan! Why? Why was he doing this? She'd rejected him. Why was he so determined to have her? To get back at Ares and Apollo? Because he wanted the throne? Or something else? She couldn't decide.

She'd expected Titan to demand she agree to mate him the moment she'd woken up on the first night. She'd expected him to demand a lot of things, actually, but he hadn't. In truth, he'd not spent any time with her since her kidnapping.

She knew he wanted her; she'd seen it in his eyes, but there was something else there as well, something she couldn't put her finger on. An expectation of something, though she had no clue what.

River got up more easily from the bed since her body had some sugar in it. She looked down at the clothes she'd woken up in a week prior. Her shredded mating dress lay in a crumpled heap in the corner; she could only assume Titan had ripped it up. But more than that, it bothered her to think he had seen her naked and had redressed her.

She looked over at the destroyed dress, and a pang of sadness flowed through her. It had been the twins' mother's dress. She could only imagine what Ares and Apollo were going through.

She swallowed hard- if they were even still alive.

Apollo. Her precious Apollo. The last time she'd seen him, he was only semi-conscious. So many injuries and bullets. And Ares. He'd been shot at least twice with the poison-laced bullets.

A tear leaked from her eye, and she breathed deep. No. She wasn't going there again. They were alive. Apollo was alive. She knew it. Mainly because if he weren't, she would know that so much more… wouldn't she? Wouldn't her wolf?

Apollo's gentle smile and warm eyes flooded her mind, and she whined. She couldn't lose him. She couldn't. Not her gentle protector.

The ribbons connecting her wolf to theirs were still intact. Would they be if her mates were dead? Or would they snap like the one that she'd broken with Titan? Or thought she'd broken with him…

The red ribbon from Titan wove tighter than ever.

She swiped the tears from her eyes. Why couldn't she have an extraordinary power like in books? Telepathy or something to tell them where she was?

She shook her head. She had to be strong. She couldn't let herself fall apart. Not for them. Not for her. Not for their child.

She brushed her fingers through her hair and caught a whiff of herself. Blech!

She hated to admit it, but Titan was right; she needed to shower and burn her clothes.

And then… she needed a plan.

CHAPTER THREE

APOLLO

"Where's my daughter?"

Shouting woke Apollo, and he blinked several times, trying to orient himself. A beeping sound sounded next to him, and he recognized the hospital equipment.

He sighed. Still in the safe house. How many days had it been?

His wolf whined as he sniffed the air.

Still no River.

He sat up and groaned as pain shot through him. The wolfsbane mixed with silver bullets had done more damage than he'd thought they would.

He remembered very little after being shot and Titan taking River. He vaguely remembered Silas and Thomas picking him up. Ares had been shot as well as Cherry. And someone else… someone- Bennett.

His wolf whined. Titan had killed Bennett.

His best friend had sacrificed his life to protect Apollo and River.

He hadn't expected that to ever happen. Yes, Bennett had put his life on the line every day for Apollo, but Apollo had never felt like he was in danger until that night. That moment. And now, Bennett was gone.

It was like losing his parents all over again. His gut squeezed tight, causing more pain than it should.

"I don't care! I'm leaving. If you assholes can't find her, then I'm gonna have to do it myself!"

He rubbed his face. Cherry was finally awake. Good. He did not want to have to tell River her mother had died. Somehow, he thought that would be worse than telling Cherry River died.

He threw his legs over the side of the bed and stood. His legs wobbled, and his head spun, but he forced himself to stay on his feet.

The monitors went crazy, and Apollo pulled the wires off his torso and fingers.

"Sweetheart, they're looking." Strider's calm voice floated through the door.

"These buffoons couldn't find their asses to scratch them," Cherry retorted.

"Cherry-" Tension laced Ares' voice.

Apollo shuffled to the door and opened it. Cherry stood so close to Ares, he was surprised that Santiago hadn't stepped between them.

Cherry shoved Ares, but he didn't move. "Get out of the way."

"You need to go back to bed," Ares replied.

"Screw bed. I need my daughter back!" She pushed him again, but stumbled. Strider steadied her, but she pushed him off.

"Cherry-" Ares tried again.

"Love, you need to get back in bed. You just woke up. You need-"

She shook her head at Strider. "I should have kept them safe. I should have done more. I need to do more. I can't lie around while… who knows what is happening to my daughter."

"Cherry," Apollo finally said, making every eye turn his direction. "Please. You and I both know that if we let anything happen to you, River will murder us all when she returns."

Cherry stared at him for a moment and then dropped to her knees, heaving with sobs. Strider knelt beside her.

Steps cracked up the staircase, and Zeke and Bianca came into view holding bags of food. Bianca took one look at Cherry and dropped her bags.

"Mom!" Bianca ran to her and wrapped her arms around Cherry. "You're awake," Bianca cried. "You're awake."

Bianca clung to her, and Cherry patted Bianca on the back. "Okay, Baby girl. Okay."

Bianca let go. "We haven't found her yet. We have been looking in shifts day and night. Everyone. Me. Zeke. Ares. Apollo's guys. Even the Alphas who stayed have been searching for her."

"We have to find them. We have to."

"We will, Love." Strider lifted her into his arms, and she wrapped her arms around his neck.

In that moment, Apollo's arms ached to hold River. To smell her. Taste her. Feel her and know that she was okay, that she was safe.

"He won't harm her," Apollo assured them. "He wants her for himself. He won't get that if he hurts her. He saw what she did last time. He won't make that same mistake."

Cherry looked so small in Strider's arms. "You don't know that. You don't know what he'll do when…" She trailed off.

"When what?" Ares asked.

Cherry shook her head and pressed her lips together. "Find her. You need to find her. Fast."

Strider turned and carried Cherry back into the room she'd been in. As Apollo watched them go, he got the feeling there was something Cherry wasn't telling them. However, there was no way she would tell him until she was ready. He just hoped it didn't cost them anything in finding River.

"Hey." Ares walked to him. "Get your ass back in bed, too."

"How long has it been?"

Ares chewed his lips. "A week."

A week? They hadn't found her in a week? Apollo opened his mouth to say something, but seeing the look on Ares' face, he changed his mind. Ares' cheeks were sunken in, as were his eyes. For the first time that Apollo had seen in over five years, he wasn't wearing a suit. Instead, he wore a T-shirt and slacks.

"I'll get back in bed if you tell me what's been happening."

Ares nodded and followed Apollo into his room. Apollo sat on his bed, waiting. Ares shut the door and dropped into a chair across from him. He sat forward and hung his head in his hands.

"Are there any tracks?"

Ares shook his head but didn't look up. "Nothing. It's like they disappeared. They could be anywhere."

Apollo's wolf paced, and the longer he was conscious, the worse his wolf reacted. He wanted to be let out. To find her himself. To save her from the man who had murdered his parents and bring her home to safety. Damn rogues from the woods. He should have kept them alive longer. Forced them to give up Titan. He should have tracked Titan down and killed him that night. Then none of this would have happened. River would be at home with him and Ares.

"Stop."

Apollo looked up.

"It won't help," said Ares. "I've been doing the same thing for the last week. What if I'd tracked the rogues and Titan when we were in New York? What if I'd done this? What if I'd done that? Trust me, it doesn't help. We have to think of now. What can we do now?"

"Kill him." Apollo surprised himself at his total lack of hesitation.

"That's the plan, Brother. But first, we need to find him."

"What about rogues? Find them. Question them. Whatever it takes."

"Done that. Every Alpha has provided a list of all their rogues and their last known locations. They've been using all their resources to track them down, but most have gone underground."

"Or sided with Titan."

“Maybe.”

Apollo’s stomach growled.

Ares stood. "I'll get you some food."

Apollo shook his head. "Don't bother. I can't eat when my wolf is this wound up."

Ares snorted. "Tell me about it. It's taking everything inside me to keep him from running through Montreal and tearing everyone to shreds."

"There has to be something. Some way…" Apollo looked at Ares. "Wait. You said there was no trail beyond the gates."

"Yeah. Nothing. I should have at least been able to smell her going one direction or the other."

"Come to think of it, I don't remember smelling any of them. I smelled blood, and the Alphas and their mates, but not the rogues.”

"And not Titan either."

Apollo thought for a second. "Right before Titan took her, after he…"

"Forced her to kiss him."

Apollo's wolf snarled. "Yeah. That. Someone approached her from the side. A woman, I think."

Ares thought. "Wearing a cloak."

Apollo nodded. "And a moment or so later, River passed out."

"She must have been given something."

"An injection?"

"What if that injection didn't just have a sedative in it? What if it was a blocker? Like the ones the rogues were using in the woods. What if they are all on blockers?"

"It would make sense why there was no scent. Nothing."

"Nothing. That's the exact word River used. She said they didn't smell like anything, they smelled like nothing."

Ares nodded. "That's why there was no trace of her. But why do that if they were already getting into cars to take off? Eventually her scent would have faded."

"Maybe," Apollo mused. "Or maybe it's because she isn't as far away as we think."

"You mean they didn't leave town."

Apollo shrugged. "It would explain why he gave her a blocker. And how he kept tabs on us in the woods."

"But why stay close? Why not take her halfway around the world, where we would never find them?"

"That is the question, isn't it? It could be that this is about more than just River. If he can prove to the Alphas that he's stronger than us. That he can attack us in our own home, and has an army of rogues at his disposal..."

Ares' eyes went black. "He wants the crown."

Apollo hated to admit it, but it was very well possible.

Ares growled and, without warning, turned and punched a hole in the wall. Several sets of rushed footsteps made their way up the stairs and down the hallway. The door flew open, and the men looked at each other.

Apollo waited as a shift rippled through Ares, and he turned to Apollo, fangs lengthened, talons thick and dark.

"I don't give a shit about the crown. If he wants it, he can have it. Or you can have it. All I want is her. Nothing else matters."

Apollo's chest squeezed, and he nodded. "Then we agree. We will do whatever it takes to get her back."

"Including burning the whole damn nation to the ground."

"How many did we lose to the rogues?"

Ares shook his head. "Too many. Ten Alphas and six Lunas."

Sixteen people. Sixteen people under their protection had died at the hands of Titan and his rogues.

Ares and Apollo stared at each other for a long moment, and for the first time in his life, Apollo knew what it meant to be a twin. For the first time, they had a common goal. They were united. The idea burned inside Apollo. Titan was truly in trouble.

"We will make sure they are avenged," said Apollo. "But first, we need to talk to Cherry."

Ares' brow wrinkled. "Why?"

"We need to find out where she got those blockers for River. If we can find out where Titan gets the blockers, we can follow the trail."

Ares nodded. "Thank you."

Apollo blinked twice. "What?"

"Thank you."

Apollo had never heard the words from his brother before, and he was tempted to ask Ares to say them a third time just to make sure he heard right.

"For the first time in a week, I feel like I'm not completely helpless." Ares' eyes held genuine gratitude.

Damn. If Ares didn't stop being so nice to him, he might begin to like his twin.

What the hell would that be like?

CHAPTER FOUR

TITAN

Titan took the stairs out of the basement two at a time and headed to the first floor behind Vanessa. Inside the kitchen, he locked the door behind himself before heading down the hall. Half a dozen rogues sat at the expansive kitchen table, eating. Another dozen ate in the dining room. He nodded to them as he passed, and they bowed their heads. In the living room, other rogues assembled guns and categorized their most recent shipment of weapons, preparing them for distribution. He didn't like the people he had to deal with to procure the weapons. Scum, all of them, but he couldn't deny that the money he received for the merchandise was more than enough to keep his plans rolling forward. In a couple more years, he'd have as much money as the twins, maybe more.

Titan strode past the rogues, scrutinizing their work as he went. His wolf relished the aroma of fear and respected that wafted off them, but Titan couldn't care less. He didn't want their fear or their respect. He only wanted two things: the crown and River. Nothing else mattered. Not anymore. Before River, he'd wanted to make a new world for them. Gather them all together and bring them out of the shadows- now he couldn't care less about them. They were a means to an end and nothing more. And when he took the crown, he would be the king, and they would be the army he used to keep all the others in line. Nothing more.

As he reached for the door handle to his study, Vanessa stopped and flirted with one of the newer guys. Vanessa had come to him desperate and begging for help a month ago. But within a week, she'd started acting like the lady of the manor- something he would not tolerate. And now that River was with him, he needed to figure out a way to get her out, especially after her most recent stunt. He'd had a fling with her about six or seven years prior, but had thought nothing of it because so had most Lycans. But somehow, with age had come desperation. A desperation he recognized. The same desperation his mother had shown when his father had found his fated mate, and she knew she would be sent away.

Titan's gut twisted, and he shook his head at the memory of his mother. Now was not the time for memories. He had to talk to the most recent returning rogue and find out what was going on with Ares and Apollo.

Titan opened the door. Vince lay on his leather couch, appearing to be already dead. His Beta turned from the window.

"Kane."

Kane nodded. "Brother."

Kane had been the first rogue Titan met after his father had sent him and his mother away. He'd found Kane when his mom had taken him to the park. Kane was a good five years older than Titan, and his Alpha had kicked him out because Kane had been the fated mate of one of the Alpha's daughters. With no remaining family in the pack and no rank, the Alpha had forced his daughter to reject Kane and kicked him out.

With nowhere to go and no family or pack, Titan's mom had

taken Kane in and adopted him. From that day forward, Kane never left Titan's side. Several of Titan's men had similarly come to him. Titan's mom had spread the word that her home was open to any werewolf or Lycan who had no pack. By the time she'd died, ten of them had formed their own pack, and over a dozen more called them family at one point or another before moving on to find their way in the world.

But all of that had changed when Titan had found River. Every one of his adopted brothers had come back, and many of them brought friends or mates. Now, Titan took care of fifty-plus rogues across Montreal. That didn't even include the hundred more he had searching the world for more like them.

His father may have disowned him, but at least the substantial payout he'd paid his mom off with had allowed Titan to help rogues and start several businesses under the table. One of which was gun running.

"Vince?" Titan walked to the couch and touched his friend's arm.

Vince sucked in a shuddering breath and groaned as he opened his one remaining eye.

"What can I get you?" Titan asked.

Vince shook his head. "Nothing, Highness. I'll be fine."

The bruises that marred Vince's face looked like he'd gone ten rounds with Conor McGregor. His arm was out of its socket, and he had a compound fracture of the leg. That didn't even count the cuts, scrapes, and burns that covered his body.

Titan's wolf snapped his jaws.

"Who did this?" Titan growled.

He shook his head. "Ares' and Apollo's men."

"What about Ares and Apollo?"

Again, he shook his head. "Maybe… I don't remember all of it."

Titan nodded. "How did you get back?"

Vince sucked in a breath.

Titan patted his arm. "It doesn't matter. You rest. We'll talk tomorrow." He turned to Kane. "Get Doc. Then take Vince to his old bedroom."

"That's Vanessa's room now," said Kane.

Titan snorted. "No. It's not. It's Vince's. Move her into the guest house. Or she can pick one of the other houses. I don't care, move her out of his room."

Kane stared at Titan. "She won't like that."

"Do you think I give a shit what she likes?"

Kane shook his head. "I simply meant that her loyalties switch as quickly as her bed partners."

"One more reason to move her out of here."

"What if she goes back to Ares and tells him where we are?"

"She won't. She can't. She helped us. She's the one who got us on the grounds. And she's the one who knocked River out. Ares would decapitate her before she got out a word. We are her last choice, and she knows it."

"I still suggest we tread carefully."

"I tread carefully with no one but my mate. Put her in the guest house. Tell her it's so she can have the whole place to herself. It's a gift."

Kane nodded, but didn't move.

"What?"

Kane clenched his jaw several times before speaking. "I don't understand why we don't attack them now when they're weak. Take the estate. Take the throne."

"I need her to accept me first."

"What if she won't?"

"She will."

Kane shook his head. "We've worked too hard to throw it all away over a girl who doesn't even want you."

"I worked this hard for her. She is the reason I did all this, you know that."

Kane growled. "She isn't the reason we started this. Why your mother started this."

"She is now."

"She's not worth it. You should cut her loose. Attack the twins. Take the crown."

Titan bit his tongue. They'd had this conversation so many times over the last four years it irritated Titan like a thousand bug bites. Titan understood that the need for revenge powered Kane. It was why Kane had stuck by Titan. Supported Titan. Did... everything he did. But Titan didn't only want revenge anymore. He wanted what he was owed as the firstborn of the Lycan King. His crown and his Omega. But not necessarily in that order.

"I don't want the crown if I can't have her."

Kane shook his head. "This obsession with that female is going to get you killed. Going to get all of us killed."

"You can't tell me that if you had a choice to go back and get Alyssa from her father and mate her today, that you wouldn't do it."

The look on Kane's face told Titan he'd hit a nerve. Kane hadn't talked about Alyssa in over five years. But Kane still wanted her. And he wanted her father dead for kicking him out and making her reject him.

Without a word, Kane stormed out of the room.

Titan's gut twisted. Kane was the truest brother he'd ever had. Kane had been pivotal in Titan's planning of taking the throne. He'd been essential in organizing the rogues. Without Kane, he was nothing. At the same time, Kane had to understand that River was no whim. Wasn't an obsession, or a weakness. She was everything.

CHAPTER FIVE

RIVER

River's stomach roiled as footsteps stomped down the stairs toward her door again. She'd had it with Titan coming and going from her room at will.

She squeezed her eyes shut and blew out a breath, trying to calm her wolf. The longer she was awake and away from Ares and Apollo, the more feral her wolf became- even if she couldn't do anything about it because of the drugs. It was only a matter of time before her wolf tried to get out and attack Titan, even if she couldn't fully transform. But that wasn't her primary concern. Her biggest concern was keeping Titan from finding out about her baby. And the constant nausea didn't help.

Her wolf whimpered.

A lock clicked on the door, and metal scraped against metal before another lock undid itself.

She clenched her jaw and gripped the blanket covering her. She hated that she'd given in to lying in the bed Titan had provided her, but her hips could not take the cement any longer.

The door creaked open and then closed again. She breathed as evenly as possible, but when bile rose in her throat and she had to swallow it down, there was no hiding the fact that she wasn't sleeping.

"You haven't eaten," Titan said.

She tried, oh, she had tried.

"You need to eat, my Luna, otherwise you'll end up sick."

She didn't reply, but her wolf snarled at being called 'his Luna'.

Not his. Never his.

Titan sighed, and the chair at the table scraped against the floor.

"At least you bathed. That must make you feel somewhat better."

Again, she stayed silent.

"River, you can't stay in here and sleep your life away."

"Says who?"

"Me."

She opened her eyes and glared at him as her wolf growled. "You have no say over what I do."

"I do. I am your mate. Your Alpha and I say you need to eat and get used to your new home."

Her gaze flickered Omega golden, but she couldn't hold it. "First, I don't have to do shit. Second, you are not my mate or my Alpha, so I refer back to my first statement. Third, even if you were either of those things to me, I still don't have to do shit, I'm an Omega."

His eyes went Alpha gold, but she refused to look away. She didn't know how long they both fought for control before his eyes went black and then golden again.

Finally, he looked away.

Her wolf chuffed. *Weak male.*

"I'm thirsty," she said.

He got to his feet like an obedient pup. "What would you like?"

The eager expression on his face told her she'd made a mistake.

To wolves, providing for someone was a sign of affection and respect. She didn't want him to take it that way, but if she didn't at least put something in her body, she was pretty sure she'd pass out.

"Cola. A twenty-four pack."

He chuckled but stopped. "You're serious."

"You should know about my love of soda; you've watched me long enough."

His smile fell.

"Also, if you are going to keep me in here, I want a refrigerator. Warm soda is gross."

"I had hoped that you'd join me in my rooms."

She blinked. "Are you serious?"

"Of course."

She barked out a laugh. "Let me understand this. You attack me, bite me without consent, and I reject you. Then, four years later, you attack me again, as well as one of my fated mates. Two weeks later, your men attack me, shoot, and almost kill me. And then at my mating ceremony with Apollo and Ares, you try to murder not only my fated mates but also my mother and father, my Alpha, and all the other people there. You kidnap me, and you seriously think I am going to wake up from being kidnapped and fall into your arms? Are you insane or stupid?"

He growled. "Those Alphas got what they deserved."

"They deserved to die? And what about their mates? They deserved to die as well?"

"Yes," he snapped. "My pack, my brothers and sisters upstairs, are rogues because of those Alphas. Unjustly kicked out under the pretext of being too old and still unmated. Do you think that's insane or stupid? A lot of them weren't even kicked out because of age; they were kicked out because they threatened the secure little lives those Alphas had made for themselves. Because they were deemed not worthy to be in their packs, or because they ended up being the fated mate of someone that the Alpha disapproved of. So, you tell me, did they deserve it? Did those Alphas deserve to see what they had done to good Lycans and shifters who were tossed out of their packs and families? Of everything they'd ever known? Thrown away like trash, never to be acknowledged again?"

Titan's eyes had gone completely black, and his nails and fangs had lengthened. Rage shook his frame.

River didn't know how to answer. She'd always thought that how Alphas exiled wolves for age or no good reason was wrong. But did they and their Lunas deserve to die for it? Lunas didn't even have a say about who was exiled.

The more she peered at him, the more she wondered if he was using the rogues as an excuse to enact his revenge on the ones he deemed responsible for his own exile. Apollo and Ares. But they hadn't been the ones to send him away; their father had. In a blink, Titan's nails and fangs retracted. He took a breath and said, "A refrigerator stocked with soda. Is there anything else?"

She cocked an eyebrow. "Do you really want me to answer that?"

"I suppose not." Without another word, he opened the door.

A memory sprang to the forefront. "Actually, I do have other things I need."

His grip tightened on the doorknob.

"Candy."

He looked over his shoulder at her. "Candy."

She cocked an eyebrow at him, and he nodded.

"Any special requests?"

"Peppermint patties. Lots of them. And those mint pillow things. Butter mints."

"Anything not mint?"

If she didn't say something else, he might become suspicious. "Gourmet chocolates. Expensive ones. Toffee and caramels. And bags of red licorice."

"Maybe I should kidnap Willy Wonka."

"I wouldn't put it past you."

He growled and told someone on the other side to make a list before the door slammed behind him.

She'd almost blown it by asking for all the mint candies. But she needed them in hopes that the mint might help settle her nausea. Back in her pack, the Luna had used a lot of herbs she grew or found to help people out. And she remembered the Luna bringing her some mint tea when she had the flu once. Besides, if the food was where he was putting the blockers, she had to eat; even a mouthful was better than just soda.

River looked at the door, wondering who was out there and whether it was Vanessa.

Her wolf roared.

If River got her talons on Vanessa, that bitch was dead. It had taken her several days to remember everything that had happened when she'd been taken, and when she had remembered, it had been Vanessa who had stuck her with the syringe. She'd decided that if she ever saw the bitch again, Vanessa was as good as dead.

An hour later, River's door opened again, and a man walked in backward carrying a significant black something. He turned sideways, and Titan entered carrying the other end. A refrigerator.

They walked toward the kitchenette, and the man she didn't recognize dropped his end.

"I'll put this in place and hook it in," he said.

Titan nodded and headed out of the room. The man shimmied the fridge toward the wall and plugged it in. Then he stripped off the plastic and label from it. He opened it and stuck his hand inside before closing it again and tossing the wrap in the trash can.

He turned and looked at her. Large and fair-skinned with light brown eyes and a nose that looked like it had been broken at least once. His right cheek sported a long scar that ran from his forehead down through his eye and cheek to his chin and throat.

Damn! Who had he pissed off?

"Who are you?" she asked.

"No one."

Her wolf growled.

"Okay, No One. You can leave now."

His lip curled, and his eyes narrowed. "I'm not one of your servants, Princess."

"No, I just don't like you in my space."

He snorted. "So this is your space now?"

"Until I leave."

He shook his head.

"What?"

"I never thought my little brother would fall for a girl like you."

Little brother? A girl like her?

"What the hell does that mean?" she growled.

"Haughty. High maintenance. A pampered princess. Basically, you."

Was he joking? She dug her nails into the blanket as they lengthened, and her wolf tried to rise to her feet unsuccessfully.

He snorted. "Just like you're looking at me right now. You see me as scum."

Anger swirled inside her, and she narrowed her eyes. "All I see is an asshole."

"See, scum."

"Scum is someone you think you're better than. Being an asshole is a personality defect. I don't think I'm better than you, but I do think you are an asshole. That's on you, not me."

He snarled. "You don't belong here."

She gave him a mocking smile. "Agreed. How about you walk me out?"

He opened his mouth to say something, but the door opened again, and Titan sauntered in holding twenty-four packs of soda and several plastic bags. He looked at the man and then at River, and growled.

"Leave."

The man inclined his head and shot River a sideways glare before stalking out.

Titan took the soda to the fridge and stuck it inside. He paused for a moment and then turned to her.

"What did he say to you?"

"Who is he?"

Titan blew out a breath. "Kane."

"He said he is your brother."

"He's as much my brother as Bianca is your sister."

River snapped at the mention of her sister. "You stay the hell away from her."

"I will as long as she doesn't get in my way."

River leapt off the bed in an instant. She glowered at him, her Omega gaze going golden. She fought with everything she had to keep her stare golden and on her feet at the same time, but it wouldn't last long.

"You touch one hair on my sister, and you won't have to worry about Apollo and Ares, I'll rip your guts out myself."

She leveled her gaze on him until he turned from her and dropped the bags on the counter.

"I won't touch your sister."

"Swear that *no one* will touch my sister."

He let out a small laugh. "Don't trust me?"

"Not a single ounce. Swear it."

He turned, and his lips drew into a thin line, and then he licked them and crossed his arms. "Fine. I swear no harm will come to your little sister."

"From you or anyone else."

"I can't promise that."

She bared her teeth even though she couldn't produce her fangs. Hell, she'd rip him apart with her human teeth if she had to. Every muscle tensed, ready to attack.

"I promise I, nor any of my pack, will harm her."

Her wolf tried to stand, but couldn't because of whatever cocktail of drugs Titan was giving her.

"Now I want you to do something for me," he said.

"No."

He ground his teeth together. "I want to show you why I'm doing what I'm doing."

"You already told me why."

"Yes, but I want you to see why."

River had no interest in anything Titan wanted, but showing her meant that she would at least leave the room. Maybe see the house and the grounds. Perhaps she'd discover something that would tell her where she was. Or a flaw in their security, she could exploit. She couldn't keep sitting around doing nothing to help herself and her baby.

"On one condition."

He chuckled. "That's not how this works, sweetheart. I already gave you something."

She cocked an eyebrow at him.

He sighed. "What do you want now?"

"I want to know who is alive and who's dead."

His eyebrows drew together. "What?"

"From the attack. I want to know who is alive and who is dead."

"How would I know that?"

She shrugged and walked to the bed. "You get me that information, the real information, and not made-up crap, and I'll go with you. That is, if my mom, stepdad, and sister are okay." She wanted to include Ares and Apollo, but didn't want to push him too far.

Besides, she'd said she wanted to know everyone who had died, so she assumed he would tell her about them anyway.

His jaw worked hard, and then he nodded. "All right."

He headed toward the door.

"And," she said.

"Yes?" Irritation laced his voice, though he kept his face impassive.

"I want a television."

"Fair enough."

He headed toward the door.

"One more thing."

He didn't turn.

"I need clothes. Sweats, lounge suits, underwear, socks, pajamas, comfortable stuff."

"What size?"

"Medium, large. I'm not picky. But nothing cheap or scratchy."

She hoped he got more mediums than larges. She didn't know if a large would even stay on her body, but the bigger the clothes, the better. The more she could hide her changing figure, the safer.

"Wow. I had no idea the twins could spoil you so badly in such a short amount of time."

"You can always send me back."

He looked as if he might say something, but instead turned and left. The door locked, and she waited before going to the fridge, ripping open the cardboard packaging, and grabbing a cola. She sank to the floor and chugged it. The soda burned as it slid down to her stomach. She burped, then curled into a ball, letting the semi-cool air from the fridge wash over her as she battled to keep the liquid down. It tried to make a reappearance several times, but she managed to prevent it from resurfacing.

Finally, her stomach settled, and her wolf sighed and laid down to rest. River stayed there for several more minutes before getting to her knees, grabbing another can of soda, kicking the door shut, and crawling to the bed.

She hauled herself up on it and melted into the foam. The interaction with Titan swam in her mind.

One thing was certain. If he came back with that list and her mom's name, or Strider's or Bianca's, Apollo's, or Ares' names were on it, she would disembowel Titan. She didn't know how, but she would- even if it killed her in the process.

CHAPTER SIX

ARES

Cherry gave Ares the information for the man who made River's suppression pills. Apollo had tried to insist on going with Ares to interrogate the man, but Ares refused. His brother still wasn't at full strength after having so much silver and wolfsbane pumped into him, and Ares was going to need Apollo at full strength for the battle to come. It surprised Ares how worried he'd been about his twin over the last week. So much had changed in so little time. But he couldn't focus on everything at the moment because thoughts of finding River consumed him.

Besides, Apollo had work in Montreal. Calls to Alphas. Condolences given, and support secured. All the kinds of diplomatic stuff that Apollo was brilliant at, like their mother had been. Ares was the hammer, Apollo was the glove, always had been. Only now did Ares realize what an asset that could be, and would need to be in the future. Titan hadn't gotten all those rogues to help him by sheer force. Somehow, he'd gotten them with finesse. Finesse that Ares mostly lacked, amongst other things.

As Ares' wolf's mournful whine pierced through him, it wasn't merely a sound, but a visceral ache. An echo of loss reverberating through his very soul. The wolf's raw, primal sorrow clawed at Ares' heart with an unrelenting ferocity. His breath caught as if the weight of the grief had physically struck him. His hand pressed against his breastbone, as though it could somehow ease the hollow ache spreading there. But no amount of pressure could muffle the truth that raged within him.

The weight of their failure to protect her bore down on him. The memory of her cries haunted him. Her voice, desperate and tinged with pain, had been a dagger to his soul. Ares clenched his fists, his nails biting into the armrests of his seat. He still saw her face in those final moments before she was ripped away from them: wide eyes filled with terror, reaching for him, trusting him to save her.

But he hadn't.

His wolf growled low and guttural inside him, a sound drenched in self-loathing and fury. We should have done more. Ares' fists clenched. He hadn't just failed her; he had failed them all.

Guarding her had been their sole purpose, yet they had faltered in that crucial moment. Every fiber of his being had been attuned to her presence since the day they bonded, her laughter like sunlight breaking through storm clouds, her touch grounding him when the world spiraled out of control. She was everything, not just to him but to the wolf that shared his soul. And now, emptiness took root where she should have been.

How could he safeguard his entire species when he couldn't even ensure the safety of his beloved mate? The thought sank like he'd swallowed a granite slab, cold and unrelenting. He let out a shuddering exhale, running a hand through his hair as if trying to pull himself together.

His mind flashed back to the elders' words during their last gathering. "You are our strongest warrior, Ares, the one who will lead us into a new era." The memory felt like mockery, a cruel joke. What kind of leader couldn't even protect his mate?

A mournful whine escaped his lips, not from his wolf but from somewhere deeper.

Ares opened his eyes, their usual stormy gray now tinged with an eerie golden glow as the wolf's presence surged to the surface. His breathing steadied as determination replaced despair.

"I'll find you," he vowed, trying to access the bond they shared, the white ribbon that connected them even across impossible distances. "I'll bring you back, or die trying."

The stewardess walked up next to him and took his empty whiskey glass. "We will be landing in thirty minutes, Mr. Wolvenguard."

Ares nodded without looking up.

"I've been told your car is already waiting to take you where you need to go."

Ares glanced out the window above the midwestern US. He'd only ever been to Chicago a few times, but he'd never once been to Indianapolis. The man he was looking for didn't know Ares was coming, and that was just fine. He didn't want the guy refusing to meet with him, or worse, running.

How he had not known about a suppressor chemist before now, he had no idea. Probably because Lycans never used suppressors. There was no point. But in that moment, Ares realized there were a lot of things he probably didn't know about the world he'd grown up in, especially when it came to shifters. And that could not continue, particularly if Titan was gathering an army of them.

As soon as he had River back, he was going to need to meet with all the shifter Alphas. Every single one. And if they didn't come, they'd be removed. There were going to be changes made. And more than that, there was going to be a lot more involvement with the ruling of shifters as well as keeping an eye on what was going on in their entire kingdom, not just with the Lycans.

CHAPTER SEVEN

RIVER

River scanned the list for the fifth time to make sure she didn't recognize any more than one of the names. Bennett. They'd killed Bennett. And as much as her heart ached from the knowledge, a part of her was relieved her family's names weren't on there. As well as Ares and Apollo.

"Satisfied?" Titan asked from where he lounged casually against the door. His blond hair hung down, covering one bright blue eye, and his T-shirt pulled tight over muscles she would usually admire on any other man. Hell, before Ares and Apollo, she might have even had a one-night stand with him, but good looks were deceiving. Especially his.

"Why would I be satisfied knowing so many people were murdered for no reason?"

His jaw tightened. "There was a damn good reason."

She snorted. "Right, so you could take me."

"To send a message."

"What message, you're all murderers?"

Her wolf bristled. *Don't Like.*

Titan growled. "To tell the Alphas and my little half-brothers that we mean business. We won't be ignored anymore, and we won't be mistreated."

"And you had to murder to do that?"

"Yes."

River's wolf growled. River glared at Titan, trying to figure out whether or not to ask her next question.

"I don't know where your mother is, or your sister and stepdad. They, as well as Ares and Apollo, haven't been seen since the attack," he said as if reading her thoughts.

They needed medical attention for sure. River could only assume they were in hiding somewhere, recuperating. She wished more than anything to hear their voices and know for herself that they were okay.

A knock sounded on the door, and Titan opened it. A man stood on the other side holding two plastic bags. A sense of familiarity raced over her. She knew him. Knew his face, but his eyes were… different. Hard. Angry. A memory flashed into her mind of kinder eyes. Smiling and joking.

His gaze met hers and widened.

Austin. His name was Austin. She opened her mouth to say something when Titan took the bags from him and shut the door in his face.

"That was rude. I know him," she said.

Titan walked to the bed and handed her the bags. "Do you?"

"Yes. He was in our pack. He left about six or seven years ago. What's he doing here?"

"Same as the rest of us. We were kicked out. He had nowhere to go. So, he found their way to me."

"What do you mean kicked out?" River hadn't really known Austin, but he was a decent guy. Solid, kind, funny.

"Are you that naïve? How could you not know what has been happening?"

"Because I was never really part of the pack. My mom kept me separate, and I never fit in. I had nothing to do with pack politics or anything else except to keep my head down and help when asked."

Titan chewed his lip. "I'll wait for you outside. You can put on clean clothes, and then I'll take you around. You won't be keeping your head down while in my pack. You are strong, and we need your strength to help pave the way for a new future for Lycans and shifters."

"And what if I don't want anything to do with paving the way to a new future with you?"

"Then you are welcome to warm my bed while I do it."

A bark of laughter escaped River. "I'd rather bite through my tongue and eat it ."

An eerie smile spread across his face. "We shall see, my Luna." He walked out.

Her wolf snarled. *Not him.*

What was with Titan? One minute he was a total asshole, and the next he was asking her to give him a shot. She couldn't pinpoint what his game was, but she had to find out if she wanted to escape.

River emerged from her room several minutes later, dressed in a velour pink lounge outfit. She couldn't remember a time when she'd worn pink before, but it was the largest of all the clothing. Luckily, they'd brought her sports bras and white cotton underwear, so though she had no desire to wear anything Titan had gotten her, at least it was comfortable.

Titan looked her up and down and then held out his hand for her. She shoved her hands in her pockets, and he started up the dark staircase.

River glanced around. A hall ran down to her right, and stairs lay straight ahead with a locked door at the top. That was it. The walls were bare white, and the floors cement, as if it were a fake set on a TV show. It surprised her how much effort he'd put into making her room look so normal.

"Coming?" he asked from the top of the stairs.

River sighed and started up the stairs. "Do I have a choice?"

Her stomach cramped and growled, and she coughed to try to cover the sound.

Come on. Not now. Keep it together for just an hour, will ya?

She'd chugged a cola, but it wasn't enough to satisfy her hunger. Nothing was though, so she wasn't about to risk eating something and puking in front of everyone. That would raise more questions than simply refusing to eat. Not eating, she could explain away. Vomiting not so much. She popped a small butter mint into her mouth and sucked on it, letting it dissolve.

She stopped a step below Titan, and he pulled out a key ring and unlocked the door. Natural light flooded the stairwell, and River shielded her eyes. How many days had it been since she'd seen real sunlight? Sure, there was a fake window with simulated light, but it was nothing like real sunlight.

Her wolf whined and lifted her head, but couldn't do more than that.

Don't worry, girl, I'll let you out when the time is right. For now, let's enjoy the sunshine and air.

Her wolf grumbled.

Titan stepped to the side, allowing River to exit. A dozen locks adorned the outside of the heavy metal door.

She glanced around the hallway, surprised by its grandeur. She wasn't sure what kind of house she'd expected Titan to live in, but this was not it.

Rooms shot off in both directions. The house was decorated in whites and creams. White wainscoting, cream wallpaper, contemporary furniture, light colored flower arrangements. It looked so...

normal. Elegant. It reminded her of her mating ceremony, and her heart squeezed.

Wait... She looked around again, taking better stock of the setup. It... it was the same configuration as Ares and Apollo's house. A chill ran through her.

"Come on," said Titan. "I want you to meet some people."

She didn't say anything, but when he placed his palm on her back to lead her, she shrugged out of his reach as her wolf gnashed her teeth.

"This way." He motioned for her to walk in front of him.

She didn't know if it was because he was afraid she might make a run for it, or if he feared she might stab him in the back. Either scenario was possible.

They walked down the hallway toward the grand entrance, and again, it had the same glass windows on either side of the front door as the estate did. The idea that the house had been an exact duplicate of Ares and Apollo's home gave her a strange feeling, as well as a glimpse into Titan's mother's mental state and why Titan had never been able to let go of the past. How could you when you lived in a house whose construction reminded you every single day of where you weren't?

Several men stood around talking and smoking. A large gravel driveway stretched as far as she could see down to a thick tree line, which cut the house off from any street.

When they rounded a monumental staircase, Titan turned left, and they walked to double French doors that led into a grand library or something. All around, men and a few women read or talked on their phones, but every single one stopped when she entered with Titan. They all bowed their heads as her gaze traced over them to see if she recognized anyone. She didn't. Their scents washed over her, reminding her of her old pack. For a moment, a sense of longing rushed through her at the nostalgia the scents brought. But then she remembered what had forced her to leave that pack, and her gut clenched.

"This is my Luna, River Whitetail," Titan announced.

They bowed their heads until River grew uncomfortable.

"Tell them to stop," she said.

Titan looked at her. "You tell them. They're your pack, too."

River's gut clenched, but he was right. As High Luna and mate to Ares and Apollo, they were her people.

"That's enough," she commanded.

They lifted their heads to look at her, and she felt like she should say something profound, but the only thing she could think to say was, "Thank you for your welcome."

The wolves didn't move.

"Please go back to what you were doing."

Slowly, they returned to what they'd been doing before she entered, even though they still stole glances at her.

"This is the den," said Titan. "As you can see, we have a great many books as well as computers and anything else wolves might need."

River nodded, and Titan ushered her forward. Computers. Many computers. And every wolf had a cellphone. She cataloged the information for future use.

As she wove between couches, chairs, and tables, she didn't miss the fact that the wolves would lift their heads to sniff her as she passed.

She wondered what they smelled. Or if they smelled nothing like others on suppressors. Suppressors... most of the rogues in the house were on suppressors, she realized. Did that mean only the ones who left used suppressors? Because the ones who had attacked in New York, the woods, and at the ceremony had all been on suppressors.

At the far end of the library, Titan opened double doors into what she could only call a gamer's room. Giant screens, luxury gaming chairs, headsets, speakers, you name it, all lined the room. Several males sat on a comfortable-looking leather couch playing a racing game on the biggest TV screen she'd ever seen. She couldn't imagine the price tag on all the equipment. But more than that... it all seemed so normal. Like a group of roommates living together and sharing the expenses of a large house. As if they hadn't gone out and slaughtered people a week ago. As if they weren't plotting to overthrow kings. Just... stupid twenty-somethings having a beer and gaming all day.

Titan watched her as she inspected the room. One of the males spotted them and hit the one next to him. Suddenly, the group all dropped their controllers, took off their headphones, and bowed to her.

"Luna," they all said.

River looked at them for a moment and recognized two of them. They'd been in the tunnel with Titan. They'd attacked the Alphas.

Her wolf snarled.

She took half a step forward, her teeth bared, but Titan moved in her way.

"Move." She shoved at him, but damn if he wasn't as hard and big as her mates.

"River-"

She shoved his torso again. "They attacked my ceremony."

He nodded. "They did."

"They deserve to pay for it."

He cocked an eyebrow and made a gesture with his hand, and the TV turned off.

"Jameson, come here."

One of the men she recognized stopped a step behind Titan.

"Where are you from, Jameson?"

"Washington, Highness."

"How long has it been since you were kicked out of your pack?" Titan's gaze never left hers.

"Five years, six months, and two days, Highness."

"And why were you kicked out?"

Jameson's eyes widened, and then he swallowed hard as he clenched his fists. "The Alpha's son raped my sister. So I beat him."

"Did his son survive?"

"Yes."

"And your sister?"

A low whine escaped Jameson. "She was forced to mate him."

River gasped without meaning to. How the hell could that happen? What kind of monsters would do that?

"Was the Alpha's son at the mating ceremony?"

"Yes," Jameson growled.

"Was his mate?"

"Yes."

"Where is that Alpha's son now?"

"In the ground."

"And where is your sister?"

"Upstairs in my room. She hasn't left it since I brought her here. She's too afraid that he isn't dead and he will find her."

Titan's eyes hardened.

Her throat dried, and she searched for words.

"Thank you, Jameson," said Titan. "I appreciate you sharing your story with my Luna." Then Titan tore his gaze from hers and turned to Jameson. "Please let me know when your sister is ready to see Dr. Higginson, and we will send for her."

Jameson bowed. "Thank you, Highness."

Titan nodded to the gamers, and they each returned to the couch, turning the TV back on.

Titan ushered her toward another door.

"Who's Dr. Higginson?"

"A psychiatrist who has been helping the rogues deal with their trauma."

He opened a swinging door which led into a spacious kitchen.

She wanted to ask if he'd ever talked to Dr. Higginson about his trauma, but she already knew the answer. No one who had dealt with their trauma would do what Titan had done.

At the counter, half a dozen more rogues ate and chatted. They bowed the same as everyone else. All except one. In the corner, at a table with a laptop open and dozens and dozens of guns, sat Kane. He glanced up from his laptop and sneered before going back to it.

"This is River Whitetail, my Luna. You will give her the same respect you give me. All of you."

Kane looked up again, and his gaze locked with Titan, and for a moment, nothing happened, but then Kane inclined his head.

"Please continue eating," said River. "I don't need you to bow to me every time I enter a room."

"You may not need it," said Titan. "But they will do it out of respect anyway,"

The rogues nodded, and she and Titan headed through the kitchen toward Kane.

He stiffened as they drew closer.

"How goes it?" Titan asked.

Kane's gaze flicked to hers and then back. "We're short."

"How many?"

"Twenty."

Titan nodded. "Reach out to Rodolpho. See what he's got in stock."

Kane nodded and went back to his computer.

Guns? They had guns? And what did he mean by, short? They had dozens on the table, which meant they had more elsewhere. Her heartbeat kicked up at the thought of those guns being used on her loved ones. But… they hadn't carried any guns when they'd attacked before. So what were they for then?

River turned to the back windows that overlooked the expansive yard, and her wolf whined.

"I need fresh air," she blurted.

Titan nodded. "Of course."

They walked toward a back door, and when River looked over her shoulder, everyone in the room was staring at her.

Her skin prickled. She didn't like being watched, especially by Kane. The other rogues she could handle with a simple command, but Kane… she didn't know about.

All thoughts fled from her mind like a deer from a hunter, the moment she exited the house, and her entire body relaxed. She stopped, frozen on the expansive wrap-around balcony, just taking in the scents of the outdoors. Trees, dirt, flowers, fertilizer, water. Her body flooded with so many emotions, she couldn't catch them all. Happiness, joy, excitement, longing, sadness, anger. All of them mixed like a volatile cocktail, and she had to stop herself from either screaming or crying.

Memories surfaced of being in the woods with Apollo. For a moment, she let her memories flood her. Running. Chasing. Sleeping out under the sky together. His passionate kisses. The hard lines of his body pressed into hers. Emotions bubbled up, threatening to drown her.

No. She would not show weakness. She had to keep it together. Showing weakness would be worse than anything in Titan's pack. They'd eat her alive if they spotted weakness, especially with her being pregnant.

She gazed at the enormous yard. Several medium-sized guest houses, a bright blue pool, and a few smaller units lined the property.

Titan moved to her side. "Would you like to go down and walk around?"

She swallowed hard. If she agreed too fast, he would think

something was up, but she wanted nothing more than to sink her toes into the grass.

"If you want to go down, that would be fine," she said as neutrally as possible.

The corner of his mouth quirked up.

"What?"

"You can say you want to go down. Agreeing with me on something won't mean I think you suddenly like me or anything."

She scowled at him, and he chuckled and shook his head.

He pointed to the left. "The stairs are over there. Feel free to head down. I'll join you in a moment."

She narrowed her eyes. "You aren't going to guard me? You trust me not to run?"

He shrugged. "You could try, but you can't leave our property unless you go out the front gate, and you can't get out without permission and a code. Or if you scale a ten-foot-high wall topped with razor wire. Not that there's anywhere for you to go. Feel free to test the theory if you're so inclined."

"If I can't get out, why keep me locked in the basement?"

"For safety."

"Afraid I'm going to try and fight my way out?"

"Well, I've seen you with a knife. You are pretty impressive, but no. It's not because I'm afraid you might fight, it's because I'm afraid of how many males I will have to kill to keep you from them."

"You afraid someone will bite me without permission?" she challenged.

His eyes turned black, then returned to normal. He gritted his teeth. "Something like that. You don't even have a potato peeler this time."

"You could give me one."

He nodded. "I think not, Princess."

She shrugged and turned from him, heading for the stairs. "Then whatever happens to me will be your fault."

He didn't say anything as she headed to the balcony's edge and marched down the stairs. She half expected him to follow her, but he didn't, surprisingly. Guess he really didn't think she'd be able to escape.

She hit the grass below and sighed in relief. The past week, cooped up, floated away as her bare feet sank into the grass, and she sucked in a breath. Her wolf lifted her head and sniffed the air. Being outside stirred her wolf, who stood for the first time since arriving.

Run.

River scanned the area. *I don't think I can right now.*

Run. Escape. Apollo. Ares.

Yes. Apollo and Ares. I want to be with them, too, but we have to be smart. We'll look around. See if there are any ways out, but not now. Not our first time out. We have to let him think we aren't going to bolt. Otherwise, he will put us back in that room, and we'll never be free.

River's wolf grumbled.

River didn't like it either, but it was the truth. River needed Titan to at least think she wouldn't try anything. River sat on the ground and let the cool grass and soil soak into her limbs through her clothes.

She doubted Titan would believe she'd stay with him after everything he'd done, but if he hadn't believed it, he never would have brought her there, would he? So some part of him had to think, or at least hope, she would stay. And that belief, that hope, she could work with. She could use that. Not that she'd ever been good at trying to be coy or lying to people. It was the curse of being Cherry's daughter. Her mom had always told her to speak her mind, and damn the consequences of what other people thought. But Cherry's advice wouldn't help her in this situation. In this situation, she needed to channel her father and Strider. She needed to be observant and collected. Then, and only then, would she be able to find her way out of the mess she'd gotten into.

"Enjoying yourself?"

River's head whipped up, and her wolf roared.

Vanessa strolled across the grass toward her, wearing jeans so tight they looked like body paint and a shirt so short it was no better than a sports bra. River dug her fingers into the dirt to keep from jumping up and attacking the bitch.

Vanessa stopped feet from her. Their gazes locked, and Vanessa smirked.

"I don't know what it is about you that has all these Wolvenguard boys in such a tizzy."

River threw on a fake smile. "Maybe it's the fact that I don't put out for anyone with a dick."

Vanessa's smile faltered for a second, and fire made her eyes narrow.

River snickered. As if Vanessa could do anything that would intimidate River.

"Let me ask you," said River. "How did you see this going? You help Titan kidnap me, and then what? You rush to Ares and Apollo and pretend to be so sorry I am missing, and they'll take you back, and somehow fall for you, though they didn't before they found me?"

Vanessa crossed her arms over her breasts.

"Well, I have news for you bitch, if that was your plan, go for it. I can't wait to see what they do to you." River cocked her head to the side. "I wonder if they will disembowel you outright or if they'll torture you first to see what you know."

"They wouldn't do that."

River got to her feet. "You think so? Then what are you still doing here? Titan doesn't want you. So why haven't you left already?"

Vanessa swallowed hard.

"Ahhhh..." River chuckled. "You have nowhere else to go, do you? You may put on a good act, but inside, even you don't believe your bullshit. You know if you go back, they will execute you. Hell, I'd slit your throat myself if I had a knife. Or even access to my claws. It's only the suppressors Titan has me on that has kept me from doing it already."

"You think you're so special. You-"

"No." River stepped up to her. "I don't think I'm special. I know I am." River let her golden stare fall hard on Vanessa. It wasn't easy, but River managed to hold it for several seconds.

Vanessa tried not to look away from River, but she began to shake and then lowered her eyes.

The second River turned away, Vanessa lunged at her, but River sidestepped her and kicked Vanessa in the rear, sending her sprawling to the ground. River's stomach roiled at the sudden movement, and nausea flowed through her, but she refused to let it take hold. Instead, she jumped on Vanessa's back, pinning her arms to the ground with her knees. She seized Vanessa by the back of the head and smashed her face into the dirt before lifting it and baring her teeth at the side of Vanessa's throat.

Vanessa screamed and howled as she struggled to get out of River's hold.

River chuckled. "You know, when my mates and I bonded, and they marked me, and I marked them, I didn't have to beg. They were so ready to mark me and make me theirs that I had to hold them off."

"Get off me!" Vanessa yelled.

"No. I am the High Luna. Omega and mate to Ares and Apollo Wolvenguard. If I wanted to rip your throat out right now, I could. If I wanted to disembowel you in front of everyone here, I could. If I wanted to banish you from ever living on the North American continent for the rest of your life, I could. I can do whatever I want, and there isn't a single person besides Ares or Apollo who could stop me. So I'll give you a choice. You can either stay the hell away from me, or I kill you. Personally, killing you seems rather more pleasurable to me, but I try to give people a choice. I'm nice like that. So what will it be? Stay away or death?"

"Yes, Vanessa, which will it be?"

River looked over her shoulder at Titan, watching the scene unfold from feet away.

Vanessa tried to look over at him. "Titan I-"

"I believe my Luna asked you a question," he said.

Vanessa's mouth opened and shut several times.

River yanked her head back. "Sorry, I didn't hear that."

Tears sprang to Vanessa's eyes. "I'll stay away."

River sighed. "Damn. I was hoping you would choose death. But just so you remember your promise to stay away..." River raked her human nails down the side of Vanessa's face. The marks wouldn't last more than a day, but River didn't care. She wanted to send a message. A message that everyone who came in contact with Vanessa would see over the next twenty-four hours. The message that River would not take shit from anyone. And that she didn't need Titan to enforce that message, she could do it herself.

River slid off Vanessa, being sure to dig her knees into Vanessa's arms before she rose to her feet. River's wolf chuffed. River backed away. Her head grew fuzzy, and her eyes dimmed at the mix of sudden movements. Her belly flopped, and she dug her nails into her palms to keep from passing out.

Vanessa lay on the ground for a moment before getting up and turning to face River and Titan. Her blouse and jeans were stained with mud and grass, and blood smeared her face. Tears rolled down her cheeks as she squared her shoulders and inclined her head to River and then Titan.

"May I go?" she asked Titan.

"I don't know, my Luna, what do you think? Can she go?"

"Yes," River commanded. "And stay out of my sight."

Vanessa looked like she might say something. Instead, she spun away, back straight, shoulders stiff, and strode to the guest house nearest the pool. As soon as she was out of sight, River let out a low breath. The nausea that had been a slight flutter before had turned into a tidal wave, and River sat shakily on the ground again. A moment passed as she put her head between her knees and took several slow breaths.

Titan's body heat burned River's skin as he brushed her arm with his.

"You did well," he said. "Leading comes naturally to you."

River didn't look up as saliva pooled in her mouth, and she spat it on the ground.

Don't throw up. Don't throw up. Don't throw up.

"It's not leading that comes naturally; it's the fact that I'm sick of everyone thinking they can do whatever they want to me, and I won't defend myself. Like, I am somehow unfit to have an opinion or a say in my own life. I'm sick of it. Sick of being told what to do. Sick of being tossed around. Sick of people coming in and out of the room I'm staying in without knocking or asking or anything."

"I get it," he said. "It's why I'm doing what I am. I'm tired of being told I'm not worthy to be the king because my mother wasn't my father's fated mate. I'm tired of others being shoved out, banished, beaten, and treated like dirt because someone else says they are better. See, we're the same River."

"No, Titan, we aren't. I gave Vanessa a choice: leave me alone or die. You wouldn't have. You would have simply killed her."

He shrugged. "Maybe. Maybe not."

She straightened. "If your father were here, right now, would you give him the option to take you back or die? Or would you have just killed him?"

Titan's eye twitched.

"Exactly. There are huge differences between you and me. I value life, everyone's lives. And I value allowing them to make their own choices. You don't. You want to make the choices for people and have them thank you for it later. But you know what that is? Slavery. Not freedom."

Titan swallowed hard. "Maybe you're right. Maybe I think some people don't deserve the opportunity to make a choice. Not after everything they've done."

"Like me? What did I do to you to make you take my right to choose away?"

His eyes hardened and then softened. "I shouldn't have done that to you. I know it doesn't make a difference, but I didn't know what I was doing that night I bit you. My wolf... All I can say is that it wasn't me."

"And that's supposed to make it all better?"

He shook his head. "No. It's just that night..."

"That night, what?"

He licked his lips. "I-"

"Highness," Kane called from the balcony.

How long had he been standing there? How much of what had happened with Vanessa did Kane see?

Titan nodded and got to his feet. "I'm sorry, I have to cut this short. I have a meeting I need to be at."

He held his hand out to River, and without thinking, she took it, and he pulled her to her feet. His body pressed against hers, and her throat dried. They stared at each other for a moment before she slid her hand from his and backed away.

"I suppose I'm headed back to my cell now?"

"It's not a cell, River. As I said before, I would like to give you free rein of the entire house, but..."

"I thought you said I couldn't escape even if I wanted to. So what does it matter if I'm out here or in the basement?"

"My meeting shouldn't take more than a couple of hours. How about if I take you to the art studio I made for you? You can stay in there while I'm gone."

"I told you I don't paint."

He shrugged. "Why don't you try? You might like it."

River looked up at Kane, who still watched them like a vulture waiting for her to die so he could pick at her carcass.

"Fine," she said. "But I'm going to need some different clothes and my soda and candy."

Titan nodded. "Of course. I'll take you to your room, and you can get everything you need."

He held his hand out to her, and River shoved her hands into her pockets.

Once again, he dropped his hand as if he'd expected nothing less and turned and walked to the stairs of the balcony.

Run. Escape.

"Yeah, yeah," River told her wolf. *Me too.*

CHAPTER EIGHT

TITAN

Titan waited by River's door as she changed her clothes. Watching her take down Vanessa had been thrilling. Seeing the power she possessed. The fire. The grit. He wondered if that was something she'd inherited from her mother or something she'd had to learn for herself. One of the things he'd learned about River over the past four years was that her upbringing had been almost as hard and isolated as his had been. Losing her father. Never belonging to her pack. People looking at her differently. They were so similar… So why couldn't she see that she fit better with him than with those asshole twins? What did those bastards have that he didn't?

River emerged from her room, and Titan's breath caught. She'd changed into a pair of black yoga pants and a loose-fitting gray t-shirt. Her silver hair was pulled back in a messy bun, exposing the graceful curve of her neck. For a moment, Titan imagined pressing his lips to that spot just below her earlobe, marking her as his for real. Feeling her arms wrap around him as she begged him to take her.

His wolf growled in approval.

"Ready?" he asked, keeping his voice neutral.

River nodded, not meeting his eye. As they walked down the hallway, Titan noticed how she kept a careful distance between them. His wolf whined, wanting to close that gap. Wanting to kiss where Titan had imagined. To pin her to the wall and rip her clothes off.

"The art studio is down here." Titan gestured to a door halfway down the hall.

He unlocked it and stepped aside, allowing River to enter first. The large room flooded with natural light from windows high on the west wall, and French doors that led to the backyard. Easels, canvases, and a variety of art supplies filled the space.

River's eyes widened as she took it all in. "This is... impressive," she admitted reluctantly.

Titan's wolf chuffed.

"I wanted you to have everything you might need. There's a small fridge stocked with soda and snacks."

River walked to an easel, running her fingers lightly over the smooth wood. "I told you, I don't paint."

"Maybe you'll discover a hidden talent." Titan smiled. "After all, you learned to carve wood recently."

She tensed.

He thought about saying something to smooth over the fact that he'd been watching her. He didn't want to ruin the moment. But what was the point? He'd apologized enough.

"I have to go to a meeting, but I'll be back in a couple of hours. Will you be alright?"

River's eyes narrowed. "I'll manage."

So feisty.

Titan nodded, fighting the urge to pull her into his arms. "If you need anything, press the intercom button by the door. Kane will come."

As he turned to leave, River's voice stopped him. "Titan?"

He looked back, hope rising. "Yes?"

"Earlier, you started to say something about the night you bit me. What did you mean when you said it wasn't you?"

Memories of that night flooded back. The primal urges that had overtaken him. "It's... complicated," he said.

Before River could respond, Titan exited and locked the door behind him. He leaned against it for a moment, taking a breath to steady himself. He'd told her that he'd not been himself when he'd bitten her, but that wasn't entirely true. Yes, he'd been his wolf at first… but biting her had been all him.

CHAPTER NINE

ARES

Ares disembarked his private jet with Santiago waiting for him at the bottom of the steps and Theo at his back. He sniffed the air, and his wolf grumbled.

I know. I'm moving.

Ares' wolf didn't like how long he'd been apart from River any more than Ares did. If anything, he thought his wolf might miss her more. Well... not miss her more, but he was far more out of control than he ever had been before, that was sure. It was all Ares could do recently to keep his wolf from taking over. Even letting his wolf run the estate as well as the neighborhood to smell for himself that her scent didn't linger had only angered his wolf further. Every day since her absence, he'd taken to running a minimum of twenty miles. Double what he was used to, but it didn't matter. It was as if he'd not exercised at all within an hour of finishing.

A black SUV sat at the steps of the plane, and a driver exited. Ares recognized him, but didn't know his name. He was the son of the local Alpha.

Santiago shook hands with the man, and Ares walked down the steps to the vehicle. Theo opened the door.

"Prince Ares, this is Romero."

Ares nodded.

"Highness." Romero gave a slight bow. "It's an honor to have you in our area. My father was upset that he couldn't meet you himself, but my mother is still not healed."

A pang of guilt struck Ares. Romero's mother had been one of the Lunas injured in the attack. "Is there anything she needs? A specialist? Anything?"

"No, Highness. Just rest. Thank you."

Ares held his hand out to Santiago. Santiago dug in his coat pocket and handed Ares a business card. Ares handed the card to Romero. "If your family needs anything at all, you call Santiago, and he'll make sure you get it."

Romero bowed. "That is most generous of you, Majesty."

"Not at all. It is the loyalty of Alphas and Lunas like your parents that is most generous."

Ares slid into the back seat, Theo slipped behind the wheel, and Santiago shut Ares' door before walking to the passenger side and getting in.

Romero bowed one last time before walking to a flashy yellow Corvette and getting in.

Ares sat back and closed his eyes. "How long?"

"Thirty minutes." Theo turned the SUV around and headed off the tarmac.

They needed to get to Dr. Emerson, find out where the hell he was sending the blockers, and make him stop. Period.

THEO PULLED THE SUV UP TO THE FRONT OF A TALL, MODERN GLASS building and came to a stop. Ares hadn't quite decided how he was going to obtain what he wanted from the humans inside. He wasn't used to dealing with humans without some sort of introduction from the people he employed to deal with his businesses beyond the shifter world. This was a first. Most humans were unaware of his status; therefore, they never felt the same compulsion to acquiesce to his demands as wolves did. Not unless he was introduced as Prince Ares. Even in the human world, a royal title carried considerable weight.

Ares buttoned his suit jacket and strode to the front door. Theo opened it for him, and he proceeded inside to the security desk. Theo moved forward and handed the guard Ares' business card before Ares spoke.

The man looked at it and then looked between Ares and Theo. "Can I help you?"

"I'm here to see Dr. Emerson."

The guard glanced at his computer screen. "I'm sorry, sir, but Dr. Emerson doesn't appear to have any appointments scheduled today."

"He'll want to see me," Ares said firmly.

The guard hesitated. "I'm afraid I can't let you up without an appointment, Mr...?"

"Wolvenguard," Ares supplied. "Call Dr. Emerson and let him know Ares Wolvenguard is here to discuss his special pharmaceutical projects. I'm sure he'll make time for me."

"I'm sorry, but we can't just let anyone into the building, as I'm sure you understand."

"This isn't just anyone," said Theo. "This is Prince Ares Wolvenguard."

"I'm sure if you tell Dr. Emerson my name and let him know I am here to discuss the special project he has been working on and that my mother-in-law, Cherry, gave me his information, he will see me."

"I'm sorry-"

Ares' wolf leapt to his feet. Ares slammed his fist on the granite counter and took a calming breath.

He's a human. He doesn't understand. He doesn't know what's going on.

"Surely you can ask," Theo offered. "After all, you wouldn't want to be the reason Dr. Emerson missed such an important meeting, would you?"

The man licked his lips, wetting his Tom Seleck mustache, and looked at Ares' business card again. He picked up the phone and dialed an extension, speaking quietly for a moment before hanging up.

Ares struggled not to rip the phone from the man's hand and demand to be let up.

He shook his head. "I'm sorry, but Dr. Emerson has already left for the day."

"Left?"

"Yes. His assistant said that he went home about an hour ago."

"Can I get his home address?"

The guard slid Ares' card back across the counter. "If you would like to call his assistant and make an appointment, I am sure she will find a time to fit you in."

Theo opened his mouth, but Ares stopped him. "Since I'm already here, may I go up and speak to her?"

"I'm afraid not. But I'll call and see if she will come down to talk to you."

Ares nodded, jaw clenched. "Thank you."

The guard pointed at a pair of couches several feet away. "You can wait over there."

Ares picked up his card and handed it to Theo, who put it back in his jacket pocket.

"I could knock him out, and we could find the information on the computer."

Ares unbuttoned his suit jacket and sat on the couch. "We can't risk scaring the doctor or his assistant. Or the police being called.

That would waste too much time. As much as I would love to choke the information out of that guy, I think employing a more Apollo-style approach might be better this time."

Theo cocked an eyebrow.

Ares snorted. "Trust me, he isn't rubbing off on me that much. I just think that if we are dealing with humans, the last thing we need is human police involved. We have enough problems at the moment."

Theo nodded as an elevator opened and out walked a pretty, petite brunette in a simple black dress and sensible heels. She walked over to the security desk and then turned to look at Ares before striding toward them.

Ares stood. If he hadn't been mated, he would have done whatever it took to get the information out of the woman. While he needed the info more desperately than he'd ever needed anything in his life, even he couldn't stoop that low. He just prayed it wouldn't take something like that to get the assistant to tell him where Dr. Emerson was and how he could meet with him.

"Hello," the assistant said nervously. "I'm Amanda, Dr. Emerson's assistant. I heard you would like to make an appointment."

"It's imperative I speak with him today. I need to speak to him about some pills that he sold my mother-in-law for my wife."

The assistant glanced over at the guard, who watched the interaction.

"I'm sorry, Dr. Emerson is a chemist; he does the research, he cannot prescribe or sell pills of any kind. It's against the law."

"Of course," said Ares, fighting to keep his tone friendly. "Maybe I'm mistaken, but my mother-in-law gave me the doctor's name. If I could speak to him, I'm sure he can help me figure out who I should be looking for."

"What's the name of the pills you say he gave her or told her about?"

"Uh… I'm not sure they have a name."

She scoffed. "How do you expect him to help you then?"

Ares growled, and his wolf got to his feet.

The assistant backed up, but Theo touched her hand and smiled.

"Please," said Theo. "We came all the way from Canada. We just need to speak to him for a moment. If there is any way you could help. Prince Ares'… wife's life could depend on it."

Amanda's eyes drifted to where Theo held her hand and then to his gentle smile.

Damn, he was good. If Ares weren't mated or so ready to shift at any provocation, he would have thought of using the same tactic. But since finding River, he couldn't even imagine touching another woman, let alone flirting with her.

"I… well… I could call him, I suppose…"

Theo's smile widened. "I appreciate that, but I wonder if maybe there was any way you could tell us where he lives."

She shook her head violently. "I can't do that; he would fire me."

"I'll pay you," said Ares. "A hundred thousand dollars."

Her eyes widened, and her mouth dropped open. "I… Surely you're kidding."

"Two hundred." Ares' patience hung by a silken thread.

"I…"

"Three hundred."

The assistant pulled her hand from Theo's and blinked several times before swallowing hard.

"Five hundred," she whispered.

"Done." Ares held out his hand. "Give me your phone."

"You're serious?"

"If you end up getting fired, you call me, and I'll have you employed somewhere else in twenty-four hours at double your current salary."

She held her phone out with a shaky hand.

He used her phone to call his cell and then handed it back.

"Text me the doctor's address and your bank account number."

She looked between them like she couldn't tell if it was some kind of trap.

Ares sat back on the couch. "I'll wait here until you send me the information. I'll send the money immediately. You can watch if you want."

"I have to get the address."

Ares nodded. "Go ahead. As you can see, I'm not leaving without it."

She turned quickly and headed for the elevator.

Theo sat next to him. "I'm sure she would have taken the one hundred if you'd waited."

"I would have gone up to five hundred million if it got me one step nearer to finding River. Five hundred thousand was a bargain."

THE SUV STOPPED BY A SPRAWLING RANCH-STYLE HOUSE ON THE outskirts of Indianapolis. Ares exited, his senses on high alert as he scanned the area. The property appeared quiet, with no visible signs of activity or security measures beyond a few basic cameras.

He marched to the front door and knocked. After a few moments, he heard shuffling inside. The door cracked open, revealing a wiry man with thinning gray hair.

"Can I help you?"

"Dr. Emerson?"

The man looked over Ares' shoulder to Theo, and then he licked his lips. "Sorry, you have the wrong house."

He started to shut the door, but Ares wedged his foot in the gap.

"I'm Prince Ares Wolvenguard."

The doctor's eyes widened in recognition.

"I'm not here to harm you. I just need information about the suppressants you make. Tell me what I need to know, and I'll leave, and you won't have to see me again."

Dr. Emerson hesitated. "You can come in. But I warn you, I have security measures in place."

Ares wanted to laugh at the threat, but he didn't. Instead, he nodded and followed the doctor inside to a cluttered living room.

The doctor gestured for him to sit. "What do you want to know?"

"Everything. But let's start with who you've been supplying lately. Particularly any large orders."

The doctor shook his head. "I can't reveal client information. That would violate-"

Ares leaned forward, his eyes flashing gold. "Doctor, I don't have time for games. Rogues have taken my mate, and I believe they're using your suppressants."

Dr. Emerson swallowed hard. "I... I understand your concern, but I am unable to divulge that information. My clients trust me with their privacy."

"And I'm trusting you to do the right thing," Ares growled. "These aren't ordinary clients. They're dangerous rogues who have killed people. Innocent people."

The doctor's eyes widened. "Killed? I had no idea..."

"Now you do," Ares said firmly. "So I'll ask again- who have you been supplying large orders to recently?"

Dr. Emerson wrung his hands. "I... there was a substantial order about a month ago. Much bigger than anything I'd filled before. But I don't know the client's name. It was all done through intermediaries, very hush-hush."

Ares leaned in. "Tell me everything you remember about that order. Every detail."

The doctor nodded shakily. "It was for a new formulation- stronger, longer-lasting. They wanted it in both pill and injectable form. The quantity was... massive. Enough to suppress hundreds of wolves for months."

"Where was it shipped to?"

"I don't know the final destination. They had me deliver it to a storage unit in Cincinnati, Ohio. After that, I have no idea where it went."

Ares' heart raced.

"I need the address of that storage unit," he said. "And anything else you can tell me about these people?"

Dr. Emerson hesitated, then sighed. "There's something else. The formulation they requested. It isn't just stronger- it has some unusual additions. Components I'd never worked with before."

Ares' brow furrowed. "What kind of additions?"

"Compounds that would not just suppress shifter abilities, but... alter brain chemistry. Increase suggestibility."

A chill ran down Ares' spine. The implications were horrifying. What was Titan planning to do with suppressants like that?

"I need samples," Ares said. "And formulas. Can you provide those?"

The doctor nodded. "I can. But you have to promise me protection. If these people find out I helped you..."

"You have my word," Ares said. "The full protection of the Royal Wolvenguard family. Just get me what I need. Did they place another order?"

"Yes. I'm supposed to deliver more in two days."

Two days? He had to wait two more days for answers? "Give us the package. We'll deliver it."

"It's not finished."

"Doesn't matter. It won't be getting to them anyway."

Dr. Emerson chewed his lip and then got up, hurrying from the room.

Ares' mind raced. They had a lead- a tangible connection. But he would have to wait two whole days.

His wolf grumbled. N*o wait. Now.*

"Ares, we need to keep him from making any more for them."

Ares nodded.

"Suggestibility?" Theo muttered. "The implications of that are limitless."

"It's possible he means to use them on the rogues to keep them compliant," said Santiago.

"Or on us, or the Alphas."

Ares chewed his lip. Was it possible that Titan didn't have the same command that he and Apollo did? He was an Alpha, yes. He was their father's son… but he wasn't their father's offspring by his fated mate. Did that make a difference? Was there something more to it than that?

He didn't know. But the possibility was intriguing.

Ares rubbed the center of his sternum. The following 48 hours, waiting for the drop, would be the longest two days of his life. He had no clue what the hell he would do in the meantime.

CHAPTER TEN

TITAN

Titan walked briskly down the hallway, his mind racing. He shook his head, trying to clear his thoughts as he approached the meeting room. Now wasn't the time to dwell on River and what she had said to him, or had not said. What she thought of the art studio, or didn't think. He had more pressing matters to attend to.

As he entered, Kane and several other high-ranking members of his pack stood from their seats around the large oak table.

"Report." Titan took his place at the head of the table.

Kane moved forward, his face grim. "The shipment of new suppressors should be here in three days."

"Did Doctor Emerson contact us with a total?"

Kane shook his head. "Not yet. He's most likely still working on it. You doubled the order this time."

Titan nodded. "As soon as he delivers to the storage unit and it's been picked up, send the money. We need to make sure he stays invested in helping us."

Kane nodded.

"Ares and Apollo?"

"Nothing."

"And the safe house?"

“We have everyone on it. The estate is under total surveillance. If they or any of their missing guards show up, we'll know."

"We need to accelerate our timeline," Titan said. "How soon can we be ready to move on the estate?"

The room fell silent as the others exchanged uneasy glances.

"Highness," Kane began, "are you sure that's wise? We're still outnumbered, and many of our people aren't trained."

Titan's eyes flashed. "Are you questioning me, brother?"

Kane held his gaze. "I'm advising caution. We've come too far to risk everything on a hasty attack."

For a long moment, tension crackled between them. Then Titan sighed. "You're right," he admitted. "We can't afford to be reckless. But we also can't afford to let Ares and Apollo gain ground. We need a new strategy."

He turned to address the room. "I want options by morning. I also want a complete inventory of our weapons and supplies. If we can't outfight them yet, we'll have to outmaneuver them."

As the others nodded and began discussing potential plans, Titan's thoughts drifted back to River. He wondered what she was doing in the art studio. If she was plotting her own escape, or if maybe, just maybe, she'd started seeing things differently.

He shoved the thought aside.

One thing at a time.

CHAPTER ELEVEN

RIVER

As soon as Titan left, River let out a harsh breath she hadn't realized she'd been holding. She scanned the extensive art studio again, taking in all the high-end supplies and equipment. Part of her was impressed- but another part unsettled.

She walked over to the mini-fridge, retrieved a can of cola, cracked it open, and took a long swig. The cool liquid soothed her still-unsettled stomach. Inside sat fruit, a sandwich, yogurt, and even a couple of candy bars. As much as she wanted to rip into the candy bars, she had nowhere in the art room to throw up. River wandered around the room, running her fingers over easels and examining the various paints and brushes.

"What do you think?" she murmured to her wolf. "Should we try our hand at painting after all?"

Her wolf gave a noncommittal grumble in response. River couldn't blame her- this wasn't the time for artistic exploration. This was an opportunity to identify weaknesses and plan their escape. River placed the soda on a table and began her search.

Twenty minutes later, after River had methodically inspected every inch of the room, looking for anything that could be useful. The windows were reinforced and didn't open. The solid door locked from the outside. The French doors had three locks on them and an alarm at the top that would sound if they were opened. And with her wolf out of commission, there would be no way for her to rip the wood between the small panes of glass apart enough to get out anyway.

She sighed and turned, inspecting the room again. A small wisp of AC caressed her ankle. She looked around again, and her eyes stopped at a corner where a large table sat. She walked to it, and the breeze grew stronger. She dropped to all fours and looked under the table.

Aha!

Under the table stood an 18-inch square vent. River hopped to her feet and looked around. She found a palette knife on the table and took it before dropping to her knees again. She crawled under the table and unscrewed the vent cover. It dropped to the ground, and the slats shook. River caught it and muffled the sound before holding her breath.

She waited. Seconds ticked by, and nothing happened. Finally, she breathed again and moved the vent to the side.

She stuck her hand into the vent, but there was no metal shaft inside. Instead, it felt like the same cement she sat on. She tried to look inside but couldn't see anything. Air flowed out, but not from a connected vent; it was from something else. The sound of whirring filled the air. She thought about climbing in, but without a way to see what was inside, it was too dangerous to risk it.

She replaced the vent cover, screwed in the screws with her fingers, then crawled out from under the table and put the palette knife back. She thought about taking it to use as a weapon, but it was too short, thin, and dull ever to be effective. It was effective at removing screws, though. That could come in handy. She went to snatch it back up but stopped, wondering if there were cameras in the room. She scanned the ceiling and walls but didn't see any.

If she were a prisoner, and Titan didn't want her to escape... why didn't he have cameras on her at all times?

She moved slowly back to the main easel, inspecting every surface as she went. Still, she didn't see anything that looked like a camera. She folded her arms over her chest and chewed the inside of her lip as she inspected the few items that could potentially be used as weapons in a pinch. Wooden paint brushes, more palette knives, palettes. Paint thinner would be great if she had a lighter, which she didn't. Several ceramic mugs. She could break one and use the shards, possibly, but Titan would notice for sure. She looked at the paintbrushes in the mug again and stopped. She pulled out a smaller, shorter brush with an acrylic handle. She ran her fingers down it to the angled tip. Now that she could use as a weapon, but nothing would help her break out.

With a sigh, River sank onto a plush armchair in the corner. She rubbed her belly, thinking of the life growing inside her. A tidal wave of protectiveness washed over her.

"We'll find a way out of here. I promise."

She stared at the blank canvas, and her thoughts drifted to Ares and Apollo. Were they looking for her? Of course they were. But would they find her? And if they did, would they live through the encounter? Titan seemed to have planned everything meticulously. And he had an arsenal of guns…

She shook her head. She had to stay focused on finding a way to escape and get back to her mates. If she could escape, Ares and Apollo wouldn't need to come to Titan's place. They wouldn't be put in further danger. But she needed to get out.

River stood and shuffled to the easel. Maybe painting would help her think, give her subconscious mind space to work on the problem. She squeezed some paint onto a palette and picked up a brush, staring at the blank canvas.

Without thinking, she ran the soft brush over the canvas, leaving a long, dark streak. She looked at it, and an image formed. Using broad strokes of sky blue and purple, the image began to take shape. River painted a night sky as seen from the forest where she'd gone with Apollo.

RIVER BACKED AWAY FROM THE CANVAS, SURVEYING HER WORK. THE night sky she'd painted was hauntingly beautiful, stars twinkling against the midnight blue backdrop. It was far from perfect, but if she was going for impressionism, it wasn't bad.

She snorted and then chuckled.

She continued to dissect the painting. Something was missing.

She picked up a smaller brush and dabbed on more detail. Three wolves emerging from the shadows at the edge of the canvas-one silver, one black and white, one russet brown. River's ribcage tightened as she painted, memories flooding back.

The bond with Ares and Apollo warmed her. The sense of belonging, of being seen and accepted. The fierce protectiveness and love that had enveloped her. Being with both of them. Loving them unconditionally and without restraint. Feelings she never thought she'd experience.

A tear slipped down her cheek, and she swiped it away. She couldn't afford to break. She had to stay strong, stay focused.

River placed the brush on the easel and walked over to a window, pressing her forehead against the cool glass.

Her hand drifted to her abdomen again. How long before she started showing? How long could she keep her pregnancy hidden?

Her wolf grumbled. *Escape. Ares. Apollo. Home.*

"I know," she murmured. "We'll get out of here. Somehow."

CHAPTER TWELVE

APOLLO

Apollo paced in the safehouse, his muscles tense with pent-up energy. It had been a day since Ares left for Indianapolis, and Apollo was going stir-crazy waiting for news. His wounds had mostly healed, but he still hadn't regained full strength. Doctor Keller insisted on more rest, but how could he rest when River was out there somewhere, in danger, and he sat doing nothing?

Okay… that wasn't true. He'd been busy. More than busy. Calling Alphas. Coordinating transportation. Sending condolences. Smoothing things over. Asking for more support. Demanding loyalty from those who seemed unsure before. Reinforcing the fact that they still ruled. Ensuring everything ran smoothly despite the disaster surrounding them.

Apollo paused by the window, staring out at the wooded property surrounding the safehouse. His wolf whined, desperate to break free and search for their mate. Apollo gritted his teeth, forcing the urge down. Charging off half-cocked would do more harm than good. But every instinct in his body screamed for him to act.

A knock at the door interrupted his brooding. "Come in."

Silas entered, a tablet in hand. "We've got an update from Ares."

Apollo's heart raced. "Did he find something?"

Silas nodded, his expression grim. "He tracked down the chemist making the suppressants. Titan ordered a substantial quantity about a month ago- enough for hundreds of wolves. But that's not the worst part."

Apollo's gut clenched. "What do you mean?"

"The suppressants aren't just stronger. They've been modified to increase suggestibility. Almost like..."

"Mind control," Apollo finished, a chill running down his spine. "Shit." He ran a hand through his hair, mind racing. "Where were they shipped?"

"They are to be delivered tomorrow to a storage unit in Ohio. Ares is heading there now to investigate."

Apollo nodded, already moving towards the door. "I'm going too. Have the jet ready in thirty minutes."

Silas blocked his path. "Apollo, you're not ready. The doctor-"

"I don't give a damn what the doctor says," Apollo growled, his eyes flashing gold. "That's my mate out there. And if Titan's planning something with those suppressants, we don't have time to waste."

Silas held his gaze for a long moment, then sighed and moved aside. "I'll have the team ready to move out in twenty."

As Silas left to make the arrangements, Apollo picked up his phone and dialed Ares. His brother picked up on the first ring.

"I'm on my way," Apollo said. "Send me the address for the storage unit. I'll meet you there."

There was a pause on the other end of the line. Then Ares spoke, his voice tight with contained emotion. "No, brother. You have to stay there. I need you there. I need you to keep things running."

Apollo swore. "I never should have let you go. I'm the oldest. I'm the Alpha of Alphas. It's my job-"

"To keep tight reins on our kingdom. That's your job. You know when shit hits the fan, I can barge in and make things happen, but this isn't the time. If we are to stay ahead of Titan and on top of the whispers and rumors that are more than likely flying around right now, we need a king. A king who is logical but also caring. You are that king. Let me do my job, and you do yours. It's what we do. You're the mercy. I'm the justice. Two sides to the same shit sandwich."

Apollo snorted. "Wow. Couldn't think of a better analogy?"

"Nope. That's why I'm not the brains."

Apollo rubbed his forehead. "Fine. I'll stay here. But no more talking to Silas or any of the others. You call me."

"Will do."

"Every two hours."

"Okay. Except, I'm going to grab some sleep. Theo will wake me if anything changes. I'll call you immediately if it does. Otherwise, we both need sleep."

Sleep? How the hell could he even think of sleeping with River still gone?

"Apollo?"

"Yeah."

"Go to bed. You're no good to her if you aren't fully healed and you're exhausted."

Apollo swallowed hard. "I hate it when you're right."

Ares laughed. "Then you must hate me all the time."

Apollo shook his head. What an ass.

CHAPTER THIRTEEN

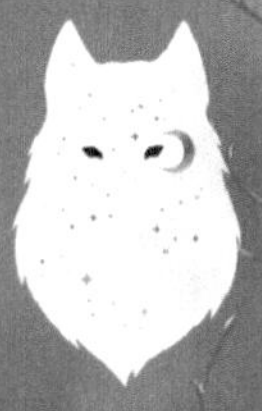

RIVER

The intercom by the door buzzed, startling River. She hesitated, then walked over and depressed the button.

"Yes?"

"Luna," a voice responded. "The Alpha requests your presence for dinner in an hour. May I come in and take you back to your room?"

River's wolf grumbled at the thought of sitting across from Titan. River grumbled at the idea of making polite conversation while pretending she wasn't his prisoner. But she couldn't refuse either. Not if she wanted to maintain the illusion of cooperation.

"Fine."

The door opened, and Austin, the guy from her old pack, gave her a small wave.

Her eyes widened. What was he doing there? Had Titan sent him for some specific reason? He had to have. Titan wouldn't let just anyone come near her. He had to have chosen Austin for a reason.

"Hi," she said.

"Luna." He inclined his head.

"Stop that," she said. "I hate that crap."

He looked at her and smiled.

"What?"

"Same girl I knew all those years ago."

Her eyes narrowed. "You remember me?"

He snorted. "How could I not? There aren't many females who look like you, but at the same time, not a single male is interested in her. And has no scent at all."

She swallowed hard. "It was the blockers."

"Your mom is a smart lady. Tough too. She was the one who made sure I packed up and left."

A pit opened up in River's stomach. Had her mom done that? There was so much she didn't know.

"I don't blame her," Austin said. She did what she was ordered to do. And now that I realize how much she was trying to protect, I understand even better."

"Why were you told to leave?"

"I thought everyone knew why."

She shook her head. "Cherry kept me out of the pack politics."

Austin shoved his hands in his jeans pockets. "Makes sense. Well, officially, I was accused of hugging the Beta's mate and trying to kiss her."

"Officially?"

"That's what the Beta and Alpha told everyone."

"That's not the truth?"

"The truth was, my great-grandfather was the original Alpha of the pack. My grandfather left when the current Alpha's grandfather beat him for control. My mother returned after my father died, and the Alpha was afraid I would try to take the pack back. I assured him the last thing I wanted was to lead. He didn't believe me, I guess. So he made up a reason to get rid of me."

River had no words. She walked back to her painting, starting to clean the brushes in a can of water. "Your mom is still with the pack, though."

"I told her to stay. She'd already been through enough when she lost my dad. I didn't want her to lose her pack again to leave with me. I still see her once a month. We meet for lunch. It's been tough on her."

"So we are near enough to the pack that you and your mom get together?"

Austin opened his mouth, stopped, and smiled. "Smart. Try to get me to tell you where we are. Sorry, Luna. If Titan wants you to know, he will tell you himself."

Her wolf sighed.

It had been worth a try. "Do you want revenge on our Alpha?"

"He's not my Alpha anymore, and yes, I do want revenge for what he did to me. I don't want him dead, but I don't want him to do to anyone else what he's done to me."

"And how do you think that's gonna go? You think Titan is just going to sit down and have a friendly chat with the Alpha about not kicking others out?"

"Come on, Luna, you and I both know he won't. Do I want to hurt people? No. But do things need to evolve? Yeah, they do. If violence is the only way to get it, then that's the only choice they've given us."

River stared at him, then wiped the brushes down with a cloth and set them on the table. "That's why Titan had you come fetch me, isn't it? He was hoping you would connect with me and convince me to come over to the dark side."

He shrugged.

"Sorry, it won't work."

He shrugged again. "It's worth a shot. We'd be much more powerful with you by Titan's side. And look what you had to go through just to keep you safe. You think that if everyone had known you were an Omega, you wouldn't have been sold off to the most powerful bidder?"

"You think my mom would have let that happen?"

He shrugged. "Your mom is tough, but even she can't say no to an Alpha."

"I can."

He looked at her, and his eyebrows drew together. "Really?"

"I told Titan no. Rejected him on the spot four years ago when he found me. You do know Titan bit me without permission, right? That members of his pack, your pack, attacked and shot me to kidnap me. That Titan shot my mates and tried to murder them, and then kidnapped me and is now holding me hostage here?"

Austin's eyes widened, and he licked his lips. "I didn't know he bit you without permission. He told us you are his mate and that Apollo and Ares had tricked you, and he brought you here to learn the truth."

She snorted. "That's about as truthful as what the Alpha said you did. So, what were you saying about me being sold off to the highest bidder under Ares and Apollo's rule? I would rather have taken my chances with any Alpha of the shifters than what Titan did to me. In the end, it wouldn't have mattered anyway, though, would it? I was not the fated mate of a shifter Alpha. I'm the fated mate of Ares and Apollo. My wolf rejected Titan the first time she saw him."

For a moment, Austin looked conflicted.

"You could help me. Do the right thing. Help me escape. I promise you, Austin, when I return home, I will ensure they are aware of what is happening to shifters and put a stop to it. That no one else is kicked out. That the Alphas are held accountable for what they've done."

The sound of loud footsteps descended the stairs. River rushed to Austin, clutching his arm.

"Please, Austin," she begged.

Kane walked into view, and River dropped her hand as Austin turned.

"You should be dressed by now," said Kane. "Titan is waiting."

"I was just taking her back to her room," said Austin.

"I'll do it."

Austin inclined his head and left before River could say another word.

Dammit. River backed away from Kane as he moved further into the room.

She bumped the table, and several of the brushes rolled to the floor.

"Come on. You need to get dressed."

River squatted down and picked up the brushes. She looked at them momentarily and then set them down slowly on the table, being sure to cover them with her frame. She snatched up the acrylic brush and shoved it up her sleeve before folding her arms and turning back to Kane.

She kept her breathing and heartbeat even as she followed Kane silently back to her cell. Had she gotten through to Austin at all? Or had she made things worse by revealing that Titan had lied to his followers?

Kane opened the door to her room and gestured for her to enter. "You have five minutes to get ready, then I'll escort you to dinner."

River nodded, not trusting herself to speak. As soon as the door slammed behind her, she let out a shaky breath and ran to the bed. She watched the door for a moment and then slid the paintbrush from her sweatshirt sleeve. She glanced around for a place to hide it and walked to the fridge. She opened it, but there was no place to conceal it. She opened the freezer and then the ice maker. She shoved the brush inside the compartment and shut it again.

She couldn't think of another place Titan may not search at some point. Cliché but effective.

She pulled her hair from the scrunchie.

Her conversation with Austin gave her a lot to think about. She'd known many of the rogues following Titan had legitimate grievances against the current Lycan power structure. However, hearing Austin's story firsthand drove home the complexity of the situation.

Still, that didn't justify Titan's actions. Or make her captivity any more acceptable.

River shuffled to the closet, surveying the clothes Titan had provided. Most were casual, wearing jeans, T-shirts, and sweaters. But there were a few dresses as well.

As she undressed, River caught sight of herself in the mirror. The slight swell of her belly seemed more noticeable than ever. She ran a hand over the bump. Soon, she wouldn't be able to hide it. She had to escape before she reached that point.

She pulled on a simple navy-blue sweater and a pair of wide-leg cotton pants, grateful for their flowing designs. As she knotted her hair into a simple braid, the bag of makeup sitting on her bathroom counter caught her eye. No way in hell was she going to make herself look any better than she had to. Hell, if he'd gifted her makeup to make her look worse, she would have put it all over her face. Though she doubted it would have helped. Titan had the crazy idea in his mind that she was his mate, and she doubted even goth clown makeup would deter him.

She threw the makeup bag in the trash can. She needed to find something to turn him off. Maybe she could eat like a pig. Slop food all over herself.

She glanced at the fake window in the corner, suddenly missing the real windows in the art room that let her feel real sunlight. A fake garden played on the video screen with the grass swaying in an unnatural breeze. If she hadn't known it was fake, she would have believed it was a real window. Titan had spared not even a penny when putting together her prison. She closed her eyes and imagined the real grounds of the Wolvenguard house stretched out before her, lush and green. The feel of grass between her toes. The smell of the trees, soil, and water from the pool. The scent of wood shards and motor oil in the barn.

Her wolf whined, and River swallowed down her own whine.

A knock at the door signaled Kane's impatience, bringing her back to reality. River steeled herself.

Whatever game Titan was playing, she had to stay sharp. She had to look for any opportunity or weakness she could exploit. For her sake, for her baby's sake, and for the sake of everyone counting on her.

CHAPTER FOURTEEN

TITAN

Titan paced the length of the formal dining room, tension radiating through him. He'd instructed Anna, a former executive chef and the rogues, to prepare an elaborate meal to demonstrate to River that life with him could be good and comfortable. Luxurious, even. The twins weren't the only ones who could spoil her.

Rich tapestries and exquisite paintings adorned the formal dining room. A crystal chandelier hung from the ceiling, casting a warm glow across the room. Fine china and silver cutlery adorned the table. And every inch of their opulence had him almost as on edge as waiting for River. None of it was his. His mother had designed every foot of the house. Every painting her choice. And every dollar's worth of finery his mother's dream. To Titan, they were nothing more than a waste. However, he was more than happy to use them in his favor if it meant he might be able to win over River.

Titan's dark navy suit clung to his broad shoulders, making it tighter than it should. The last time he'd worn the suit had been at his mother's funeral. His heart squeezed at the memory. Though it had been years, he felt like every day was the day he'd found his mom's body in her bed. A wave of grief washed through him, and he locked it away, refusing to give in to sadness, knowing that she would be proud to see what he'd become and what he'd built for her. And even more so that he was going to be king with an Omega as his mate.

He glanced at the wall clock. River should have been there over fifteen minutes prior. Was he fooling himself? Would she refuse to come? Could he ever win her over after everything that had happened? Everything he'd done?

The door opened, and Kane entered with River close behind. Titan's breath caught at the sight of her. The simple blue sweater hugged her curves in all the right places, and her hair gleamed silver in the soft lighting. The comfortable-looking pants seemed to dwarf her petite frame, but also suited her. He'd never seen her wear anything like it before. That pleased him. She was trying new things. First painting and now new styles. It was a good sign.

"River. You look lovely."

"It's a sweater and knit pants." She scanned him. "Guess I underdressed for the occasion."

"No. You're perfect." Titan strode forward and pulled out a chair for her.

His wolf whined and paced.

Keep it cool. Stay cool.

She eyed him and sat.

He felt Kane's harsh gaze and nodded to him. He didn't need Kane's presence upsetting dinner.

Kane glanced at the back of River's head and left without a word.

Titan lifted River's chair and slid her into the table. "Would you like some wine?"

"Cola."

He looked over at the wine he'd picked out specifically for dinner, and his smile fell.

His wolf growled. *No. Respect.*

Shut it.

Titan had spent an hour looking over the bottles in his cellar. "Of course."

He turned to Austin, standing in the corner. "Get my mate a cola from the fridge, please."

Austin nodded.

"Bring a whole six-pack, please," River said.

Austin smiled. "Of course, Highness."

Titan's wolf leapt to his feet and bared his teeth. *No talk. No smile. Mine. My mate.*

Titan's wolf surged forward, wanting to rip Austin apart for smiling at River.

Titan swallowed hard and walked to the other end of the table before sitting.

He knows River. They grew up together in the same pack. We want her to be comfortable, he reminded himself, as well as his wolf.

Titan poured a large glass of wine, downed it, then refilled the glass. "You can go, Austin. I'll call you when we are ready for the main course."

Austin nodded. "Of course, Highness."

Titan waited for Austin to disappear before blowing out a breath. Why the hell was he so nervous? Why was he like an anxious pup on its first pack run?

He sipped his wine and swirled it on his tongue. He forced a smile on his face as River scrutinized him.

"How did the painting go? Did you like it?"

Austin returned with the six-pack, tore one from the pack, and handed it to River before retreating to the corner. River popped the tab on the cola and took a sip. "The supplies are impressive."

Titan beamed. "I'm glad you liked them. I wanted to make sure you had everything you might need."

"Except my freedom," River muttered.

An awkward silence fell between them as the first course was served- an elegant salad with candied walnuts and goat cheese.

River picked at her food, and Titan searched for something to say.

"I hope you're finding your accommodations comfortable," he ventured.

River dropped her fork with a clatter. "My accommodations? Are we going to do this? Pretend I've been allowed accommodations, not a holding cell. That this is a dinner date and not you kidnapped me and forced me to come up here?"

Titan clutched his fork so tight it bent. He laid it on the table, trying to figure out the best response. How much longer could he put up with her constant rejection without lashing out? He'd never had a woman not want him before. Rebuff him at every turn and look at him like he'd murdered her toy poodle and laughed while he'd done it.

"I'm trying to make the best of a difficult situation. For both of us."

"Both of us?" River scoffed. "You're the one who chose to attack my mates to take me against my will, and to lock me up in your house as a prisoner. How in the world is this 'difficult' on you at all?"

"I had no choice but to take you!" Titan growled. "You're my mate. I couldn't stand by and let you bond with them."

River leaned forward, her eyes glowing with anger. "I am not your mate. I rejected you. You have no claim on me."

Titan stiffened, trying to keep his wolf at bay.

Take. Mine. Mate. Take now. Make her submit.

No!

His wolf tore at his chains to be let free. *Weak. Insignificant. Human.*

Titan shoved his wolf away. If he lost it now, she'd never accept him.

His wolf growled, but Titan refused to back down.

Finally, his wolf backed off but didn't entirely lie down.

He opened his eyes to find River staring at him.

"I know you don't believe me now," he said, trying to keep his voice even. "But in time, you'll see. We're meant to be together, River. Everything I've done, building this pack, gathering these rogues, it's all been for you. To create a world where we can be together without interference from the old guard."

River shook her head. "You're delusional, Titan. What you're doing is wrong. These rogues have genuine grievances and real pain. But you're using them for your own selfish ends."

Titan's wolf lunged forward, and Titan slammed his fist on the table, making the dishes rattle. "I'm trying to change things for the better. To create a world where no one has to suffer like I did, like my mother did, and like the other rogues have."

River's lips thinned. "Is that what you are doing? Or are you just trying to enact some petty vengeance on those you perceive as having wronged you?"

Titan stared at her, unable to look away. A strange sensation raced through him. Her steady, heavy stare told him he should cower. He should look away and submit to her. He didn't like it. Didn't like how her stare made him feel. Weak. Out of control.

Though Titan refused to look away, his wolf laid down and submitted to her.

Holy shit.

His wolf had never done that to another wolf ever. Not his mother. Not his father. Not Kane. No one. Shifter or Lycan.

"Enough of this," Titan growled. "Eat. You need to keep up your strength."

Titan downed his second glass of wine before pouring a third.

River picked up her fork again and stabbed her salad. He waited for her to eat first, and when she didn't, he gave in and ate.

CHAPTER FIFTEEN

APOLLO

Apollo stretched his arm, trying to loosen the tightness in his ribs. He glanced at the clock. It was five a.m., and even though he'd gotten less than five hours of sleep, he was sick of being in bed. Sick of sitting around waiting. Sick of feeling utterly useless.

A knock sounded on his door, and it opened before he could tell the person to enter.

Cherry stood in the doorway, anger vibrating off her like a tidal wave.

"Well," she said. "Where's my daughter?"

Apollo tensed. He'd known this confrontation was coming, but he'd hoped to have more information from Ares.

"Cherry," he said. "We're doing everything we can to find her."

Cherry strode into the room, her eyes flashing, lips pulled into a snarl. "Everything? Because from where I'm standing, it looks like you're lying in bed while my daughter is out there with that psychopath."

Apollo winced, both from the pain in his ribs and the truth of her words. "I swear to you, we have every available resource working on tracking down Titan and his rogues here, and Ares is in the States following the lead we got from Dr. Emerson."

"And what are you doing?" Cherry demanded. "Other than recuperating in luxury while River suffers?"

Apollo's jaw clenched. He understood Cherry's anger and fear-he felt it too, constantly. But her accusation stung.

His wolf growled. *Make her submit. We are King.*

If it had been anyone but Cherry or River, he would have done it in an instant. Strider, Zeke, even Bianca wouldn't have gotten away with speaking to him like that. But Cherry… she was a different animal. On top of that, if he had a daughter and she'd been kidnapped, he would be acting the same way.

Apollo winced. "I assure you, we haven't stopped searching for a moment-"

"Not good enough," Cherry snapped. "Get up. We're going to find her ourselves."

"Rushing out with no plan of action or idea where we are even going won't help River. We need to be smart."

Cherry strode forward and yanked the covers off Apollo's legs. "I don't care about being smart. I care about my daughter. Now get dressed, or I'll drag you out of here in your underwear."

"I'm coordinating our search efforts. Analyzing intel, directing our teams. And as soon as I'm physically able, I'll be out there myself."

Cherry scoffed. "Coordinating from your bed. How convenient."

Apollo's temper flared. He pushed himself up straighter, ignoring the stabbing pain in his side. "You think I want to be here? You think I wouldn't trade places with River in a heartbeat if I could? She's my mate. My other half. Every moment she's gone feels like I'm missing a piece of myself. My wolf wants to tear me apart. He grows more feral and uncontrollable by the day."

Cherry's expression softened at the raw emotion in his voice. She sank into the chair by his bed.

"I'm sorry," she said quietly. "I know you love her. I just... I can't stand feeling so helpless. My baby is out there, and there's nothing I can do."

"I promise you, we will find her. No matter what it takes. I will bring her back to us."

Cherry nodded, blinking back tears. "Tell me everything you know. I want to help."

Apollo hesitated. "Cherry, I'm not sure that's a good idea. It could be dangerous-"

"Don't you dare try to sideline me," Cherry growled, her eyes flashing. "I may not be a Lycan, but I'm not helpless. I want in on this. All of it."

Apollo studied her for a long moment. He thought of all Cherry had done over the years to protect River, to keep her safe in a world that would have used and abused her. If anyone deserved to be part of this fight, it was her. He wondered how much more formidable she would be if he made her a hybrid. But as soon as he thought it, he dismissed the idea. She was hard enough to handle as a shifter. Gods help them all if she became a hybrid.

He nodded. "Alright."

CHAPTER SIXTEEN

RIVER

River had slowly chewed two small pieces of meat and mushed the rest of the food around her plate to make it at least look like she'd eaten. She'd managed two dry rolls and a large glass of cola, but that was it. She hoped it was enough to keep Titan's suspicions at bay for the moment.

"So, what now?" she asked. "Are we going to watch a movie together, continuing this charade?"

Titan's eyes flashed, and he slammed his fist on the table. "Can't you just try?"

She narrowed her eyes. "No."

"Why? You tried with them."

"They didn't kidnap me."

"Ares all but kidnapped you. He hunted you down and found you at your exhibit and forced you to go with him to his hotel."

"Where I was free to leave whenever I wanted." With a bodyguard, of course, but she didn't mention that part. "You can't be comparing what happened with Ares and me with what happened with you."

Titan shook his head. "I don't understand. You are bonded to me."

"No, I rejected you."

His eyes narrowed and then widened. "But I haven't rejected you."

The words hung in the air between them. A cold chill shivered down River's body. That was it. She'd rejected him, but he hadn't rejected her. It was why he was still determined to have her, but she had little to no feelings for him at all.

The wheels turned in his head. Wheels trying to figure out how to undo what River had done. Wheels trying to decide if he bit her again, if it would change anything. Wheels that churned over the idea of how a fated mate could do what she did with no repercussions. Wheels she did not want churning at all.

River scraped her chair back and stood. "I'm tired. I'd like to go back to my cell now."

Titan growled. "The sun just went down."

"Yes, but-" River stopped. Out of the large picture window, blues, purples, and greens danced across the sky. She blinked, trying to process what she was seeing. Blues, purples, and greens? And they weren't static, they were… moving.

She took a step toward the window. "Are those… the Northern Lights?"

Titan glanced at them and back at her distractedly. "Yes, you can see them sometimes when the night is clear. River, I wish you would stop calling your apartment a cell. I-"

"I had no clue you could see the Northern Lights here."

Titan waved his hands and growled again. "It's not common, but it's been known to happen every once in a while, in Montreal."

River's gaze snapped to Titan. *Montreal?*

His eyes widened and then turned black. His nails lengthened as did his fangs. Quick as a blink, he was in front of her.

He grabbed her arms. "You tricked me."

River's heart slammed into her ribs. "No, I didn't."

"You've been playing me this whole time. Waiting for me to slip up. Trying to find a way to get information from me."

Her mind raced, and her wolf snarled but was unable to do more.

Venom wafted off Titan as his nails dug into her arms, pinching her skin. His wild black eyes bored into her the way he had the night he'd bitten her, sending a trickle of fear through her.

She couldn't back down. She needed to stay in control.

"Let go of me," she said.

His nails dug deeper, and the scent of blood hit her nose. Her stomach roiled, and she forced herself not to throw up.

"Let go of me, or I'll make you let go."

A snarl curled Titan's lip, and he shoved her into the wall. Her head bounced against it, forcing her to struggle against another wave of nausea.

He leaned in. "You are mine. I am Alpha. You do what I say."

She had to leave before she puked all over his fancy suit. River did the only thing she could think of. She gripped Titan's balls and squeezed.

His eyes widened, and he bared his teeth. When she squeezed tighter, she tried not to notice his length hardening against her forearm.

Neither moved for several seconds, and then River squeezed. Not hard enough to cause incapacitating pain, but enough to let him know she was serious. Again, his arousal grew against her wrist.

"Do that again, it feels good, Princess."

She wondered if she'd made a fatal mistake, but then twisted her wrist, and his grip slackened on her arms slightly.

"Let. Go."

He growled, but his eyes went from black to blue and then flickered back.

She leveled her gaze on him and twisted further.

He hissed and his nails retracted, leaving only blunt fingers gripping her arms. She waited until his fangs shortened before speaking.

"You, don't touch me. You don't ever touch me. If you touch me again without my permission, I will rip your balls off and shove them down your throat. Do you understand?"

Titan didn't move.

She squeezed tighter, and he gritted his teeth.

"Do. You. Understand?"

"Yes," Titan croaked.

"Yes, what?"

The strain on his face and the pulsing tendon in his neck told her she was pushing her luck, but she refused to back down. If she did, he'd think he'd bested her. And if that happened, who knew what he would do?

"Yes, my Luna," he ground out.

She waited a moment longer, and he let go of her arms. She took a breath and then released him.

Any human male would have doubled over in pain from what she'd done, but Titan didn't move a muscle. Tension crackled in the air like lightning, and she wasn't sure what he would do next. Finally, he turned and strode from the room without a word. Several moments later, a door banged open and then slammed shut. Afterward, a roar sounded from the backyard. It turned into a howl and then disappeared in the distance.

The door to the kitchen swung inward, and Kane burst in. He took in the dining room, and then his gaze landed on her.

"What did you do?"

"I'm ready to go back to my cell."

He stared at her intently and then sniffed the air; his eyes drifted to her arm. Blood trickled through her sweater where Titan had gripped her. And because of the blockers, she wasn't healing immediately. Even as the wounds burned and stuck to her sweater, she ignored them to focus on Kane.

He didn't move.

"Or you could let me go," she said. "It's what you want, isn't it? To get me out of here? Now's your opportunity. He's gone. He probably hates me. You can see he already injured me. Let me leave. Then you can have him back all to yourself."

Kane prowled toward her, his eyes hard, calculating. "I would love nothing more than to kick your pampered ass out of this house and out of his life. Unfortunately, if I did, he would do something reckless and stupid to try to bring you back, getting all of us killed, including himself. And I care for him more than I hate you."

She detested admitting it, but she understood Kane's feelings. They were the same feelings she had for her sister. She loved Bianca even more than she hated Titan. And if she were in Kane's position, she would do the same thing to save Bianca.

"Let's go."

River didn't move as she tried to find something to say.

"Don't make me pick you up," he threatened.

"Put your hands on me," she said. "And you'll find out why your master bolted out of this house so fast."

"Try anything with me, and you'll find out just what I did to receive the scar I have."

River bared her teeth, and Kane pointed to the door, unfazed.

"I'm going to kill you one day," she said.

Kane leaned into her and bared his teeth. "Not if I kill you first."

TITAN

TITAN STOPPED A MILE FROM THE HOUSE AND FORCED HIMSELF BACK into human form. His wolf howled in anger, but Titan pushed him away. He couldn't believe it. He'd done it again. He'd lost it, and he'd almost hurt River… again.

No. He had hurt River. Titan looked down at his hands. Small flecks of her blood tinged his fingertips.

Mine. Take. Submit.

Now she'll never trust us.

Take.

Titan turned and slammed his fist into a tree, splitting the skin open. Blood trickled down his hand, mingling with beads of sweat.

NO! No take. No submit asshole!

His wolf snapped his jaws and roared to be freed.

Titan battled his wolf. Trying the techniques he'd taught himself to stave off the shift.

Memories bombarded him. Times of running with Kane. Killing. Fighting. Screwing anyone he wanted.

But not her. Why not her? He'd bitten her, claimed her almost four and a half years ago. He'd fought to change, fought to become stronger. To prove what he could offer her. To make penance and have her see him for who he was meant to be- King of the Lycans. Yet still he wasn't good enough. His work wasn't good enough. He went against every instinct of his nature to be better for her. To win her. But it hadn't worked. None of it had worked. Even now, with his giving her everything he possessed, she didn't want it. Didn't want him.

His anger shifted. He thought, with enough time away from his bastard half-brothers, she would feel the bond he'd started with her, and she would return to it. Embrace it even. But that would never happen. Not as long as Ares and Apollo lived.

Steps crunched up behind him, and he sniffed the air.

"What?" he asked without turning.

Bones crunched as Kane shifted to human form. "Are you okay?"

"Just fine."

Kane didn't say anything. Finally, Titan turned over his shoulder and glared at him.

"I took your mate to her room."

Titan nodded.

"We have a drop-off tonight. If you aren't up to going-"

"I said, I'm fine," Titan growled.

Kane stared at him.

"What?"

"We have an hour, want to hunt?"

Yes. Hunt. Kill.

Titan shifted before he even realized it. He hadn't hunted in almost four years. He'd sworn off hunting moments after she'd rejected him. But now he wanted to hunt more than anything. To hunt and to kill.

And what he wanted to hunt most of all were Apollo and Ares.

CHAPTER SEVENTEEN

ARES

Dr. Emerson told Ares to drop the drugs off at a storage unit about two hours from Indianapolis. After finally getting more than a couple of hours of sleep in more than a week and a half, Ares had awoken in the hotel, eaten a full three meals, showered, and had changed into clothes he could move in more easily. Wearing the sweats and hoodie, he wondered why he had never let himself dress down before. He feared that if he got too comfortable in workout clothes, he might never wear a suit again. He now understood why Apollo never wore a suit at home. What was the point? Who the hell was he trying to impress? At the very least, he might put on sweats while still wearing a button-up shirt and jacket for virtual meetings.

Ares crouched in the shadows of the storage unit, his muscles coiled with tension as he surveyed the rows of shelves stacked with illicit goods. The acrid smell of gunpowder and chemicals hung in the air, mingling with the musty odor of cardboard boxes and rusted metal. He turned to Theo, his voice barely above a whisper.

"We need to move. Grab anything that looks important."

Theo nodded, his eyes darting towards the entrance.

Ares rifled through a nearby crate. Dust hung thick in the stale air, swirling faintly in the weak beam of light cutting through the open door. The crate's contents seemed louder than they should under his touch, brittle paper rustling against paper. The smell of mildew mingling with oil and rust.

Nearby, Santiago moved with equal parts precision and tension. His boots scuffed against the concrete floor, echoing faintly in the cavernous space. Neither spoke; words would only waste time they didn't have. Instead, they communicated in glances, quick, sharp looks exchanged between them like silent signals on a battlefield.

The silence stretched thin until it was interrupted by the faint clink of something metallic, a sound that cut through the stillness like the blade of a knife. Ares froze mid-motion, his breathing stalling. He looked at Santiago, who picked up the metal coin from where he'd dropped it.

"Sorry," he mouthed.

Ares' hand hovered for a moment over the jumbled mess inside the crate before plunging back in. His fingers ran under something weighty. He pulled free a thick accordion folder, its edges worn as though it had passed through countless hands before landing in the box.

He turned the folder over in his hands, brushing off a fine layer of dust that left smudges across his fingertips.

"What is it?" Theo asked.

"Not sure yet." Ares pried open the metal clasp on the envelope

Ares slid out the contents, a stack of legal documents and deeds.

Ares' shoulders tightened again as he flipped through the papers, scanning each page with efficiency. "It's all here. Buildings. Companies. Addresses. Holdings."

"Is there an address in Montreal?"

Ares scanned the dozen or so documents. "No. However, this address is included, as is one in New York. A warehouse."

"You think that's where they operate out of in the US?"

Ares nodded. "Maybe."

A low growl echoed from outside, and hushed whispers of voices arguing. Ares' head snapped up, his nostrils flaring at the scent of unfamiliar wolves.

"Rogues," he snarled, already beginning to shift.

The door burst open with a crash, and five werewolves poured into the unit. Ares met them head-on, his own wolf erupting from his skin in a blur of fur and fangs. He slammed into the lead rogue, feeling ribs crack under his mighty blow.

Theo shifted a heartbeat later, smaller than Ares but quick and vicious. He darted between the legs of a hulking gray wolf, tearing at its underbelly.

The storage unit erupted into chaos. Shelves toppled over, their contents spilling across the floor. The air filled with snarls, yelps, and the metallic tang of blood. Santiago and Theo tore through the rogues with brutal efficiency. The rogues were strong, but they were shifters and no match for three Lycans.

One managed to sink its teeth into Ares' flank, eliciting a roar of fury. Ares whirled, his meaty paw connecting with the rogue's skull with a sickening crunch, and then he sank his teeth into the rogue's exposed neck.

The remaining two snarling wolves had pinned Theo. With a surge of primal instinct, he leaped across the unit, crashing into the rogues and sending them flying. Theo scrambled to his feet, panting heavily, blood matting his fur.

The end came almost as quickly as it had begun. Four rogues lay dead, and one breathed shallowly on the blood-soaked floor, Santiago's jaws at his jugular.

Ares stood over the remaining rogue, body vibrating. "Where's Titan's house? Tell me."

The rogue's eyes darted between Ares, Theo, and Santiago. "I have no idea. I was only recruited a few weeks ago. I've never seen him."

"Then who is running things here in the US?"

Again, the rogue shook his head. "I know nothing. I swear. I was told by a friend there was a new pack of rogues forming and that the new King was the Alpha of it."

"New King? I am the King. Do I look like I'm forming a new pack?"

The shifter shook his head. "Please. I swear-"

"That you know nothing. You said that. Where were you headed from here?"

"Somewhere in New York. I've been a few times, but I don't have the address or anything."

Ares shook his head. It didn't matter. If they were tasked with bringing the shipment to New York, there was only one address it could be going to.

With a swift, merciless movement, Ares snapped the rogue's neck, letting the body fall to the ground.

"We need to move," Theo said.

Ares nodded in agreement. "We also need clothes."

"I have some in the trunk," said Santiago.

Ares snatched up the now-splattered folder and headed for the exit.

"Are we going to leave all this here?" asked Theo.

"Burn it."

Theo cocked an eyebrow at him. "Gee, wherever did I put my lighter?"

Ares growled. "Then I guess we're leaving it, aren't we?"

The trio stalked out of the building naked for anyone to see and headed for their car. The acrid smell of blood still clung to them. Theo opened the trunk and tossed Ares a pair of underwear and a new pair of pants. Ares tossed the folder into the back seat and pulled on his clothing as his phone rang.

The words 'Pompous Asshole' appeared on the screen. Ares picked up the phone and answered as he tugged a T-shirt over his head.

"We've got a lead," Ares said. "New York. Some kind of warehouse."

"New York?" Apollo's voice crackled through the speaker. "That's unexpected. What's your plan?"

Ares ran a hand through his hair, his eyes scanning the darkened parking lot. "We're heading there now, but I've got a bad feeling about this. Someone is running things down here, and it isn't Titan himself. That means it has to be someone with some pull. He wouldn't leave an entire portion of his operation to just a peon."

"Be careful," Apollo warned. "How did you find the warehouse?"

"I found a file with a bunch of deeds and receipts in it."

"Send me photos of what you've got, and I'll see what I can find out."

"Check back in a couple hours."

"Please do. If we don't make some headway soon, I'm afraid Cherry is going to start going door to door."

As Ares hung up, Theo's head snapped up, his nostrils flaring. "We've got more company."

Damn. Ares had just gotten dressed. He stripped his shirt off when a voice sounded from around the corner.

"No. Wait."

Ares stopped moving, but Santiago pulled a gun from his shoulder holster and aimed it in the direction of the voice.

Ares sniffed the air. "What do you want?" he shouted.

"To help."

"Who are you?" asked Theo.

A man older than Ares, possibly mid-thirties, walked around the corner of the building with his hands out. "My name is Duncan."

"You're a rogue."

"Yes. But a rogue of my own making. I disagreed with some of the things my pack did. So I left."

"Why are you here?" Santiago asked.

"I was sent with the others, but I've never been one to attack first and ask questions later."

"What do you want?"

Duncan stared at them. "You're one of the Princes, aren't you?"

"Prince Ares Wolvenguard," said Theo. "And if you don't show some respect, I'll make you."

"I'm just here to help."

"Help kill us," said Santiago.

Duncan shook his head. "No. Not that I could. I'm not as stupid as the others."

"What do you want then?" Ares asked.

"To help you."

"Why?"

"Because I understand both sides of this battle."

"Meaning?"

"Meaning I understand you are the better choice for a king than Titan. But I also understand why he is doing what he's doing."

"For revenge."

"Titan says he's doing it to make things better. At least that's what he's telling the rogues. It's how he has gotten so many on his side."

"You don't believe him?"

“No.”

"Why not?"

"Because I know what's really in those pills in your car."

CHAPTER EIGHTEEN

RIVER

River was woken up by her wolf freaking out.

No. Away. No. Away.

She tried to tune her thoughts to those of her wolf.

Yeah. I know. We will get away.

No. No touch!

River thought for a moment and realized how warm she felt. She tried to push the covers off but found her body pinned down by a substantial weight.

Panic stirred as she found a bulky arm draped over her. A light snore sounded behind her, and she threw the arm off and jumped from the bed. Her heart thundered as she took in Titan's naked form lying in her bed, dirty and caked in blood.

"What the hell are you doing?" she yelled.

Titan's eyes shot open, and he glanced around.

"I asked what the hell you are doing? Naked. In my bed."

He seemed conflicted, but then his eyes frosted over, and he sat up.

"I believe I was sleeping," he replied.

"Get out. This isn't your room. It's mine."

"Actually, it's my room. Every inch of this house is mine. Therefore, I can sleep wherever I want."

She clenched her jaw to keep it from falling open. "And I am the High Luna and deserve the respect not to be accosted while I'm sleeping."

"Trust me, Princess, if I were to accost you, you'd remember."

"Oh, believe me, I do."

He huffed. "That again?"

"Yes, that, again."

He grumbled and lay back on the bed, stretching out every inch of his large, naked frame.

"When are you going to stop complaining about that and just move on?"

His cold tone shot right through her. He could not be serious.

River stared at Titan in disbelief, her mind reeling from his abrupt shift in demeanor. Gone was the man who had carefully prepared an elaborate dinner, who had tried to win her over with art supplies and promises of a better world. In his place lay a cold, demanding Alpha, his muscular body sprawled across her bed as if he owned it- and her.

"Move on?" River sputtered, her voice rising. "You bit me without consent, kidnapped me, and now you expect me to forget all that and what... fall into your arms?"

Titan's eyes flashed dangerously. "I expect you to honor the bond between us. To take your rightful place as my Luna and help me build a new future for our kind."

River shook her head, backing away until she hit the wall. "There is no bond. I rejected you. And even if there was, that's not how this works. You can't force someone to love you."

A muscle twitched in Titan's neck as he stood, seemingly unconcerned with his nudity. River averted her eyes, her cheeks burning despite her anger.

"I'm done playing nice, River." Titan stalked towards her. "I've given you time. I've tried to show you the benefits of what joining me can offer you. But my patience has limits."

River's heart raced as he approached, her wolf snarling. She wanted to lash out, but the suppressants still dulled her strength and reflexes.

"What happened to you?" she demanded. "Last night, you practically begged me to accept you. Now you're acting like... like..."

"Like the Alpha I am," Titan finished, his voice low and dangerous. He braced his hands on either side of her head, caging her in. "I realized something at dinner, River. I've been weak. Trying to win you over like some lovesick pup. That's not who I am. It's not who we are. We aren't weak, and we don't beg; we take. You and I both."

His scent enveloped her- earth and pine and something wild, tinged with the metallic tang of blood. River stiffened as memories of their first encounter flooded back. The primal hunger in his eyes. The feel of his fangs ripping into her flesh.

"I'm a Lycan," Titan said, his breath hot against her ear. "The rightful oldest son of the former king and I will not be denied my right to take the High Luna as my mate."

River shoved him, but it was like pushing against a brick wall. "I am not yours," she hissed.

Titan's hand shot out, gripping her chin and forcing her to meet his gaze. "You are. Whether you want to admit it or not. I feel it, River. The pull between us. Stop fighting it."

River's mind raced, staring into Titan's cold, demanding eyes. The abrupt shift in his demeanor left her feeling like she was finally seeing the real him. The man underneath the mask of civility. The monster that she'd met that night in the pantry closet of her old pack.

"I won't stop fighting. Not now, not ever. Whatever you think you're going to accomplish by acting like this, it won't work."

Titan's grip on her chin tightened, his fingers digging into her skin. "I'm not acting. Not anymore. This is who I am. Who we are meant to be together."

She searched his face, looking for any sign of the man who had earnestly tried to win her over just hours before. But his expression stayed hard, unyielding.

"What happened last night?" she asked. "After you left the dining room?"

A dark smile curved Titan's lip. "I remembered who I am. What I'm capable of."

A chill ran down River's spine. "What does that mean?"

Titan's hot breath fell against her ear. "It means I'm done holding back. Done pretending to be something I'm not just to make you comfortable."

River's heart raced. "You're lying," she said, more to convince herself than him. "This isn't you. The real you wouldn't-"

"The real me?" Titan interrupted with a harsh laugh. "You don't know the first thing about the real me, Princess. But you're going to learn. Just like all the rogues that live under my roof, you will learn to respect me, and if you don't respect me, then I'm fine with you fearing me."

He stepped back suddenly, releasing her. River sagged against the wall, her legs weak with relief.

Titan strode across the room, his muscular form silhouetted against the early morning light streaming through the fake window. He paused at the dresser but didn't look at her.

"I've given you everything," he said, his voice low and dangerous. "A home. Safety. The opportunity to be part of something greater than yourself. And still you resist."

River watched him, her mind working furiously to understand his motivations. Was this all some elaborate manipulation? Push her away to make her want him? Or had he given up on winning her over gently?

"I never asked for any of that," she said. "I had a home. I had safety. I had a purpose with Ares and Apollo."

Titan whirled to face her, his eyes flashing. "They can't give you what I can. Power. The freedom to reshape our world."

"Is that what this is really about?" River asked, a spark of understanding blooming inside her. "Power?"

Titan's eyes darkened. "It's about creating a better future for our kind. One where we don't have to hide or bow even to human laws. Where we can live freely, as we were meant to."

Whoa. What? Not bow to human laws? What the hell did that mean?

River shook her head, her silver hair catching the morning light. "You're talking about tearing down everything our people have built, everything we've worked for."

"Sometimes you have to tear things down to build them back stronger," Titan growled. He stalked towards her again, his powerful form radiating aggression. "I'm offering you the opportunity to be part of that. To stand by my side as we create a new world order."

World order? What the hell was he talking about? River held her ground, even as her heart raced. She searched Titan's face, but his eyes stayed cold, his jaw set in a hard line.

"I don't know what you are doing right now, but trying to scare me is a hell of a lot worse idea to get me to your side."

For a moment, something flickered in Titan's eyes- a flash of uncertainty, quickly masked. "Being nice didn't work, did it? Didn't make you like me one ounce more. And if I'm being frank, it was exhausting being that guy. I didn't realize it until I let loose. I ran. Ran and hunted and killed last night. I haven't let myself go like that since I found you. And it felt so fucking good. Freeing. It reminded me who I am and what I wanted in the beginning. Before you. When it was just me, my mom, and Kane. I'm fully awake for the first time in years. This hold that you've had over me these last years is gone. And now it's time to get back to who I was before."

"And who is that? A tyrant? A conqueror? Because the Titan I've seen glimpses of, the one who cares about the rogues, who wants to make things better, he wouldn't act like this."

Titan's nostrils flared, his hands clenching into fists at his sides. "You don't know anything about me, River. You've seen what I've allowed you to see. Nothing more."

"Then show me," River challenged, taking a step towards him. "If this is who you are, prove it. Because right now, all I see is a man lashing out because he's scared."

Titan's eyes flashed. "I'm not scared of anything."

"You're scared I'll never choose you willingly. Scared that no matter what you do, no matter how much power you gain, it won't be enough to make me love you. This is you protecting yourself from being hurt."

The words hung in the air between them, charged with tension. Titan's chest heaved, his breathing ragged. For a long moment, neither of them moved.

Then, with a low growl, Titan's hand shot out, tangling in River's hair as he pulled her roughly against him. His lips crashed down on hers in a bruising kiss, demanding and possessive.

River's body reacted instinctively, a jolt of heat racing through her despite her best efforts to resist. The red ribbon attached to her wolf's leg tightened momentarily.

She shoved him away, and then her hand connected with his cheek in a resounding slap.

Titan staggered, his eyes wide with shock. But it was gone in an instant, replaced by a snarl.

"You dare strike me?" he roared.

River's heart pounded, but she stood her ground. "I told you not to touch me without permission."

Titan's eyes flashed gold, his muscles tensing as if preparing to pounce, and then he did. His lips on hers again, demanding, claiming.

River struggled in his grasp and brought her knee up to his balls.

Titan grunted and doubled over, letting go of her.

"Do you want to know how I know you aren't my mate?" she spat. "When I first saw Ares and Apollo, my wolf went crazy trying to get to them. Even when I ran from Ares and wanted to reject Apollo's claim on me, she was the one who wouldn't let me. She claimed them the first time she smelled them. Mine. My Alpha. My mate. But do you know what she said when she first saw you? No. Not him. It doesn't matter how much you push me, or what you try to do to make me yours, I'm not your fated mate. Just like your mother wasn't your father's fated mate, and that will never change."

Titan straightened. "Fated or not, you are mine. I am the rightful Alpha King. And I will never, ever, let you go. Ever."

She prepared herself for him to kiss her again, but he didn't.

Instead, he moved in close, his hot breath tickling her neck. "You will have to kill me if you want me ever to let you go."

Ice trickled through River's veins. She looked up into his black eyes. "And I'll die before I give in to you."

Titan chuckled. "Then let the game begin."

CHAPTER NINETEEN

ARES

Ares and Theo sat across the table from Duncan as he ate a steak and vegetables. Santiago sat at a table nearby, watching people enter and leave the restaurant.

"How did you even know we would be at the storage unit?" asked Theo.

Duncan shrugged. "I didn't. Not until I saw you. Ares came to a tri-pack meeting once. I saw you both there."

"So no one in Titan's organization knows we are in the States?" asked Ares

Duncan shook his head. "Not as far as I know."

Theo glanced at Ares, who turned his glass of wine before sipping it. The restaurant buzzed with the low hum of conversation and the clink of silverware. Soft jazz played in the background, creating a stark contrast to the tension at their table.

"Tell us again," said Theo.

Duncan took a colossal bite of his steak and then put down the knife and fork before finishing his beer.

"I told you three times already."

Ares wolf growled. "And if you want me to believe you and not slaughter you, you will tell me one more time."

Duncan held up his hand to the waiter and ordered another beer before pushing his plate away a few inches.

"I'm Duncan McShane. Raised in the East Valley pack in West Virginia. When our Alpha died, our packlands were claimed by the West Valley pack, and instead of dealing with the politics and back-stabbing and ass kissing of a new pack, I took off on my own. I traveled all over the US and ended up in New York a few years back, where Titan found me and convinced me to join him."

"And now you don't agree with him?" Ares asked.

Duncan's beer arrived, and he thanked the waiter before sipping it.

"I agree with what he said he wanted to do. I don't agree with how he is going about getting it. Plus, I'm not okay with the drugs and gun running."

"What, you're a lover, not a fighter?" asked Theo.

Duncan snorted. "Oh no, I'm a fighter, but only for the things I agree with. And Titan isn't one I can agree with any longer. Plus, I don't agree with Titan kidnapping your Luna. That's not okay."

"So you want to help us now? Why? What do you want out of it?"

Duncan twirled his beer. "I'm tired of being alone. I need a pack. Under current law, the only options available to me are to return to my pack or to marry into another. Problem is, as a rogue, no pack will have me. And no female will even give me a chance unless she's a rogue herself. I'm done traveling. I want a place. A home. A family."

Ares studied Duncan, searching for any sign of deception. The rogue met his gaze, his brown eyes clear and unwavering. There was a weariness in those eyes, a loneliness that resonated with something inside Ares. He knew all too well the pain of feeling like an outsider, of not belonging.

His wolf paced, not ready to trust Duncan. But he'd told the same story four times now, and it added up. Besides, he had to have at least considered the fact that Ares or Theo would kill him on sight, and yet he chanced showing himself anyway.

Ares sipped his wine, savoring the rich flavor as he considered Duncan's words.

"A pack," Ares mused, his voice low.

Duncan leaned forward. "I understand your hesitation. But I swear on my life, I want no part of what Titan's planning. I've seen firsthand the destruction they're capable of. The way they manipulate others to further their agenda." He paused, running a hand through his shaggy hair. "I joined them because I believed in change, in creating a better world for our kind. But this... this isn't the way."

Theo shifted in his seat, his hand never straying far from the concealed weapon at his side. "Pretty words," he said. "But actions speak louder."

Duncan nodded, a rueful smile tugging at his lips. "Which is why I'm willing to put my life on the line to help you. I know where they're storing the drugs in New York, and I can get you inside."

Ares raised an eyebrow. "Inside, where precisely?"

"They have a warehouse, heavily guarded, where they're coordinating everything- the drug distribution, weapons shipments, recruitment of new rogues."

Ares and Theo shared a look. They already knew about the warehouse in New York, but Duncan telling them about it showed that he might mean what he said.

"Alright," he said slowly. "Let's say we believe you. What's your plan?"

Duncan's eyes lit up with a mixture of relief and determination.

"I can get us past the outer security. I know the weak points in their defenses."

Duncan's voice dropped to a hushed whisper as he outlined his plan. "The compound is an old factory on the outskirts of Brooklyn, heavily fortified and surrounded by abandoned warehouses. They've got a rotating security detail, but I know the blind spots in their patrols."

He pulled out a napkin and began sketching a rough map. "There's a drainage tunnel here that leads into the basement. It's narrow and partially flooded, but it's our best shot at getting in undetected. Once inside, we'll need to move fast. The main storage area for the drugs is on the ground floor, but the boss is two levels up."

Theo leaned forward, his brow furrowed. "Who's in charge? Titan?"

Duncan shook his head. "No, the compound is managed by an Alpha named Rudy. Mean son of a bitch, built like a tank. He's Titan's enforcer, keeps everyone in line through fear and brute force."

Ares' eyes widened, and his wolf's hackles raised. "Rudy? He was one of the Alphas there the night River was taken."

A cold fury settled in Ares' bones as he remembered Rudy as one of the men who had gotten away unscathed with his Beta and their mates. How many other Alphas had turned against them? How deep did the betrayal go?

Duncan nodded. "Rudy's got a personal grudge against the royal family. Says you've grown soft, forgotten what it means to be true Lycans. He's been itching to prove himself against you."

Ares' lip curled in a snarl. "He'll get his shot soon enough."

Duncan watched them with a mixture of curiosity and concern. "Rudy's dangerous," he warned. "Loyal to Titan and Kane, and not afraid to get his hands dirty. If we meet him, we'll need to be prepared for a battle."

Ares took a long swig of his wine, letting the rich flavor ground him. "I'd welcome one at this point," he said. "How soon can you get us inside?"

Duncan's eyes gleamed with determination. "Give me a few hours to make the necessary arrangements. But we need to get to New York."

"I'll take care of it," said Theo.

"Aren't they going to miss your group? Won't someone come looking?" Ares asked.

"Not for at least twenty-four hours. We drive the products to New York. That's about twelve hours, give or take. Trust me, if I thought I couldn't pull this off, I wouldn't have offered. Rudy is cocky and overconfident. He doesn't think anyone would dare cross him or betray him. Not with Kane and Titan at his back."

Ares nodded, then fixed Duncan with a piercing stare. "I'm trusting you with a lot here. If this is a trap..."

"It's not," Duncan said. "I swear it on my life. I want out of this mess as much as you want to find your mate."

As they settled the bill and prepared to leave, a concoction of hope and trepidation coursed through Ares. They were close. But not close enough. Not for him and not for his wolf.

CHAPTER TWENTY

APOLLO

Apollo's wolf paced and whined and paced and growled, wanting to be let out. Apollo still felt weak, but his injuries had finally healed. Neither of them could stand it any longer. The fact that Ares was tracking down their mate while he sat on his ass, was something he could no longer tolerate. He needed to be back in his own home so he could think logically.

Apollo grabbed his coat, jammed his feet in his boots, and marched to his bedroom door. Silas stood from a chair, and Regan rose as well.

"We're leaving," Apollo announced.

"Where to?" asked Silas.

"Home."

His men looked at each other.

"Problem?"

"No," replied Silas.

"Good. Then get everyone together, I'm not hiding anymore. It's time to do something."

"About bloody time," Cherry said behind him.

Apollo had no idea where to start, but if he didn't take action, he'd never feel like he deserved to be River's mate.

TWENTY MINUTES LATER, THEY ALL PULLED UP TO THE ESTATE. A sense of dread washed over him momentarily. He swallowed it down as his wolf bristled, uneasy with being back at home after what had happened. They drove up the drive and parked by the front door. All of his men and Ares' remaining men exited their bikes and vehicles, checked the area, then let Apollo, Cherry, Strider, and Bianca out.

Apollo took in a breath of fresh air. Home. The familiar smells and sounds of home soothed him somewhat, but the moment he walked inside the house and was slapped by the lingering scent of River's fragrance, he almost crumbled to his knees.

His wolf paced and clawed to be unleashed so he could search for any sign of her.

Out. Mate. Find.

Apollo forced his wolf to calm down so he could concentrate. *We are. Be patient.*

"Okay," said Cherry. "We're here. Now what?"

Apollo bit his tongue at the retort that almost passed his lips. "Now we look for clues."

"Where?" asked Cherry.

Despite her tough exterior, Cherry appeared smaller and frailer than she had the first time he'd seen her a month before.

"The ballroom first."

"Boss," said Silas. "I don't know that that's such a good idea."

Apollo pinned him with his gaze. "Are you saying you don't think I can handle it?"

"No, Highness." Silas shook his head. "I just…"

"I've seen carnage before, Silas. I may not like it, but it is part of our life."

Silas nodded. "Of course."

"I'm going to take Bianca upstairs," said Zeke.

"We'll go with you," Strider replied.

Cherry shook Strider's hand off her shoulder. "Go with them if you want. I want to find my daughter."

For the first time, anger flashed across Strider's face. "You think I don't?"

"Well, she isn't your daughter, is she?"

The growl that escaped Strider surprised Apollo.

"How can you possibly say that to me?" his voice came out more as a snarl than actual words. "I've raised her for more than half her life. Taken care of her. Loved her as much as I love Bianca. And you think you have the right to say that to me after everything we've been through?"

The air crackled with tension as the hair on Strider's arms lengthened and his eyes darkened. His teeth elongated, and he loomed over Cherry.

Her expression changed and then hardened again. "Go with Bianca. I'll let you know if I find anything."

Strider didn't move for a long second, his body so rigid that Apollo was afraid he might snap.

"No," Bianca said, startling everyone.

Cherry and Strider turned to her.

"Dad is right. He loves her as much as you do, Cherry. She is as much his daughter as she is my sister. You don't get to have a monopoly on who loves her most. And you don't get to treat dad like he doesn't love her as much as you do just because she came out of your hoo-ha."

The way Cherry's eye twitched made Apollo think that Bianca had never spoken to her that way before.

Cherry looked between Strider and Bianca. She blew out a breath, her shoulders sagging.

"I know how much you love River. Both of you."

Strider's posture relaxed, the feral energy dissipating from his form. It was the best apology Strider or Bianca would receive at the moment. "Alright then. Let's head to the ballroom."

"Come on," said Zeke. "Let's head upstairs."

"No." Bianca straightened. "I'm tired of being babied. My sister, my mom, and my dad almost died. It's time for me to step up and help. I'm not as helpless as everyone thinks I am. I may not be the sharpest tool in the shed, but I love my family just as much. And I want to help."

Zeke chewed his lip. "B-"

"If you can't handle it, feel free to go to your room. But I'm going with my parents, and I dare you to try and stop us." Bianca walked to Cherry and locked arms with her.

Zeke looked to Cherry, who cocked an eyebrow at him.

He shook his head and swore under his breath before ushering them inside.

The group made their way through the grand foyer, their footsteps echoing in the eerie silence of the house. As they approached the ballroom, Apollo paused, steeling himself for what lay beyond. With a deep breath, he opened the doors.

The scene of chaos and violence frozen in time greeted them. Dark, dried blood stained the once-gleaming marble floor; the metallic odor of blood clung to the air. Shattered crystals from the chandeliers glittered like diamonds strewn across the room. Overturned tables, smashed chairs, and moldy food lay scattered about, silent testaments to the struggle that had taken place. His gut clenched, remembering the battle that had ruined everything. And where he'd lost Bennett. He huffed out a breath and coughed to keep himself from breaking down. They would have a proper memorial for Bennett when River returned.

Apollo moved into the room, taking in every detail. He crouched down, running his fingers along a pair of claw marks gouged into the wooden floor. His wolf growled at the memories of the rogues who had invaded their home.

Apollo made his way around the perimeter of the room, pausing occasionally to examine a particular spot more closely. He lifted an overturned chair, studying the splintered wood and torn upholstery. The violence of the attack evident in every destroyed object, every splash of blood.

Finally, he approached the area where Bennett had fallen. The floor was darker where the blood had pooled and congealed. Apollo closed his eyes for a moment, remembering his loyal friend who had given his life protecting them. Grief and anger surged within him.

"I'm so sorry, my friend," he murmured. "Your sacrifice will not be forgotten."

Taking a shaky breath, Apollo forced himself to focus. He couldn't let emotion cloud his judgment now. River needed him to be strong, to be the leader he was born to be.

His gaze landed on a section of paneling. Moving to it, he ran his hands along the woodwork until he touched a subtle catch. With a soft click, the hidden door swung open, revealing a dark passage beyond.

"The tunnel," Apollo murmured. "This is how Titan got in. I didn't even know it was here."

Apollo approached the passage, the musty air thick with dust. He ran his hand along the rough stone wall, the damp walls cool to the touch. The tunnel stretched before him, a dark maw swallowing what little light spilled in from the ballroom.

"Silas," Apollo called. "Bring a flashlight."

As Silas hurried to comply, Apollo breathed deeply, steeling himself. His wolf paced, eager to get going. Silas handed him a flashlight, and with a nod to the others, Apollo plunged into the darkness, his footsteps echoing off the narrow walls.

The tunnel twisted and turned, leading deeper under the bowels of the estate. Apollo's keen senses picked up the acrid stench of fear and the metallic tang of blood.

After several minutes, a glimmer of light appeared. Apollo quickened his pace, emerging at the northern edge of the property. The late-afternoon sun filtered through the dense canopy of trees, dappling the ground with shifting patterns of light and shadow.

Apollo stood near the northern fence, behind the barn. He located the security camera mounted on a nearby tree. Its lens had been shattered; wires dangled uselessly from its housing. He inspected the damage.

"This isn't random destruction." He ran his fingers along the shattered lens. "They knew where to hit it to disable it without triggering any alarms."

His eyes scanned the perimeter, spotting the section of fence that had been compromised. A neat hole had been cut through the metal links, the edges curled back with surgical precision. Apollo crouched down, examining the ground around the breach.

"Here," Cherry called, pointing to faint impressions in the soft earth. "Tracks."

Apollo inspected where Cherry pointed. "Multiple sets," he confirmed.

Silas nodded grimly. "They came prepared. Titan had this planned down to the last detail."

Rising to his feet, Apollo crouched through the gap in the fence, his senses on high alert as he moved into the dense underbrush beyond. The tracks led away from the estate, winding through the trees with purpose.

After a hundred yards, the forest opened up onto a narrow dirt road that cut along the edge of the property. Apollo's heart raced as he spotted tire tracks imprinted in the soft earth.

"Photograph these tracks. We need to identify what kind of vehicle they used," Apollo called.

As Silas documented the evidence, Apollo stood.

"Regan," Apollo called. "Has anyone watched the security tapes?"

"The tapes were wiped. Cloud too."

Apollo looked at him and smiled. "But not the server in my room."

APOLLO RUSHED UPSTAIRS, HIS HEART POUNDING. HE TOOK THE stairs two at a time as he strode towards his private quarters. The door swung open at his touch, revealing his bedroom.

For a moment, the lingering aroma of River's perfume threatened to overwhelm him. Apollo shut his eyes, forcing himself to focus. He crossed to an intricately carved mahogany panel on the far wall. His fingers danced across the woodwork, finding the hidden latch with practiced ease.

The panel slid open, revealing a state-of-the-art server rack humming with quiet efficiency. Apollo pulled a laptop from inside and sat at his desk. His fingers flew across the keyboard, bypassing layers of security protocols. The screen before him flickered to life, displaying an array of data and security footage.

"Any other secrets we should know about?" Cherry asked. "Like maybe hidden cameras in the bedrooms?"

Apollo snorted. "Trust me, I have no interest in what people do in the privacy of their rooms. Especially my mate's parents."

"Good to know."

"Come on, come on," Apollo muttered, scanning the feeds. He navigated through weeks of archived footage, searching for anything out of the ordinary with Cherry hovering over his shoulder and the others not far away. He realized in that moment he'd never had anyone in his room before besides River.

His wolf didn't like it. *Mine. My room.*

Yeah. Let's make an exception just this once.

Just as Apollo was about to lose hope of finding anything, a flicker of movement caught his eye.

There, on the screen, a figure emerged from the tree line. The timestamp corresponded with the second day he and River had been in the woods.

He recognized Vanessa, her lithe form moving with predatory grace across the grounds. She marched straight for the camera, her gaze fixed on the lens.

Apollo's hands clenched as Vanessa climbed up to the camera. For a moment, her face filled the screen. A smile played across her lips, and then the feed died.

"Damn it!" Apollo slammed his palm against the desk. How long had Vanessa been working against them? How much information had she fed to Titan and his rogues?

He rewound the footage, studying every detail of Vanessa's approach. The confidence in her stride spoke volumes about someone intimately familiar with the estate's layout and security measures.

As Apollo pored over the footage, a chill ran down his spine. He realized that the camera had been disabled weeks before the attack.

This was more than a breach of security; it was a long-term infiltration. Titan and his rogues had been watching them, studying their routines, waiting for the perfect moment to strike.

How many other weaknesses had Vanessa exposed? How much of their defenses had been compromised? He'd have to redo everything. Start from scratch with the security to ensure their safety. Thank the goddess he had the backup security system locked away in his room; otherwise, they may never have known who was responsible for betraying them.

Apollo's mind raced, wondering how long Vanessa had been working with Titan.

"I know her," said Bianca. "She's Ares' secretary. River told him to get rid of her."

Apollo nodded. "She must have come back to grab her things when River and I were away."

"She did," said Zeke. "Ares told us to let her in."

"Did anyone stay with her?"

"I don't think so."

Apollo shook his head at Ares' stupidity. He should never have left her unsupervised in the house. But then he couldn't blame his twin for being distracted. After all, his mate had been with another man. So it was as much Apollo's fault as it was Ares'.

Silas entered the room. "I took photos of the vehicle tracks and sent them to Terrance."

Apollo nodded and closed the closet, which contained the server. "Which way did those SUV tracks go?"

"North."

"North? But north just takes you further into the area. The only way out is to go east."

"You think they didn't leave the neighborhood?" asked Cherry.

"I'm sure they are gone by now, but they could have been hiding out near here."

"It would explain how they got so much intel on what was going on here."

Apollo nodded. "Let's go."

"Where?" asked Zeke.

"To research every house in this gated community." He looked at Silas. "Except for you. I have something else I need you to do."

CHAPTER TWENTY-ONE

ARES

Ares' nostrils flared, taking in the dank, musty odor as Duncan pried the rusted metal grate open enough for them to slip through, leaving jagged edges threatening to snag their clothes. He glanced at Theo and Santiago, nodding before squeezing into the opening.

The faint glow of their phone lights barely illuminated the space. Ares moved carefully, on high alert for any sign of danger. Moisture slicked the walls, covering them in a thick layer of slime, making every step treacherous. Shallow water sloshed around their ankles, its murky surface concealing who knew what.

As they progressed deeper into the tunnel, the air grew thicker, heavy with the stench of decay and stagnant water. Ares fought the urge to gag, focusing instead on the steady rhythm of his breathing. Behind him, Theo coughed, and Santiago gagged and spat on the ground.

"Are you sure this is the only way in?" Theo croaked.

Duncan chuckled and shook his head, but didn't say anything.

The tunnel seemed to stretch on, twisting and turning like the bowels of a great beast. Ares lost all sense of time and direction, trusting Duncan's guidance as they navigated the labyrinthine passages, he realized that if Duncan screwed them, he would never figure his way out again. Every so often, they would pause to listen, straining for any sound that might indicate they'd been detected.

Duncan tapped Ares' shoulder. "We're here."

Ares peered ahead toward a faint square of light in the distance and spotted the outline of a metal grate similar to the one they'd entered through. Duncan produced a small tool from his pocket and worked on the bolts holding the grate in place.

With agonizing slowness, they eased the grate open, wincing at every creak and groan of protesting metal. Ares exited first, hauling himself up into what appeared to be a dimly lit storage room. Boxes and crates were stacked on top of each other haphazardly around them, providing ample cover as Theo, Santiago, and then Duncan emerged.

Duncan checked his phone. "Shift change is in two minutes."

They crept towards the door, pausing to listen for movement. Ares eased the door open, peering into a long, sterile hallway. Fluorescent lights buzzed overhead, casting harsh shadows across the concrete floor. He sniffed the air, and his wolf growled. The scents of shifters mixed with chemicals and gun oil.

Easy, boy. We don't want to make a bigger mess than necessary.

Though truthfully, Ares was willing to slaughter, maim, or torture anyone he had to to get River back.

Moving swift and silent, they made their way towards the main storage area. Ares' heart pounded, every nerve on edge as they rounded each corner. Voices sounded in the distance, growing louder as they approached.

Just as they reached the door, Ares held up a hand. Voices carried from the other side of the steel door, low and gruff. He honed in on their words, ignoring the sounds of machinery in the building.

He sniffed the air. Two males.

"... shipment's late again," one growled. "Rudy's going to rip someone's ball off if this keeps up."

"Better them than us," another chuckled nervously. "I don't trust him. Rudy thinks he's untouchable, but Titan would gut him if it suited Titan's purpose."

Ares exchanged a look with Theo. His wolf growled at the mention of Rudy's name, the beast demanding action. Duncan was becoming more trustworthy than Ares had anticipated.

The other guard snorted. "As long as Rudy keeps the guns and suppressors moving, he's safe. But did you see how much was in the last shipment? They've got enough suppressors now to dose half the damn continent."

"Not me," said the first guy. "I ain't never taking those things. Screw that. I'll leave before I let them force me to take those."

"You think Titan will let you go? You've obviously never met him."

They'd been right. Titan was using suppressors on his rogues. Ares gestured for Theo and Santiago to ready themselves at the opposite side of the door while Duncan edged back toward the shadows, keeping watch on the room they'd come from.

Theo raised three fingers, silently counting down. On one, Ares shoved the door open, slamming it against the wall and catching the two wolves inside off guard. The first rogue hardly had time to turn before Ares surged forward, shifted mid-leap, and sent both of them crashing into a stack of crates.

Theo and Santiago followed like shadows, their claws slashing the second guard's torso before he could draw his weapon. The sound of gurgling filled the air as blood spattered across the floor.

The first guard struggled under Ares' weight, managing to shift partially before Ares sank his teeth into his neck. The body went limp, and Ares rose, shifting and wiping blood from his mouth as Santiago and Theo fanned out looking for more threats.

Theo trotted back and shifted. "Clear."

Duncan's dark eyes darted between the bodies on the floor and Ares' blood-streaked form. "That was fast," he muttered.

"No time to waste," Ares growled. "Where to?"

"This way." Duncan gestured toward another door at the far end of the room. The four of them moved efficiently, weaving through narrow rows of boxes and crates lit up by buzzing fluorescent lighting. Every turn felt more claustrophobic than the last, but Ares' determination fueled him forward.

His wolf surged, clawing to take over.

Kill. Kill. Kill.

He couldn't give in yet. *Soon. I'll let you kill them all soon.*

They reached another door, this one heavier and reinforced with multiple locks. Duncan cursed under his breath as he examined them.

"Can you open it?" Theo kept watch down the aisle as footsteps echoed in the distance.

"Give me a second." Duncan pulled a phone from his pocket and texted someone.

Ares' wolf's restlessness bled into him until he couldn't control himself.

He snarled and gripped the reinforced handle in both hands.

"Wait-" Duncan started, but Ares didn't listen.

With a guttural growl, Ares' muscles strained as he wrenched at the reinforced door, the metal groaning under the force of his strength. The locks gave way, and the door flew open with a resounding crash.

The group surged forward into a small antechamber, their eyes adjusting to the dim lighting. A bank of elevators stood before them, their polished doors reflecting the harsh fluorescent lights overhead.

"Third floor," Duncan panted. "That's where Rudy will be."

The elevator arrived with a soft ding, its doors slid open, revealing a plush interior that seemed wildly out of place in the industrial setting. They piled in, tension crackling between them as the elevator began its ascent. Soft music played over the speakers, and Ares glimpsed himself in the mirrored walls. Blood splashed his torso and face. His gaze slid to his neck, and he touched the mark River had left on his skin. He stared at the marks and then reached for the ribbon that connected them. It remained intact. Those two little things, scars and a ribbon, were the two things he held on to hardest. Having those two small reminders spurred him on in his determination to find her.

Ares' heart pounded. His wolf clawed at the surface, desperate to make someone pay for what had been taken from them.

The elevator slowed to a stop, and Ares tensed. As the doors slid open, he glimpsed movement in the hallway beyond. He launched forward, shifting mid-leap, and attacking without thought.

Ares' powerful jaws snapped down on the throat of the nearest male, cutting off his cry of alarm. Theo and Santiago were right behind him, their own shifts fluid and practiced as they engaged two more rogues.

Duncan hung back, watching the Lycans tear through Rudy's men with brutal efficiency. Blood spattered the walls, the sound of snarls and breaking bones echoing through the hallway.

Amid the melee, a booming voice cut through the din. "What are you idiots doing out there?"

Ares' head snapped up, his golden eyes locking onto the hulking figure of Rudy at the end of the hall. The rogue Alpha's face contorted as he recognized the intruders.

"You," Rudy snarled, already shifting. "I should have known you'd come sniffing around."

Ares growled, stalking forward as the last of Rudy's men fell. Rudy completed his shift, his massive brown wolf form filling the narrow hallway.

The two Alphas collided in a fury of snapping jaws and slashing claws. Rudy was strong, but he was a shifter, and Ares was a Lycan. A Lycan fueled by desperation and rage.

They tumbled down the hallway, a whirlwind of fur and fangs. Rudy's claws rake across Ares' flank, but he hardly registered the pain. His world narrowed to a singular focus- slaughter Rudy.

Ares and Rudy crashed through a pair of double doors, tumbling into an opulent office space. The stark contrast between the industrial corridors and this lavishly furnished room jarred him, but Ares had no time to dwell on it. He rolled to his feet, snarling as Rudy lunged at him again.

The two powerful wolves circled each other, eyes locked, muscles coiled and ready to strike. Rudy made the first move, feinting left before darting right, his jaws snapping shut inches from Ares' throat. But Ares was ready, twisting away and sinking his teeth into Rudy's shoulder.

Rudy roared, and Ares charged forward, using his superior bulk to slam Rudy into an ornate bookcase. Books and trinkets crashed to the floor as Rudy struggled to regain his footing.

Ares pressed his advantage, his enormous paws pinning Rudy to the ground. Rage pulsed through Ares, fueled by thoughts of River and all she had endured because of Titan and his traitors.

In a blur of motion, Ares' jaws clamped down on Rudy's throat. Rudy thrashed and snapped, but Ares held firm, slowly increasing the pressure, enjoying the terror in Rudy's eyes.

Just as Rudy's struggles began to weaken, Santiago rushed to Ares.

"Ares. We need him alive!"

No. Kill. Revenge.

With tremendous effort, Ares forced his beast to release his grip. His wolf writhed and tried to retake control, his howls becoming more desperate for vengeance. But Ares forced him back and shifted. Rudy collapsed to the floor, wheezing and coughing. He shifted as well but stayed on his hands and knees, blood dripping from the puncture wounds on his neck.

"Where is she?" Ares demanded.

Rudy looked up, confusion mingling with the pain and fear in his eyes. "Who?"

Ares grasped a fistful of Rudy's hair, yanking his head back before punching Rudy in the face. Rudy's bones crunched under his fist. "Don't play games with me. My mate. Where are you keeping her?"

Rudy's brow furrowed. "The High Luna? She's not here."

Ares' grip tightened, eliciting a pained gasp from Rudy. "I know that asshole. Where is she?"

"With Titan, I assume."

"Where?" Ares demanded. "Where has Titan taken her?"

Rudy's gaze darted between Ares, Santiago, and Theo, panic evident in his eyes. "I... I don't know," he stammered. "Titan doesn't share that information with me. I just handle shipments."

Ares exchanged a glance with Theo.

"Then perhaps you'd like to tell us about those shipments," Theo said. "Where are the drugs going?"

Rudy's eyes widened, beads of sweat forming on his brow. "I can't... Titan will eviscerate me."

Ares leaned in to Rudy's ear. "And what do you think we'll do if you don't?"

The room fell silent for a moment, the only sound Rudy's ragged breathing. Then Ares drove his fist into Rudy's kidneys. The Alpha doubled over, gasping for air.

"That was a warm-up," Ares growled, hauling Rudy upright once more. "Now, let's try again. Where are the shipments going?"

Rudy spat blood onto the plush carpet, his defiance crumbling under Ares' relentless stare. "Canada," he wheezed. "The main distribution center is in Canada."

Ares extended his claws into Rudy's skin, drawing blood. "Be more specific."

"A... a mailbox place," Rudy gasped. "Montreal. That's where we send paperwork and the bulk of the suppressors. From there, it gets distributed to wherever Titan wants it."

Ares' mind raced, connecting the dots. Montreal. It made sense-close to the border, access to major shipping routes. And if Titan were operating out of Canada, it would explain why they'd had such a hard time tracking him down.

"Why does he want so many suppressors?" Santiago asked.

"I don't-"

Ares slammed his fist into Rudy's mouth, and Rudy groaned before spitting out a tooth. "Lie all you want," Ares said. "I'll just keep punching until every tooth is gone. Then I'll move on to bones."

"He wants to control the rogues," Rudy groaned. "The suppressors are supposed to help him keep them compliant."

"But why does he need such huge shipments?"

"He's stocking up."

"For what?"

"For when he takes back the throne."

There it was. Titan didn't just want River; he wanted the throne, and he was determined to keep it at any cost, even if it meant drugging shifters and Lycans to keep them in line.

"The address of the mailbox place," Ares demanded. "Give it to us."

Rudy hesitated, and the internal struggle played out across his face. With a growl of impatience, Ares crushed Rudy's hand, bending his fingers back until the bones snapped.

Rudy screamed, his body convulsing against Ares' iron grip.

"16249 Meganese Ave."

"How do we know he isn't lying?" asked Santiago.

"Because it's right here," Duncan chimed in from behind them.

Ares turned to find Duncan typing away at Rudy's laptop.

"Shipping info is here in his shipping account."

"Are there any other addresses in there?"

Duncan scrolled through the screen and shook his head. "Nothing."

Ares swore. The address for the shipments was fine, but clearly, River wasn't being held at a shipping and mailbox business.

"What are you going to do with him?" Duncan pointed at Rudy.

Kill. Kill him. Kill-

Stop. You aren't helping.

Ares studied Rudy before giving Theo a sharp nod.

Theo didn't hesitate; he moved with precision and punched Rudy in the temple.

Rudy crumpled to the floor.

Ares exhaled harshly as he ran a hand through his hair. Every second wasted was another moment River was in Titan's grasp. And with the new information about his plans... River was in worse danger than Ares had imagined.

"Tie him up. We'll take him with us." Ares strode for the elevator.

Hold on, River. I'm coming.

CHAPTER TWENTY-TWO

APOLLO

Apollo scanned his computer, reviewing the recorded deeds of all the estates in a five-mile radius. They all appeared legitimate. But looks could be deceiving.

Regan knocked on his door. "Highness?"

Apollo shook his head. "Regan, good. Go through this entire list and see how many have been sold and or renovated in the last ten years. Are any vacant or rented out? Find every owner and do a thorough background check on them."

Regan nodded and headed out as Apollo's phone rang. The words, 'Selfish Bastard', flashed on the screen. He should probably rename the title now that he and Ares were getting along. He wondered if Ares had changed his name from 'Pompous Asshole' on his phone yet.

"Have you found her?"

"No. But, I've made progress."

"Where are you?"

"New York."

"Where are you headed?"

"Home."

The news didn't surprise him. "You think Titan is here?"

"Yeah."

"Me too."

"Where are you?"

"At home. I've been looking over the video footage, as well as the lack of footage."

"Meaning?"

"Meaning Vanessa cut the feed to a back section of the fence when you let her in to get her things. We followed the tunnel Titan used, and it led straight to the area. And when we went back and checked, the fence had been cut, and there were tire tracks on the dirt road."

"Leading out of the area?"

"No. Leading further in."

Silence deadened the line. "He took her somewhere nearby."

"I'm looking at all the houses in the area. When I have a list of sales in the last ten years, I can narrow it down, and we will search each of them."

"I'll be back in two hours. Let's regroup. I have the address where Titan's drug shipments are sent."

"I'm getting everyone ready to start the search."

"Sounds good." Ares paused for a moment. "How are you healing?"

"I'm fine."

"How's Cherry?"

"Fiery as always."

"Good. We're gonna need her fire. I have a feeling we are in for a bigger fight than we realized."

"Agreed."

"Check in with all the Alphas who came for the mating ceremony. Feel them out."

"Already started. Did something happen? Are you thinking some may have traded loyalties?"

"I know some have. We just need to see how many. I'll call when I land."

"Ares?"

"Yeah?"

Apollo didn't know what to say.

"Don't go all mushy on me now, brother, or I'll kick your ass when I return, whether you're injured or not."

Apollo chuckled. "Fair enough."

Apollo laid down his phone.

His wolf whined.

Don't worry, boy, we're close. Very close.

CHAPTER TWENTY-THREE

TITAN

"You need to calm down," Kane said without emotion.

Titan growled in response. "I should take her tonight. Force her into submission. Being soft didn't work. Now it's time for a new tactic. Do what I should have done from the beginning. Take her."

"You let her rattle you," Kane said. "Don't. Focus on what we need to do to complete our goal. Forget her and focus on our original plan."

His original plan. His mother's original plan. "So you think I should let her go?"

"What's the alternative? Lock her up for the rest of your life? You think that will make her love you?"

Titan's harsh breathing heightened the tension between them before he spat out angrily, "At this point, I don't care if she loves me. All I want is her submission. And the moment that happens, I'll take her and get her to give me a child. Then I'll have everything I need to secure my legacy."

Kane blew out a breath.

"What?" Titan demanded.

Kane shook his head. "I dealt with you wanting her. I dealt with you, building our empire for her. I dealt with you going in and kidnapping her. But forcing yourself on her… That I can't be ok with."

Titan's roar echoed through the room as he whirled to face Kane. "You dare question me? After everything we've been through, everything we've built together?"

Kane stood his ground, his face grim. "I'm not questioning you, Titan. I'm trying to protect you from yourself. This obsession with River is clouding your judgment. Making you reckless."

Kill him. Force him to submit.

Shut it.

"Reckless?" Titan snarled, advancing on Kane. "I've never been more focused in my life. Everything we've done, every move we've made, has led to this moment. And now you want to back out?"

Kane shook his head slowly. "I'm not backing out. But forcing yourself on her... that's a line I can't let you cross. It goes against everything we stand for."

Titan's laugh came out harsh and bitter. "Everything we stand for? We're rogues, Kane. Outcasts. We make our own rules."

"There are some rules that shouldn't be broken," Kane said. "Some lines that, once crossed, you can never come back from. Just ask that tortured girl upstairs who we promised to protect. We promised not to let the same thing happen to another female under our watch. Was that a lie?"

For a moment, Titan became conflicted. He had promised her, but this was different. River was his mate. His.

Mine. Take. Mark.

Titan's wolf spurred him on. He grabbed Kane by his shirt, yanking on him. "You're either with me or against me. There is no middle ground."

Kane's face remained impassive. "I've always been with you, brother. But this... this isn't you. The Titan I know wouldn't even consider-"

"The Titan you knew is exactly who I am. I've been weak for far too long. Now I understand, though. I understand why my mother did what she did. She did it for me. For us. All of us. And it's time I repay her for it."

"Then you'll have to do it without me."

Titan's grip tightened, and his wolf roared to be let out. To rip out Kane's throat. "You'd betray me? After everything?"

"It's not betrayal to try and save someone you care about from themselves. If you go through with this, if you force yourself on River... then you're no better than the monsters we've been against all these years."

Titan's fangs burst into his mouth, and his claws lengthened, tearing through Kane's shirt.

Do it. Kill. Make him submit. We are Alpha. We are King.

Titan shoved Kane away. "Get out," he growled. "Get out before I do something we'll both regret."

Kane straightened his shirt, his eyes locked on Titan's face. "Think about what you're doing, brother. There's still time to stop."

Titan turned away and gripped his desk. "Go."

As Kane's footsteps faded down the hallway, Titan stood alone in the room, his mind a whirlwind of conflicting emotions. Part of him knew Kane was right. Forcing himself on River would destroy any chance of ever restoring what little connection endured between them. And yet, the thought of giving her up, of allowing Ares and Apollo to win, sent fury surging through him.

His wolf roared. *Take. Claim. Make ours.*

Titan raked a hand through his hair and stormed toward the window, staring out at the dark expanse of his lands. The Northern Lights still flickered in the sky, their colors eerie and unnatural against the pitch-black night.

Go. Hunt. Run.

A knock at the door interrupted his thoughts.

"What?" he barked.

The door creaked open, revealing Vanessa. She slipped inside, her usual confidence tempered by something else, hesitation.

"I heard your... conversation with Kane."

Titan scoffed, turning away from her. "Is that what you've stooped to? Listening at doors now?"

"When you're losing allies left and right, you can't afford to ignore those who are still loyal."

"Don't lecture me about loyalty when you can't even spell the word."

"Then maybe you need something else." Her voice dropped to a seductive purr as she closed the distance between them, her fingers trailing along his arm. "You're wound too tight. You're overthinking when you should be acting."

He clenched his fists, trying to keep from shoving her away.

"Your problem-" She circled him like a predator scenting weakness, "is that you're obsessed with making her come to you willingly." She stopped in front of him, placing a hand on his torso. "But she's never going to."

Titan growled. "Careful, bitch."

Vanessa only smiled wider. "You think I don't know what you're planning? You want an heir. A child with royal blood to solidify your claim to the throne." Her lips brushed his ear. "I can give that to you."

His wolf snarled.

Titan wrenched her wrist and shoved her away before she touched him again.

"You're not her," he snapped.

Vanessa's eyes narrowed briefly before she let out an amused hum. "No," she admitted. "But I'm willing. Are you going to waste your time chasing after a female who will never love you? Or do you want to secure the throne?"

Titan exhaled sharply through his nose and turned away from her again.

"Think about it." Vanessa sauntered toward the door. "River will never accept you." She paused in the doorway, looking over her shoulder. "But I will. I'll give you the child you want. You don't even have to mate me for it."

She slipped out before he could respond.

Damn it all.

His wolf demanded they find River and force her compliance if necessary, but something held him back.

Kane's words echoed in his mind: Some lines, once crossed, you can never come back from.

For the first time in years, doubt crept into Titan's heart.

Titan stood frozen for several long moments, his mind racing. Vanessa's offer tempted the darkest parts of him. The parts that craved power and dominance above all else. If Vanessa had his child, but he could make everyone believe the child was River's... His wolf recoiled at the thought.

He stalked over to the bar and poured himself a glass of whiskey, downing it in one burning gulp.

River's face flashed in his mind. Her silver hair gleaming in the moonlight, eyes flashing with defiance. Even in her anger and fear, she was breathtaking. The thought of replacing her with Vanessa or anyone else made his gut churn.

But Vanessa's words nagged at him. River had made it abundantly clear that she would never accept him willingly. But Vanessa...

Titan poured another drink, his hand shaking. He had come so far, sacrificed so much. To give up now seemed unthinkable. But forcing River, breaking her spirit... that felt equally as impossible.

With a roar of frustration, Titan hurled his glass against the wall, where it shattered into a thousand glittering pieces. The crash echoed through the room, matching the chaos in his mind.

He had to clear his head.

Titan strode from the room and made his way through the winding corridors of the mansion, ignoring the nervous glances from the pack members he passed.

He burst out into the cool night air, inhaling deeply. Without conscious thought, his feet carried him towards the dense woods surrounding the property. As he reached the tree line, he stripped off his clothes, piling them on the forest floor.

The shift came easily, his human form melting away as his wolf surged forward. In moments, his black wolf stood where Titan had been.

With a low growl, Titan took off into the forest, his powerful legs eating up the ground beneath him. He ran without direction or purpose, reveling in the primal freedom of his wolf form. The scents of the forest filled his nose: Evergreens, earth, and a myriad of small creatures that scurried out of his path.

As he ran, memories flooded his mind. The first time he'd smelled River. Biting her, only to be rejected by her. The years he had spent building his empire, always with her in mind. Watching her from afar but never touching, never tasting. Only to then have her claimed by the two men he hated most in the world.

Titan recognized a scent and turned instinctively toward it. In minutes, he'd taken down the doe and tackled her to the ground. As he ripped out her throat, he reveled in the feel of her warm blood in his mouth.

This was who he was, who he was meant to be. The monster that everyone feared. King of the Lycans. King of everything.

CHAPTER TWENTY-FOUR

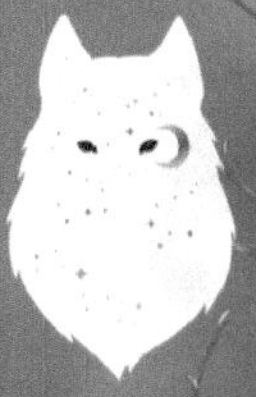

RIVER

River sat on her bed, staring at a random TV show and rubbing the fading bruises on her arms. Titan had gripped her hard, but that wasn't what unsettled her most; it was the look in his eyes when she'd defied him. The push and pull of anger and longing, dominance and something dangerously similar to desperation.

She traced a fingertip over the marks, anger simmering beneath the surface. He thought he could wear her down. That if he applied the right amount of pressure, she would fold. Submit. But River wasn't raised to be anyone's captive queen. As the anger rolled through her again, her stomach flopped, and she lurched for the bathroom just before throwing up soda. She heaved again and again until she broke out in a sheen of sweat.

Damn, being pregnant was not all it was cracked up to be. No wonder her mom had only had one kid. This might be her only one, too.

She flushed the toilet and lay down on the cement floor, letting the coolness seep into her face.

Her wolf whined.

"I'm fine," she croaked. "After being bitten, shot, and kidnapped, I'm not about to let nausea take us out."

Her wolf whined again.

River pushed herself from the cool bathroom floor, her limbs trembling with exertion. She gripped the sink, staring at her pale reflection. Dark circles shadowed her eyes, a stark contrast to her silvery hair. Her skin held a waxy pallor, and she was sure her face was thinner.

Shit. Was she losing weight? That wasn't good, was it? But what did she expect when all she possibly managed to keep down daily was a couple of hundred calories of sugar? Just walking seemed to fatigue her. Not good. Not. Good. She needed to escape before she died or, worse, miscarried.

The thought made her wolf yowl.

"No. We're going to make it through this," she murmured. Her hand drifted to her abdomen. "I'll get us out. I promise."

Her wolf stirred restlessly. River took a deep breath, trying to calm both herself and her agitated other half.

Stay strong. Keep your wits about you.

Titan grew more unstable by the day, and she couldn't afford to be off her game.

A soft knock at the door startled her from her thoughts. A knock? No one knocked.

River tensed, she rushed out of the bathroom, and her eyes darted to the fake window. It was too early for her usual meal delivery. The sun hadn't set yet.

"Who is it?" Her voice came out steadier than she felt as she shuffled to the bed and sat quickly, hoping her room didn't smell like vomit.

She popped a mint from the nightstand into her mouth and

crunched it between her teeth as she tensed, ready for another confrontation with Titan. But when the door eased open, it wasn't him.

Kane entered, his face unreadable as he shut the door.

River turned off the TV. "Came to deliver another threat?"

Kane exhaled through his nose and crossed his arms. "No threats tonight."

River narrowed her eyes and finished chewing her mint. Silence was often more unnerving than words. His eyes narrowed as he sniffed the air and then looked at her.

He studied her for a long moment before leaning against the dresser. "You're driving him insane, you know."

"Good," she said flatly.

Kane huffed a quiet laugh but shook his head. "Not good for you." His gaze flickered to the bruises on her arms. "He's losing it."

River swallowed hard but kept her expression blank. "Then maybe you should talk some sense into your almighty Alpha before there's nothing left to salvage."

"You think I haven't tried?" Kane shot back, voice low and sharp. "I told him this would go sideways if he forced it. But he's ready to… do something I just cannot agree with."

"You created the monster but can no longer control him, huh?"

"Believe me when I say I didn't create him. But that isn't the point. Look, I don't like you."

"Obviously."

"And you don't like me."

"Truth."

"But even I don't want to see you forced into something that will destroy you both."

She snorted. "You mean mating?"

"That's exactly what I mean."

River stared at him as his meaning sank in, making her gut twist.

"He wouldn't," she whispered. But even as she said it, she knew Kane wouldn't be there unless Titan would.

For a long moment, neither of them spoke.

Kane muttered a curse under his breath and ran a hand through his hair. "I wanted to fix the system. I thought Titan would do that."

"As long as he listened to you."

"We had a goal. A plan. But you screwed the whole damn thing up."

"You do know I don't want this, right? I don't want any part of it. If you let me go-"

"He will kill me and get himself killed trying to get you back."

"Then help me," River said softly.

Kane looked away.

But she saw it, the flicker of doubt tightening his shoulders, the war waging inside him.

And for the first time since being taken, she saw a crack in Kane's armor. He cared for Titan and believed in what they were doing.

Kane stared at the wall, visibly wrestling with himself. When he looked back at River, his eyes held a storm of conflicting emotions.

"I can't betray him," he said. "He's like a brother to me. We've been through hell together."

River took a cautious step toward him. "Then don't betray him. Save him. You know what he's planning will destroy him in the end."

"You don't understand what's at stake," Kane growled. "This is bigger than just you and Titan. It's about changing our entire society."

"By drugging innocent wolves? By tearing apart families?" River challenged. "Is that the change you want to see? Help me understand. What is all this for? The drugs, the rogues, kidnapping me... what's the endgame?"

Kane exhaled slowly. "Freedom," he said simply. "Freedom for our kind to live as we're meant to, not hiding in the shadows, not bowing to ancient traditions that keep us weak."

"And you think forcing me to be Titan's mate will accomplish that?"

Kane shook his head. "It was never supposed to go this far. You were meant to be a symbol- the Luna who would stand beside the true Alpha King. Together, you would usher in a new era for wolves everywhere."

"But I'm not his true mate," River said. "My wolf rejected him from the beginning."

"He doesn't believe that. He thinks the bond needs time, that your connection to the twins is what's blocking it."

A chill ran through River. "What do you think?"

Kane's expression darkened. "Our system is defective. The Council and the royal family have all failed us. Do you have any idea what it's like for rogues? For those who don't fit into your perfect little hierarchy?"

River's eyes flashed. "And your solution is what? More violence? More control? How does that make you any different from the system you're trying to overthrow?"

Kane fell silent, his gaze drifting to the fake window where the faint glow of lights still flickered in the distance. "We were going to build something better. His mom had a vision, a world where wolves lived without shame, without hiding. Where strength and love were valued over heritage. I believed in that vision. I still do."

"What changed?"

Kane's eyes hardened. "The Council rejected Titan's petition for recognition as a legitimate son of the king. And then... His father died."

"You mean he killed his father."

Kane looked at her and shook his head. "No. He didn't."

Ares and Apollo had said he'd killed their parents. They wouldn't lie about that.

"Who did then?"

She didn't think he would answer.

"His mother," he finally said.

River shook her head. "You're lying."

"I was there. I saw what happened. Titan had nothing to do with it."

"Then why did he take the blame?"

"Because he loved his mother. He felt she'd suffered enough, and he didn't want her name tarnished as well."

River's mind reeled. Titan hadn't killed his father or the twins' mother.

"We had to go underground after that. We'd gone to the States for a while and tried to make a new life, but then Titan's mom killed herself, and it sent Titan into a tailspin. He'd been out of control for a year and then-"

"And then he found me," she finished for him.

"It became... personal after that. His goal shifted from changing the system to conquering it. To prove he deserved you, deserved everything they said he couldn't have."

River sank onto the bed, absorbing this information. "And now?"

"Now he's lost in his obsession," Kane said. "With you, with power, with revenge. I don't recognize him anymore."

"Help me, Kane," River said. "Not just for my sake, but for his too. This path he's on will destroy him."

Kane's eyes met hers. "What would you have me do? I can't just let you go."

"Then help me reach him," River said, a plan forming in her mind. "The real him, not this twisted version consumed by vengeance and obsession. You said it yourself, he wasn't always like this."

Kane ran a hand over his face, looking suddenly exhausted. "Even if I wanted to help you, it might be too late. He's not listening to reason anymore."

"There has to be something. Some way to get through to him."

A thick silence fell between them, marred only by the distant howl of a wolf somewhere in the forest surrounding the compound. The sound sent a shiver down River's spine, a reminder of her mates, still searching for her.

Kane paced the room. "Even if I wanted to help you, what could I do? There are cameras everywhere. Patrols. Dozens of rogues. Not to mention the fences. Titan would know immediately you were missing."

"There must be something. A way out, a way to contact Ares and Apollo..."

"And then what?" Kane challenged. "They'll come storming in here, and people will die. Good people, who believe they're fighting for a better world."

River stood, her eyes flashing with determination. "Then help me talk to him."

Kane laughed bitterly. "You think you can reason with him? After everything?"

River struggled for something to say. Something that would convince Kane to act.

No. Not that. She couldn't…

"I have to try," River blurted. "For my child's sake."

Kane froze, his eyes widening as they dropped to her abdomen. "You're pregnant."

River's hand moved to her belly. "Yes."

"That must be why your scent is stronger. I couldn't smell you before, but now…" His eyes widened, and he scanned the room. "Have you stopped eating the food?"

Well, in for a penny… "Yes."

"Shit. Then you know that's where the suppressors are."

"I'm not a total idiot. Not that I'm keeping much of anything down. I'm lucky if my body will accept soda and mints."

He sniffed. "I take it Titan doesn't know?"

"Do you think I'd still be pregnant if he did?"

"You'd be surprised. With how twisted he is now, he'd likely claim the child was his."

The thought made River gasp. There was no way she would ever let Titan claim Apollo and Ares' child.

Kane ran a hand over his face. "This changes everything. It's only weeks, possibly days, before Titan realizes you aren't on the suppressors and blockers. He's said he's always been able to smell you even when you were on them before, but the others will notice soon, too. If you go upstairs, there will be no hiding it from them."

"Why doesn't Titan have cameras in here or in the art studio?"

"Because he doesn't want anyone else watching you. Believe me, if he weren't so paranoid about another male getting at you, he'd have every angle of the room covered by cameras."

The thought angered River. She wouldn't have put it past Titan to put cameras in the bathroom as well, so he could get his rocks off watching her.

"Help me," River begged. "Help my child. Please. I don't want him brought up in this world. Imagine what Titan would do to a baby. How much worse his obsession would become. If you do, I'll make sure Apollo and Ares give you whatever you want. I'm the High Luna, I can-"

"I don't want anything from you or them for myself. That's not why I'm here. I'm here for all the other wolves upstairs who didn't ask for this. All I want is for them to have an opportunity to live a normal life. It's all I've ever wanted."

"Then call Ares. Tell him what you want. He'll make sure it happens. I'll give you my word."

Before Kane could answer, the door burst inward. Titan stood in the doorway, his broad frame blocking the exit, his eyes blazing.

"What. Is. This?" he growled to Kane.

Kane straightened. "Talking."

"Talking," Titan repeated, his voice dangerously soft. "Behind my back. In her room. My mate's room."

River's heart pounded as Titan guided the door behind him with deliberate slowness. The air crackled with tension, and her wolf stirred anxiously.

Escape. Run.

"It's not what you think," Kane said evenly.

"No?" Titan's eyes narrowed. "Then tell me, brother, what is it? Because from where I'm standing, it looks an awful lot like betrayal."

Kane held his ground. "I'm trying to prevent you from making a mistake you can't take back."

"A mistake?" Titan's laugh barked out harsh and brittle. "The only mistake was thinking I could trust you."

"Titan-" River began.

"Don't," he snarled. "Don't you dare speak right now."

River's wolf growled at the disrespect.

Easy, girl.

The situation teetered on the edge of violence. She had to defuse it to prevent Titan from killing Kane.

"You think I don't know what's happening?" Titan stalked forward. "You think I can't smell your deception? Your guilt?"

Kane didn't move. Didn't speak.

"You're plotting against me." Titan's voice dropped. "My oldest friend. The only person I thought I could trust."

"I'm not plotting against you. I'm trying to save you."

Titan snorted. "Save me? Is that what this is?" He gestured between Kane and River. "Conspiring with my mate behind my back?"

"She's not your mate," Kane said quietly. "Not truly. And deep down, you know it."

The words hung in the air between them, explosive and dangerous. River held her breath, her heart pounding so loudly she was sure both men heard it.

Titan's face contorted with rage. "You dare-"

"Yes, I dare," Kane interrupted, taking a step forward. "Because someone has to tell you the truth. This obsession is destroying you, Titan. It's corrupting everything."

For a moment, something flickered in Titan's eyes, a flash of uncertainty, quickly masked by fury. "Get out," he growled.

"Titan-"

"GET OUT!" Titan roared, his voice reverberating through the room with such force the television rattled.

Kane held his ground a moment longer, his eyes locking with Titan's in a silent battle of wills. Then, with a nod, he turned to leave. As he passed River, he gave her a look that spoke volumes, half apology, half warning.

Kane slowly exited the room, leaving River alone with Titan. The silence stretched between them, taut as piano wire.

"What did he tell you?" Titan asked, his voice calm.

River swallowed hard, weighing her options. Titan would detect a lie immediately. But the truth might provoke him further.

"He told me about your past," she answered carefully. "About your vision for changing things."

"And?"

"And about your mother."

Something dark and pained flashed across Titan's face. "He had no right to speak of her."

"Maybe not," River conceded. "But it helped me understand you better."

Titan scoffed. "You don't want to understand me, River. You want to escape me."

"Can you blame me?" River asked, a flash of defiance breaking through her caution. "You bit me without consent and then kidnapped me."

Titan's eyes darkened. "I claimed what should have been mine from the beginning. If my father hadn't thrown me away, you would have been mine."

River stood her ground, refusing to be intimidated. "That's not how it works. That's not how any of this works."

Titan stalked toward her, looming over her like a towering skyscraper. "The old laws and traditions you cling to are just tools of control. Ways for the powerful to maintain their grip on us."

"And what you're doing is different?" River challenged. "Forcing a bond I don't want? How does that make you any better?"

Titan's nostrils flared as he inhaled deeply, his golden eyes studying her face with unsettling intensity. "You're different today." His voice dropped to a dangerous murmur. "Something's changed."

River's heart skipped, and her hand moved to protect her stomach before she stopped herself. Titan followed the movement, his eyes narrowing.

"What are you hiding?" he demanded.

"Nothing," River replied too quickly.

Titan moved closer, invading her personal space. "Lie to me again," he growled, "and see what happens."

River's wolf snarled, and for the first time in a week, jumped to her feet.

River approached him, her chest almost touching his.

"Threaten me again, and see what happens."

He growled, and his eyes went black.

In a flash, he pinned her to the wall, teeth bared.

River's wolf struggled to stay upright.

Before River could think, Titan's hot lips slammed down on hers.

Her wolf roared, and River thrashed against Titan's giant form as he crushed her against the wall, his lips trying to part hers, his tongue fighting to invade her.

River twisted her head away, breaking the brutal kiss. "Stop!" she gasped, pushing against him.

Titan growled, his hands tightening around her wrists. "You're mine." His hot breath hit her neck. "Mine to claim, mine to take."

His lips slammed down on hers again, making her teeth ache.

River's wolf surged, lending her strength. She bit down hard on Titan's invading tongue, the metallic taste of blood filling her mouth as he jerked back with a roar.

"I will never be yours," River spat. Her wolf lunged forward. With a sudden movement, she brought her knee up hard between his legs.

Titan grunted in pain, his grip loosening enough for River to wrench herself free. She stumbled away from him, putting the bed between them as she struggled to catch her breath.

"You little-" Titan's face contorted and shifted, his snout elongating and then shortening again.

"I told you not to touch me," River cut him off. "I warned you."

Titan straightened, probing her with his unnerving black eyes. "And I told you, the game had begun."

"This isn't a game," River shot back. "This is my life. My body. My choice."

Something shifted in Titan's eyes, a flicker of... what? Uncertainty? It vanished as soon as it appeared, replaced by cold calculation.

"You think you're so different from me," he said. "So righteous. But we're the same, River. Both of us trapped by circumstances beyond our control, both fighting for something we believe in."

"We are nothing alike," River insisted. "I don't hurt people to get what I want."

Titan snorted. "What about your precious twins? Do you think their hands are clean? That their royal bloodline wasn't built on violence and conquest?"

River faltered, unsure how to respond. Titan seized on her hesitation, taking a step forward.

"They've filled your head with lies. Made you believe they're the heroes of this tale. But they aren't. You've seen the rogues. You've heard their stories. Your precious twins let that happen."

"And that needs to be changed. But not by kidnapping, rape, and murder."

Titan looked at her, confused, and shook his head. "Rape? Who's been raped?"

"That's what you want to do to me, isn't it?"

"You can't rape what is meant to be yours."

River couldn't stop her mouth from falling open. "You don't believe that. You can't."

He didn't answer.

She glanced at the freezer and the only possible weapon at her disposal, the paintbrush. No. She would never reach it in time.

All right, girl. If you have any strength left right now, I need it if we want to make it out of this unmolested.

River focused all of her strength into her eyes. Her wolf lifted her head, lending what little she could manage.

Finally, River's gaze grew heavy, and she leveled it at him. At first, he looked at her in confusion and then with defiance.

"Do you feel that?" she asked softly. "That weight? Your wolf telling you to bow to me and look away? That feeling means I'm not yours."

"No, it-"

"Don't speak," she commanded.

His mouth snapped shut, and he swallowed hard. He growled and opened his mouth, but when nothing came out, he snapped it shut again.

"That command I have over you, I don't have it over my mates. Ares and Apollo do what they do because they are my fated mates. But when it comes to me telling them what to do, they don't do it because they feel compelled to or because I command them to, they do it because they choose to."

Titan's body began to shake, and he bared his teeth.

"Stop," she commanded. "I am not your mate. I will never be your mate. When my wolf saw you for the first time, she said two words: not him. When I met Ares for the first time, she all but clawed her way out of me to go to him and submit. But she will never do that with you. She will never choose you. She will never submit to you. We. Reject. You."

Titan roared and stormed to the bed. River backed toward the kitchenette as he flipped the bed without any effort. He swiped at the table and chair, and they shattered against the wall. He ripped the curtains from the fake window and punched his fist through the screen, making it crack and go black.

River took another step away from him and glanced at the freezer. No matter what happened, she would not let him harm her or her baby.

He ripped the television from the dresser and broke it over his knee. Then he tipped the dresser sideways, spilling her clothes everywhere. He roared and then broke the footboard of her bed in two pieces before ripping into the mattress and shredding it with his claws.

When there was nothing left to break, he stopped, chest heaving with each ragged breath. The room lay in ruins. The bed overturned, furniture splintered, the fake window's screen now a spiderweb of cracks with a gaping hole at its center, and barely still planted in the wall. His knuckles dripped blood on the cement floor, but he seemed not to notice.

River's wolf prowled anxiously, ready to fight if, though they both knew it would be futile against Titan's superior strength.

When he turned to face her, his expression had transformed. The anger still simmered, but his face wore a mask of cold calculation.

"You think you've won something here," he said. "You think your rejection means anything?"

River said nothing.

"I've been patient. I've tried to make this pleasant for you. To give you time to adjust." His lips curled into a bitter smile. "That ends now."

"Meaning?"

Titan's eyes morphed back to normal in the dim light. "It means no more luxuries. No more privileges. No more kindness." He gestured to the destruction around them. "You'll stay in here until you learn your place."

"My place is with my mates," River shot back.

"Your mates," Titan sneered. "They haven't found you yet, have they? And they won't." He slid closer. "You're mine, River. The sooner you accept that, the better this will go for all of us."

River lifted her chin and met his eye. "I will never accept it."

"We'll see. I won't force myself on you again. You will either see things my way or die in this room."

He strode toward the door, reached for the handle, and paused. "One week of isolation. No visitors, minimal food. Think about your situation carefully, River. It can be comfortable or challenging. It's up to you. But whichever way you choose to go, you are never leaving this property. Oh, and if you try to use your Omega gaze on me again to force me to do something you want, I'll rip your tongue out before the words leave your pretty lips."

With that, he left, the door slamming behind him with finality. The locks clicked into place, followed by the sound of something metal being slid across it.

River waited until his footsteps faded completely before she allowed herself to exhale. Her legs trembled with the aftermath of adrenaline, and she sank to the floor and dry heaved.

"Apollo. Ares. We need you."

CHAPTER TWENTY-FIVE

ARES

The house loomed before them, its stone walls and wrought iron gates both welcoming and imposing in the fading twilight. The familiar aroma of wet earth filled Ares' nostrils as they drove past the magnificent silver maple trees that had stood as sentinels for generations.

Theo drove with Santiago sitting beside him, his face a mask of concentration as he checked out his windows. Duncan shifted beside Ares, his eyes darting from window to window, taking in the expansive grounds.

They pulled up to the entrance, where the ornate double doors stood. A warm light spilled out the windows onto the stone steps. It should have welcomed them. Instead, all Ares could think about was the emptiness which would greet him inside. The absence of River's laughter, her eyes, her presence.

The car stopped, and Apollo strode out of the house, his lean frame silhouetted against the light from inside. Despite his evident exhaustion, he moved with purpose, his eyes locking with Ares' as he exited the vehicle.

The twins stood face-to-face for a moment, then embraced each other.

The sensation raced through Ares, consoling him in a way he'd never experienced before with his brother.

"Good to see you aren't still lying in bed while I do all the work."

Apollo chuckled and pushed away. "Thanks for letting me join in this time."

Apollo's gaze moved over Ares' shoulder as Duncan exited the vehicle.

"That him?"

Ares nodded and turned to Duncan.

"Duncan, my brother, Prince Apollo. Alpha of Alphas. Apollo, Duncan."

Apollo raised an eyebrow at Ares.

Ares chuckled.

Duncan bowed his head to Apollo. "Highness."

"Thank you for your help."

Duncan nodded.

Ares was about to ask where everyone was when Cherry burst through the door.

"Where's my daughter?" She strode down the steps with Strider in tow.

Ares groaned. He hadn't had enough sleep to deal with Cherry. "Good to see you feeling better as well, Cherry."

"Where is she? Do you have any leads at all, or do I start knocking on doors?"

"Let's go inside," said Apollo.

"No. We've been sitting on our asses too long. Who knows what that bastard could have done by now."

"River's strong," said Strider. "She'll hold her own until we can get her out."

Cherry turned on him. "How do you know that?"

"Because she's our daughter. And for as much as she's tried not to be like you, she has a stubborn streak in her that rivals even your own."

Ares' other guards exited and moved to Ares' side.

"Boss," said Zeke. "Tell us what to do, and we're ready."

Ares nodded. "Let's all meet in the conference room in an hour."

"An hour?" Cherry demanded.

Ares sighed and swallowed his emotions. "Yes, an hour."

Without another word, he headed inside. He needed a moment to himself. He'd not had a second alone in over a week, and if they wanted him to keep the shred of sanity he still possessed, he needed a shower, a breather, and a drink.

Ares stood at the window of the conference room, staring out at the sprawling grounds. The sky had darkened to indigo, stars beginning to pierce the velvet canvas above. The Northern Lights flickered behind the stars.

Apollo took his place at the head of the long mahogany table, Cherry and Strider settling into chairs, their bodies tense with anxiety. Zeke, Regan, Silas, Theo, Santiago, Lachlan, Drew, and Thomas all took their seats as well. Ares looked at the vacant seat where Bennett should have been and couldn't help the sense of guilt that wracked him at the relief it hadn't been one of his guys who'd been killed.

Duncan entered last, hanging near the doorway as if uncertain of his welcome.

"Duncan, sit," said Ares.

Apollo watched Duncan fill the last seat, and his gaze lingered on it before connecting with Ares.

Ares gave his brother a nod of understanding and then took his seat at the far end of the table.

The conference room, once a place of strategy and Lycan business, now felt like a war room. Maps spread across the table, surveillance photos pinned to a corkboard, and a whiteboard covered in Apollo's precise handwriting detailing everything they'd learned about Titan's operation.

Ares wolf paced, demanding action, demanding they find their mate. But rushing forward without a plan would only lead to disaster.

"Alright." His voice cut through the tension. "For those of you who haven't been introduced to Duncan, he provided us with important intel about Titan's operation." Ares centered himself as all eyes turned to him. "We have confirmation Titan's main operations are based in Canada, specifically here. But the exact location is still unknown."

Apollo nodded. "While you were in New York, we discovered something interesting." He gestured to a series of photographs pinned to the board behind him. "The security camera footage revealed Vanessa tampering with our systems weeks before the attack. She disabled a section of our perimeter defenses."

"That bitch," Cherry muttered, her fingers curling into fists.

"We also found evidence that when Titan took River, he may have stayed in the area for a bit," Apollo continued. "The tracks we found led north, deeper into our gated neighborhood rather than out of it."

Strider leaned forward, his face creased with concentration. "You think they had a house nearby? Somewhere to lay low before moving her?"

"It's possible," Apollo confirmed. "We've compiled a list of properties in the area that changed hands in the last few years. Fifteen estates total."

"There's also a mailbox business we found where the shipments of suppressors go to," said Ares. "We will check the estates first. If that doesn't pan out, we will go to the P.O. box store. It's Saturday.

No one will be able to get mail until Monday anyway. So we can wait on that."

Ares studied the map where Apollo had marked each location with a red pin. His wolf growled at the thought of River being held so near, right under their noses. So near, and they'd missed it. Maybe if they hadn't gone to the safe house… No. He had no way of knowing they would stay nearby, and even so, with their defenses shattered, they never could have stayed. They had no choice but to retreat and regroup.

No retreat. No surrender.

"We need to search them all," Apollo declared, breaking through Ares' thoughts.

"That could take days," said Ares. "Titan is bound to find out by tomorrow at the latest what's going on."

Apollo gave his brother a tight smile. "That's why I've brought in extra help."

CHAPTER TWENTY-SIX

RIVER

River lay on the remains of the foam mattress, with the shredded blanket on top of her. She had no idea how long she'd been lying there. True to his word, Titan had only returned to place a tray of food on the floor by the door and then leave again. No words. No questions. Nothing.

A stack of now four trays sat mostly untouched where he'd left them. He hadn't even questioned the fact that she hadn't eaten much or that the trays hadn't moved. As with all the trays before, she removed a small portion of food from each and flushed it down the toilet. She took the cans of soda and put them in the fridge to save for when she really needed them, since the twenty-four-pack hadn't lasted. She had so much candy and soda over the last weeks, she wasn't sure she'd ever have either again after getting out of her prison. But she couldn't afford to eat anything else. She needed her wolf to get up. She needed help if she intended to escape. But the additional strength her wolf had exerted to get Titan to leave her alone had depleted her. The suppressors may be working their way out of her system, but whatever Titan had used on her hadn't entirely left yet. She just hoped it didn't affect her baby.

After Titan's tirade, she had searched every inch of her room for hidden cameras. Even though Kane had told her there weren't any, she wanted to be certain.

Titan had done so much damage to the place that her making a bigger mess wouldn't be noticeable. When she was certain there were no cameras in the room, she went to work.

She'd walked to the fake electric window, which had previously displayed an outdoor scene, and inspected the area where it'd shattered and dangled on the wall. Titan had put a hole through the wall beside the fake window. Not too big. Roughly the size of a fist, but it had been enough to catch her attention. Upon examination, she found space on the other side of the wall.

First, she reached her hand in and then up to her elbow. She'd almost been able to fit her entire arm in the space when she felt cinderblock on the other side. River peeled back the drywall enough to see inside the hole. The room was a facade. She ripped the drywall more and stuck her head inside. Though pitch black inside, she made out that the space ran down the entire length of the room, like a movie studio on a sound stage she'd seen once on a documentary. She assumed it was because it had been made specifically for her.

River pulled her head out of the hole and looked at the shattered window. It was a good forty-inch screen. She reached her hand through the hole and felt around behind it. It sat on a wooden beam, and wooden beams surrounded it. Cables connected it to an extension cord below. River unplugged the LED screen and wrapped her arms around it. She shimmed it from side to side until it tipped forward into her arms. She held it for a moment, checking the weight. It was light for a flat screen. She lowered it to the floor and took a breath. She looked at the door and then scanned the room. She walked to a piece of the footboard from the bed and lifted it. It might be big enough. She crossed to the door and wedged the wood under the handle. It just fit. She kicked it in tight and then went back to the hole.

She hoisted herself up on the wooden beam and looked both ways into the small space inside the wall, but saw nothing. She dropped down inside the passage and headed to the left.

River crept along the narrow passage, her hands outstretched, groping through the utter darkness as she shimmied forward. The space felt impossibly tight, only wide enough to accommodate her shoulders, and it carried the stale smell of dust and mildew. Her heart pounded, the sound echoing in her ears and mingling with the loud thump of her pulse. She inched ahead, every sense on alert.

Her wolf whined, but excitement also coursed through her at the prospect of an escape.

After only a few feet, her fingertips touched solid resistance. She ran her hands along the surface, feeling the rough texture of the cinder block. Pressing her weight against it, she pushed as hard as she could, but the wall didn't budge.

"Damn it."

She turned around awkwardly in the cramped, stifling space, scraping her shoulder against the drywall and biting back a hiss of pain where her bruises healed. The passage extended in the opposite direction, disappearing into darkness. Sweat dampened her forehead as she slowed her breathing, desperate not to let the feeling of entrapment sink its claws in any deeper. With no other option and her determination rising, River moved to the right, more urgently.

As she crept along, her mind raced with possibilities. If this passage ran the length of her prison, where did it lead? Was there a way out? Was this finally her opportunity to escape?

A swell of emotions threatened to overtake her. Anger, hope, desperation, all tangled together, pushing her forward. The passage stretched endlessly, and claustrophobia threatened to overwhelm her. Suffocating. Endless. Just when she thought she might have to turn back, the space widened slightly. Her outstretched hands brushed empty air, and she realized she'd reached the end of the wall.

Feeling around carefully, River discovered another passage branching off at a right angle, running along what must be the back wall of her room. Hope surged through her as she considered the new path.

River pressed on, her wolf sluggishly stirring with her heightened pulse. New energy spurred her forward, though the familiar pressure of the enclosing walls soon reasserted itself. When nothing but blackness lay ahead, her hope began to shrink along with the passage. Her arms ached from stretching out. Her eyes watered from the grit in the air, but she dared not stop to wipe them. She couldn't afford to stop. The terror of her confinement began to build again, gnawing at the edges of her mind.

A whirring sound floated from somewhere up ahead.

She swallowed down the panic as her hand snagged on a splinter of wood, and she twisted it free with a grimace. The splinter pierced her palm, burning her skin. She ripped it free and sucked on her bleeding palm, realizing anything could lie ahead of her. Wires. Nails. A drop off. Who knew? She could be putting herself in more danger by walking around outside the room than inside it.

She had to keep moving. Despite the risk, she had to try.

She continued in the same direction, and at last, the space widened once more. Her hands brushed against open air, and she discovered not only a wider turn but another branching passage. The whirring sound grew louder still, and she turned right but ran into a wall.

Left it was then.

River made a mental map of her location in relation to her room and took a step into the open area when a sudden noise froze her in place.

A thud sounded distantly behind her. Then another.

"River!" Titan's voice boomed, muffled but unmistakable in its fury. "Open this door!"

Her heart leaped into her eyeballs.

River scrambled backward, away from the promising escape route. If he discovered the passage, he'd seal it or move her, or worse.

River scrambled back through the passage, her heart hammering against her ribs. Another crash echoed from her room, the sound reverberating through the walls.

"River!" Titan bellowed again, his voice nearer now. "Open. Now."

She moved faster, scraping her elbows in her desperate rush to return. The darkness seemed thicker now, more oppressive, as if conspiring to slow her down. Her wolf whined and paced before dropping again.

She reached the hole behind her broken LED screen.

"What do you want?" she called out, trying to keep her voice steady as she hoisted herself up onto the wooden beam.

"Open this door!" Titan demanded, the handle rattling violently.

River gripped the LED screen, her fingers trembling and blood slicking her hand as she maneuvered it back into position.

"I don't want to see you," she shouted, buying seconds as she reconnected the power cord.

"Either you open this door right now, or I'll break it down!" His voice was a growl, primal and threatening. "And trust me, you won't like it if I have to do that."

"Just leave me alone!" River positioned the screen in its frame, her heart nearly stopping when it wobbled precariously. The wood of the door shook.

Just as she secured the last corner, Titan's boot slammed against the door. The piece of footboard wedged under the handle shuddered but held. River scrambled across the room, throwing herself onto the mattress and pulling the shredded blanket over her body. She forced her breathing to slow as the door exploded inward with a deafening crack. The footboard crashed to the floor, making her jump.

River didn't move, feigning sleep as Titan's footsteps approached the mattress. He loomed over her, his breathing harsh and angry. The thin blanket whipped away, exposing her to the cold air.

"Get up," he growled.

River's eyes snapped open, genuine anger flaring. "What the hell is wrong with you?"

Titan's eyes narrowed as they swept over her, then around the destroyed room. "Why didn't you answer me?"

River stood, her hands clenched into fists at her sides. "Just because I'm your prisoner doesn't mean you have the right to burst in here whenever you feel like it. I have a right to privacy! And I did answer you, you just didn't like the answer."

Titan's nostrils flared as he sniffed the air. "Privacy? In my house?"

"Yes, privacy," River shot back, refusing to be intimidated. "You've taken everything else from me- my freedom, my choices, my mates. The least you could do is knock before entering."

He scanned the room, lingering on the broken LED screen. "I did knock."

"Doesn't mean I have to let you in."

"Yes," he said. "It does."

River crossed her arms over her breasts. "What the hell do you want anyway? Just wanted to come and see what? If I am miserable? If I learned my lesson? If I'm ready to beg you to take me as your mate because you left me alone? Am I ready to be a good girl?"

Titan growled.

River snorted and snatched up the blanket from where he'd thrown it on the floor, covered herself up, and lay back down, turning her back to him.

She tried to keep her breathing even, though her nerves held on by a thread of dental floss. She just needed him to leave so she could explore the passage again.

Titan didn't move, and finally, he yanked off her blanket for the second time and looked over her.

"Now what?" she demanded.

He sniffed the air and then looked at the bed where she'd been lying. "Why is your hand bleeding?"

She snorted. "Why do you think? Because there is glass and debris everywhere in here. People tend to get cut when they live in a wrecked rage room."

He growled at her and looked over her as if searching for a lie.

"What time is it?"

He blinked and looked at his phone. "Four p.m."

"Great. That means dinner in a couple of hours, and then I can get some sleep without the fear of you barging in again until morning."

"Maybe by then you'll have a change of heart. We have work to do, and this childish behavior won't serve you at all."

She snorted. "Why don't you try holding your breath until then and see how it turns out. What did you want anyway?"

Titan watched her, then strode from the room.

River waited as his footsteps receded.

Four p.m. She just had to wait until after dinner, then she would try again. Titan wouldn't wait much longer for her to change her mind. If she didn't escape soon, she was likely not to get out alive.

CHAPTER TWENTY-SEVEN

APOLLO

Thirty minutes after the meeting, the teams assembled. Apollo stood in the driveway, watching as Ares and his squad headed east while Strider and Zeke led another group west. Cherry insisted on joining Apollo's team with Silas, Regan, and Thomas, her fierce maternal energy radiating like heat from her slight frame.

"Let's go," Apollo commanded.

The exclusive neighborhood lay eerily quiet as they walked to the first property on their list, a sprawling colonial with manicured gardens. Apollo signaled for his team to spread out, covering the perimeter while he and Cherry stepped up to the front door.

A middle-aged woman answered, her eyes widening at the sight of Apollo's imposing figure.

"Good evening, ma'am," Apollo said, his charm slipping into place like a well-worn mask. "I apologize for the intrusion, but we're conducting a neighborhood security check. Have you noticed anything unusual? Strangers or suspicious vehicles, possibly?"

"Uh… I don't know. I don't think so," she stammered. "Are you a police officer? Did something happen?"

"My house is a few streets down on Wolf Place-"

"Oh, the big one behind the trees, with the large gate with a 'W' on it?"

Apollo gave a patient smile. "Yes, ma'am."

"You know, we've always been curious about that place. We moved in fifteen years ago and have never really seen anyone come or go. Everyone I've spoken to says they've never seen it for sale or anything. Honestly, we weren't sure if anyone even lived there."

Apollo's wolf growled.

Go. Find mate.

"The land has been in our family for generations."

"Have you seen anything or not?" Cherry asked.

Apollo turned and glared at her before turning back to the homeowner, whose mouth hung open in shock.

"I apologize for my mother-in-law," said Apollo. "We just had someone break in, and it's left her a bit upset. Something very precious was stolen."

"Oh my goodness, when was this?"

"On October twenty-third."

The woman thought for a moment, and then she shook her head. "No. I'm sorry, I didn't see anything."

Apollo nodded. "Thank you. If you can think of anything, will you please call?" He pulled out a business card and handed it to her.

She stared at the thick matte black card, running her fingers over it. "Do the police have any leads?"

Apollo's wolf barked, tired of wasting time.

"I have my security looking into it. Thank you for your time."

Before the woman could ask any more questions, he turned with Cherry and marched down the steps.

"Maybe I should do the questioning," said Cherry. "I could help people remember better."

"Maybe you should go home. Your people skills are-"

"Are what?" she snapped.

Apollo looked at her, and his wolf growled. "Are better left for people guilty of doing something worth having their head bitten off for."

Cherry looked at him and huffed. They joined the others at the end of the driveway and headed for the next house.

The pattern repeated at each house: polite questions, careful observations, and ultimately, dead ends. By the fourth property, Cherry's patience wore thinner than a piece of paper in a thunderstorm.

Apollo's team moved through the neighborhood with methodical precision, each property revealing nothing but ordinary lives. The fifth house on their list sat back from the road, partially obscured by ancient oak trees. As they moved closer, Apollo touched Cherry's arm.

"Wait," he said softly. "Something's off."

Cherry froze, her eyes narrowing as she scanned the property. "What?"

Apollo inhaled deeply, his enhanced senses picking through the layers of aromas. "No one's been in or out of this place for more than a week. But there's something else..." He frowned, concentrating. "A faint trace of chemicals. Industrial-grade cleaners."

Silas appeared at Apollo's side, his hand resting on the weapon concealed in his jacket. "Windows are covered. Security cameras at every corner, but I don't think they're on."

"Excessive for this neighborhood," Apollo murmured. "Also, look at the lawn. It's overgrown. Even for this time of year, it hasn't been cut in weeks. Same with the hedges." He signaled to Thomas and the others to circle around back while he, Cherry, and Silas headed for the front door.

No lights emanated from inside the house, and the whole building felt utterly silent. He rang the doorbell, and it echoed hollowly inside off the walls. No footsteps sounded, no lights flickered on. Apollo rang again, then knocked firmly.

"No one's home," Cherry stated, impatience edging her voice.

Apollo scanned the property once more. "Or they don't want to be disturbed." He backed up, examining the brick exterior. It wasn't rundown, but it hadn't been cleaned in a long time. Something strange for someone who had paid almost five million dollars for a house.

He pulled out his phone and scrolled down the list he'd made. "This place was purchased eight months ago by a shell corporation. Paid in cash."

"That's not suspicious at all," Cherry muttered.

Apollo moved to a window, peering through a tiny gap in the thick curtains. The interior remained dark, but he made out nothing but pristine surfaces. Too pristine.

"This place has been cleaned recently. Thoroughly." He turned to Silas. "Get the others. We're going in."

They regrouped at the rear of the property, hidden from street view by a high privacy fence on all three sides.

"No alarms visible," Regan reported. "But there's a keypad entry."

Apollo studied the door for a moment, then stepped back and, with a swift, powerful kick, shattered the lock. The door swung inward, revealing a darkened kitchen. The team moved in, weapons drawn.

The interior smelled of bleach and industrial solvents. Every surface gleamed with unnatural cleanliness. They moved room by room, finding nothing but minimal furniture and bare walls.

"Basement." Apollo pointed to a reinforced metal door. Unlike the rest of the house, the door sported multiple locks and reinforced hinges.

Apollo's wolf paced, hackles raised.

Regan worked quickly, his lock-picking skills making short work of the sophisticated mechanisms. As the last tumbler clicked into place, Apollo pulled the door open, revealing a steep staircase descending into darkness.

The scent hit him immediately: blood, fear, and something else. Something familiar.

"River," Cherry whispered, her voice breaking. "She was here."

Apollo descended the stairs first, heart hammering against his ribs. He reached the bottom and felt around for a light switch. He flicked it on, and everyone else filed down the stairs.

The basement stretched out larger than expected, divided into several rooms by stark white walls. Clinical. Sterile. Like a laboratory or hospital ward.

"Check everything," Apollo commanded.

They each took a different section. The main room contained a metal table bolted to the floor. Though not a drop of blood appeared anywhere, the fragrance lingered underneath the cleaners. Medical equipment lined one wall, monitors, IV stands, and instruments whose purpose Apollo didn't want to contemplate.

"In here," Cherry called, her voice echoing from an adjoining room.

Apollo rushed to join her, finding her standing frozen in the doorway of what appeared to be a bedroom. A narrow bed sat against one wall, its sheets perfectly straight. Beside it stood a small table with a lamp. The walls were bare.

"This is where they kept her," Cherry whispered.

Apollo moved through the space, his senses straining for any trace of his mate. But the overwhelming odor of bleach and chemicals masked everything. Someone had meticulously erased all evidence.

Apollo said, fury building inside. "They've sanitized everything."

Thomas and Silas appeared in the doorway. "Boss, you need to see this."

Silas led them to another room, smaller than the others. A desk stood against one wall, its surface empty. A chair sat perfectly centered before it. On the opposite wall hung a large corkboard, completely bare.

"Look." Thomas pointed to tiny holes in the corkboard's surface.

Apollo examined the puncture marks.

"They've taken everything," Regan said from behind them. "Every room is the same. Cleaned top to bottom. No personal items, no papers, nothing."

Apollo's fist slammed into the wall, the impact creating a crater in the drywall. "Damn it!"

Cherry placed a hand on his arm.

Regan returned from checking the upstairs. "Boss, the entire house is the same. Not a fingerprint, not a hair, not even dust. It's like no one ever lived here."

"But they did," Apollo said, moving through the space with renewed purpose. "And they were careful. Too careful."

"Check for hidden compartments," Apollo ordered. "False walls, hollow spaces under the floors, anything."

FOR OVER THIRTY MINUTES, THE TEAM SPREAD OUT, TAPPING WALLS and examining baseboards, running their fingers along the seams of the wooden floorboards.

"Nothing," Regan reported. "If there was anything here, they took it with them."

Apollo's frustration mounted as he moved to the windows, examining the thick blackout curtains. "They didn't just clean this place," he murmured. "They erased it."

Cherry joined him, her face tight with anxiety. "But why leave it standing? Why not burn it down or destroy it if they were so concerned about leaving evidence?"

"Because that would draw attention," Apollo replied. "This way, it just looks like another empty luxury home. Nothing suspicious about that in this neighborhood."

He pulled out his phone and redialed Ares. His twin answered on the first ring.

"We found it," Apollo said without preamble. "The house on Oakridge Place. They kept her here, but they've cleared out. The place has been professionally sanitized, no evidence."

"On our way," Ares replied, his voice taut with urgency.

Apollo pocketed his phone and turned to his team. "Keep searching."

They searched the house for nearly an hour with nothing new to show for their efforts when a sharp knock at the front door startled everyone. The team exchanged tense glances, hands moving instinctively to their weapons.

Apollo motioned the others to stand back. He inhaled deeply, catching the scent of a human male, alone, anxious, but not threatening. With a slight nod, Silas positioned himself out of sight but still in striking distance, and Apollo opened the door.

A middle-aged man with salt-and-pepper hair and wire-rimmed glasses stood on the porch, his brow furrowed with concern. He wore a cardigan despite the unusually warm evening, and his hands fidgeted at his sides.

"Can I help you?" Apollo asked, his voice neutral as he positioned himself to block the man's view of the interior.

The man peered around Apollo's shoulder, trying to see inside. "I should be asking you that," he replied. "Who are you people? I've been watching all evening, different groups coming and going from houses all over the neighborhood."

Apollo straightened to his full height, allowing a hint of his natural authority to surface. "We're looking for someone," he said. "A missing person."

The man's eyes widened. "You're police?"

"Something like that," Apollo replied. "Where do you live, sir?"

"Just there," the man pointed to a beautiful two-story home one property down. "I'm Douglas Whitaker. Been here twelve years."

Apollo studied him for a moment. "And you've been watching this house?"

Whitaker nodded, glancing nervously over his shoulder. "There have been strange things happening here for months. Cars and vans coming and going at all hours. Black SUVs with tinted windows. Men in suits carrying things inside. Never the same people twice, it seemed."

Apollo's pulse quickened. "When did this start?"

"About six months ago, right after the new owners moved in. Though I never actually saw the owners, come to think of it." Whitaker adjusted his glasses. "It was always these... workers, I guess. And they were careful, always parked in the garage, never left anything in the driveway."

Cherry appeared at Apollo's side, strangely composed despite the intensity in her eyes. "Did you ever see a young woman? Silver hair, about this tall?" She held her hand up to indicate River's height.

Whitaker hesitated, then nodded. "Maybe. Late at night. They were helping her from a car to the house. She looked... unwell. I almost called an ambulance, but then I thought better of it."

"Why?" Apollo asked.

The man swallowed hard. "Because of the way they were holding her. Not like someone who was sick, but someone drunk, maybe."

Stiff footsteps tapped on the floor from behind Apollo.

"Mr. Whitaker." Ares moved beside Apollo, his eyes intense as he studied the man. "Do you recall any details about these vehicles? Make, model, anything distinctive about them?"

Whitaker looked between the brothers.

"I have better than descriptions," Whitaker replied. "I wrote down the license plate numbers."

Ares and Apollo exchanged a glance, hope flaring between them like a sudden flame.

Whitaker adjusted his glasses. "I'm a retired accountant. Details are important to me. When things didn't seem right, I started keeping records. Dates, times, descriptions... and the license plates whenever I could see them clearly."

"Where are these records?" Apollo demanded, fighting to keep his voice steady.

"At my house." Whitaker gestured toward his home. "In my study. I've been collecting them for months."

Ares moved out the door before the man finished speaking. "Show us, please."

Apollo looked at Silas. "Round everyone up and meet us back at the house."

Silas nodded, and Apollo followed Ares and Douglas across the street to a manicured lawn and his beautiful classic colonial-style home.

Douglas opened the door and wiped his feet on the mat before removing his shoes and waving the twins inside.

The interior hallway and rooms to the left were meticulously organized, with bookshelves lining the walls and the books organized by color and size. Family photos arranged meticulously on the mantle.

"This way." Whitaker led them to a study off the main hallway.

The room was exactly what one might expect of a retired accountant; an antique wooden desk dominated the space, with neat stacks of papers arranged at precise angles. A tall filing cabinet stood against one wall, its drawers labeled with color-coded tabs.

Whitaker moved to the cabinet, pulling open the second drawer and extracting a thick leather-bound notebook.

"Here." He placed it on the desk. "I recorded everything."

Ares snatched up the ledger, flipping it open with barely controlled urgency. Inside, in precise handwriting, were pages of detailed notes. Dates, times, weather conditions, and, most importantly, license plate numbers, along with descriptions of the vehicles and their occupants.

"This is..." Ares trailed off, his fingers tracing the entries. "Amazing."

"Thank you," Douglas smiled.

Apollo scanned the pages. "Is there anything about when they left? When they cleared out?"

Whitaker nodded, reaching over to flip to the back of the notebook. "Two weeks or so ago. Around 3 AM. The exact details are in there. Four black SUVs arrived and then left within an hour. A day later, two vans pulled up with cleaning supplies. No one has been there since."

"These license plates." Apollo ran his finger down the list. "We need to locate them."

Ares turned back to Whitaker, his eyes intense. "Did you notice anything else? Anything at all about the people who came and went?"

Whitaker removed his glasses, polishing them with the hem of his cardigan. "There was one man who came more often than the others. Tall, built like a linebacker. He had this way of moving, like a predator." He shrugged apologetically. "Sorry if that sounds dramatic, but there was something... different about him."

"Titan." Ares' fists clenched.

"Was there anything more about the woman?" Apollo asked. "Did you ever see her again after that first night?"

Whitaker shook his head. "No. I'm sorry. Is she the one who is missing?"

Apollo straightened and smiled. "Mr. Whitaker, we need copies of everything you have, please."

The man nodded. "Of course. My copier is right here." He moved to a small machine in the corner, beginning to duplicate the pages with efficient movements.

While Whitaker worked, Ares pulled Apollo aside, his voice low. "She's still here. I can't believe she's still here."

"Makes sense if he wants the throne. He can't take it from halfway across the world."

"We're close. So close."

Ares placed his hand on his brother's shoulder. "We're going to find her."

Apollo's wolf howled.

He just hoped they were in time.

CHAPTER TWENTY-EIGHT

TITAN

Titan paced his study. His footsteps resounded against the hardwood floor. His mind raced with conflicting thoughts, each pulling him in a different direction. Kane's possible defection had shaken him more than he cared to admit. For years, Kane had been his right hand, his brother. Now, that bond was fractured, perhaps beyond repair.

A knock at the door interrupted his brooding. "What?" he snapped.

Vanessa entered, her movements fluid and calculated. "The twins are on the move," she said without preamble.

Titan stopped pacing, his golden eyes fixing on her. "Explain."

"Our sources report increased activity around their estate. They've assembled teams, armed and ready." Vanessa crossed the room to stand before him. "They're searching properties in their area."

A cold weight settled in Titan's gut. "How many?"

"Three teams. They're being methodical." She paused, her eyes studying his reaction. "They've already checked seven properties."

"How did they even realize we'd hidden there? What tipped them off?" Titan resumed his pacing, faster. "They're getting closer."

"Yes," Vanessa agreed. "They'll find the Oakridge house."

"It's been sanitized," Titan said dismissively. "They'll find nothing."

"Perhaps," Vanessa conceded. "But the neighbor-"

"What neighbor?" Titan whirled on her.

Vanessa's composure faltered. "The retired man. He was... observant."

Titan's roar shook the bookshelves, sending several volumes tumbling to the floor. "And you're just telling me this now?"

"I didn't think it was a big deal, but now…"

Titan's mind raced through contingencies, calculating risks and responses. "We need to accelerate our timeline. River is the priority. Once she accepts her place, the rest will follow."

"And if she doesn't?"

Titan turned away, staring out the window at the dense forest surrounding the compound. The Northern Lights still flickered in the distance, their glow eerie.

"She will," he said with finality. "She has no choice."

Despite his threats, he couldn't keep her isolated forever. The woman was stubborn, challenging him at every turn. And yet, something about her defiance only made him want her more.

He opened the door to his study. Kane waited for him, a troubled look on his face.

"What is it?" Titan demanded.

Kane straightened. "Rudy hasn't checked in."

"What do you mean he hasn't checked in?"

"I've been trying to reach him for twelve hours. No response from him or anyone in his crew." Kane's voice stayed neutral, but his concern was evident. "We haven't received a receipt for the shipment either."

Titan roared. "That worthless piece of-" He cut himself off, inhaling deeply. "Have you sent anyone to investigate?"

"Not yet. I wanted your authorization."

Titan muscles stretched taut with barely contained fury. However, the fact that Kane was still seeking permission and not trying to make decisions on his own gave Titan hope that they might still be able to repair their relationship.

"Send Markus and his team. Tell them to be discreet. If that traitor Rudy has sold us out, I'll personally tear out his guts and slaughter his entire pack." He leaned forward, his voice dropping to a deadly whisper. "No one betrays me. No one."

Kane nodded once, already reaching for his phone. "I'll dispatch them immediately."

"And Kane," Titan called, "increase security around the compound. We need to prepare for unwelcome visitors."

Once alone, Titan moved to the large map spread across the wall. Colored pins marked key locations across North America, distribution centers, allied packs, and strategic assets. His empire, built piece by piece over years of careful planning. He wouldn't let one weak link destroy everything he'd worked for.

His thoughts returned to River, locked in her room below. Perhaps it was time for a different approach. The isolation clearly hadn't even bent her spirit. If anything, it seemed to strengthen her resolve. He'd tried the carrot. He'd tried the stick. What was left?

CHAPTER TWENTY-NINE

RIVER

River waited in the darkness, counting the minutes. Titan's footsteps had stomped up the stairs hours ago, following the delivery of her evening meal. Once the house fell silent, she lay her ear against the wall, listening for any sign of activity.

Nothing.

Her heart hammered against her ribs as she crept toward the damaged LED screen. The jagged hole Titan had punched through it gaped like a dark mouth, beckoning her. With trembling fingers, she removed the TV screen and slid through the hole once more.

Her heart hammered, and she took a slow breath. Her wolf's desire to escape spurred River on. River inched along, every sound- her ragged breathing, the soft scrape of her clothing against the wall, the pounding of her pulse in her ears- seemed impossibly loud. She moved quick as she dared, terrified that at any moment, Titan would discover her absence.

Following the path she'd explored earlier, River navigated the passages. Left at the junction, straight, and then right at the wider section. Her muscles burned, but desperation drove her forward. This might be her only shot.

After minutes which stretched out like hours, she reached the second passageway, the one she hadn't fully explored before. Slightly wider than the first, it allowed her to move with marginally more speed. Dust tickled her nose, and she held back a sneeze, freezing in place until the urge passed. The whirring sound grew louder as she moved toward it.

The passage curved, and River realized she must be following the outer wall of the house. Her wolf stirred, offering what little strength she could. The pregnancy had drained them both, but the instinct to protect all of them burned fierce and bright.

The passage opened into a small maintenance alcove. Moonlight spilled through a narrow window, casting silver patterns across the dust-covered floor. River gasped. An actual window, not a screen, not a simulation, but real glass separating her from the outside world.

She rushed to it, drinking in the sight of the night sky. The moon hung full and luminous, bathing the lawn beyond in ethereal light. For the first time in weeks, a flicker of genuine hope burned inside her. She reached high above her head and pressed her fingertips against the cool glass, a sob of relief threatening to escape her.

The small window, hardly eighteen inches square, was real.

River scanned the space, but there was nothing to stand on for her to reach the window. She took several steps back and examined it, almost bursting into tears. It was a fixed piece of glass that didn't open. So even if she did find something to help her get up there, she'd have to break the glass to get out.

River slid to the floor and hung her head.

No. Give up.

I'm not. I just… need a sec.

River stared at the cement floor, her back against some kind of heating unit.

Please, goddess, get me out of this.

A soft creak echoed in the small space, and River froze, her heart nearly stopping. After several agonizing seconds of silence, she breathed again. She couldn't stay there. She had to do something.

Air whooshed against her feet, and she looked to her right. Light parallel shadows cast across the floor.

She stared at them for a moment before realizing what they might be.

She crawled over and placed her hand on the wall, casting the shadows. A metal ping sounded as she ran her fingers down the area.

"Yes."

She pushed on the metal, and it fell forward. She caught it before it hit the floor. She sat, not moving, not believing what she saw. She let out a breath and placed the metal grate on the floor. Her heart leapt as she crawled through the hole and into the paint studio.

River scooted out from under the table and looked around the space. Everything sat as she'd left it days before. She ran her fingers over the table, feeling for the tools. She found two palette knives and hurried to the doors in the corner that led to the backyard. She tried to keep her hand from shaking as she located the lock and wedged the first palette knife in the joint between the door and the doorjamb. She tried wiggling it, but nothing happened. Then she tried sliding it up and down. Still nothing.

She groaned and tried twisting it harder, and the knife snapped in half.

"Shit." She looked at the knife handle in her hand and then dropped it.

A palette knife wouldn't cut it. She needed something more substantial. But there wasn't anything stronger. She'd looked already.

She touched the glass on the door. Maybe she could break one of the smaller panes, and it wouldn't make too much noise. Then she could open the lock from the outside. She glanced around and grabbed a rag, wrapping it around her hand.

Don't screw up. Don't screw up. Don't screw up.

Her wolf made a worrying sound, but wanted freedom as much as River did.

River punched the glass, and it cracked. She prodded it, and the glass crunched but didn't break.

She took a breath and punched it again, not as hard. The glass cracked again, and one of the pieces fell to the grass below.

Yes!

She wiggled the glass shard by shard and placed them on the table until she'd cleared as much as possible. She reached through the hole and felt for the handle on the other side, only to discover it took a key on both sides.

She swallowed a scream. Tears washed her eyes. The broken door would be discovered. And when it was... who knew what Titan would do. She had to make it happen now. There was no other option.

She looked around, and her gaze lit on a stack of quart-sized cans of paint. That. She could use that.

Quickly, River walked to the stack and counted the cans. Twelve cans. She didn't know if it would be enough, but what choice did she have? She had to try.

In groups of three, she moved the cans from the middle of the room to the vent in the corner. She crawled through the vent hole and then carried the cans to the wall below the small window. She stacked them in two columns, and they rose over two and a half feet off the floor. It might just be enough.

She stepped up with one foot on each stack of cans. They wobbled but didn't fall. When she straightened, she stood torso-high to the window. Rewrapping her hand, she punched the glass once again. Struggling to hold back her impatience, as well as her wolf's pestering. The window shattered, and the cool night air rushed in, carrying the fragrance of trees, flowers, and earth. Smells so vibrant they nearly overwhelmed her after weeks of recycled air.

River paused, listening for any reaction to the noise, but everything stayed silent. Her wolf urged her to move. River dropped the rag and, with trembling arms, hoisted herself up to the narrow opening. Her muscles screamed in protest. The window frame scraped against her sides as she squeezed through, her breath coming in short, painful gasps. Small shards of glass scraped her skin, and she swallowed a yelp of pain as the odor of blood hit her nose.

Dammit! Someone was going to smell that. She has to move.

River shimmied faster, trying to pull herself through the window. For one terrifying moment, she thought she might be stuck, as her hips wedged in the frame. Panic flared, but she forced it down, twisting to find a better angle. With a final shove, she tumbled out onto the damp earth below, landing awkwardly in a tangle of limbs.

Pain shot through her shoulder, but River bit back the pain. She lay still for several seconds, the cool grass caressing her cheek, feeling impossibly luxurious. The night air filled her lungs, sweet and clean. Above her, stars glittered, and the full moon bathed everything in silver light.

Freedom. So close. She was so close.

River crawled toward a dense cluster of bushes, her movements slow and deliberate. Her wolf, though weak, was fully alert now, sensing both danger and opportunity. Once concealed among the foliage, River took stock of her surroundings.

The house, or rather, compound, rose three stories. Its cream stone facade gleamed pale in the moonlight. High walls surrounded the property, topped with what appeared to be security cameras and motion sensors.

Dark figures patrolled the grounds. River's heart sank as she counted one, two, five, guards moving with military precision along predetermined routes. Each carried weapons, not standard firearms, but what looked like automatic rifles.

River shrank deeper into the bushes as two guards passed nearby, their voices carrying in the still night air.

"...doubling the patrols on the east side," one said, his voice low but distinct.

"Waste of manpower," the other replied with a snort. "If those royal pricks find this place, a few extra guards won't make a difference."

River's pulse quickened. Ares and Apollo.

The first guard glanced around. "Don't let Titan hear you talking like that. Besides, they're getting closer. That house in the city was compromised."

"How close?"

"Close enough that Kane's pulled in everyone from the satellite locations.

"Titan's got us all on high alert." The first guard moved closer to River's hiding spot.

The second guard spat on the ground. "Just because of her? All this for one female? That's why he's keeping her locked up tight? Breeding stock?"

"Watch your mouth," the first guard growled. "That's our future, Luna, you're talking about."

"Luna? Ha! You've seen how she looks at him. That woman would sooner cut his dick off than bear his pups."

The first guard glanced around. "She's an Omega, and she's mated to the twins. That makes her the High Luna. Whether or not she accepts Titan, she is still a crap ton higher up than you or me. So be respectful."

The second guard snorted. "Yeah. True. Wait."

The men stopped.

"Do you smell that?"

"What?"

"It's blood, I think."

River's gut twisted, and her wolf prepared to move. Could she sprint past them? Even if she did, they could mow her down in an instant.

"I don't smell anything. Come on."

Their voices faded as they disappeared around the corner of the building. River stayed frozen. Ares and Apollo were close. They were looking for her.

She had to move.

More guards appeared, gathering near a side entrance to the house. Their voices carried across the quiet night.

"Extra patrols on the north perimeter," a burly man said. "We've got reports of activity in the sector. Could be nothing, could be them."

"What about the Luna?" another asked.

"Locked down tight. Titan's orders. No one goes in or out."

"And if they do find us?"

The leader's face hardened. "Then we fight. Or we run. Depends on what the Alpha commands."

The group dispersed, heading in different directions to take up their posts. River waited, calculating as the guards moved into position. There was a small but noticeable gap in their coverage on the edge of the property, where the forest grew thickest.

She would have one shot. Just one.

River gathered what strength remained, her muscles trembling with exhaustion and anticipation. Her wolf stirred, lending its fierce maternal instinct to her determination.

The moon slipped behind a cloud, casting the grounds in a dark shadow.

Now.

River burst from her hiding place, keeping low to the ground as she darted across the open space between the bushes and the tree line. Her bare feet made almost no sound on the damp earth, but her heart pounded.

Twenty yards. Fifteen. Ten.

A shout rang out behind her. "There! By the trees! Someone's out there."

River didn't look back. She pushed her weakened body harder, drawing on reserves she would quickly deplete. The forest edge loomed ahead, promising temporary sanctuary under the thick canopy of trees. Her lungs burned as she gulped the night air, each breath a desperate prayer for escape.

The crack of a rifle echoed behind her, followed by the whistle of something sailing past her head. River zigzagged, making herself a more challenging target as she plunged into the dark embrace of the woods.

Dense underbrush tore at her legs and feet as she crashed through the forest. Branches whipped across her face, leaving stinging welts, but she didn't slow. Behind her, the shouts grew louder as Titan's men gave chase, their powerful flashlight beams cutting through the darkness.

"Spread out!" someone bellowed. "Don't let them reach the perimeter!"

River rushed deeper into the trees, her bare feet finding purchase on the soft earth despite the rocks and fallen branches that threatened to trip her. The darkness was both ally and enemy, hiding her from her pursuers but concealing obstacles in her path.

Her wolf surged forward with energy she didn't know she had.

Run. Protect. Survive.

The primal commands pulsed through her with each frantic heartbeat, overriding the screaming protest of her muscles and the stabbing pain in her side.

The voices behind her grew more distant, then louder again as the pursuit organized itself. Flashlight beams swept through the trees, occasionally illuminating her path for precious seconds before plunging her back into darkness.

River's breath came in ragged gasps, her lungs burning with each inhale, and her side and shoulder ached from their damage when she'd gotten out the window. She'd been confined too long, her body weakened by poor nutrition and lack of exercise. Her pace slowed, and her movements became less coordinated.

Not yet. She couldn't fail now. Not when freedom was feet away.

A stitch tore through her side, forcing her to clutch at her ribs as she ran. Still, her wolf spurred her onward. The sound of pursuit grew louder; they were gaining on her.

River veered left, hoping to throw off her trackers. The underbrush grew thicker, and the trees more densely packed. She ducked under low-hanging branches, weaved between trunks, and scrambled over fallen logs.

The forest floor sloped downward, and River used the momentum to increase her speed, half-running, half-sliding down the incline. At the bottom, she paused, leaning against a thick tree to catch her breath. Her legs trembled, threatening to give out.

"I heard something! This way!"

The voice was too close. River shoved off the tree, forcing her exhausted body into motion once more. She couldn't stop. Couldn't rest. Not until she was far from Titan's reach.

The forest blurred around her as River's legs grew heavier with each step. Her lungs burned, desperate for oxygen; she couldn't seem to draw fast enough. Sweat plastered her silver hair against her head despite the cool night air.

Her wolf surged with renewed determination even as her human body faltered.

Veering left at a young tree, River stumbled through a dense thicket, branches tearing at her already tattered clothing.

Suddenly, the trees ended. River skidded to a halt, her heart plummeting as moonlight illuminated what stood before her: an enormous concrete wall stretching in both directions. Ten feet tall at least, its top bristling with coils of gleaming razor wire that glinted in the moonlight like silver teeth.

"No," she whispered, her voice breaking. "No, no, no."

River laid her palms against the cold concrete, tears of frustration welling in her eyes. Titan had told her about the wall, but she hadn't thought it would stretch the entire property. She had to be at least half a mile from the main house.

So close. She'd been so close to freedom.

"There they are!"

The shout came from behind her, accompanied by the harsh glare of flashlights. River spun, pressing her back against the wall as three of Titan's men emerged, their weapons trained on her.

"Don't move," the leader commanded, approaching her.

Murmurs started between the men.

"Luna?"

"It's the Luna."

River searched desperately for an escape route. Her muscles screamed from exertion. Even if she could outrun them again, where would she go?

"Please," she said. "Let me go."

The guards exchanged uncomfortable glances, but their weapons remained steady. "We can't do that," the leader said, almost apologetically. "Alpha's orders."

As they moved in, terror surged through her. Her wolf rose to the surface with a final burst of protective fury. She wouldn't go back. Couldn't go back. Not to that room, not to Titan's possession.

With a feral growl, River launched herself at the nearest man, catching him off guard. Her nails, human, not claws, raked across his face as they tumbled to the ground. Shouts sounded around her as hands grabbed at her, but she fought with the wild desperation of a cornered animal.

"Sedate her!" One of them yelled.

"Don't injure her!" the leader shouted as River thrashed wildly. "Titan will have our heads!"

River's eyes widened with sudden clarity. Of course, they couldn't harm her. Titan's precious mate, his obsession. Her wolf surged with renewed purpose, and River channeled her strength with calculated precision.

She twisted away from the man trying to restrain her, using his momentum against him. As he stumbled forward, she brought her knee up hard into his solar plexus. He doubled over, gasping for air, and River wasted no time. She gripped his head and slammed it against her rising knee. The male crumpled to the ground.

"Shit!" The second wolf lunged for her, but hesitated at the last moment. That split-second of indecision was all River needed. She feinted left, then spun right, sweeping his legs out from under him. As he fell, she delivered a precise strike to his temple. His eyes rolled back as he joined his companion on the forest floor.

The leader backed away, raising his tranquilizer gun. "Luna, please. Don't make this harder than it needs to be."

River circled him warily. "I am the Luna. The High Luna. Mate to Apollo and Ares Wolvenguard, and I command you to let me go."

He hesitated. "I… I can't."

Dammit. She'd exerted too much energy to make her Luna gaze work.

He fired, but River was already moving. The dart whistled past her ear as she ducked and charged forward, driving her shoulder into his midsection. The gun flew from his hands as they both went down. River recovered first, scrambling atop him and delivering two quick, sharp blows to his face. His head lolled to the side, and she picked up the rifle and fired it at him.

A dart lodged between his pecs, and his eyes fluttered.

A crackle of static broke the sudden silence. "Team three, report. Have you located the intruder?" The walkie-talkie at the leader's belt came to life with an urgent voice. "Repeat, team three, what's your status? I'm sending reinforcements."

River snatched the device and hurled it against the wall, where it shattered. She had seconds before more came to investigate. She shot the other two men with darts and then tossed the gun away.

Her gaze traveled up the concrete barrier looming above her. Ten feet of smooth surface, topped with cruel coils of razor wire. Impossible for a human to scale.

But not for a wolf.

River reached for the last reserves of her strength.

I need you. We need you.

Her wolf answered, surging forward with ferocity. The shift rippled through her, painful after so long suppressed, but desperately welcome.

Bones cracked and reformed. Muscles stretched and contorted. River cried out as she stood still, human.

Please, goddess, please help me.

River tried again, and this time her vision sharpened, and her sense of smell grew stronger as her body transformed into her sleek silver wolf.

With a power born of desperation, River's wolf gathered herself and leaped. Her claws scrabbled against concrete, finding tiny imperfections to grip into and dig deeper in. Higher, higher, her powerful legs drove her upward in a desperate climb.

She reached the top and carefully tried navigating between the coils of razor, but voices rang out behind her, and she panicked. River's wolf leapt from the wall to the ground below, and the razors hooked into her skin. Her leg snagged, and she scrambled to get free. Yanking hard, her leg flayed open. Blood gushed from the wound, but the razors dug deeper into her muscle. She yelped. She has to keep going. Screw the pain. River yanked her leg hard and cried out as she tumbled to the asphalt below. The air rushed from her lungs, and she lay on her side, unable to move for several seconds. Stars blinded her eyes, and her heart thundered. Blood slicked her fur, and the smell made her gag. Even so, she couldn't help but smile. She'd done it. She was out.

River's wolf tried to stand, but her rear leg couldn't hold weight. She yelped as sharp burning pain shot through her all over. Blood slicked down her leg and pooled around her feet.

Not good. Not good.

River had no idea how long she had before she might pass out from blood loss. She had to move. River spurred her wolf forward, and on three legs, hobbling down the road with no idea where she headed.

She'd gone several blocks when she dropped to the ground, half on the sidewalk, half in the road, and breathed heavily. Exhaustion threaded through every muscle. She had to keep going. Titan could find her there.

Her wolf howled in pain, and her body shook. River tried to get her wolf to her feet, but she couldn't lift her head. She tried to force a shift back to human, but it was all she could do to stay conscious.

The sounds of a vehicle approaching sent a shiver of fear through her. She needed to hide. She looked around but couldn't make her limbs work. Her heart pounded as the vehicle drew closer. Pop music blared out of the open windows. A van slowed and then stopped, its lights blinding her.

Please, goddess, don't let it be Titan. Please don't let it be Titan. Not that she could imagine Titan or any of his men listening to the latest female pop star belt out a song about breaking up with her boyfriend.

The driver's side door opened, and a teenage boy hopped out. He rounded the van and raced to her.

"Holy crap! Who did this to you?"

He stroked River's ear, and she whined.

The boy looked over her, stripped off his shirt, and wrapped her leg. Then he slid his hands underneath her side.

"Don't worry," he said. "I'll get you help. Just... please don't bite me, okay?"

The boy struggled to lift River into his arms, and for a moment, she thought he might drop her, but he didn't. He opened the back of his mommy van and laid her on the itchy carpet inside. He covered her with a small blanket.

"I promise I'm going to help you. Just don't die."

The van door lowered shut, and then the driver's side door slammed, and the vehicle lurched forward. The teenage boy's voice drifted back to her, a stream of worried muttering as he navigated the streets.

"Hang on, girl. Just hang on. There's an emergency vet clinic about ten minutes from here."

Relief washed over River in waves. She was out. Away from Titan, from the compound, from the prison that had held her for so long. Her wolf body trembled, partly from pain and partly from the overwhelming realization that she'd done it. She'd gotten herself out. She thanked the goddess, thanked herself, and, most of all, thanked her wolf.

We did it, girl. We did it. We're safe. Our baby is safe. Thank you. Thank you.

The boy talked to her, his voice a comforting anchor as darkness began to encroach on the edges of River's vision. "My mom's gonna shoot me for getting blood all over the van, but whatever. You're gonna be okay. You have to be okay."

River wanted to thank him, to communicate her gratitude, but her strength and consciousness faded rapidly. Blood seeped through the makeshift bandage, her leg throbbing with each beat of her heart.

The last thing River remembered was the gentle sway of the van as it turned a corner, and then blackness claimed her.

BRIGHT LIGHTS PIERCED THROUGH RIVER'S CONSCIOUSNESS, dragging her back to awareness. Voices surrounded her, urgent and confused.

"...never seen anything like this..." said the teenage voice she recognized.

"...losing too much blood..." said a female. "...need to stabilize her before..."

River blinked, her vision swimming as shapes gradually came into focus. She was still in the back of the van. Fumes from the van burned her nostrils. A woman in scrubs examined her leg while the teenage boy hovered under the neon sign, muttering.

"The laceration is extensive." Her voice was clinical yet concerned. "She's lost a significant amount of blood. This isn't something we can handle here."

"What do you mean?" The boy's face paled.

The vet straightened, fixing him with a stern look. "This isn't a dog, young man. This is a person."

"No, it's a wolf or a husky or something. I found her on the side of the road!"

"Do you think I'm blind? Or crazy?" The vet gestured toward River. "This is clearly a woman with a severe injury."

River realized she'd shifted back to her human form. The pain, blood loss, and unconsciousness of her wolf must have triggered the involuntary shift. She lay exposed, nothing but the small blanket covering her.

The vet turned to River, her eyes softening with concern. "Miss, did this boy harm you?"

River struggled to find her voice, her throat parched and raw. "No," she managed to croak. "He... helped me. He saved me."

The teenage boy froze, his eyes wide with shock. "But ...you were a dog." His face contorted in confusion. "I saw you. You were a dog with silver fur."

"We need to call an ambulance." The vet reached for her cellphone.

"No!" River's voice came out stronger than expected, stopping the woman's hand mid-air. "No hospitals. He'll find me." River clutched the blanket as a wave of dizziness washed over her.

The teenage boy shuffled forward hesitantly. "Who? Who's after you?"

River's eyes darted between them, weighing her options. These strangers had shown her kindness, but involving them further put them at risk. Still, she needed to reach Ares and Apollo.

"My name is River," she said, her voice growing weaker with each word. "I need you to call Apollo Wolvenguard. Tell him where I am."

The vet's eyebrows shot up in recognition. "Wolvenguard? The businessman?"

"Please," River begged, darkness creeping at the edges of her vision again. "He'll come for me. He's my mate."

"This is ridiculous," the vet argued, reaching for the phone again. "You need a hospital now. You could be in shock or delirious from blood loss."

"If I go to a hospital, Titan will find me," River insisted, her words slurring. "Please. Call Apollo or call Ares Wolvenguard. Tell them River is..."

Her vision tunneled, the van spinning around her as consciousness began to slip away once more.

The last thing she heard was the teenage boy's voice. "I think we should do what she says."

Then darkness claimed her again.

RIVER FLOATED IN AND OUT OF CONSCIOUSNESS, FRAGMENTS OF conversation drifting through the haze of pain and exhaustion. She was lifted, and something warm was draped over her naked body.

They laid her on something hard and cold, and then she bumped across the asphalt toward a blue neon sign.

"...stabilized the bleeding..."

"... can't keep her here..."

"...said Wolvenguard, like the billionaire?"

"...dogs don't just turn into people..."

A cool hand brushed her forehead, followed by the sharp sting of a needle in her arm. River wanted to protest, but her body refused to respond. Her wolf lay dormant, completely unconscious.

Time became meaningless; minutes or hours might have passed as River drifted through layers of awareness. Images flashed behind her eyelids: Titan's wrathful face, the concrete wall looming over her, the desperate flight through the forest. And last of all, the faces of her mates, calling her home.

CHAPTER THIRTY

ARES

The small postal store stood silent in the darkness, its windows blank and empty. Three figures moved swiftly toward the rear entrance, their footsteps slapping on the wet pavement. Ares led the way. Cherry followed behind, while Duncan brought up the rear, a small electronic device clutched in his hand.

"Security system looks basic," Duncan murmured, scanning the building. "Probably an alarm that triggers if the door opens after hours."

"Can you disable it?" Ares asked.

Duncan nodded, already moving toward the electrical panel. "Give me two minutes."

While Duncan worked, Ares examined the door. Heavy metal with a deadbolt, formidable to humans, but not to an Alpha Lycan. Cherry paced behind him, her anxiety rolling off her in waves.

"We're wasting time," she hissed.

"And this is our best lead until we get information back on the vehicle registrations," Ares said without turning. "Duncan?"

"Almost there." Duncan's fingers moved deftly across the small device in his hands, connecting wires and typing commands.

Ares wondered where Duncan had learned the skills to break in, but being a rogue, he'd probably had to do whatever it took to survive. And though Ares was grateful for his skills, he was determined to pay Duncan back by inviting him to stay with them permanently. Making him part of the pack.

A small light on the security panel blinked from red to green, and Duncan gave a satisfied nod. "We're clear. Alarm is disabled."

Ares nodded and texted Apollo.

> Put the cameras on a loop. We're going in.

Apollo replied with just one word.

> Done

Ares gripped the door handle and wrenched it open. The lock gave way with a muted crack, and the three of them slipped inside.

Rows of metal shelves stacked with empty boxes and bins full of packages to be mailed lined the walls of the back room. Ares moved with purpose through the racks toward the front of the store.

"Box 437."

The three fanned out and examined the numbers on the boxes.

"Here." Cherry pointed to a larger box near the bottom of one wall.

Ares crouched, inserting his claws into the seam where the door met the frame, and with a single powerful motion, ripped the metal door clean off its hinges.

Inside a stack of mail sat, waiting with envelopes and packages jammed inside. Ares pulled them out, spreading them across the floor as Cherry and Duncan crouched beside him.

Duncan examined an envelope. "They're all addressed to North-Star Holdings. That's the name of the company I heard Rudy mention before."

"Yeah. The building in New York was registered to it as well."

Ares rifled through the stack, his movements urgent. Bills, advertisements, and business correspondence- nothing that screamed "kidnapping" or "hidden location."

Then, at the bottom of the pile, a legal envelope slid out. Unlike the others, this one had no return address. Ares tore into it, spilling its contents onto the floor.

Photographs. Dozens of them. Of... all of them. Ares. Apollo. Cherry and Strider. Luckily, there were no photos of Ares going to the States. Maybe Titan hadn't learned that part yet.

Ares motioned for Duncan and Cherry to follow him as he stalked back out of the building, and he pulled out his phone.

"Ares?"

"Apollo. Did you find anything more about NorthStar Holdings?"

"Not yet. The paper trail is huge. Looks like a shell company. Dozens of smaller companies underneath it."

"Dig deeper. In the meantime, call anyone you have to. Put a block on every bank account associated with any of those companies. If they've paid anyone who doesn't check out, stop those, too. Call every contact. Pull every string. I don't want money flowing in or out of any company that may have helped finance Titan. Check every single one. I want to know who runs each company and where to find them."

"Got it."

Ares disconnected the call and turned to Cherry, whose eyes burned with hope and fierce determination.

"What now?" she demanded. "This is just more confirmation Titan's been watching us. It doesn't tell us where River is."

"Trust me, I'm as frustrated as you are."

"Then what do we do?"

"I don't know," Ares yelled. "I haven't slept. I haven't eaten. I am doing absolutely everything I can. You think you want her back? I want her back more. Apollo wants her back more. No one on Earth wants her back more than we do. So you tell me, Cherry, you tell me. What do we do now?"

Cherry flinched at Ares' outburst, then her eyes narrowed.

"We think like River," she said. "My daughter is resourceful. If she has the opportunity to escape, she'll take it."

Ares ran a hand through his hair, his frustration ebbing. "You're right. River wouldn't sit passively waiting for rescue. She'd fight."

"Exactly," Cherry nodded. "And if she's fighting to get out..."

"Then Titan would be scrambling to keep her contained," Ares finished, a new energy surging through his exhausted body. "He'd need extra security, resources diverted to watching her."

Duncan cleared his throat. "If that's the case, we might be able to track unusual patterns. Increased influx of rogues to the area. Ones not necessarily already on suppressors. Increased supply deliveries, that sort of thing."

Ares' phone rang, interrupting their discussion. Apollo's name flashed on the screen.

"Tell me you found something," Ares said without preamble.

"I might have. The neighbor's notes mentioned deliveries through a secondary company, Evergreen Supplies. We traced it to a warehouse outside Montreal, but that's not the interesting part."

"What is?"

"The supplies. Specialized equipment for creating a contained living environment. Air filtration systems, water purification, and custom lighting panels that simulate natural daylight cycles."

Ares' heart pounded harder. "They were building a prison."

"Not just any prison. One designed for long-term captivity, with attention to psychological comfort. Why bother with simulated daylight unless you're planning to keep someone for months?"

"Where were these deliveries sent?" Ares demanded.

"That's what we're working on now. The warehouse records show shipments to various locations, but there's one address that stands out, a property about thirty miles northwest of here, registered to a hunting club that doesn't seem to exist."

"Text me the coordinates." Ares moved toward the car. "We'll meet you there."

Ares ended the call, and his phone buzzed with an incoming text from Apollo with the location. He pulled up the map, studying it before showing it to Cherry and Duncan.

"It's semi-remote," Duncan observed. "Surrounded by forest, minimal road access. Defensible."

"Perfect place to hide someone you don't want found," Cherry added.

Ares nodded, a cold determination settling over him. "Let's go. Duncan, call Theo and tell him to bring everything we have. If River's there, we're getting her out tonight."

CHAPTER THIRTY-ONE

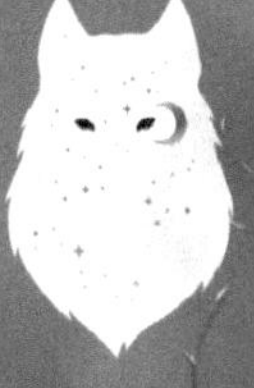

APOLLO

Apollo searched his computer for the Hunter's Club, which owned the house, when he heard a commotion in the hallway.

"Move! Move!" Regan yelled.

Apollo looked up as Regan raced through the door, phone in hand.

"It's for you." He held out the phone.

"Who is it?"

"The answering service forwarded a call to me since you told them you didn't want to be disturbed."

He looked back at his computer screen. "I don't have time for business crap. Don't you know-"

"Apollo!"

Apollo looked up and growled.

"You need to hear this." Regan shoved the phone at him.

Apollo took the phone. "Hello?"

"Mr. Wolvenguard?" A woman's hesitant voice came through

the line. "My name is Dr. Sarah Mitchell. I'm a veterinarian at Pine Creek Emergency Animal Hospital."

Apollo frowned. "I don't have time for-"

"Sir, I have someone here. A young woman named River. She asked specifically for you."

Apollo's heart stopped. The world around him froze as the words registered. "River?" he whispered. "You have River?"

Apollo stood.

Apollo's wolf leapt to his feet, howling. *Mate. My Luna.*

"Yes, sir. She was brought in as an injured dog, this kid says, but she's clearly human. She's severely injured, suffering from blood loss and exhaustion. She insisted we contact you rather than take her to a hospital. But she needs a doctor badly."

Apollo snatched up his jacket with one hand while keeping the phone firmly against his ear. "Where are you located?"

The veterinarian rattled off an address that Apollo committed to memory. "She's stable for now, but she needs proper medical attention. She has a troublesome gash on her leg and-"

"I'm on my way," Apollo cut her off, his voice deadly calm despite the storm raging inside him. "Keep her safe. Don't let anyone else near her. Do you understand?"

"Yes, but,"

"No one," Apollo repeated, his voice dropping to a dangerous growl. "No matter who they claim to be."

He ended the call and turned to Regan. "Get two teams ready. Now."

Regan nodded, already dialing.

Apollo moved with controlled urgency, checking his weapon before sliding it into his holster. "Have Dr. Keller meet us at the Elm house. Tell her to prepare for trauma care."

As Apollo raced from the room, his wolf surged forward, nearly overwhelming him with its desperate need to reach River. After weeks of searching, false leads, and dead ends, River had found her way to safety. He wouldn't lose her again.

Apollo leapt the staircase to the foyer and ran out the door. Silas screeched the car to a halt right in front of him, and Apollo jumped in.

"Drive."

THE RIDE TO THE VETERINARY CLINIC WAS A BLUR. APOLLO'S HANDS gripped the armrests with white-knuckled intensity as Silas pushed the vehicle to its limits. In the back seat, Apollo's two most trusted guards stayed silent.

When they pulled up to the small building with its blue neon sign proclaiming "24-Hour Emergency Animal Care," Apollo jumped out of the car before it came to a complete stop. He burst through the front door, scanning the reception area.

A startled receptionist jumped to her feet. "Sir, can I-"

"River Wolvenguard," Apollo cut her off, his voice vibrating with uncontrollable emotions. "Where is she?"

The receptionist paled, her eyes darting to a hallway behind her. "I'm sorry, who are you?"

"Apollo Wolvenguard, her husband."

"Uh..." The receptionist swallowed hard. "May... may I see some ID, please?"

Apollo growled. He didn't have time for this, but he had told the doctor not to let anyone else near River, so he pulled out his wallet and showed it to the girl.

She inspected it and nodded. "Dr. Mitchell is with her in exam room three, but-"

Apollo was already moving, Silas, Regan, and Thomas behind him as they strode down the corridor. The clinic's antiseptic smell mixed with something else, blood- River's blood. His wolf howled, desperate to reach their mate.

My mate. My Omega.

When he pushed open the door to exam room three, the world narrowed to a single point. River lay on an examination table, her silver hair matted with dirt and blood, her slender frame covered with a blanket. Eyes closed, her face ashen beneath smudges of dirt and scratches. An IV line ran into her arm, and a makeshift pressure bandage wrapped her thigh.

"River," Apollo breathed, his voice shaking.

Dr. Mitchell turned, her eyes widening. "Who are you?"

Apollo barely registered her words as he moved to River's side, reaching to touch her.

"River," he called again. "I'm here, love. I found you."

River's eyelids fluttered, then opened. For a moment, confusion clouded her gaze before recognition dawned. "Apollo?" Her voice came out barely audible.

"Yes, it's me." His voice broke as he gathered her hand in his. "I'm here. You're safe now."

Tears welled in River's eyes as she struggled to sit up. "I escaped," she managed, wincing with the effort. "I got out. I had to... the baby..."

Apollo froze, his eyes dropping to her abdomen. "Baby?"

River nodded weakly, tears spilling down her cheeks. "Our baby. I had to protect our baby."

A wave of emotions crashed through Apollo: joy, fear, and fierce protectiveness. His hand trembled as he placed it gently on River's abdomen.

"Our baby," he repeated, his voice thick with renewed fury at what Titan had put them through.

River reached for him and pulled him to her to rub her nose against his. Apollo's wolf howled, and Apollo held back the desire to hold her against him as tight as he was able.

Dr. Mitchell cleared her throat. "She needs a hospital, Mr. Wolvenguard. I've done what I can, but she's severely dehydrated, malnourished, and has lost a significant amount of blood. And if she's pregnant-"

"No hospitals," Apollo said firmly. "We have a private family physician. Our doctor is waiting."

"She most likely needs surgery for that leg and a blood transfusion."

Apollo looked at the doctor. "I assure you, our doctor can do whatever is required."

Apollo unhooked the IV and gathered River into his arms. She whimpered softly. The pain and fear wafted off her like an overly scented candle in a small enclosed space. He stopped and inhaled. He could smell her. Not strong, but he could.

"Hold on." The doctor stopped him and retrieved a cotton ball and Band-Aid, and covered River's arm where he'd removed the IV.

"Titan." She clutched weakly at Apollo's shirt. "He'll come for me."

"Let him try," Apollo growled, his eyes flashing. "I won't let him near you again. Ever."

Dr. Mitchell moved forward, concern etched on her face. "Mr. Wolvenguard, I really must insist-"

"Thank you for your help, Doctor," Silas interrupted smoothly, pressing a thick envelope into her hands. "We appreciate your discretion. I promise Prince Apollo will do whatever is necessary to ensure the health of his wife and unborn child. You need not worry."

She blinked at the envelope, then at River's frail form cradled against Apollo. "I... I don't understand what's happening here, but she needs proper care."

"She'll get it. My wife will get whatever she needs. Whatever the cost." Apollo assured her, already moving toward the door. "You have my word."

As they exited the clinic, Apollo scanned the parking lot with predatory intensity, his senses on high alert for any sign of danger.

He stopped and glimpsed a teenage boy standing awkwardly by the entrance, his face pale with shock.

"He brought me here," River whispered.

"Thank you," Apollo said. "You saved her. I owe you mine."

The boy nodded, but looked completely overwhelmed. "I was just doing Uber Eats, and there she was… on the sidewalk… bleeding… She was a dog," he said. "And then when we got here, she wasn't."

Regan placed a hand on the boy's shoulder. "You did the right thing, son. But it would be best if you forgot what you saw tonight."

Apollo looked at the boy. "What's your name?"

"Jack Wilson."

"Jack. I am in your debt forever." He nodded to Regan. "Call Wolvenguard Limited and tell them I said to get your information so I can repay you. Whatever you want. College tuition? Covered. Debts wiped out. Done. You just tell me what it is and I'll make sure it happens."

Regan handed Jack a card. Jack took it, but his eyes never left River. The boy's mouth opened, but before he could respond, Apollo moved toward the waiting SUV, River held securely against him. His wolf howled with fierce protectiveness as her shallow breaths fell against his neck.

His wolf sniffed River. *Hurt. Needs help.*

I know.

Silas hopped in the driver's seat and Regan in the front as Thomas slid in the third row. Apollo settled with River in the second row, her head resting on his torso.

The vehicle pulled away from the clinic, and Apollo stroked River's silver hair, his heart thundering with a mixture of relief and fear. She was alive. She carried their child. And Titan would pay for every second of pain he had caused her.

"Stay with me, Kitten."He pressed his lips to her forehead. "Just stay with me."

River's eyes fluttered open, focusing on his face with effort. "I knew you'd find me," she murmured.

Apollo's throat constricted. "Rest. I've got you."

"I'm cold," she said.

Thomas handed Apollo a blanket, and he spread it over both of them.

She wrapped an arm around him and inhaled deeply. Squeezing him tighter.

"I love you, Apollo. I'm so glad you aren't dead."

He chuckled. "Me too." Tears sprang to his eyes, and he kissed her head. "I love you, too, Kitten."

River's eyes drifted closed again. "Where's Ares?"

Shit! Ares. He hadn't even called him. Apollo pulled out his phone, his fingers trembling as he dialed Ares' number.

His twin answered on the first ring. "Apollo, did you find-"

"I have her," Apollo said, his voice thick with emotion.

"What?"

"I have her. She's alive, Ares. She escaped somehow. We're bringing her to the safe house on Elm."

Silence stretched out on the line.

"I… I can't…" Ares' voice cracked, and he whined.

"I know, brother. I know."

"Is... she okay? Let me talk to her."

Apollo stroked River's hair. The blanket fell away from her leg, and the huge bandage peeked out from underneath.

His wolf whined and paced.

"She's badly injured. I have Dr. Keller on her way already."

There was a discussion on the other end of the line, and then Cherry's voice rang through.

"Is she going to be okay?"

Apollo suddenly remembered Cherry's words: *"I couldn't save them. I have to save them."*

She'd known. She'd known River was pregnant.

"She's going to be okay, Cherry. They both are."

"Both?" Ares asked.

"Yes. Our mate is pregnant."

A roar erupted from the phone, so loud that Apollo winced and River stirred.

"I'll kill him," Ares snarled, his voice dropping to that deadly register that meant Ares' wolf was just below the surface. "I'll tear out his throat with my teeth. I'll-"

"Ares," Apollo cut in sharply. "River needs you. Our child needs you."

"That bastard kept her prisoner while she was pregnant with our child?" The sound of something cracking came through the phone. "I'm going to eat his heart."

Apollo glanced down at River's pale face, her silver hair tangled with blood and dirt. She stirred, her brow furrowing as if sensing her mate's pain even from a distance.

"Brother, listen to me," Apollo said, his voice firm but gentle. "Come to the house. Be with your mate. Let the Alphas handle the investigation of the house for now."

"The Alphas?" Ares spat. "This isn't their fight."

"It is now," Apollo insisted. "River escaped, which means Titan knows she's gone. He'll be looking for her. We need to protect her, and we need allies. The Alphas can secure the location and gather evidence."

"While Titan escapes?" Ares growled.

"While we ensure River and our child survive," Apollo countered. "Brother, she's weak. She's lost a lot of blood. She's thin, too thin. She needs us both."

The line went silent save for Ares' harsh breathing. Apollo could almost see his twin torn between bloodlust and the primal need to protect his mate.

"Ares..." River whispered. "Please..."

Ares whined. "Beloved."

"We're coming," said Cherry.

"How far away are you?" Ares asked, his voice marginally calmer.

"Fifteen minutes."

"I'll be there in twenty." The line went dead.

Apollo returned his attention to River. Her breathing steadied somewhat, but her skin stayed alarmingly pale. The bandage on her thigh had soaked through with blood, and numerous more minor cuts and scratches marked her exposed skin. Her side also held several jagged cuts. What she must have been through, he could not begin to imagine. But one thing he swore right there, for every scratch, scrape, and cut she suffered, Titan would suffer tenfold.

"How is she?" Silas asked from the front seat, his eyes meeting Apollo's in the rearview mirror.

"Holding on." Apollo brushed a strand of hair from River's face. "She's stronger than any of us knew."

The SUV sped through the darkened streets, Silas taking corners with practiced precision. Regan and Thomas stayed vigilant, constantly scanning for any sign of pursuit, their guns at the ready.

She was going to be fine. She had to be, just had to be, because if she wasn't... Apollo would slaughter every rogue in North America.

RIVER

River's eyes fluttered open as the SUV pulled up to a modest two-story structure nestled among towering, overgrown trees, its exterior deliberately unremarkable to avoid attention. Dr. Keller waited on the porch, her face tight with concern.

"Quickly," she called as Apollo emerged with River. "Bring her inside."

Apollo moved with swift precision, carrying River through the front door and following Dr. Keller down a hallway to a prepared bedroom. Though he tried to be gentle, River couldn't help but moan in pain at being jostled.

"I'm so sorry, my love. I'll get you settled in just a moment."

Medical equipment had been set up. Monitors, IV stands, and various supplies were arranged on a rolling cart.

"Put her on the bed," Dr. Keller instructed, already pulling on latex gloves.

River hissed as Apollo's arms grazed her cuts.

Apollo laid River down with exquisite care, his hands lingering as if unable to break contact. River's eyes found his, pain and exhaustion evident in their depths.

"Don't leave." She grasped at his sleeve.

"Never," Apollo promised, stepping back just enough to give Dr. Keller access while still holding River's hand.

Dr. Keller worked methodically, cutting away the makeshift bandage on River's thigh to reveal a wound seeping blood. "What happened?"

"Razor wire," River managed, crying out as the doctor began cleaning the wound. "Had to... escape."

"She needs blood," Dr. Keller declared, glancing up at Apollo. "And fluids. She's severely dehydrated."

The doctor hooked up an IV bag to a rolling device that resembled a small hat rack and then examined River's other injuries. Her eyes grew concerned as she prodded the cuts on River's side from the window and a large bruise on her shoulder from where she'd fallen onto the grass.

"When was the last time you ate?" she asked River.

"Don't... remember." River shook her head, but a pain shot

through her neck, and she stopped. "I've been only drinking soda and eating candy to avoid the blockers in the food."

Apollo's jaw clenched, his hands balling into fists. His eyes went black, and she squeezed his hand. He knelt by her and kissed her knuckles.

"You're going to be okay now," he promised.

"And you believe you're pregnant?" Dr. Keller's hands gently prodded her.

River nodded weakly. "Morning sickness... bad. Everything smells too strong. My wolf is protective but weak." She swallowed hard. "I've been so tired, and my breasts are tender. And I haven't had a period in at least two months."

Dr. Keller nodded. "We'll confirm it right away."

Apollo's hand tightened around River's as Dr. Keller prepared the IV needle and slid it into River's arm with practiced precision.

River winced at the expected pinch, but it happened so fast she didn't even notice.

The sound of a vehicle screeching to a halt outside broke the relative quiet. Everyone froze, and River gripped Apollo's hand.

"Apollo-"

"No one will get you here. I promise."

Seconds later, thunderous footsteps pounded down the hallway.

The bedroom door burst open with such force it slammed against the wall. Ares stood in the doorway, his massive frame filling the space, golden eyes wild, full of fear and desperate relief as they locked on River.

"For heaven's sake, calm down!" Dr. Keller snapped. "This is a medical situation, not a battlefield! Besides, the Princess doesn't need any more stress."

Ares ignored her, crossing the room in two long strides to reach River's bed. He dropped to his knees beside her, hands trembling as he cupped her face. His lips caressed her forehead, her cheeks, her lips, her chin, everywhere he could reach, as if he couldn't believe she was real.

"River," he breathed between kisses, his voice breaking. "My River."

"Back up," Dr. Keller ordered, attempting to shoulder between them. "I need to finish my examination. You do want her to live, right?"

River's weak laugh turned into a cough as tears streamed down her face.

Ares growled but pulled back. He moved around to the other side of the bed and took her free hand, standing opposite Apollo, both her mates flanking her like protective sentinels.

Dr. Keller looked between them with exasperation, shaking her head as she turned back to her medical supplies. "Alpha males," she muttered under her breath. "Biggest babies in the animal kingdom."

"I heard that," Ares growled, though his eyes never left River's face.

"Good," Dr. Keller retorted. "Now stay out of my way while I check on your mate."

She pulled out a small device shaped kind of like a microphone and attached the cord to a laptop sitting on the nightstand. She squeezed gel onto River's stomach, the coolness making River flinch slightly. As Dr. Keller depressed the wand against her abdomen, the room fell silent except for the steady beep of the heart monitor.

River held her breath. Please, goddess, let my baby be okay.

A moment passed, and then another, as Dr. Keller moved the wand in one direction, the other, and then back again, her face never straying from the laptop screen.

"Figures." Dr. Keller shook her head and snorted.

"What?" Ares and Apollo asked together.

"Twins," said Dr. Keller.

"Twins?" River asked. "As in, two babies?"

Dr. Keller nodded. "That's what 'twins' means."

Cherry growled and looked at the doctor. "No one in this room is allowed to be a bigger bitch than me. Especially to my daughter."

Dr. Keller raised an eyebrow at Cherry but didn't flinch as she turned back to the monitor.

River hadn't even noticed her mom enter. She looked over at her mom and smiled. Her mom smiled back.

River looked at Apollo and then Ares. "One for each of you."

"No," said Apollo.

"Two for both of us," Ares finished.

Both of her mates covered her in kisses again, whispering to her about their love and never letting her be endangered again. River's heart squeezed. She wanted nothing more than to climb into an enormous bed with both of them and be smothered by their strong arms.

"Well," the doctor finally said, "Everything looks normal. Babies are fine. We just need to get River on the mend. The babies will take from her what they need, so we need to get ahead of them and nourish her to health swiftly. She needs blood-"

"Take mine." Cherry, stripped down to her tank top, and moved toward the bed without being asked. "We have the same type."

Dr. Keller directed Cherry to sit in a chair beside River's bed. "This won't take long, but you might feel lightheaded afterward."

Cherry complied without hesitation, her eyes never leaving her daughter's face. "Take as much as she needs," she said. "Every drop."

Tears watered Cherry's eyes, and River gave her a weak smile.

"Hey, Mom."

"I swear if you ever disappear like that again, I'm going to kick your ass."

River snorted. "I'll make sure my next would-be kidnapper knows."

Dr. Keller inserted the needle into Cherry's arm, and the door opened again. Zeke walked inside with Strider. Zeke's usually stoic expression softened at the sight of River.

"Luna," he said, giving her a gentle smile. "It's good to see you."

"Zeke. Good to see you too."

"Hey, kiddo," said Strider. "I'm glad you're back with us."

River's heart squeezed. "Me too, Dad."

Tears welled in Strider's eyes. It was the first time River had ever called him that.

He shifted slightly and then coughed. "Bianca's been driving everyone crazy with worry. She says she loves you and wants to video chat as soon as you're able."

River nodded. "Tell her I'd like that."

Zeke nodded, then turned to Ares. "Highness, I hate to interrupt, but one of the Alphas is on the phone. Says it's urgent."

Ares growled, his hand tightening around River's. "They can wait."

Dr. Keller looked up from where she connected the transfusion line between Cherry and River. "One of you needs to move anyway. I need access to hook up this transfusion properly, and unless someone is volunteering to have me shove the line straight through their torso, you need to go."

Ares hesitated, torn between his duty and his desperate need to stay with River.

"Go," River told him softly. "I'll be here."

With visible reluctance, Ares rose to his feet, leaning down to press his lips to River's forehead. As he turned to leave, River's wolf whined, the sound escaping her before she could stop it.

"Stay where I can see you," River said, her fingers reaching for him. "Please."

Ares hesitated like he might refuse to move after all, but she gave him a reassuring smile that she didn't feel, and he walked to the corner of the room where Zeke handed over his phone.

"This better be important," Ares growled.

River's gut twisted tight as she watched Ares' reactions to the conversation. Had the Alphas found Titan's estate? Had they gotten in? Was Titan even there, or was he out looking for her? Questions swirled in River's mind, and she had to bite her tongue to keep from screaming.

Apollo shifted nearer to River and stroked her hair as Dr. Keller finished connecting the transfusion line. He bent over her and kissed her softly.

"It's going to be all right," Apollo said.

River tipped her head back and brushed his lips with hers. The feel of him on her lips, the taste and smell of him, all had her wanting to jump into his arms and wrap herself around him.

"There," the doctor said with satisfaction. "Cherry's blood will help stabilize you while your body works to replace what you've lost."

Cherry's blood flowed through the clear tube toward her arm. It seemed fitting somehow, Cherry giving life to her once again.

"Thank you," she whispered, meeting her mother's eyes.

Cherry's tough exterior cracked as she gave River a watery smile. "I didn't get you this far in life to let you and my grandbabies die now."

River chuckled. "We all thank you, Granny Cherry."

Cherry's eyes flashed. "Then again, all I have to do is pull out this little tube..."

River laughed. Apollo kissed her knuckles, and she looked up at him, seeing him clearly for the first time. He hadn't shaved in days, and his eyes were sunken in.

"When was the last time you slept?" she asked.

"For more than a couple of hours at a time? The last night we spent together. In the last forty-eight hours? None."

River's mouth fell open. "Apollo. You need sleep. Especially with all the injuries you sustained."

"I'll rest when Titan is dead."

River hated how much Apollo and Ares had suffered at her absence. But she, too, had suffered. It had taken a whole week before she'd been able to confirm they were both even still alive, and that had been agonizing. But they'd known nothing. They had no idea where she was or what was happening to her.

"I was so worried about you. I was so afraid I'd lost you," she said.

Apollo pressed his lips to hers. "And I, you."

They stayed that way for several seconds, and then Apollo pulled his lips from hers.

"Don't go away again," Apollo murmured.

"Don't almost die without me again."

He chuffed, and when he straightened, his eyes swam with tears. River's chest squeezed so tight she thought her heart might stop.

"Okay," said Ares. "We've found the house."

"Really?" asked River.

Ares nodded. "It's identical to our estate on the outside."

"On the inside, too," River said.

Ares shook his head. "He's such a freak. Anyway, we currently have about forty Betas and Alphas surrounding the place and making sure no one leaves or gets in."

"Call everyone," said Apollo. "Everyone answers the call. No exceptions. Every Alpha. Every Beta. Even the Council. They all go and surround that place. No one makes a move until we're there."

Ares nodded and turned to Zeke.

"We'll get on it." Zeke started dialing on his phone as he left the room.

Regan peeked his head in.

"Every Alpha. Every Beta. They all come, or they'll deal with me," said Apollo.

"With both of us," Ares corrected.

"No," said River. "They'll deal with all of us."

All eyes moved to her. With everything she'd learned from Titan and the rogues, she didn't want a massacre, but she was not about to let what had happened go unpunished either.

CHAPTER THIRTY-TWO

KANE

Titan hurled the crystal decanter against the wall, sending shards of glass and amber liquid spraying across the room. The sweet, heady scent of bourbon filled the air as he overturned the heavy oak desk with a single, violent motion, scattering papers and electronics across the floor.

"She can't be gone!" he roared, veins standing out on his neck as he seized a leather armchair and smashed it against the stone fireplace. "Not possible!"

Kane stood in the doorway, keeping his face a mask at Titan's destructive rampage. He'd seen Titan angry before, had witnessed his temper after Council rejections and territorial disputes, but this was different. This was unhinged, primal fury.

"Titan," Kane said, his voice firm but careful. "We need to think clearly. Tearing apart your office won't bring her back."

Titan whirled on him, black eyes blazing with an almost feverish light. "Those guards." He stalked toward Kane with predatory intensity. "The ones she overpowered. Bring them to me. Now."

Kane didn't move. "What for?"

"What for? They failed me. They let my mate escape." His thick fist slammed into the wall beside Kane's head, cracking the plaster. "They deserve to die for their incompetence."

"They're loyal soldiers who made a mistake. We both know they weren't prepared to find her out there. We never thought she might be able to escape. They didn't know what they were supposed to do. You made it beyond clear if anyone touched her, they would die." Kane stood his ground despite the murderous intent emanating from Titan. "Killing them won't solve anything."

Titan's nostrils flared as he leaned in, his face inches from Kane's. "You dare question me? After everything?" His voice dropped to a deadly whisper. "Perhaps you've forgotten who's in charge here."

"I haven't forgotten. But someone needs to remind you of the plan. Our goal was never about one woman. It was about changing the system, creating a better world for rogues. Those rogues. The ones you are threatening to murder. The ones who have already been through enough."

Titan stared at Kane for a moment before turning away. He didn't move for several seconds, giving Kane a glimmer of hope that he might be getting through to Titan.

Titan turned back. "Get everyone armed. We're going after her."

Kane blinked in disbelief. "Going after her? She could be anywhere."

"She's injured. Bleeding. She won't get far." Titan's eyes gleamed with obsessive certainty. "The twins will come for her. When they do, we'll be ready."

"Listen to yourself," Kane said, stepping further into the room. "You're talking about starting a war over one woman who clearly doesn't want to be your mate."

"SHUT UP!" Titan roared, hurling a heavy bookend and narrowly missing Kane's head. "She is MINE!"

"Screw River Whitetail!"

Kane's wolf leapt to his feet, gnashing his teeth at Titan. *Spoiled. Pup. No Alpha.*

Titan ignored his wolf. "When we started, this was about helping those who couldn't help themselves. But it isn't anymore. Your father disowned you. He found his fated mate. He had the twins. It sucks. If you want to take the throne to change things. If you want to take back your birthright, okay. I'm with you. But if you are just doing all this to get River as your High Luna, you are no better than all the others who promised change and were out for themselves in the end. And I'm not going to be part of that."

Titan's face twisted. "Get the guards. Tell everyone to arm themselves. We're going after her now."

If Kane didn't stand up to Titan now, it could cost everyone they'd been trying to help.

"No." Kane planted his feet. "I won't."

Titan froze. "What did you say to me?"

This moment would either save Titan or get Kane killed... but there was no other way.

"I said no." Kane stood his ground despite the dangerous energy radiating from Titan. "This is irrational, Titan. You're not thinking clearly. We need to secure the compound, not charge out half-cocked into what could be a trap."

"You dare defy me?" Titan's voice dropped to a deadly whisper.

"I'm trying to save you," Kane insisted. "Look what this obsession has done to you. Look at what it's done to everything we built."

With a roar that shook the walls, Titan launched himself across the room. His fist connected with Kane's cheek with bone-crushing force, sending him crashing into the bookshelf. Volumes rained down as Kane stumbled, tasting blood.

"I gave you everything!" Titan bellowed, stalking forward. "I made you who you are! I built all of this. Me. I built it. It's mine to do with as I please."

Kane spat blood onto the polished floor, wiping his mouth with the back of his hand. "And I've stood by you through everything," he countered. "But I won't follow you into madness."

Titan struck again, a vicious uppercut that Kane narrowly avoided. As Titan's fist crashed into the wall, splintering wood paneling, Kane countered with a sharp jab to Titan's ribs.

"Stand down." Kane circled him. "This isn't you. This isn't who we are."

"You don't tell me who I am!" Titan launched another attack.

This time, his blow landed square in Kane's sternum, driving the air from his lungs and sending him staggering backward. Kane recovered quickly.

Years of teaching Titan how to fight meant Titan's patterns were Kane's patterns. He ducked under Titan's next swing and delivered a punishing blow to Titan's kidney.

Titan howled, his movements becoming less calculated and more frenzied. He seized a severed chair leg and swung it like a club, catching Kane across the shoulder. Pain exploded through Kane's arm, but he delivered a powerful kick to Titan's knee.

The two men crashed through what remained of the desk, grappling in a deadly dance they'd performed countless times in training, but never with such raw intent to harm. Blood spattered the floor as Titan's elbow connected with Kane's nose, the cartilage cracking audibly.

Kane retaliated with a headbutt that sent Titan reeling. Both men bled, their breath coming in harsh pants.

The door burst open as several guards rushed in, drawn by the sounds of combat. They froze at the sight of their Alpha and his second-in-command locked in a brutal struggle.

"Stop them!" someone shouted, and four wolves rushed forward, attempting to separate the men.

Titan roared, his fist connecting with the first guard's temple, dropping him instantly. The second guard received an elbow to the windpipe. He collapsed, clutching his neck as he gasped for air that wouldn't come.

"Stay back!" Kane shouted to the remaining guards, but it was too late.

Titan was lost to his mind, his movements fluid and lethal as he tore through anyone who approached. A third guard screamed as Titan's hand closed around his throat, lifting him off the ground before hurling him across the room. His head hit the stone fireplace with a sickening crack, his body going limp as it slid to the floor.

"Enough!" Kane roared, tackling Titan from behind.

They slammed to the floor, wrestling amid battered furniture and shattered glass. Kane managed to pin Titan, straddling his torso as he delivered punch after punch to the face of the man who'd been his best friend and younger brother for more years than he hadn't. Blood sprayed with each impact, Titan's features becoming a crimson mask.

Kane's wolf spurred him on. *Take it all. Make him submit.*

But Kane had no desire to take what Titan had built. He didn't want to be Alpha. He only wanted his little brother back.

Titan struggled against him. Trying to buck Kane off.

"Stop!" Kane shouted between blows. "It's over!"

"Never! Traitor. Bastard."

The remaining guards watched in horror as their leaders balled, but none dared intervene.

Footsteps clicked rapidly across the floor as Vanessa appeared, eyes widening at the carnage. Without hesitation, she rushed forward, a syringe clutched in her hand.

She dropped to her knees beside the struggling men.

Kane pinned Titan's shoulders with all his strength as Vanessa jabbed the needle into Titan's neck, depressing the plunger in one swift motion.

Titan's roar shook the room as he bucked upward with inhuman strength, throwing Kane off him. He staggered to his feet, swaying as he turned toward Vanessa.

"You're dead, bitch." His voice slurred as he lunged for her.

Vanessa tried to dodge, but Titan's backhand connected with her face, the impact lifting her off her feet and sending her into the remaining guards. Blood streamed from her split lip as she crumpled to the floor.

More wolves gathered at the doorway, drawn by the commotion. They watched their Alpha, the man they'd followed in exile and rebellion, stagger to the center of the destroyed room.

Titan swayed, his blue eyes glassy as the sedative took effect. His blond hair plastered to his bloodied face as he stumbled forward, before his knees buckled.

"You..." Titan snarled, his voice growing thick, but eyes still burning. "You… my brother! You… betrayed me? For her?" Spittle mixed with blood flew from his lips as his voice rose to a thunderous roar. "For the Luna that is MINE!"

Vanessa pulled herself up, pressing a hand to her split lip. "No one's betraying you, Titan. We're trying to save you."

"LIES!" He slammed his fist into the floor, leaving a crater in the wood. "When I wake..." He stumbled, catching himself against the bookcase. "I will hunt each of you down," he slurred. "I will tear… your throat… my teeth. I will bathe in your…"

His gaze swept over the assembled wolves, many averting their eyes from the madness.

Kane moved forward. "Titan."

Titan lunged for Kane but collapsed to the floor instead. "I'll save the longest death for you." His voice slurred into incoherence as his eyes closed.

Silence fell like a shroud, broken only by the labored breathing of the injured. Blood pooled on the hardwood around Titan, spreading like a crimson halo.

Kane wiped blood from his face, wincing as his fingers brushed his broken nose. That made what, three times, four times broken?

"Everyone out," he ordered. "Except you." He pointed to Vanessa.

The guards hesitated, looking between their fallen Alpha and his lieutenant.

"Now!" Kane barked, and the wolves scattered, dragging their injured comrades with them.

Kane turned to Vanessa. "What was in that syringe?"

"Strong sedative." She touched her split lip. "Enough to take down a bull elephant. He'll be out for hours."

Kane nodded, limping to what remained of the liquor cabinet. He extracted a miraculously unbroken bottle of whiskey, uncapped it, and took a long pull before passing it to Vanessa.

"What now?" Her eyes never left Titan's prone form.

Kane stared down at the man who had been his brother in all but blood. The man whose vision had once inspired him, whose strength had been a cornerstone of his life. Now that man lay twisted by his obsession, consumed by madness that had been growing for months. The same madness and obsession he'd watched Titan's mother succumb to.

"We evacuate," Kane said, his decision crystallizing with each passing second. "We get everyone to safety. Now."

Vanessa's eyebrows shot up. "Evacuate? The entire compound?"

"Yes." Kane turned to face her fully. "The twins are close. It's only a matter of time before they find us."

"But we have defenses. Security systems, armed guards-"

"Against two royal Alphas and whatever force they've assembled?" Kane shook his head. "They won't be taken by surprise a second time. They'll be prepared and with as much backup as they can get. We'd be slaughtered."

"But we have guns. Ammunition."

“Not as much as we’d need. The shipment went out days ago.

The armory is all but empty. Even so, only a handful of the rogues even know how to use them. Titan called in reinforcements, but they haven't even arrived yet, and who knows when or if they will. Most of the rogues here aren't fighters; they're scared wolves who wouldn't win against other rogues, let alone Alphas, Betas, and Lycans."

Vanessa shook her head. "You're right. Most of the rogues here don't have what it takes to fight." She glanced at Titan's unconscious form. "Okay. But what about him?"

Kane stayed silent for a long moment, the weight of the decision pressing down on him. Not that there was anything to decide. "We take him with us. Contain him until he's... himself again."

"If that's even possible," Vanessa murmured.

"It has to be." Uncertainty tinged his voice. "The Titan I know is still in there somewhere."

Vanessa shrugged. "I wouldn't be too sure. I know you want him to be, but from where I stood, he would have killed you if I hadn't intervened."

"What? Do you want me to thank you or something?"

"No. I just want you to face the truth that it is very well possible he won't come back from this."

Kane growled. He didn't want Vanessa's words to be valid. But even he had his doubts about what Titan would do when he woke up.

It didn't matter, though; that was the least of his worries at the moment.

He moved to the intercom on the wall and pressed the button that would broadcast throughout the compound. "This is Kane. All persons, begin evacuation procedures. This is not a drill. Secure essential documents and equipment per protocol. We move out in one hour."

Releasing the button, he turned back to Vanessa. "We need to stabilize him for transport."

"And the others?" she asked, gesturing toward the door. "Some of them are loyal to Titan, not to you."

"They'll follow orders, or they'll be left behind," Kane said. "I won't sacrifice everyone for his obsession. But you can't help those who won't help themselves."

Vanessa nodded and hurried from the room. Kane knelt beside his brother. Blood had congealed on Titan's face. For a moment, Kane rested his hand on Titan's shoulder.

"I'm sorry, brother. But this ends now."

Rising to his feet, Kane surveyed the destruction around him. The shattered furniture, the splintered walls, the blood-soaked floor. A fitting metaphor, he thought, for what Titan's obsession had done to their cause.

He would salvage what he could. He had to. Even if it meant betraying the man he had followed for so long.

Austin rushed in. "The estate is surrounded."

"What? By who?"

"Alphas and Betas."

Kane's wolf leapt to his feet. *Fight. Kill.*

"Which ones?" Kane asked.

Austin swallowed, his eyes wide as tennis balls. "All of them."

Shit. Kane sighed. "Turn on the electric fencing."

CHAPTER THIRTY-THREE

RIVER

The safe house hummed with activity as the sun rose, painting the eastern sky in hues of pink and gold. River lay propped against pillows, her body weak, but her spirit strengthening with each passing hour. The transfusion from Cherry had helped immensely, bringing color back to her pale skin and clarity to her mind. Even her scrapes had begun to heal.

She rested her hands on her belly, still unable to believe she was having twins. Twin boys for her twin mates. She smiled.

Dr. Keller changed the bandages on River's wounds, which were now clean and properly sutured. Though healing faster than a human would, the wound would still take time to mend completely.

Dr. Keller packed away her equipment. "You've healed somewhat since last night." She gave River a stern look. "But you need rest. Proper nutrition. And absolutely no more escaping through razor wire fences."

River smiled weakly. "I'll try to restrain myself."

Apollo sat beside her on the bed, his fingers intertwined with hers, while Ares paced near the window, his powerful frame silhouetted against the morning light. Both twins had refused to leave her through the night, taking turns holding her as she slept fitfully, plagued by nightmares of concrete walls and endless darkness.

A gentle knock at the door preceded Strider's entrance. "How are you feeling, kid?" he asked, his face creased with concern.

"Better." River squeezed Apollo's hand. "Much better."

Strider nodded, relief evident in his posture. "Can I get you anything? Cola, cookies?"

"No," Dr. Keller answered. "The girl needs meat, vegetables, fruit. You know, stuff that is going to feed her body, not just fill up her belly."

River smiled. "I'm okay, thanks. I'll let you know if I need anything."

Strider nodded, and Santiago entered.

"I'm sorry to bother you, but we have a situation developing."

Ares turned from the window, his golden eyes sharp. "What kind of situation?"

"The compound is surrounded," Theo reported. "Every Alpha and Beta in the region answered the call. They've formed a perimeter, no one in, no one out."

Apollo tensed. "And Titan?"

"No sign of him trying to escape yet," Santiago replied. "But there's movement inside. Looks like they're preparing for something."

Ares growled. "I should be there."

"No," River said firmly. "You should be here. With me."

Ares nodded. "Of course, Beloved."

"The Council is there," Santiago continued. "They're demanding to speak with both of you."

"They can wait," Apollo's thumb traced circles on River's palm.

Santiago shifted uncomfortably. "They're insisting. They say this is unprecedented, nearly every Alpha in North America gathered without Council authorization. They're threatening sanctions."

Ares snorted. "Sanctions against who? Us? What can they do? Nothing. Absolutely nothing."

"It's not just that," Santiago added. "There are rogues inside that compound. Dozens, maybe more. The Council wants to know what to do with them."

River's eyes widened. "They're not all bad."

Both twins looked at her questioningly, and she continued.

"The rogues. Some of them were just trying to survive. Titan and the others told me about how they were treated. They were hunted and driven off because they were perceived as competition to the Alphas. Or because they didn't like who the goddess had chosen as their fated mate," River's voice grew stronger as she spoke. "The ones who followed Titan, many of them were desperate. They believed his promises of a better life, of equality. They wanted a pack, a home, something to believe in."

Apollo's brow furrowed. "That doesn't excuse what they did. What he did to you."

"No," River agreed, wincing as she shifted position. "But if we slaughter them all, we're no better than the Alphas who judged them unfairly and without proof of them doing anything worth being exiled for."

Ares stalked back to the bed, his expression intense. "What are you suggesting?"

"Justice, not vengeance. The Council needs to hear what I learned. About the rogues, about the corruption in some of the packs." She took a breath. "They need to hear it from me."

"Absolutely not," Ares growled.

"Out of the question," Apollo said simultaneously.

River's eyes flashed golden. "I wasn't asking permission."

The twins exchanged a look of equal parts frustration, admiration, and resignation.

"River," Apollo began, "you can hardly sit up. You're pregnant with our children. You need rest and recovery, not a confrontation with the Council."

"And I'll rest," River assured him, "after I make sure those rogues get a fair hearing." Her hand moved to her stomach. "Our children deserve to be born into a world where justice matters more than bloodlines or vengeance."

Strider cleared his throat. "For what it's worth, I think she's right."

Ares glared at him. "Of course you'd say that. You're her father."

"Yes, I am," Strider agreed, unintimidated. "Which is why I know that stubborn look on her face. She's going with or without your blessing."

Dr. Keller, who'd been observing silently, stepped forward. "If, and I stress if, she goes, it must be brief. No more than an hour. She needs to be seated the entire time, with medical support nearby."

River smiled at the doctor. "Thank you."

"Don't thank me," Dr. Keller retorted. "I think it's a terrible idea. But I've worked with enough Alphas to know when I'm fighting a losing battle."

Another knock at the door preceded Cherry's entrance. She took in the tense atmosphere with a raised eyebrow. "What did I miss?"

"Mom." River seized the opportunity. "Tell them I need to speak to the Council."

Cherry nodded. "About the rogues?"

River nodded, surprised. "How did you know?"

"Because I raised you. And because I've heard your nightmares." She crossed the room to sit on the bed. "You've been talking in your sleep. About rogues, about justice, about things being not what we thought."

River squeezed her mother's hand. "There's so much the

Council doesn't know. Or has chosen to ignore. But this can't continue to be ignored."

Cherry nodded, then turned to the twins. "She needs to be there. Not just for the rogues, but for herself. For closure."

Ares ran a hand through his hair, his frustration evident. "And if it's too much? If she collapses? If Titan somehow-"

"Titan won't get near her," Cherry interrupted. "Not with every Alpha in North America standing between them."

Apollo studied River's face for a long moment, his golden eyes searching hers. Finally, he sighed. "One hour. You speak your piece, then we bring you straight back. And you stay in a wheelchair the entire time."

"Agreed," River said before he could add more conditions.

Ares growled, clearly unhappy but unwilling to argue further. "Fine. But we take every precaution. Full security detail. And at the first sign of trouble, we leave."

River nodded, relief washing over her. She hadn't been sure they would agree, and she'd been preparing for a much longer argument. "Thank you."

Dr. Keller shook her head disapprovingly. "I'll prepare something for pain and get a portable monitor ready. You'll wear it the entire time."

As the doctor left, Santiago pulled out his phone. "I'll let the Council know you're coming. And arrange transportation."

Cherry stood, determined. "I'll help you dress. Something that makes you look strong but doesn't put pressure on your wounds."

Left alone with her mates, River found herself the focus of twin golden gazes burning with protective intensity.

"Are you sure about this?" Apollo thumb tracing her palm.

River nodded. "I have to. Not just for the rogues, but for us." She looked between them. "I've seen the darkness in our world, and I can't unsee it. I can't pretend it doesn't exist. How can I be the High Luna and allow these things to continue?"

Ares moved to her other side, the mattress dipping under his weight as he sat. "We'll be right beside you. Every second."

River reached for his hand. "I'm counting on it."

The twins exchanged another look over her head, some unspoken communication passing between them.

"What?" River asked.

"We're just wondering," Apollo said. "Whether we are going to rule now or if you are."

"Don't get us wrong," said Ares. "I'd happily leave everything to you and just be your sexy arm candy from now on."

"Not me," said Apollo. "I'd be a stay-at-home dad."

Oh my goddess, were they serious?

Her wolf chuffed for the first time in weeks, making River chuckle.

"I don't want to rule. I don't want to be king, but if I am to be your queen, things have to change. Did you know Alphas were kicking out males they felt were competition?"

Apollo and Ares looked at each other.

"You did," she said. "How could you allow that to happen?"

"Beloved, we have a lot on our plates, small things here and there are not something we can get in the middle of. Do you know how much of our time would be consumed with that stuff?" said Ares.

River withdrew her hands from theirs and folded her arms. "If you want me to be your Luna, then you will make time. Several of those rogues were kicked out because the Alpha didn't like who they ended up with as a fated mate. They thought the males were not worthy enough, but that's not their call. It should never be their call. And a wolf shouldn't be banished to wander alone with no pack or family because of fate's decision. Or what about the female forced to mate the Alpha's son because he wanted her. He raped her. Over and over. And he did it all under the banner of the mating bond. She is forever damaged. They were at our mating ceremony."

"We didn't know about that," said Apollo.

"Of course not. Who would tell you? A rogue? Would you have even listened?"

"Probably not," said Ares.

"Exactly. The whole society has to evolve, or we will end up with another rogue like Titan organizing and murdering people out of revenge. We can't look away. We need a system to handle this stuff. It's our duty to take care of everyone. Not just those with money or power. I know you don't see shifters as equal to Lycans, but they deserve the same rights as everyone else."

Ares smiled.

"What?"

He wrapped an arm around her and kissed her head. "You said we. As in, all three of us. I like that."

"Of course. Unless you two don't want me anymore."

Apollo growled and pulled her into him. "Don't be ridiculous."

"Besides," Ares continued. "Until I found you, you're right, I didn't see shifters as equals, but now… I find nothing lacking."

He kissed her softly, and her wolf howled in happiness. Until his lips touched hers, she hadn't realized just how painful it had been being away from her mates. She'd been so focused on her babies and getting out and defying Titan at every turn that she'd not allowed herself to process the pain. The weight of missing Ares and Apollo. She'd missed them desperately, infinitely, but now awake and in their arms, the realization of what she and her babies had been through fully sank in.

River began to sob.

Apollo held her, mindful of her injuries, as her body shook with sobs. His hands stroked her hair, her back, offering comfort as the emotional dam broke. Ares moved closer, enveloping both of them in his powerful arms, creating a protective cocoon around her and Apollo.

"It's okay," Ares murmured against her temple. "Let it out. We've got you."

River clung to Apollo's shirt, her tears soaking the fabric as weeks of terror, pain, and uncertainty poured out of her. Then she turned, and Ares kissed her, and she gripped him tightly as Apollo stroked her hair. The twins held her through it, their bodies warm and solid around her, anchoring her to safety.

"I was so scared," she confessed between sobs. "Not just for me, but for our babies. Every day, I thought it might be my last chance to escape."

Ares growled, the sound both protective and pained. "I should have found you sooner. We should have-"

"No." River pulled back enough to look at both of them through tear-drenched eyes. "You did everything you could. I know you did."

Apollo swiped the tears from her cheeks with his thumbs. "We never stopped looking. Not for a single moment."

River's wolf whined as she took comfort in the protection of her mates.

"I knew you wouldn't." River's breathing began to steady. "That's what kept me going. Knowing you were searching for me."

Mine. My Alphas. My mates.

Yes. Ours. Home.

The twins laid River down on the bed and spooned her on both sides as she cried and processed and then cried some more. She shed tears of pain, of terror, of rage. She cried out all the tears she'd been shoving down for weeks. All the words she hadn't said. All the screams she'd not screamed. Everything. All of it. And when she finished, she let it all go.

Titan may have taken her. He may have held her against her will. He may have tried to force her to be his mate. But that didn't matter anymore. It was over, and she refused to let what he'd done to her ruin the rest of her life.

TWENTY MINUTES LATER, CHERRY APPEARED IN THE DOORWAY, A garment bag draped over her arm. She took in the scene before her.

"I can come back," she offered.

River shook her head, wiping at her face. "No." She took a steadying breath. "Let's get ready."

"The council can wait," said Ares.

"You don't have to do this now," Apollo intoned.

"The sooner we do this, the sooner we can move forward and be together as a family."

With gentle hands, Apollo and Ares helped River onto the side of the bed. Her legs dangled over the side, the bandaged thigh exposed underneath her cotton gown.

"This might hurt a bit," Cherry warned.

River snorted. "Pain seems to be my new state of being."

"Let's hope that ends after today," said Apollo.

Together, the three helped River dress in a flowing silver tunic that draped elegantly over her form, leaving her wounds untouched. The fabric shimmered subtly in the light, reminiscent of her wolf's coat. Paired with soft black leggings pulled over her bandaged leg, the outfit looked both regal and comfortable.

"Perfect," Cherry declared. "You look like the High Luna you are."

River's stomach growled at the same time her head spun, and she sat again.

"You shouldn't do this," said Apollo. "You need to wait."

"She can do it," Ares assured.

Apollo glared at Ares, but Ares squeezed his shoulder. "She's stronger than both of us."

Apollo looked like he might argue, but stopped. "Thirty minutes, no more. And we are picking up a double cheeseburger, fries, and a huge soda for her on the way."

"Actually," said River. "I think I'll stick to seltzer water for a while. But a double bacon cheeseburger with fries sounds amazing. If my body lets me keep it down."

"Whatever you want," said Apollo. "I'll have an entire palette of bubbly water here by the time we return."

"I want to go home," she said.

"We do too, Beloved," said Ares. "But until we have Titan in silver shackles, we need to keep you in hiding. The only people who know about this particular safe house are us, your parents, Zeke, Silas, and Theo; that's it. I won't put your safety at risk ever again.

River sighed, too tired to argue. "Is there at least a room with a bigger, more comfortable bed? A memory foam one?"

Apollo smiled. "We'll have that here by the time we are back as well."

She gave a tight smile as exhaustion began to weigh her down. "We should go."

Dr. Keller returned with a wheelchair and medical equipment. "The car is ready when you are," she announced, attaching a small monitor to River's wrist. "This tracks your heart rate, blood pressure, and oxygen levels. If any of them drop below acceptable parameters, we leave. No arguments."

River nodded as Ares lifted her from the bed and placed her in the chair. She clung to his neck a moment longer than necessary. Just having him and Apollo so close gave her strength, but at the same time, made her feel like she might burst into tears again. She let go and took a cleansing breath. She had to do this. She had to stick up for the rogues. After that, whatever happened, her conscience was clear.

CHAPTER THIRTY-FOUR

RIVER

The armored SUV wound through the roads, each curve bringing them closer to the secret meeting place. River sat between her mates in the backseat, their warmth enveloping her from both sides. Dr. Keller monitored her vitals from the front passenger seat while Theo drove, his eyes constantly checking the mirrors for any sign of pursuit.

Cherry reached forward from the third row to squeeze River's shoulder. "Remember, say what you need to say, then we'll bring you home."

"I know," River's voice came out stronger than she felt.

The SUV slowed as a beautiful stone church came into view.

"The Council's emergency meeting place," Apollo explained. "Used only in times of crisis."

Theo pulled the vehicle into an underground deserted parking lot, except for five other cars. A bodyguard stood by each vehicle, watching the SUV approach.

"Pull up to the door," said Dr. Keller.

"Are you ready?" Ares asked as the vehicle came to a stop.

River nodded, steeling herself. "As I'll ever be."

Apollo and Ares exited the vehicle. Ares retrieved the wheelchair as Apollo lifted her out of the back seat.

"You know my legs do still work," she said.

"Don't fight him," said Ares. "This may be one of the only times in his life you actually let us feel like we're the heroes."

River looked up at Apollo. "You are my heroes."

Apollo kissed her and smiled before setting her in the chair.

She grabbed Ares' hand and kissed his knuckles and then rubbed them on her cheek. "Both of you."

Ares kissed her head. "Good to know."

"What does that mean?" she asked.

"It means," said Strider. "That sometimes Whitetail women are so independent and strong-willed that it leaves us males feeling like they might not need us as much as we need them."

Cherry elbowed him. "That's not true."

Strider shrugged.

"Would you rather I were a damsel in distress who required you for everything? Oh, Strider, I can't open this jar. Oh, Strider, I can't lift this box. Oh, Strider, someone was mean to me. Go kick their ass for me."

"I don't know," he said. "I've never had those things said to me."

Cherry shook her head. "Males. Their egos are so fragile." She strode to the heavy wooden doors and turned back. "Oh, Strider, can you please open these huge doors? I can't manage with my puny little female arms."

River chuckled.

Strider walked to Cherry and said something so softly in her ear that River couldn't hear it, but it made Cherry smile and blush. Blush. What the heck? River didn't even know her mother could blush.

Strider opened the door with a grand flourish, and Cherry

shook her head as she strode through. Strider winked at River, and Apollo wheeled her in. She was beyond tempted to ask him what he'd said to her mom, but decided that she probably didn't want to know.

Dr. Keller walked beside River's wheelchair, while Apollo flanked them protectively with Zeke in the rear. The scents of old stone and candle wax filled the air, reminding River of her night at the cathedral with Ares. It felt like they'd done that years ago, rather than mere weeks ago.

The inner chamber of the church formed a perfect circle, with three ornate chairs positioned on a raised dais. Behind them, ancient Lycan symbols had been carved into the wall, as well as the history of their kind. River had never even known a place like that existed. But then, she assumed not many Lycans even knew of the place.

The three elders, Osmodius, Mercule, and Nathian, rose as River wheeled to the center of the room. Their usually impassive faces showed concern as they took in her weakened state.

"High Luna." Osmodius greeted her with a formal bow. "We are relieved beyond words to see you alive."

Mercule stepped forward. "Our dear High Luna, what ordeal you must have suffered. Are you well enough to be here?"

"I insisted," River said, her voice steady despite her exhaustion. "I thank you for your concern."

Nathian, the middle of the three, in his early fifties, studied her with piercing eyes. "What happened to you, Luna?"

Apollo's hand rested supportively on her shoulder.

"Titan kidnapped me, as you are aware. He believes himself to be the rightful heir to the throne. He kept me prisoner, hoping to force a mating bond." She paused, collecting herself. "But that's not why I'm here today."

The elders exchanged glances.

"With respect, Luna," Osmodius began, "your abduction and

the subsequent manhunt have thrown our society into chaos. Dozens of Alphas and Betas have abandoned their territories to join the search. Others have called for immediate action against the rogues, blaming them for your disappearance."

"That's precisely what we need to discuss," River said, her voice growing firmer. "The rogues are not to blame. They're victims. At least some of them."

"Victims?" Nathian's brow furrowed. "High Luna, with all due respect,"

"With all due respect," Ares cut in, his voice a low growl, "my mate was held captive for weeks, tortured, and nearly died. She has earned the right to speak without interruption."

An uncomfortable tension fell over the chamber. River reached up to touch Ares' hand.

"What I discovered during my captivity changes everything," she continued. "Many of the so-called rogues have been exiled, hunted, imprisoned, and even executed for generations because males in power didn't like them. They're our people, wolves who've been systematically oppressed and driven to desperation. Many of them for being fated to someone or having a bloodline their Alpha didn't like."

Mercule leaned forward. "These are serious claims, Luna."

River nodded. "They aren't claims, they are truth. Talk to them. Listen to their stories. Investigate. Titan has been running guns and drugs in and out of Canada, and he didn't act alone. He had support from high-ranking Alphas who've been exploiting rogues for years."

The elders exchanged troubled glances.

"The territory restrictions, the bloodlines, they're all designed to create a permanent underclass of wolves to be exploited."

"These are ancient laws," Osmodius chimed in. "Established to maintain order and purity, but-”

"They're antiquated laws," Cherry spoke up from behind River.

"And they've been that way for longer than any of us have been alive. I am sorry to say that I've both seen and been a part of these things at the direction of my Alpha. Don't get me wrong. My Alpha is a good man, but that doesn't mean he's always made the right decisions."

"What are you asking of us?" Nathian demanded, his composure slipping.

River straightened in her wheelchair, wincing as the movement pulled at her healing wounds. "I'm asking for fairness. For an immediate review of all laws. For a stay of execution for all rogues currently in Titan's compound pending individual case reviews."

"Impossible," Nathian declared. "Sweeping changes would destabilize our entire society."

"Our society is already destabilizing," Apollo countered. "The question is whether we rebuild it with justice or continue with the corruption that nearly cost the High Luna her life."

Nathian rose from his seat, his eyes flashing with indignation. "What you are suggesting would throw our entire society into chaos. The rogues have operated outside our laws for generations. They cannot simply be pardoned because of one man's actions. The course is clear. The Alphas must enter the compound, eliminate the threat, and restore order. Once the situation is contained, they return to their territories, and we can look into how to ensure this never happens again."

Apollo's golden eyes gleamed with quiet authority. "No."

The single word hung in the air, laden with royal command.

Nathian's face darkened. "You dare refuse the Council's directive? Even you, as royal Alpha, must respect our authority in matters of-"

"What are you?" River interrupted, her voice cutting through the tension.

The elders stared at her.

"I beg your pardon?" Osmodius asked.

"What are you?" River repeated. "Are you the king of the Lycans?"

"We are the Elder Council."

"That's right," River said. "You are a council, not a board of directors. Your purpose is to advise the kings, not dictate law."

Nathian's mouth fell open. "Young lady, for centuries we have-"

"First of all, I am not 'young lady'. I am the High Luna. Mate of Apollo and Ares Wolvenguard."

She let her golden gaze fall on Nathian. He stood a moment longer before looking away and backing into his seat.

"For years," River continued, "you have overstepped your authority. The laws are clear, the Council advises; the king decides. I understand that since King Jagger died, you have been pertinent. But we have a king again. Two, in fact, which is even better in my opinion." She reached for Ares' hand. "And my mates, the kings, have decided that there will be no massacre today."

"The High Luna speaks truth," Apollo said, his voice carrying through the chamber. "We appreciate your counsel, but the decision is ours. Each rogue will be evaluated individually. Those guilty of violent crimes will face justice. Those who were merely seeking shelter will be offered the opportunity to rejoin our society."

Ares stood beside his brother. "The compound remains surrounded. No one escapes, but no one dies without a trial either."

Nathian's face flushed with anger. "This is unprecedented-"

"Yes," River agreed. "It is. But so is everything about this situation. These are our people. All of them. Even those who've been cast out and forgotten. It's time we remember that."

"And if we disagree with this course of action?" Mercule asked.

"Then we respectfully acknowledge your disagreement," Apollo said. "While proceeding as we see fit. Perhaps, as we revisit the laws and everything that has happened, it would be prudent for us to decide if an Elder Council is still necessary. Or if it might be better to go a different direction moving forward."

The silence that followed was deafening.

"I agree with the High Luna," said Osmodius.

River tried to keep the shock from her face. She studied Osmodius and saw something in his eyes she couldn't place. A softness. Pain even. It made her wonder what he had been through with the twins' mom before she'd mated the Lycan king. And what he'd been through since.

"As soon as the compound and Titan have been taken, we will come together as a group to evaluate the rogues as individuals, not as a collective," said Ares.

Nathian opened his mouth, but Osmodius cut him off. "We will await your call, your Highnesses."

Dr. Kendall gripped River's wheelchair. "We should get you back to bed."

"Is she not healing well?" Osmodius asked.

"Our Luna is healing just fine," said Ares.

"However, with her carrying our young, we are being extra careful," Apollo finished.

"The High Luna is expecting?" asked Mercule. "That is most wonderful news."

"Twins," Apollo said.

"Twins," Osmodius breathed. For a moment, a wistful smile played on his face.

"And still you won't let justice be merited out to those who kidnapped not only our High Luna but also the heirs to the throne as well?" Nathian sneered. "What kind of-"

"If you care to keep your head, I suggest you don't finish that statement," Apollo growled.

"So you will threaten me for a remark but not do anything to those who killed and maimed guests at your mating ceremony?"

"Trust me," said River. "Everyone who deserves punishment will be. But what kind of rulers are we to be if we punish an entire group of people for the actions of a few?"

"You are quite right, High Luna," Mercule interjected. His soft brown eyes crinkled in the corners. "We must celebrate in honor of our new royal family as soon as this whole mess is dealt with."

"Thank you," said River. "It will be nice to have something happy to celebrate."

Nathian growled and threw himself back in his chair. River had no idea how he'd been appointed to the Council, but he didn't seem to have the temperament for it. Something, River decided, she would need to look into at a later date.

"Then we wish you a speedy recovery and are here when you need us. As always." Mercule inclined his head and smiled at the group.

"Is there anything we can do to help?" Osmodius asked.

"No," Ares said. "Thank you, Uncle."

Dr. Kendall turned River's wheelchair toward the exit, but River stopped her and turned back.

"Actually," said River. "There is something you can do for us."

Osmodius inclined his head and smiled. "I am at the High Luna's service."

CHAPTER THIRTY-FIVE

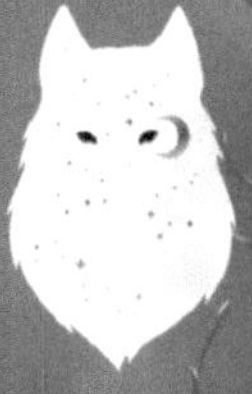

KANE

Kane stared out the front window of Titan's office, watching as yet another Alpha tested the compound's defenses. The electric fence sparked violently as claws scraped against it, illuminating the face of a wolf Kane recognized from the Southeastern territory. Behind him stood at least two dozen more, all waiting for the order.

"That's the third attempt in an hour," Vanessa observed, her voice unnaturally calm given their situation. "The security system won't hold much longer."

Kane nodded grimly. The compound had been designed to withstand attacks, but not from this many Alphas at once. Not from what appeared to be every major pack leader in North America. It had become apparent hours ago that the wolves could have overrun the compound any time they wanted, but they weren't. Which meant one thing- someone had told them they weren't allowed to attack… yet.

"How many are ready to leave?" Kane asked, turning from the

window.

"Twenty-three," Vanessa said. "Mostly the younger ones. Or the ones with someone they are looking after. The rest..." She gestured vaguely toward the main hall where nearly sixty rogues had gathered. "They want to fight."

"They'll die."

"They know that." Vanessa moved closer, her bright eyes studying his face. "But they believe in what Titan started. Or at least, what he promised."

Kane ran a hand over his face, and the dried blood from his earlier confrontation cracked at his touch. "So did I. Once."

A commotion from the hallway drew their attention. Two guards appeared, half-dragging a third between them. Blood soaked through the wounded man's shirt, spreading across his abdomen in a crimson stain.

"What happened?" Kane demanded.

"Alpha from the Western Pack," one of the guards explained, helping lower the injured man to a chair. "He found a weak spot in the fence. Joryn intercepted him, but..."

"But he's an Alpha, and I'm not," Joryn finished through gritted teeth, his face pale with pain. "He would have killed me if Ramirez hadn't pulled me back."

Kane cursed under his breath. It was starting already. The perimeter was failing, and soon the compound would be overrun with vengeful Alphas hunting for Titan and anyone who stood with him, whether the ones in charge told them to or not.

"We need to evacuate now," Vanessa urged. "While we still can."

Kane shook his head. "They've surrounded us. I don't even know how we'd get everyone out now."

Dammit. He shouldn't have waited for Titan. He should have started getting people out as soon as they found out River was gone.

His wolf growled. *No run. Fight.*

We fight, we die, idiot.

"The tunnels," said Vanessa.

"Won't get us far enough," Kane interrupted. "And they'll hunt down every last one of us as soon as they figure out we're gone."

Vanessa's perfectly composed façade cracked slightly, revealing fear. "Then what do we do?"

Kane stared at the wounded rogue, and the blood pooling under his chair, and at the faces of the guards who looked to him for leadership now that Titan was incapacitated. These weren't hardened criminals or bloodthirsty killers. They were outcasts. Wolves rejected by their packs. If they ran, they died. If they stayed, they died. There was only one choice left...

"We negotiate," Kane said, the words sounding strange on his tongue. He'd always been a fighter, not a diplomat.

Vanessa stared at him. "With who? The Alphas out there want our heads."

"Not with them," Kane replied. "With the kings."

"The kings?" Vanessa laughed. "They're the last people who would listen to us. We kidnapped their mate."

Kane shook his head. "Titan kidnapped their mate. And now Titan is unconscious, and I'm in charge." He paced the length of the office, his mind racing. "River is likely with them now. They'll be focused on her safety, not revenge."

"You're delusional," Vanessa said, but there was a hint of consideration in her voice. "They'll never agree to talk."

"They might," Kane insisted. "If we offer them what they want."

"And what's that?"

"Titan." The word hung in the air between them. "In exchange, we ask for amnesty for the others. The ones who weren't directly involved in River's kidnapping."

Vanessa's eyes widened slightly. "You'd betray him?"

"He betrayed us first when he abandoned our cause for his obsession with River. When he chose greed over equality."

"Even if I agreed," Vanessa said, "how would we contact them? It's not like we can walk up to the fence and ask to speak with the kings."

"You have connections. People who owe you favors. Call one."

Vanessa's perfectly sculpted eyebrows rose in surprise. "What makes you think I know someone?"

"Because you know everyone," Kane replied flatly. "It's what you do. Information is your currency."

For a moment, Vanessa looked like she might deny it, but then her shoulders slumped. "I might know someone. But Kane," her voice softened, "even if I can reach them, there's no guarantee they'll listen."

"We have to try," Kane insisted. "For them." He gestured toward the door, beyond which dozens of rogues waited, some preparing for war, others holding on with desperate hope. "We owe them that much."

Vanessa studied him for a long moment. "I don't owe them anything but..." She nodded. "Fine." Without another word, she pulled a slim phone from her pants. Not the one Kane had seen her with. A different one. She scrolled through contacts, her finger hovering over a name.

"Who are you calling?" Kane asked.

She pinched her brow and scrunched up her face. "Someone who owes me a favor."

She dialed a number and turned away, keeping her voice low as she spoke into the phone. The conversation was brief, mainly consisting of one-word responses from Vanessa and long pauses as she listened.

When she ended the call, she turned back to Kane, her expression unreadable. "They'll call back in five minutes. On this phone." She handed it to him. "It will be Ares."

Kane took the phone, feeling its weight in his palm like a ticking bomb. "And they agreed to this? Just like that?"

"I called in a significant favor." Vanessa avoided his gaze. "One I've been saving for an emergency. I'd say trying to remain alive qualifies."

THE FIVE MINUTES STRETCHED INTERMINABLY AS KANE PACED THE office. The sounds of conflict grew louder on the other side of the fence. Shouting, and something crashed against the perimeter fence. The crackle of electricity zapped through the air as another Alpha tested the perimeter.

When the phone finally rang, Kane answered it with steady hands despite the chaos in his mind.

"This is Kane."

"Give me one reason why I shouldn't tear your throat out personally," Ares Wolvenguard growled through the speaker.

"Because I want to end this without more bloodshed, your Majesty."

"You helped kidnap my mate," Ares snarled. "You helped keep her prisoner."

"I know," Kane acknowledged, keeping his voice level. "And I will face whatever consequences come from that. But there are innocent wolves here who had nothing to do with the abduction. They don't deserve to die for Titan's obsession. They've already been through enough."

"They sided against us. That's not innocent."

"They didn't side against you. They were looking for a pack. A home. We gave them that when no one else would."

Silence stretched for several seconds.

"Did you find her? The High Luna?" Kane asked, already knowing the answer but needing confirmation.

"Yes," Ares bit out, his voice still hard but fractionally less murderous.

"Is she okay?"

"She's safe. Not uninjured, but safe."

"Good," Kane said sincerely. "I'm glad. Please tell her that 'the asshole' says he's sorry I couldn't do more to help her."

Another pause, then Ares spoke again, his voice slightly less hostile. "What are you proposing?"

"We surrender Titan to you. He's unconscious and subdued. In exchange, I ask for amnesty for those not directly involved in the High Luna's kidnapping. An opportunity for them to plead their cases individually."

"And why would I agree to that?" Ares demanded. "I could wait until the compound's defenses fail and take everyone."

"Because it would mean less bloodshed on both sides. Your Alphas would win, eventually, but at what cost? And…"

"And?"

"Because I believe the High Luna wouldn't want that."

"What makes you think you know anything about my mate?"

Kane's wolf bristled and paced.

Kane had to tread lightly. "In the few small interactions I had with her, I could tell she is a good and generous Luna who cares for all the wolves. She met several of them, even one from her former pack. I believe she wants the rogues to have what we want for ourselves. To be treated fairly. Not like second-class citizens. We aren't asking to be treated better than everyone else, just the same as everyone else."

Another long pause. Kane heard muffled voices on the other end of the line. Ares spoke to someone. A low voice sounded through the phone, and then River's unmistakable lighter timber.

Strangely, Kane's chest squeezed at knowing she was okay. Until that moment, he'd seen River's kidnapping as a horrible mistake, but maybe, just maybe, some good would come out of it for the rogues after all.

"How do I know this isn't a trap?" Ares asked.

"You don't," Kane said. "But I'm out of options, and your

Alphas are breaching our perimeter as we speak. This is my last attempt to save lives on both sides. But you tell the High Luna the 'asshole' gives his word."

The phone crackled as Ares said something to the people in the room.

River chuckled, and her light voice rang through the line. "If Kane gives his word, he means it. Tell him, 'the Pampered Princess' gives her word as well."

Ares growled. "Here's what's going to happen. You will surrender Titan to us, bound in silver. You and the others who attacked will present yourselves for judgment. The rest will be evaluated individually, as the High Luna has requested." His voice hardened again. "But make no mistake, those directly responsible for harming my mate and killing Alphas, Betas, and mates at our ceremony, will face the harshest penalties our laws allow."

Kane closed his eyes briefly, relief and guilt washing through him. "Agreed."

"One hour," Ares said firmly. "I'll order the Alphas to stand down until then. If Titan isn't delivered by that time, we come in with full force."

"Understood."

"One more thing."

"Yes?"

"Vanessa is to surrender herself as well if she wants to live. If she tries to escape, she dies."

Kane looked at Vanessa.

The line went dead, and Kane lowered the phone.

"Well?" she asked.

"We have one hour." Kane moved toward the door. "Get Titan ready. Silver restraints, heavy sedation. I want him secured in the transport van. You stay with him and make sure it's done right."

Vanessa nodded, but hesitation flashed across her face. "Some of the others won't agree to this. They still believe in Titan and what he promised."

"Then they'll die for nothing," Kane said grimly. "Because Titan's promises died the moment he decided the High Luna was more important than our cause." He paused at the door. "Gather everyone in the main hall. I need to explain what's happening."

She nodded. "As soon as he's prepared, I'm going to find somewhere to hide until it's over, and then I'm out of here."

Kane nodded. "You do what's best for you. You always do."

Vanessa took her phone from him, spun on her heels, and marched out of the room.

Kane watched her go for a moment before sagging against what was left of Titan's desk, the weight of his decision pressing down on him like a physical force. Traitor. The word echoed in his mind, bitter and accusatory. After everything they'd been through together, he was handing Titan over to his enemies, like a cow to slaughter.

Memories flooded back unbidden. Titan, as a young wolf, fierce and proud despite the rejection from his father. The way his mom, Deleah, had extended a hand to Kane when no one else would, pulling him into their family. Teaching Titan to fight, to swim, to drive. Their days of planning together, strategizing, and dreaming of the future they'd build for everyone. All of it, gone. Over. Because of him.

"We're the same, you and I," Titan had told him one night. *"Abandoned by those who should have protected us. But we'll make our own family. Our own pack."*

Kane's wolf continued pacing. He couldn't tell if his wolf was irritated with him, with Titan, or with the Kings. Most likely, his wolf didn't want to die. Kane understood that. But if that's what it took to save the others, that's what he'd do. It was the least he could give them.

Kane shut his eyes. They had built something together. A refuge for the rejected, a home for those society had deemed unworthy. It hadn't always been about drugs and guns and revenge. Once, it had been about equality. But it had never been enough for Titan.

He remembered Deleah, Titan's mother, her elegance and kindness when she took Kane in. She had been a vision of grace, hosting dinners for other displaced wolves, creating a network of support for those with nowhere else to turn. But something had changed. The rejection by King Jagger, the humiliation of being cast aside for another woman, had eaten away at her like battery acid, corroding her once-gentle heart.

"They think they can discard us," she would say, her voice growing harder with each passing year. *"That we'll disappear into the shadows and accept our fate. But we will show them. We will take back what's ours."*

Kane had watched as her obsession with revenge consumed her, transforming her. And Titan, desperate for his mother's approval, had absorbed her bitterness, letting it shape and harden him.

"First, we build our numbers," Deleah had told them over dinner one night. *"Then, when the time is right, we strike."*

The drugs had started as a means to an end. Funding for their growing community of outcasts. The weapons came later, as Deleah's plans grew more militant. And through it all, Kane had stood by Titan's side, convincing himself they were still fighting for the right cause.

But Deleah's death had changed everything. Without her tempering influence, however twisted it had become, Titan's obsession had grown unchecked. The focus shifted from building a sanctuary for rogues to punishing those who had wronged him personally. And when River entered the picture, Titan's fixation had become all-consuming.

Kane had tried to reason with him, to remind him of their original purpose. But like his mother before him, Titan had become fixated on a single goal: taking River as his mate, proving his superiority over the twins who had everything he believed should have been his.

And now it had come to this.

Kane pushed to his feet, preparing to face the rogues who had trusted them. To tell them their leader had failed. The man who had promised protection had endangered them with his obsession.

The main hall buzzed as Kane entered. Everyone gathered, their faces drawn with fear and uncertainty. Some in small groups, whispering to one another. Others alone, weapons clutched in white-knuckled grips. All eyes turned to Kane.

"Brothers and sisters," he began. "Our situation has changed."

He explained the deal he made with Ares, watching as expressions shifted from disbelief to anger to resignation. Some nodded in understanding. Others shouted accusations of betrayal.

"You can't do this!" a young wolf named Marius yelled, pushing to the front of the crowd. "Titan took us in when no one else would. We can't just hand him over!"

"Titan is the reason we're surrounded by Alphas ready to slaughter us all," Kane replied. "His obsession with the High Luna put everyone here at risk."

"So we fight!" another voice called out. "We've been fighting our whole lives!"

Kane shook his head. "This isn't one we can win. And it's not worth dying."

An older wolf came forward, her gray-streaked hair pulled back in a severe bun. "What happens to us?" she asked, her voice steady despite the fear in her eyes. "If we surrender?"

"The kings have agreed to evaluate each case individually," Kane explained. "Those not involved in the High Luna's kidnapping will get to plead their case for amnesty."

"And you believe them?" Marius demanded. "After everything the Alphas have done to us?"

Kane met his gaze steadily. "I believe in the High Luna. And she has convinced her mates to give us this chance. She gave me her word. And I gave her mine." He looked around the room, meeting the eyes of wolves he had fought alongside, trained, and protected. "It's the only choice we have."

"It's true." Austin stepped forward. "I know River Whitetail. We grew up in the same pack, and I spoke to her when she was here. If she says we will be okay, then we will. The High Luna doesn't lie. It's not in her nature."

Outside, the sounds of the Alphas testing the perimeter had ceased. Ares had kept his word about the temporary stand-down. It was a start.

"What about you?" a voice called from the back. "What happens to you, Kane?"

He didn't hesitate. "I'll face whatever punishment comes. I was Titan's lieutenant. I helped build all of this." He gestured around them. "But I also didn't stop him when he took the High Luna and allowed Alphas and mates to die in the process."

"I'd rather die free than live at their mercy!" Marius shouted, pulling a gun from his waistband. Others followed suit, weapons appearing throughout the crowd. "After everything they've done to us, you want us to surrender?"

The room split almost instantly, those not wishing to fight backing toward Kane, while the more militant rogues clustered around Marius, their faces hardened with resolve.

"This isn't freedom, Marius," Kane argued, keeping his voice level despite the escalating tension. "It's suicide. The kings are offering us a chance-"

"A chance to be judged by the same Alphas who cast us out in the first place!" a female rogue named Lydia called out, her gun trained on Kane now. "You've gone soft, Kane. Titan would never agree to this."

"Titan has lost his damn mind," Kane countered, his patience wearing thin. "He's willing to sacrifice all of you for his revenge."

"Better to die fighting than on our knees begging." Marius' finger tightened on the trigger. "You're a coward, Kane."

An older woman, with a teen girl hugging her, stepped forward. "My daughter and I had nothing to do with the kidnapping. We came here for sanctuary, not war."

"Then go," Marius spat, gesturing toward the door with his gun. "All of you who want to surrender, get out. But Titan stays with us. We'll defend him to the death."

"That's exactly what will happen if you try," Kane warned, his voice hardening. "Death. For all of you. Is that what you want? To die for a man who was ready to sacrifice you for his obsession?"

"Get out!" Lydia shouted, firing a warning shot into the ceiling. Plaster rained down as screams erupted from the more peaceful faction. "Take the cowards and go!"

Austin moved forward, hands raised. "Put the gun down. This doesn't have to end in bloodshed."

"It was always going to end in bloodshed," she replied, her eyes wild. "From the moment they labeled us rogues, our fate was sealed."

Kane raised his arm and shoved Austin behind him, with nearly forty rogues huddled behind Kane.

Twenty or so stood with Marius and Lydia, guns drawn and faces set with grim resolve.

"You can't win this," Kane insisted, desperation creeping into his voice. "You're outnumbered, outgunned."

"We know. But we'll take as many with us as we can."

"This is insanity." Austin took a step forward. "You're throwing your lives away for nothing!"

Marius raised his gun higher, aiming directly at Austin's heart. "One more step and I'll put a bullet in you myself, traitor."

"Marius, please," a younger female wolf pleaded from behind Kane. "We don't have to die today. The kings promised-"

"Promises from Alphas mean nothing!" Marius roared. "How many times have they promised us justice? Protection? Rights? And how many times have they hunted us down like animals? Titan is the only one who kept his word to us."

Desperation shone in their eyes. The look of cornered animals who'd been pushed too far, for too long. They weren't fighting for Titan anymore; they were fighting against a lifetime of persecution.

"Take them and go," Lydia ordered, gesturing toward the huddled.

Kane looked over the group. Marius and Lydia, he could take easily, even with guns. But how many other bullets could he endure before going down?

He sighed. As much as he wanted to, he couldn't save them all. Just one more promise he'd broken.

A young female touched Kane's arm. "Please, Kane. Take us out of here."

Kane looked between the armed rogues and the frightened ones behind him. Time was running out. He had less than forty minutes to deliver Titan to the kings, or the temporary truce would end.

"Last chance," he said to Marius and Lydia. "Come with us. Live to fight another day, a better fight."

"Get out." Marius fired a shot that whizzed past Kane's ear.

Kane ducked instinctively and growled.

His wolf leapt to his feet, teeth bared. A shift ripple flowed over his skin, and his teeth lengthened.

Hurt. Teach pups a lesson.

Kane straightened. *No. Leave them to their fates.*

"Austin, get everyone to the gate."

As the larger group began moving toward the door, a shot rang out. Kane leapt in front of Austin. A bullet tore through Kane's shoulder, the impact spinning him halfway around. Blood bloomed across his shirt as he staggered, pain lancing through him.

Austin roared.

"Traitor!" Lydia screamed, her gun still raised.

Kane lobbed a knife straight at the toe of Lydia's boot. She backed up a step.

Kill. Kill them all.

"You may be okay being enemies with wolves on the other side of the gate, but trust me, you do not want to make an enemy of me right here." Kane removed his gun from the holster and pointed it at the floor. For the first time in over a decade, Kane did something he never did. He unleashed his inner wolf and leveled his Alpha gaze on the rebellious group.

The group gasped, and several stumbled backward. No one in the pack knew he was an Alpha. No one but Titan and Deleah.

"Go," Kane told Austin. "Go to the front gate and wait for me."

As they fled, Kane backed toward the door, his gun drawn but pointed at the floor.

"Feel free to tell your new Alpha masters what we think of their mercy," Marius spat.

Anger and fear radiated off the wolves standing with Marcus and Lydia, all of them driven to fight for a cause that had spiraled out of control. It was no longer just about loyalty; it was about survival.

Without another word, Kane headed to the open door, and the night air rushed up to meet him. Kane's wolf snarled at the scents of Alphas and Betas. He swallowed hard and forced himself not to shift.

"No aggression," Kane called to the others ahead of him. "We walk out slow, steady, and together. If things go wrong, return to the main house. I'll hold off as many as I can. But no matter what happens, don't give them a reason to hurt you. Your stories need to be heard. Every single one."

A nervous murmur sounded around the group. Kane headed down the front steps to the driveway below.

Please, goddess, don't let these wolves die.

CHAPTER THIRTY-SIX

RIVER

The room hummed with tension as Ares and Apollo prepared to leave. The moonlight filtered through the curtains, casting a soft, cool glow across River's new, larger bed. It did little to ease the chasm opening in her stomach.

"Please." River tried to keep the desperation from her voice. "Don't go."

Ares paused, his eyes filled with determination. "We have to, Beloved. Trust me, we want nothing more than to stay right here by your side. But if we don't go, there is no telling if the Alphas will let the rogues go. And you've made it quite clear you want us to hear what the rogues have to say."

"You think they'd betray you?"

"We don't know," said Apollo. "Desperate wolves do desperate things. Alphas even more so. They could do it to try and cover their asses and things they've done, or out of revenge for those killed."

"Should I go with you then?"

"No," they said together.

"We aren't taking any more chances with your life or the lives of our children."

River nodded.

Apollo knelt beside her, concern etched into his features. "We promise we'll do everything we can to ensure everyone's safety."

"But they have to stay contained until we figure this out," Ares added gently. "There's still a lot we don't know."

River's gaze darted between them, desperation welling inside. "Where will they be taken?"

"They'll be held in custody until we can talk to each one of them," said Ares.

Her heart sank at the thought of more imprisonment, even if it was for their good. "Promise I'll be there when you question them."

Apollo exchanged a look with Ares before nodding, though a mix of uncertainty clouded his golden eyes. "We promise."

"Even Kane?"

The brothers exchanged a look, and Apollo knelt by her. "Even Kane. And when this is over, we'll bring everyone together to build something better."

A flicker of hope ignited within River. A future where no one would live in fear of being cast aside or targeted.

She kissed each of her mates in turn.

"Please come back to me," she added. "As much as I hate to admit it… I don't like being here without you. I mean, I won't always be like this, I promise it's just-"

Ares stopped her with another kiss. "We understand. And we don't want to be anywhere but here with you either."

"Though I doubt that will ever end," added Apollo.

River chuckled.

Apollo kissed her once more, and then both of her mates placed a hand on her belly.

"We'll be back soon," Ares said, before they walked toward the exit.

As they walked into the hallway together, River couldn't help but feel a piece of herself leaving with them. A heartbeat apart yet worlds away.

She steadied herself until the sound of their footsteps faded and the front door shut behind them.

But even with the promise of safety and the knowledge that her mates were working to make things right, River couldn't shake the unease that settled over her like a shroud. A flutter of movement inside her made her heart skip.

"I know," she whispered to her unborn children. "I'm worried too."

River's wolf chuffed and yawned.

It had been a long few weeks for all of them.

Cherry appeared in the doorway, her sharp eyes taking in River's distress. "They'll be fine," she said, crossing the room. "Those two can handle themselves."

River leaned back against the pillows, exhaustion washing over her. "I keep thinking about Titan. About what made him this way."

Cherry's expression darkened. "Some wolves are born broken, River."

River shook her head. "I don't believe that. He was shaped by rejection, by a system that values power over character. The same system that created all the rogues. If we don't fix it, there will just be another Titan someday."

Cherry sighed. "You always did have more compassion than sense. That's probably my fault, just like the rest of this."

"What are you talking about?"

River's wolf lifted her head and cocked it to one side.

"This whole damn situation. It wouldn't have happened without me."

River rolled her eyes. "How do you figure?"

"I'm the one who hid the truth from you. I'm the one who sent you to New York. I'm the one who let you get taken. I'm-"

"Okay, Mom. Hold the phone. Don't give yourself so much credit. Yes, you kept the fact that I was an Omega from me, but that was it. There's nothing to say Titan wouldn't have shown up and bitten me even if you had told me. Or someone else, possibly. And if I remember correctly, I'm the one who wanted to go to art school in New York. Strider had to convince you to let me go. And as for everything since then? Even the Kings of the Lycans and a room full of Alphas couldn't stop that. I know that you think you're the baddest badass in the world, but if they couldn't stop it, I'm pretty sure you couldn't either."

"But-"

"But nothing. I don't blame you, Mom. I never have."

Cherry sniffed. "Yeah, well, let's wait and make sure those two blockheads come back safely before you say that. You might change your mind."

River sighed and shook her head. "Mom, I will never blame you. This isn't your fault. Any of it."

"Well... I do. That's what being a mom is. You'll learn that."

River touched her belly. She most likely would.

CHAPTER THIRTY-SEVEN

APOLLO

The convoy of SUVs slowed at the tall gates of Titan's compound. Apollo sat rigid in the passenger seat, his eyes fixed on the sprawling grounds that had held River prisoner for so long. The walls that had kept her in. The floors that she'd paced. The men who had held her hostage and not let her go.

His wolf snarled.

Beside him, Silas drove with practiced precision, and Duncan sat in the backseat with Regan. In the vehicle behind them, Ares rode with Theo and four other trusted bodyguards.

"Stop here," Apollo commanded as they reached the perimeter where dozens of Alphas and Betas gathered, their restless energy palpable through the tinted windows.

As Apollo exited the vehicle, Alpha Elkan from the midwestern territory strode forward, his massive frame vibrating with aggression.

"About time you arrived," he growled, not bothering with formalities. "We've been waiting for hours."

"We came at your call, but our patience wears thin." Alpha Elena, her sleek form moving fluidly through the gathered crowd. "

Ares joined his brother, his expression betraying nothing of the turmoil within, but Apollo could tell from his stiff movements that Ares barely held it together.

"The situation is delicate," Apollo said. "We appreciate your presence, but this will be handled our way."

Murmurs rippled through the gathered Alphas, some nodding in respect, others exchanging skeptical glances.

"And what way is that?" demanded Alpha Roman, his scarred face twisted in a sneer. "Negotiating with rogues who kidnapped your mate? They deserve death, all of them."

Ares' eyes flashed. "What they deserve is not for you to decide. And neither is how long you wait. You are not the kings; we are, and we decide what happens. If you don't like it, you are more than welcome to abdicate your positions and your packs now and walk away."

Tension crackled in the air as the twins moved toward the gate, their guards forming a protective formation around them. The Alphas parted, their displeasure evident, but their respect for the kings holding them in check. For the moment at least.

As they approached the iron gates, Apollo spotted a group of wolves gathered on the other side. About forty wolves, led by a powerfully built man with a bloodied shoulder, started toward the gate.

Apollo's wolf snarled. *Kill. Hurt mate. Kill them.*

"That's close enough," Apollo called. "Kane, I presume?"

Kane nodded, his face bruised and bloodied, but his posture straight as he faced them. "Yes, Your Majesty. We're here to surrender, as agreed."

Apollo's gaze swept over the rogues behind Kane. A ragtag collection of wolves, many looking more frightened than dangerous.

Women clutched younger wolves to their sides, while others supported comrades.

"And Titan?" Ares yelled, his voice hard.

"Sedated in a van in the garage." Kane gestured toward the main building. "Heavily restrained with silver, as you requested."

"Vanessa?" Apollo asked.

Kane's expression tightened. "She helped sedate Titan but disappeared in the commotion when the others refused to leave him."

Apollo's wolf growled. *Traitor bitch.*

"How many are still in there?" Ares asked.

"Maybe twenty."

"Who shot you?"

Kane looked at his shoulder and licked his lips. "Not one of your Alphas."

Apollo's jaw tightened. If the rogues inside were willing to shoot Kane, they were ready to die before surrendering. Promise or no promise to River, he couldn't save those who refused to be saved.

Kane gestured to the group behind him. "These are the refugees. Wolves cast out of their packs for various reasons. Some for challenging corrupt Alphas, others for being what their packs wanted them to be." He pointed to a young female holding the hand of a preteen boy. "Sarah was exiled when she refused to mate her Alpha's son. The boy is her cousin. Both his parents were killed during a pack run. No one would say how or why."

A low growl rumbled through several of the watching Alphas.

"This older woman, Belinda, was a healer, banished for treating rogues. Those three young males were kicked out for supporting a Beta who challenged their Alpha's decision to execute a packmate." His eyes hardened. "None of them participated in River's kidnapping. No one even learned she was here until after the fact."

Ares exchanged a glance with Apollo, both processing Kane's words against what River had told them.

"You mentioned others still inside," Apollo said.

Kane's expression tightened with regret. "They're heavily armed and determined to protect Titan. They believe death in battle is preferable to submitting to Alpha authority again."

"Led by whom?" Ares demanded.

"Marius and Lydia. Both were chased for years before Titan found them. They've... seen the worst of what Alphas can do."

Several of the gathered pack leaders bristled at the implied accusation, but Apollo raised a hand, silencing them before they could protest.

Ares huffed, his patience wearing thin. "Open the gates."

Kane nodded to one of the rogues behind him, who moved to the control panel beside the massive iron barrier. With a mechanical groan, the gates slid apart.

"Remember your promise," Kane said. "These wolves deserve a fair hearing."

"They'll get one," Apollo assured him. "But first, we secure Titan and deal with those still resisting inside."

As the gates opened fully, revealing the sprawling estate beyond, a deafening explosion rocked the compound. Glass shattered as windows blew out of the west wing, flames erupting from the upper floor. Screams and shouts erupted from both sides of the gate as debris rained down.

"What the hell?" Ares' eyes flashed.

Kane's face drained of color. "The armory. It's in the west wing."

"They're destroying everything," a rogue cried.

"Get them out of here!" Apollo commanded, gesturing to Duncan, Regan, and Silas. "Load them in the vans. Get them to the safe houses."

The guards moved with practiced efficiency, herding the surrendering rogues toward the waiting vehicles as another explosion rocked the compound, smaller this time but no less concerning.

"Keep them safe until they can be processed," Apollo added, his voice cutting through the chaos. "No one speaks to them except the High Luna and us."

As the rogues loaded into the vans, Apollo turned to Ares. "This is about to spiral out of control."

Ares' eyes remained fixed on the burning building, his face hard as granite. "We can't let Titan escape. If he gets away-"

"I know," Apollo cut him off. "But those rogues inside are armed and desperate."

"They chose their fate when they decided to side with him," Ares growled.

Before Apollo could respond, Alpha Elkan pushed forward, his face contorted with contained rage. "Enough discussion. We came here for justice!"

Ares roared before staring down Elkan.

"Justice?" Apollo challenged. "Or vengeance?"

"Is there a difference?" Alpha Elena joined Elkan, her features tight. "These rogues took our packmates, slaughtered Alphas and Lunas. They kidnapped your mate. They deserve no mercy."

Other Alphas murmured their agreement, moving closer, their wolves pushing at the surface as the scent of blood and fire filled the air.

"You are not king here, Elena," Ares shouted. "You will do as we say, or you challenge us right now for the throne."

Elena looked at Ares for a split second before inclining her head and stepping back.

"The same goes for all of you," Apollo snarled. "You need to remember you do not rule; we do. And from now on, we'll make sure you remember that. Every last one of you. If any of you have a problem with us, we will deal with it swiftly and with finality."

"My Beta died at their hands," Alpha Ronan sneered. "His heart ripped out while he begged for his life. I will not leave until I've seen justice done."

Apollo surveyed the gathered Alphas and Betas, recognizing the dangerous edge to their restlessness. If he denied them, he risked losing their loyalty, perhaps permanently. Some had traveled over a thousand miles at his call, abandoning their territories and responsibilities. All expected blood.

"Very well," Apollo conceded. "You want blood? Then you'll have blood."

Ares looked to Apollo, and he thought Ares might argue. Instead, he nodded.

"Remember," said Ares. "Any rogue who surrenders is to be taken alive. Any unnecessary deaths will be answered for with a life."

"This is your only time," Apollo added. "No matter what happens, after tonight, it's over. This ends here."

The group organized into strike teams.

Apollo turned back to Kane. "Where is Titan?"

"Underground garage," Kane replied, his voice tight. "Northeast corner of the main building. Black van with tinted windows."

"Show us," Ares demanded.

Kane hesitated, looking at the burning compound.

"Go with the others," Ares commanded Zeke and Theo. "Secure the building, look for Vanessa. Don't let her get away."

The guards obeyed as the first wave of Alphas shifted. Their massive wolf forms charged through the gates with thunderous snarls. Betas followed suit, fanning out across the grounds as more explosions shook the compound.

"We need to move," Apollo said, already striding forward.

Kane led the way through the chaos. Gunfire erupted, followed by howls of pain. The scent of blood thickened in the air as wolves clashed with the armed rogues barricaded inside.

"This way," Kane directed them toward a side entrance as flames engulfed more of the main building. "The garage can be accessed through here."

They moved swiftly through a corridor lined with opulent furnishings, a testament to Titan's wealth. Every turn mimicked their estate. Paintings adorned walls, their frames gleaming with gold leaf, even as smoke filled the hallways.

They turned into the kitchen, and Ares growled. "How much further?"

"Just ahead." Kane punched a code into a keypad beside an unmarked door that, in their estate, led to the pantry.

The heavy barrier slid open, revealing a concrete stairwell leading down. The sounds of struggle echoed from below, metal striking metal, enraged shouts, the distinctive clang of chains.

"He's awake," Kane warned, his face grim as they descended the stairs. "The sedative must have worn off."

The vast underground garage had high ceilings supported by concrete pillars. In the center, surrounded by overturned equipment and scattered tools, stood a black armored van. Its rear doors hung open, revealing a glimpse of the chaos within. Thrashing limbs, flashing golden eyes, the gleam of silver restraints

"TRAITOR!" Titan's voice boomed through the cavernous space. "I'LL TEAR YOUR THROAT OUT!"

Kane's face hardened as they neared the van. Inside, Titan strained against the silver chains wrapped around his massive frame. Blood seeped from where the metal touched his skin, but his rage seemed to override the pain. Four wolves struggled to hold him down, their faces contorted with effort.

"Your Majesties." One of the rogues gasped, relief washing over his features as he spotted the twins. "He woke suddenly and broke through the first set of restraints-"

Kill. Touched. River. Our Young. Killed Bennett. The roar that emanated from Apollo's wolf almost knocked him over.

Rage took over him in an instant, and he wanted the same thing his wolf did: to kill Titan.

With predatory grace, he lunged forward, seizing Titan by his throat, his claws ripping into Titan's flesh, and dragged him from the van. Titan slammed to the ground with an oof. The silver chains scraped across the concrete as Apollo flung Titan against the nearest pillar, the impact cracking the solid stone behind him.

"You took her," Apollo snarled. His fist connected with Titan's jaw with a crack, blood spraying across the concrete. "You kept her prisoner." Another punch, this one shattering Titan's cheekbone.

Apollo let his rage consume him. Each accusation punctuated by another devastating blow, his control slipping with every impact.

"You murdered my best friend." His wolf tore into Titan, wanting to break Titan apart, bone by bone.

Titan laughed through bloodied teeth, his face already swelling. "She should have been mine," he spat, blood bubbling from his lips. "My father's throne. My Luna."

Apollo roared, a sound so primal it sent the rogues backing away. His next blow crushed Titan's nose, driving bone fragments deeper into his face. "She was never yours to take!"

Apollo punched Titan's gut once, twice, three times until he heard the crack of ribs. Then he punched Titan in the kidneys. Every blow released the pain Apollo held inside.

Titan groaned and gasped for air as Apollo continued to punch him. Over and over and over until he couldn't see or think of anything but blood, vengeance, and death.

"Enough." Ares' calm voice cut through the haze of Apollo's rage, his hand closing around his twin's wrist.

Apollo turned toward Ares, his wolf pushing dangerously toward the surface. "He deserves to die."

"Yes," Ares agreed, his face tight with fury. "But not like this. Not by your hand alone."

Titan wheezed out another laugh, blood dripping from his ruined face onto the silver chains binding him. "The monster twin," he mocked, his voice strained. "Holding back the civilized one? That's irony at its best."

Ares' eyes flashed as he turned to Titan. "Make no mistake. I want nothing more than to tear out your tongue myself. But we are kings. And kings dispense justice, not vengeance. That is what this whole thing is about, right? Why you want the throne? What you told everyone being slaughtered upstairs? This is all for justice. But we aren't like you, Titan. We won't do whatever it takes to win."

Apollo's chest heaved with each ragged breath, his knuckles torn and bloodied from the beating he'd delivered. For a moment, he fought against his wolf, who wanted to tear away from Ares and finish what he'd started.

"Think of River, she deserves justice as well," Ares said. "Think of our children. What do they deserve?"

The mention of River reached Apollo's wolf, where nothing else could. Ares was right. This vengeance wasn't his alone to dole out. River deserved her moment as well.

"Children?" Titan's voice came out small.

Ares turned to him. "Yes. River is having our children. Twins."

"It's not possible. She only escaped a few days ago."

"She was pregnant when you took her," Apollo growled.

"No," he whispered. "You're lying."

"Why would we lie? We have no reason."

"She's mine!"

"Actually," said Apollo. "She's not. We finished the ceremony with the Council as witnesses earlier today."

Apollo and Ares raised their left hands, displaying the matching gold bands to Titan.

Titan roared in rage.

"Chain him tighter," Apollo commanded, stepping back from Titan's broken form. "Gag him if necessary."

As the rogues rushed to comply, Kane approached cautiously. "What will happen to him now?"

"He'll face trial," Ares replied, his voice hard as iron. "Before the Council and every Alpha whose pack he's harmed."

"And the others?" Kane asked, glancing toward the door.

"We'll keep our word," said Ares. "They won't be harmed unless they force our hand."

Kane nodded.

The acrid odor of burning skin scorched Ares' nose as several more pairs of silver shackles wrapped Titan's arms and legs.

Titan barely noticed the extra shackles. His eyes stayed on the floor. When he finally lifted his eyes, he looked straight at Kane.

"What did they offer you? What do you get out of betraying me to my enemies? A place at their side?"

Kane looked to Titan, his eyes sad. "Nothing. Like you, I'll take whatever punishment they dole out. That's how we wanted it, right? Fair justice for everyone."

Titan stared at Kane emotionless. "Then I guess we'll die together."

Kane nodded. "As it should be."

ARES

They hauled Titan to his feet, and Apollo turned to Ares. "Let's go before this whole place collapses."

Ares nodded and then looked at Kane. He motioned to the rogues. "Shackle him as well."

The rogues paused, looking at Kane.

Kane held out his hands, offering up no resistance. "Do it."

Ares' wolf gnashed his teeth.

No fair. Kill Titan. Touched River. Hurt pups.

I know. But we must let River decide. It won't be fair to her if we just kill him. She deserves justice. Closure.

Death. Kill him. Break bones. Rip throat.

Ares sighed. He needed his wolf to stop before he lost all sense of reason and let his wolf have what he wanted. He took the steps three at a time, reached the kitchen, and strode through it. He coughed several times and covered his nose with his sleeve.

The fires had been put out, but the air remained thick with smoke and the scent of burning hair and flesh. The main floor revealed itself as they emerged from the kitchen into the hall. Kane faltered at the threshold.

The once opulent entryway had become unrecognizable. Blood slicked the marble floors, the pristine white walls now painted crimson in sprawling, chaotic patterns. Bodies lay where they'd fallen. Alphas, Betas, and rogues alike. Their limbs contorted from the final moments of desperate struggle.

"Goddess," Kane whispered, his voice hollow as he took in the carnage.

A young female rogue crumpled against the wall, her blonde hair matted with blood, eyes fixed in a permanent stare. Beside her, an Alpha from a northeastern pack, his throat torn out, fingers sizzling and still clutching a silver dagger embedded in his heart.

The Alphas wanted vengeance, and they'd gotten it. One way or another.

Kane moved forward. He knelt briefly beside a fallen rogue. A boy, merely a teen, his ribcage ripped open and his heart on the floor next to him.

"His name was Licah," Kane said. "Seventeen. Exiled because his Alpha feared he would challenge for leadership someday." He rose, continuing through the battlefield of broken bodies.

He walked to the female with blonde hair. "This is Lydia. She was one tough wolf. She ran from her pack after they killed her mate. She never would say why." Kane closed her eyelids.

Ares scanned the room, his wolf pacing, unsure what to think or feel.

The destruction was absolute. Shattered chandeliers, splintered furniture, walls pocked with bullet holes and claw marks. In the formal dining room, three more bodies. Rogues who had made their last stand among overturned tables and broken China.

"I never wanted this." Kane's voice cracked despite his efforts to maintain composure. "None of this was supposed to happen. We were building a sanctuary, not... this."

He paused beside an older fallen wolf with silver-streaked hair. "This was Yaser. He treated everyone as equals, regardless of their status or pack affiliation. Titan found him living in the woods after his Alpha cast him out for giving rogues shelter and food." Kane's fists clenched at his sides. "He never hurt anyone."

Apollo's expression remained impassive, though his eyes cataloged every detail, every fallen wolf. Ares walked ahead.

"All of this," Kane continued, gesturing around them, "because of bloodlines, and territory, and power. Because some wolves are considered worthy of protection while others are disposable." His voice hardened. "Tell me how this is justice."

He turned and pointed at Titan. "And you. This is your fault. You promised them a better world, and they sacrificed their lives for it. They didn't even care that you'd given up on them in the end. That you only cared about yourself. They tried to protect you anyway."

"Fuck you," said Titan. "And fuck all of them as well."

Ares slammed his fist into Titan's jaw. "Do you have no respect for anyone?"

Titan spat on the floor and looked up through one barely open eye. "Fuck you, too."

Ares' wolf roared to life, wanting to rip Titan's head off. But Ares refused. To kill him would be selfish. He hadn't let Apollo kill him, and he couldn't either.

As they approached the main doors, the sounds of struggle reached them from outside. Ares pushed open the massive doors, stepping out into the darkness to find five rogues forced to their knees on the driveway.

Elkan and Elena stood over the kneeling rogues, their eyes burning with a primal hunger for retribution. Blood dripped from the prisoners' faces, their bodies bearing the marks of a brutal capture. One young male trembled as Alpha Ronan pressed a blade against his collarbone.

"We found these," Elena announced, her voice sharp with satisfaction. "Trying to escape through a service tunnel."

Ares moved forward with regal authority, his gaze sweeping over the captured rogues. "Bind them. They'll be transported with the others."

"Bind?" Ronan snarled, pressing the blade harder against the young rogue's skin. "These vermin deserve to die where they kneel. This one personally participated in an attack on my territory."

Alpha Elkan nodded in agreement, his massive hand fisting in another rogue's hair, yanking his head back to expose his throat. "This one killed three, including my Beta. Their blood demands justice."

"And they will face it." Apollo stepped forward to stand beside his brother. "But not here. Not like this."

"With respect, your Majesties," Elena countered. "These rogues have slaughtered our people. A quick death is more mercy than they showed their victims."

Ares' voice dropped to a deadly rumble. "I said bind them."

The command vibrated with Alpha authority, causing the surrounding wolves and Alphas to lower their eyes. Ronan held his ground, the blade still against his captive's throat.

"Your mate is safe now," he argued, desperation edging his voice. "You have Titan. Let us have our vengeance on these nobodies."

"This is not a request," Ares growled. "It is a royal command.

Any wolf who defies it will follow the wolf they kill straight to the grave."

Tension crackled as Ronan's eyes darted between the twins, weighing his options. With a snarl of frustration, he withdrew the blade and stepped back.

"Bind them," Apollo ordered the rogues who had followed them from the garage. "And ensure they reach the holding facility alive and unharmed."

Kane looked on, silently. The young rogue Ronan had threatened held silent gratitude in his eyes.

"This isn't over," Elkan warned, his voice low as he reluctantly released his grip on his captive. "These rogues will answer for their crimes."

"Yes, they will," Apollo agreed, his tone leaving no room for argument. "But they will answer to us and the law. Not you."

"Go home," said Ares. "We will see justice done."

"So we just walk away?" asked Elkan. "Pretend all of this never happened?"

"No," said Apollo. "You wait until you are called to testify."

"About what they did?"

"About what you did."

The Alphas and Betas looked at each other.

"You want justice? So do we. For everyone," Apollo finished.

Several of the Alphas looked unsure as they backed away.

Screams and pleading rang out behind them, and everyone turned. Theo and Zeke held a woman between them, crying and struggling to get free.

They dragged her down the steps and threw her at Ares' feet.

She crawled to him on her knees, head down. "Ares, please..."

Apollo yanked her to her feet.

Makeup melted down her face as she tried to grab onto him. "Apollo, please. Don't hurt me. Please... I... I..."

Apollo smiled at her. "I'm not going to hurt you. Your fate, like that of Titan and Kane, will be left to our mate, High Luna, River Wolvenguard."

CHAPTER THIRTY-EIGHT

RIVER

The sound of the front door opening woke River from her fitful sleep. She blinked groggily, disoriented by the unfamiliar surroundings. Her body still ached, the wound on her thigh throbbing beneath its bandages as she pushed herself up against the pillows.

Voices murmured in the hallway. Cherry's sharp tone, followed by the deeper rumble of her mates. River's heart quickened as footsteps neared her door, her wolf stirring anxiously.

When the door swung inward, Ares entered first, his bulky frame filling the doorway, followed closely by Apollo. River's breath caught at the sight of them. Apollo's crisp white shirt had soaked dark crimson, and droplets of blood marred his face, neck, and hands. His golden eyes appeared haunted and distant.

"Apollo!" River gasped, throwing back the covers and struggling to her feet despite Dr. Keller's strict instructions to stay in bed. She stumbled forward. "You're hurt!"

Apollo moved swiftly across the room, catching her before she fell. "I'm fine, Ktten," he assured her, his voice gentle as he guided her back to the bed. "It's not my blood."

River's trembling hands reached for his face, her fingers tracing his features to confirm for herself he was unharmed. "Whose then?" she whispered, searching his eyes. "What happened?"

Ares sat on her other side. "It's over, Beloved," he said, his voice rough with exhaustion. "We got him."

River's chest squeezed, and bile scorched her throat.

"Titan?" River asked. "You got him?"

Apollo nodded, his jaw tightening. "He's in a cell. Silver restraints, heavily guarded."

River sank against the pillows, relief washing through her in dizzying waves. For a moment, none of them spoke, the weight of everything that had happened, everything they had endured, settling around them like a heavy cloak.

"And the others?" River asked, remembering the rogues. "Kane? The ones who surrendered?"

"Also in custody." Ares took her hand in his. "No one who surrendered was harmed."

River nodded, gratitude swelling in her breast. "And those who didn't surrender?"

Apollo and Ares exchanged a glance that answered for them.

River closed her eyes, sorrow mingling with her relief. So much loss, so much pain, all because of a system which had failed too many for too long.

"What happens now?" She opened her eyes to look between her mates.

"That's up to you," said Apollo.

River blinked, confused by Apollo's words. "What do you mean?"

"The rogues." Ares' thumb traced circles on her palm. "Their fate. The Council has agreed to follow your recommendation, given everything you've witnessed."

"My recommendation?" River echoed, the weight of such responsibility settling on her already exhausted shoulders. The thought of deciding the fate of dozens of lives, lives shaped by circumstances beyond their control, made her head swim.

Apollo nodded. "Whatever you believe is just. The Council will honor."

River looked between her mates, seeing the trust in their eyes, but also the expectation. They, too, waited for her to make a decision that would reshape their society and set a precedent that would echo through generations.

Fatigue clouded her thoughts. The twins' blood-spattered appearance, the knowledge of what had happened at the compound, and the memory of her ordeal all swirled together in an overwhelming tide that threatened to drag her under.

"I can't," she whispered, her voice breaking. "Not now. I just... I want to go home. Our home."

She looked at them pleadingly, suddenly desperate to be surrounded by familiar walls, to sleep in her bed, to feel truly safe for the first time in weeks.

"Please," she added. "I'm too tired to think about any of this right now."

Understanding softened Ares' expression. Without a word, he rose and gathered her carefully into his arms, cradling her against him as if she were made of glass.

"Home it is," he murmured.

Apollo moved ahead of them, opening doors and issuing quiet orders as Ares carried River through the safe house. The weight of decision-making lifted temporarily, River allowed herself to sink into the comfort of her mate's embrace, her head resting against his skin.

Outside, the Northern lights painted the sky in deepening shades of pinks, greens, and blues. A convoy of vehicles waited, engines idling. Cherry appeared at the door.

"I'll go first," she said, squeezing River's hand as Ares passed. "Just to make sure everything's secure at the estate."

River nodded as Ares lowered her gently into the backseat of the lead SUV. Apollo slid in beside her, and she curled against him, seeking his warmth. He held her in a stiff embrace, and her wolf whined. Something had happened. Something Apollo wasn't ready to tell her about. But in time, he would. And she would give him time and space until he reached that point, just as he and Ares had done for her.

As the convoy pulled away from the house, River watched the building recede through the rear window. For days, it had been her sanctuary, but now it felt like just another prison she was leaving behind.

"Thank you," she whispered to both her mates. "For understanding."

Apollo pressed his lips to her temple. "You've been through enough. Everyone else can wait until you're ready."

The vehicle's headlights cut through the gathering darkness. River nestled between her mates. Ares shifted her gently until she cradled in his lap, her head resting against his broad abs. Apollo took her hand, his thumb rubbing across her knuckles.

A deep, resonant rumble began to vibrate through Ares, comforting her to the core. Apollo joined, his own purr harmonizing with his twin's, creating a cocoon of sound that wrapped around her like the safest of blankets.

River's eyelids grew heavy as the rhythmic vibration and gentle motion of the vehicle lulled her toward sleep. Her wolf fully relaxed for the first time in weeks. The babies within her seemed to settle too, as if also soothed by their fathers' presence.

"Rest, Kitten," Apollo murmured, his fingers now tracing gentle patterns along her spine. "We'll be home soon."

The purring deepened, and River surrendered to exhaustion.

River woke to the sensation of movement, her body weightless in Ares' arms as he carried her up the grand staircase of their estate. Blinking drowsily, she recognized the familiar surroundings. The ornate woodwork, the family portraits lining the halls, and the subtle scent of smoke, leather, and warm wood that permeated their home.

"We're home," she murmured.

"Yes, Beloved," Ares confirmed, his golden eyes warm as they met hers. "We're home."

Apollo moved ahead of them, opening the double doors to River's suite. The room welcomed her with its familiar comfort, her bed with its mountain of pillows, the door with new hardware, and the window Apollo had crawled through to feed her.

With infinite care, Ares laid her on the bed. Together, the twins tucked the plush comforter around her, creating a warm and secure nest.

"There." Apollo brushed a strand of silver hair from her face. "You can rest properly now."

The twins straightened, preparing to leave. Panic fluttered, unexpected and overwhelming. "Don't go," she pleaded, reaching for them.

"We need to clean up," Apollo explained. "We won't be long."

"Just a quick shower," Ares promised, leaning down to press his lips to hers.

Ares' eyes glinted mischievously as a smirk tugged at his lips. "Or you could join me," he suggested, his voice dropping to that husky register that made her heart race. "I could wash your back... among other things."

"For the love of-" Apollo rolled his eyes, grabbing his brother's shoulder and steering him toward the door. "This is absolutely not the time to be thinking with your downstairs brain."

Ares looked back at River with exaggerated innocence. "What? I'm just being helpful."

"You're being impossible," Apollo countered, continuing to push him into the hallway. "She needs rest, not your particular brand of 'help.'"

"When it comes to River, I can't help myself," Ares protested, allowing himself to be maneuvered through the doorway but throwing her a wink over his shoulder. "It's a medical condition."

"It's called being horny, and our health plan does not cover it," Apollo retorted, his stern expression betrayed by the amusement dancing in his eyes. "Now move. The faster we clean up, the faster we come back to her."

"Fine," Ares conceded as Apollo pushed him fully into the hall. "But for the record, my idea was much more fun."

"Your ideas of fun usually end with broken furniture," Apollo shot back, shaking his head as he closed the door behind them.

River laughed, soft and genuine, bubbled up from somewhere deep inside her, a sensation so foreign after weeks of fear that it felt almost strange. The sound of her mates' bickering faded down the hallway, leaving her wrapped in the cocoon of her massive bed, surrounded by their scents.

For the first time since her ordeal began, genuine happiness warmed her. She was home. She was safe. Her mates were with her, their playful banter a balm to her. They would return soon and hold her through the night, their bodies forming a fortress of warmth and protection around her.

Her eyelids grew heavy again, but this time, sleep beckoned without the accompanying dread that had plagued her for so long. Her hand drifted to her belly, resting over the tiny lives growing within her.

"We're home," she whispered to her unborn children as her eyes closed. "We're finally home."

Sleep claimed her quickly, her body surrendering to exhaustion without resistance. Her last conscious thought was of Apollo and Ares, and how, despite everything they had endured, certain things, like Ares' incorrigible flirtation and Apollo's exasperated affection, remained unchanged.

APOLLO

APOLLO MET ARES IN THE HALLWAY OUTSIDE RIVER'S ROOM. BEFORE Ares reached for the door handle, Apollo grabbed his arm.

Ares looked at him. "What? You know I was just kidding, right? I wasn't serious about showering with River. I know she's still healing."

"It's not that."

Ares studied him for a moment. "What's wrong?"

Thoughts and feelings rushed to the surface, and Apollo wasn't quite sure how to voice them. "I... I wanted to thank you for stopping me from..."

Ares patted his brother's hand. "You would have done the same."

Apollo shook his head. "If it had been you who had attacked Titan, I wouldn't have stopped you. I would have helped."

The brothers' shared moment evaporated with River's bloodcurdling scream.

The brothers shoved the doors open.

River sat rigid upright. Her silver hair clung to her sweat-drenched face as she thrashed against invisible restraints, eyes wide but unseeing.

"No! Please! Don't-" Her desperate pleas echoed through the darkened bedroom as she fought against shadows only she saw.

"River!" Apollo reached for her with gentle hands. "Kitten, you're safe. You're home."

Ares' muscular frame curved protectively around her. "Beloved, we're here. It's just a nightmare."

River's scream dissolved into ragged gasps as reality penetrated her fog of terror. Her eyes darted around the room, searching for threats. Her body trembled as she struggled to separate nightmare from reality.

"He was here," she whispered, her voice breaking. "Titan was here. He found me. He said the babies weren't yours... that he'd make sure they were his."

"Shhhh," Apollo drew her against him. "He's not here. He's locked away in silver chains where he can never reach you again."

Apollo's wolf whined, wanting to comfort her.

Ares pressed in against her back, creating a protective wall around her trembling form. "Feel us, River. We're real. The nightmare isn't."

"Breathe with me," Apollo instructed, taking exaggerated, slow breaths for her to follow. "In through your nose, out through your mouth."

River struggled to match his rhythm.

Ares' wide hand splayed across her abdomen. "That's it," he encouraged as her breathing steadied. "You're safe, Beloved. We've got you."

The terror gradually receded. Tears welled in River's eyes, spilling over to track down her cheeks.

"I hate this," River whispered, her voice growing stronger with frustration as she swiped angrily at her tears. "Being so weak. So scared. Jumping at shadows and waking up screaming like some helpless victim." She slammed her fist against the mattress. "It pisses me off. This isn't me."

His wolf chuffed.

Apollo's body rumbled with a chuckle as he stroked her hair. "It's perfectly natural. Your body and mind are still processing trauma. But I understand."

"He's right," Ares added. "Even the strongest wolves would need time to heal after what you've been through. And you're one of the strongest I know."

River twisted to look between them. "I don't want to be like this. I want to be myself again, strong, capable. Not jumping at every noise or waking up screaming."

"You will be," Apollo assured her, pressing his lips to her forehead. "Give yourself time."

Ares' golden eyes studied her face. "Do you want to talk about it? The nightmares? What happened while you were there?"

River stiffened and clenched her jaw. "If I tell you what happened, if I speak about it out loud..." She paused, her eyes darkening. "I swear I'll go straight to wherever you're keeping Titan and slit his throat myself."

Ares' eyebrows rose, a hint of approval flickering across his features before he schooled his expression. Apollo squeezed her hand.

"I understand that feeling better than you know," Apollo said. "When we found you... When I saw what he'd done to you... It took everything Ares had to keep me from tearing Titan apart piece by piece."

River's eyes suddenly widened. "My knives," she blurted out, glancing around the room. "Where are they? My blades from my mom."

The twins exchanged a quick look over her head. Neither fancied being accidentally stabbed in the night.

"You'll get them back tomorrow," Ares promised, his tone gentle but firm. "When you're feeling a bit more... settled."

"We're not keeping them from you," Apollo added. "They're here. Just maybe not tonight, when the nightmares are still so vivid."

River looked like she might argue, but exhaustion overtook her again. She sank back against the pillows with a resigned sigh. "Fine. But first thing tomorrow."

"First thing," Ares agreed, settling beside her and drawing her near.

Apollo draped his arm across her waist.

"Sleep," Apollo murmured, his lips brushing the nape of her neck. "We'll be right here."

"All night," Ares confirmed, his fingers lacing with hers. "We're not going anywhere."

River's eyelids closed.

The steady rhythm of their combined breathing, the familiar scents of home and mate, gradually lulled all three of them toward sleep.

"I love you," she whispered, the words floating between them in the darkness. "Both of you."

"And we love you," they responded in unison.

As sleep claimed them, Apollo's last thought was that they were all where they belonged. Their mate and young between them, surrounded by their love and protection in their home.

The nightmares returned, but eventually the dawn did as well.

And Apollo and Ares held her through the whole ordeal.

CHAPTER THIRTY-NINE

One Week Later

RIVER

River leaned back against the plush leather chair, her body sore but her mind clear for the first time in days. Five full days of testimonies from the rogues had taken their toll, but a sense of accomplishment settled over her as she looked over the stack of files on the table.

"I can't believe we're finished." She ran a hand through her silver hair. "Forty-three rogues interviewed."

Apollo nodded, his golden eyes scanning the final report. "And only seven left that were directly involved in the attack or your kidnapping."

"The rest were just looking for safety," River said.

Ares paced by the window, silhouetted against the afternoon light. "So now we have thirty-six rogues who need a home."

"They've chosen to stay together," Apollo noted. "Form their own pack rather than return to territories they were exiled from."

"Can you blame them?" River asked. "Would you go back to people who had abandoned you?"

"The question is." Ares turned to face them. "Where do we put them?"

River straightened in her chair, an idea taking shape. "What about Montreal?"

"Montreal?" Apollo's brow furrowed. "You want to keep them close?"

"It makes sense. We've seized all of Titan's holdings. The estate, the businesses, the accounts. We could liquidate some to help them get established."

Ares chewed his lip. "It would be a fitting use of his blood money. Using what he stole to help rogues rather than exploit them."

Apollo's jaw tightened. "I'm not comfortable with them living at what remains of Titan's compound. Too much potential for trouble."

"I wasn't thinking of the compound," River said. "What about the Wolvenguard cabins?"

Apollo stiffened. "Those cabins have been in our family for generations."

"Exactly," River said. "They're sitting empty most of the year. The town is peaceful. The locals are friendly. And there's plenty of forest for them to run."

"It would only be temporary," Ares added. "Just until we can find them a permanent settlement."

Apollo stood, his conflict evident in every line of his body. "Those cabins are special to me."

"I know." She reached for his hand. "Me too. That's why they'd be perfect. Why not let them be special for others? Plus, having the pack there would help all the small businesses in town, such as our favorite candy store."

Apollo's resistance wavered as he looked at their joined hands.

"Think about it," River continued. "They'd have privacy, security, a place to heal and rebuild. And we'd be close enough to help them out if needed."

"They'd need supervision," Apollo cautioned. "Rules."

"Of course," River agreed. "We're not turning them loose."

Ares stood beside them. "It could work. And it might be good for more than just these rogues."

Apollo looked up. "What do you mean?"

"What if," Ares said thoughtfully, "we used the cabins as a transition point for all rogues seeking to start over? A place where they could be evaluated and prepared to join existing packs."

River's eyes lit up. "A halfway house for outcast wolves. That's brilliant, Ares!"

Apollo still frowned. "The main house is off-limits. That's my place. My sanctuary."

"It's our place," River corrected.

Apollo's eyes met hers, a complex mixture of emotions.

He sighed. "Fine. But the main house remains locked."

River beamed, rising to her tiptoes to press a kiss to his cheek. "Thank you."

"Don't thank me yet," Apollo grumbled, though the corner of his mouth twitched upward. "We still have to tell the Council."

"They'll support it," River said. "Your uncle and Mercule already offered to help however they could."

"Mercule would support you if you suggested painting the moon purple," Ares chuckled.

"The old wolf has always had a soft spot for strong females," Apollo agreed.

River smiled. In the last week she'd seen a softer side of Mercule and Osmodius. Especially Osmodius. It was as if something had awakened in him. A vulnerability he'd not allowed to show in many years.

"What about the seven who were involved?" River asked. "And Titan, Kane, Rudy, and Vanessa?"

The atmosphere shifted, the brief moment of levity evaporating.

"Their trials begin the day after tomorrow," Ares said. "The Council will preside, with representatives from all affected territories present. We will review all the testimony from the rogues over the next weeks and then call the Alpha to face justice as well." He rubbed his face. "It's going to be a long, tedious month."

"But one worth the effort." River smiled at him, though if she was being honest, she was already exhausted from all the duties.

"Titan will face the harshest punishment," Apollo added, his voice hardening. "For the kidnapping, the deaths at our ceremony, the attempted coup. Same for Vanessa."

River nodded. The thought that Titan was still alive sent a shiver of fear through her. But she'd promised herself she would not allow him to rule her life anymore, so she swallowed hard and shook her head.

"And Kane?" she asked.

"His case is... complicated," Ares admitted. "He was Titan's second-in-command, but he also surrendered willingly and helped us capture Titan."

"He was kind to me," River said. "In his own way. He tried to warn me when Titan…" She couldn't finish the thought. "And he was trying to figure out a way to get me out before it all went to hell. He never agreed to Titan taking me in the first place. He'd always just wanted to help the other rogues."

"While keeping you prisoner," Apollo reminded her, his voice tight.

River sighed. "I'm not saying he should go unpunished. Just that... there's more to him than we first thought. His fated mate rejected him because she was the Alpha's daughter. He's lost a lot. "

Ares nodded. "We'll take that into consideration."

A knock at the door interrupted their conversation.

Zeke entered. "Forgive the interruption, Your Majesties, but a few of the rogues are asking to speak with you. All of you."

River exchanged a glance with her mates before nodding. "Send them in."

Moments later, Sarah, the young female exiled for refusing to submit to a Luna who physically abused her, entered, followed by four others. They bowed respectfully, though River noticed they directed their most profound reverence to her rather than the twins.

"High Luna, Your Majesties," Sarah began, her voice steady despite her apparent nervousness. "We've come to thank you for your mercy and fairness."

An older wolf with gray-streaked hair stepped forward. "We thank you for letting us form our own pack. We've chosen a name. If it pleases you, we'd like to be known as the White Tail Pack, in honor of the High Luna who gave us a second chance."

River's eyes widened, a lump forming in her throat. "I... I'm honored."

Her father's name would live on through a new pack.

"We also wanted to ask," Sarah continued. "If there might be some way we could repay your kindness. Some service we could provide to the Crown."

River looked to her mates, an idea forming. "Actually," she said. "There might be."

Apollo raised an eyebrow. "What are you thinking?"

"What if the White Tail Pack became the first guardians of the transition program? Who better to help rogues adjust than those who've been through it?"

Ares nodded. "They could screen newcomers, teach them pack protocols, and prepare them for integration."

"And report directly to us," Apollo added. "Creating a buffer between the rogues and established packs. And mitigating some of the additional workload."

Sarah and the others exchanged hopeful glances. "We would be honored," she said. "Truly honored."

"We would just need to find them an Alpha," said Ares.

"Someone willing to be their Alpha. Someone who understands their plight and is sympathetic to what they've been through."

"It will take some thinking to find the right Alpha." River smiled, a sense of accomplishment washing through her. This was what she had fought for, what she had endured for. Not survival, but the chance to build something better from the ashes of what had been broken.

"Then it's settled," she declared. "The White Tail Pack will be established at the Wolvenguard cabins, with the mission of helping other rogues find their place in our world."

As the rogues bowed and thanked them profusely, Apollo's arm slipped around River's waist.

"You're going to change our world, aren't you?" he murmured.

River leaned into his embrace, watching Ares discuss a few details with the rogues. "Our world needs to change. And we're going to do it together."

Apollo kissed her temple. "Together." His eyes reflected pride and something that resembled hope.

The rogues filed out, already discussing their new responsibilities.

"This is the beginning," she whispered.

An older rogue with gray-streaked temples stopped and turned back. "Your Majesties. If I may? Before we go, I have an idea."

RIVER RESTED IN HER ROOM WHILE ARES AND APOLLO DISCUSSED the idea brought to them by the older rogue. River thought it was a good idea, but she was done fighting for the day and had decided she was ready for a rest.

She stared at the television, watching An American Werewolf in

Paris. Man, it was silly. Sillier than the first one, but she liked it nonetheless.

A knock on her door pulled her attention. She muted the television.

"Come in."

Ares opened the door and entered with a tray of food.

She smiled. "Hey there."

"Hey, yourself."

"What did you bring me?"

"Nothing much. Just what your mom made Strider cook for you. A prime rib, baked potato, sautéed green beans, rolls, salad, a piece of carrot cake, and three cans of bubbly water stuff."

"Is that all?" she laughed. Now that she was at the end of her first trimester, her appetite had returned, and her nausea had all but gone, with a few exceptions.

Ares set the tray on the bed and then slipped out of his shoes and tie.

"Your pajama pants are in your drawer," River said, cutting her meat. "Why don't you get comfortable?"

He smiled. "Sounds good to me."

She chewed the meat that melted in her mouth, making her moan.

"Where's Apollo?"

Ares set his suit pants and shirt on a chair before pulling on his black satin pajama pants. "He went up to the cabins for the night."

River choked down the meat. "Is he upset?"

Ares shook his head and sat on the bed next to her. "He just wants to lock up the main cabin and make a list of things the rogues will need before they move in. Log things that need to be repaired and such."

"Wow, he's moving fast."

"We can't keep them where they're staying now. It's tight, and it's already been a week."

"When will he be back?"

"Probably tomorrow night."

River wished she could call him, but he wouldn't have a signal anyway. She wondered why he hadn't said goodbye to her before leaving.

"So, did you two think about Margaret's idea? Did you come to a decision?"

Ares grabbed a roll, broke a piece off, and popped it in his mouth. "Not yet."

River nodded, not wanting to press him.

"What do you want to do tonight?" he asked.

"Whatever you want to do."

"Well, I want to do what you want to do. Even watch that awful werewolf you have muted."

River chuckled. "It is awful. But that's why I love it."

"You and Apollo both. Sad to see you have the same bad taste in movies he does."

She feigned insult and threw a cherry tomato at him. It hit him in the forehead, and he cocked an eyebrow at her.

"Oh, really?"

She laughed and threw another one.

"So that's how it's gonna be, huh?"

She laughed again, realizing how good it felt. Even her wolf chuffed and bounced around. She hadn't laughed in weeks, and though the sound seemed foreign, it lightened her more than she could say.

"I have an idea," he said. "How about I give you a foot rub while you finish your food and ridiculous movie?"

A shiver ran over her at the prospect of him rubbing her feet.

"I'd have to be an idiot to pass up that offer."

Ares reached in and nibbled one of her toes through the blanket. "Give me a minute to grab some massage oil."

"Okay, but nothing perfumy. My sense of smell is in overdrive."

"Of course." He hopped off the bed and walked out of the room.

River took another bite of her meat and chased it with a piece of the baked potato. She smiled to herself. Damn, she'd missed real food while being kept prisoner. And even more, Strider's cooking. It'd been so long since she'd tasted his food, she'd forgotten how amazing he was at cooking.

The door clicked open, and Ares returned with a small bottle. His golden eyes gleamed as he approached the bed.

"Found something that shouldn't bother your nose," he said, holding up the bottle of unscented almond oil.

River wiggled her toes in anticipation as he settled at the foot of the bed. He moved the tray to give himself room, then took her right foot in his large hands.

"Keep eating," he encouraged, warming the oil between his palms before beginning to work his thumbs into her arch.

River moaned and took another bite of her meal. The combination of delicious food and Ares' skilled hands was heavenly. He applied just the proper pressure, finding knots she hadn't even realized were there.

"Oh goddess," she groaned as he worked his way to her heel. "That feels amazing."

Ares smiled, his eyes never leaving her face as he switched to her other foot. "I've missed taking care of you."

As she finished her meal, his hands moved higher, massaging her ankles and then her calves with gentle but firm pressure. The movie played in the background as River surrendered to his touch.

"May I?" he asked, fingers hovering at the waistband of her loose pajama pants.

River nodded, suddenly breathless. With infinite care, Ares eased the fabric down her legs, his eyes darkening as they fell on the healing wound on her thigh. The angry line had faded to pink, new skin forming where the razor wire had gouged into her.

Ares traced the scar with gentle fingers. "Does it still hurt?"

"Not unless the nerves flare. Just pulls a bit."

He leaned down, and his lips caressed the healing line, feathering her with kisses and sending shivers through her entire body. His kisses trailed upward, across her thigh, over the curve of her hip. He paused at the wound on her side, examining it with careful eyes before covering it too with tender kisses.

River's breath quickened as his mouth moved higher, tracing the path his hands had blazed. His lips found the sensitive spot beneath her ribs that always made her gasp.

Without hesitation, she pulled her shirt over her head, followed by her bra. Ares' eyes darkened at the sight of her, his gaze reverent as it traveled over her body.

"You are so beautiful," he whispered, voice rough with emotion.

He reached over and moved the tray to the nightstand, then stood and stripped off his pajama pants in one fluid motion. The sight of him, powerful and gloriously naked, stole her ability to speak. He was magnificent, every inch of him perfection, and he was hers.

When he returned to her, his kiss started gentle but insistent, a claiming which spoke of love rather than possession. She opened to him willingly, reveling in the familiar taste of him, the scent that was uniquely Ares.

He entered her gently, and she moaned into his mouth. Too long. It had been much too long since they'd made love. Their bodies moved together with practiced ease, finding the perfect rhythm that belonged only to them. Every deliberate caress imbued with meaning. It wasn't just passion; it was reconnection, healing, and an affirmation of love after despair.

"I love you," Ares murmured against her skin as they moved as one. "I was so scared, River. So terrified I'd lost you forever."

She cradled his face between her palms. "You'll never lose me. Never."

His movements quickened, intensity building between them. "If anything happened to you... to our children... I couldn't bear it. I would die of a broken heart."

"Shhhhh," she soothed, kissing away the fear in his eyes. "I'm here. We all are."

She held him as pleasure crested between them, waves of sensation washing away the last vestiges of fear and separation. He cried her name as he climaxed, his head falling to her neck and kissing her skin. She grabbed onto him as her climax crested, murmuring his name and pulling him close.

Afterward, they lay tangled together and still attached, his heartbeat strong beneath her ear. She traced her fingers over one of the new scars from where he'd been shot.

"Does it bother you?"

She kissed it. "No. I think it's sexy. I just hate who gave it to you."

He hugged her. "As long as you like it, I couldn't care less where I got it."

"I love you, Ares Wolvenguard." She pressed a kiss to his heart. "And I will always come back to you."

His arms tightened around her, and the tension that had plagued them for the last weeks dissipated.

As sleep claimed them, hope rooted in her heart for the first time since her ordeal began. The nightmares might return, but she would face them with the strength of her mates beside her.

Tomorrow would bring new challenges: the rogues, the trial, rebuilding their world. But tonight, in Ares' arms, everything was exactly as it should be.

CHAPTER FORTY

ARES

Morning light filtered through the curtains when Ares opened his eyes. River still rested against him, his arm draped over her waist, her breath warm against his skin. For several minutes, he lay there, savoring the moment of perfect bliss. After weeks of terror, thinking it may never happen again, having these moments meant so much more than they ever had.

River stirred, her eyes opening to him watching her. A smile spread across her face, transforming her beautiful features.

"How long have you been awake?" she asked, voice husky with sleep.

He kissed her head. "Just long enough to memorize this moment." Ares brushed a strand of silver hair from her face.

River's smile deepened as she stretched against him. "What moment is that?"

"The one where you're in my arms, and nothing can harm you." His voice dropped. "Where you're mine."

She traced the strong line of his jaw with her fingertips. "I've always been yours."

Their lips met in a kiss that started tender but quickly blazed into something more urgent. Ares rolled her onto her back, his body covering hers with protective heat as his mouth explored hers with increasing hunger. River's hands slid up his arms, across his shoulders, tangling in his dark hair to pull him closer.

"Ares," she breathed against his lips, her body arching to meet his.

He moved with deliberate tenderness, mindful of her still-healing wounds as he worshipped every inch of her. His hands traced the curves of her body with reverent appreciation, lingering where their children grew.

River's breathing quickened as he settled between her thighs. "Ares, I need you."

"And I, you." He kissed her and slid inside her at the same time. He fought to hold back his wolf's overwhelming need to take her fast and hard. He joined their bodies slowly, already close to the edge.

She moaned as her fingers dug into his shoulders, heightening his need. He wanted her, all of her, every inch. As her soft folds cradled and massaged him, he couldn't help the emotions running through him. He couldn't process them all. Need. Love. Protection. Hope. Guilt. All of them hit him in rapid succession. He pushed them away to focus on that moment and being with his mate.

They moved together in harmony. River's soft gasps and moans filled the room, her hands clutching at him as they climbed closer toward the edge. Ares broke the kiss to watch her face as passion overtook her, memorizing every expression, every sound, every shiver of his Beloved. His mate. His River. She was his and always would be. He would never let her go again.

Ares roared her name as he climaxed. She touched his cheek and ran her hand down to his hips, pulling him deeper into her and rocking him through his climax until he was utterly spent.

When they collapsed, breathless and sated, Ares gathered her against him, kissing her face.

"I love you," he murmured. "More than I ever thought possible." It was the truth. He never thought he would love someone the way he loved River. Needed River. Craved River. The thought terrified and elated him.

River smiled, her fingers tracing across his skin.

Ares slid down her body until his head rested against her stomach. He focused on the tiny lives growing within her.

"They're so strong. Their heartbeats are like little drums. Steady and determined, like their mother."

River's fingers raked through his hair. "What else do you hear?"

"Life. Beautiful, perfect life." He looked up at her. "I can't wait to meet them, to teach them everything. To watch them grow."

"What will you teach them first?"

"How to track. And swim. And shift." His expression softened. "But most importantly, how to love and protect what matters most."

"You'll be an amazing father."

"We'll take them everywhere," Ares continued. "Show them the world, teach them about their heritage, their responsibilities."

River laughed. "We should definitely take them to the giant Ferris wheel thing when they're small."

"The Ferris wheel?" Ares cocked an eyebrow. "Oh, you mean the La Grande Roué."

"We should get them used to it early, so they're never afraid of heights."

Ares smiled and kissed her belly. "Are you sure? As I remember, you didn't love it too much."

"I may need to hold your hand the entire time. But I'll keep trying."

"I'm going to hold you to that," he said, crawling back up to capture her lips in a tender kiss.

"And we need to take them to see the cathedral."

"Absolutely," Ares murmured. "And the opera."

River nodded. "Though maybe something other than Carmen."

Ares snorted. "Fair enough."

APOLLO

THE CRISP MORNING BREEZE BLEW OVER APOLLO'S FACE AS HE STOOD in front of the stone fireplace in the main cabin, his eyes fixed on the photographs that lined the mantle. His fingers traced a wooden frame containing an image of his father- regal, powerful, imposing. The man who had shaped the Lycan world for decades, whose legacy now rested on Apollo's shoulders.

"Would you have done it?" Apollo whispered to the photograph. "Would you have crossed that line? Let your emotions overtake your judgment?"

His reflection stared back at him from the glass, golden eyes troubled by memories of his rage. The way his control had shattered when he'd confronted Titan. The primal, savage need to destroy the man who had dared take River. He'd come so close- terrifyingly close- to becoming something he'd always feared lurked beneath the civilized exterior he put on.

A knock at the door pulled him from his thoughts.

"Your Majesty?" Silas entered, iPad in hand. "I've finished the inventory of the other cabins."

Apollo turned from the mantle. "And?"

"Most are in good condition, but there are repairs needed." Silas handed over a detailed list. "Plumbing issues in cabins three and seven. Roof damage on five. Almost all of them need electrical work."

Apollo scanned the document, grateful for the distraction.

"Have these addressed today. The rogues will need proper shelter when they arrive."

"Of course." Silas hesitated. "This is a generous thing you're doing."

Apollo's jaw tightened. "It wasn't my idea."

"Nevertheless, you agreed to it."

Apollo handed back the list. "Get workers out here today. I want the repairs started before I return to the estate."

"I'll make the calls." Silas turned toward the door and paused. "Do you hear that?"

Apollo listened, picking up the distant rumble of engines. Motorcycles, three of them, approached the cabin. His brow furrowed as he moved to the window, scanning the tree-lined dirt road.

His heart leapt at the sight of silver hair streaming behind one of the riders. River, her slender form wrapped in a leather jacket and jeans, navigated the winding path with natural grace. Behind her, Cherry and Strider followed on their bikes.

"What in the goddess's name..." Apollo muttered, already striding toward the door.

His wolf jumped to his feet and yipped, tail wagging.

He walked onto the porch as the motorcycles pulled up, engines cutting off in sequence. River removed her helmet, her silver hair tumbling free as she smiled up at him.

"Surprise," she called, dismounting with ease.

Apollo descended the steps, torn between joy at seeing her and concern at her riding a motorcycle alone. "What are you doing here? Are you supposed to be riding a motorcycle? Why are there only three of you? Where are your bodyguards?"

River rose on her tiptoes to kiss him. "Calm down. I missed you," she said. "And I brought lunch." She gestured to the saddle-bags on her motorcycle. "And our favorite fudge. Plus, Mom and Strider wanted to see the place."

Apollo wrapped his arms around her, inhaling her scent with relief and pleasure before pulling back to look at her sternly. "Where are your bodyguards?"

River rolled her eyes. "I brought my mom and my dad. I'm fine."

Cherry approached, removing her riding gloves. "Don't worry, Apollo. We didn't let her out of our sight the entire ride."

Strider nodded in agreement, his massive frame dwarfing the motorcycle he'd been riding. "No one followed us. I made sure of it."

"Besides," said River. "I don't have any bodyguards of my own."

Apollo growled. How had they not assigned anyone to her as personal guards? "Well, I will be remedying that. And telling Ares just what I think of him letting you come up here."

She snorted. "First, 'let me come'? You think Ares 'let me come'? I can't decide for myself? And second of all, I think maybe *I'll* remedy not having guards. After all, they will be mine. I should get to choose them."

His gaze dropped to her belly. "You shouldn't be riding. You could have been hurt. Or the babies."

"They are fine. I am fine. Everything is-"

"Fine?" Cherry smirked.

River looked at her mom and rolled her eyes. "Ha-ha."

Apollo sighed. "You should have called."

"No signal," River countered with a mischievous grin. "Besides, I wanted to surprise you."

He wanted to continue protesting, but didn't because he was overjoyed to see her.

His wolf chuffed and hopped around like a pup.

Cherry surveyed the surrounding forest. "Beautiful country. Strider and I thought we might go for a run while you two catch up."

"There's a lookout point about five miles north," Apollo offered. "The view of the valley is impressive."

Cherry nodded. "Perfect. We'll be back by evening." She glanced at Strider, who was already removing his jacket. "Ready?"

Moments later, two wolves- one honey-colored, one deep russet-loped into the trees, disappearing among the shadows.

Silas cleared his throat. "I should head into town to start calling contractors. I'll be back tomorrow with the first crew."

As Silas departed in the SUV, Apollo turned to River, taking the food bags from her. "Let's go inside. The temperature's dropping."

Inside the cabin, warmth from the fireplace enveloped them. River shrugged off her leather jacket, revealing a simple cream sweater that hugged her curves. The curve of her pregnancy protruded slightly, and Apollo's heart squeezed at the sight.

His wolf howled. *My Omega.*

"Can we watch a movie while we eat?" River asked, unpacking food from the bags. "I brought burgers and fries from that place in town you like. Or we could just dive into the five-pound box of fudge."

Apollo smiled despite his troubled thoughts. "Whatever you want, Kitten."

They settled on the couch, food spread on the coffee table before them. Apollo selected a Vincent Price film from the cabin's collection, and soon, the atmospheric sounds of "House of Usher" filled the room.

River ate with obvious enjoyment, occasionally commenting on the film's gothic atmosphere. Apollo found himself watching her more than the movie, drinking in the sight of her content beside him.

Halfway through the film, River turned to him, her eyes searching his face. "What's wrong?"

"Nothing," Apollo replied automatically.

River set down her food, fixing him with a penetrating stare. "Don't lie to me, Apollo. Something's been bothering you since you captured Titan. I told myself that I'd wait and let you talk to me about it when you were ready, but it's been over a week."

Apollo sighed. He couldn't hide his thoughts from her. Their bond was too strong. "I've been thinking about what happened with Titan."

"What about it?"

"I almost killed him, River." The words tumbled out, raw and honest. "Not in battle, not in self-defense. I wanted to tear him apart piece by piece, to make him suffer. I've never..." He swallowed hard. "I've never felt rage like that before. It terrified me."

River took his hand, her touch grounding him. "It's natural to feel that way after what we've been through."

His wolf whined.

"Is it? To completely lose control? To become something I don't recognize?"

"Yes," River insisted. "I would have done the same thing in your position. Anyone who loves their mate the way we love each other would."

Apollo turned to face her. "The thought that he took you, that he touched you..." His voice broke. "It drove my wolf and me insane. I've never been that enraged before. That kind of anger has always been Ares' thing. I've always been in control. Always been logical. But when it comes to you... logic goes completely out of my vocabulary."

"I understand." River squeezed his hand. "Believe me, I do."

A terrible thought struck Apollo. "Did he-" He couldn't finish the question, the possibility too painful to voice.

River hesitated, looking away.

"River..." Apollo's heart thundered. "Did Titan try to force you?"

She remained silent for a long moment. "He would have," she admitted. "But Kane came and warned me what might happen. We were talking about getting me out when Titan found us together and freaked out."

Apollo's wolf leapt to his feet and snarled. *Kill him. Rip out his heart.*

Apollo's blood chilled, and his mouth dried as he fought to voice the next question. "What did he do?"

"He pinned me against the wall and kissed me. His nails dug into my arms, leaving marks, but I used my Luna gaze on him. Commanded him to let go and never touch me again."

Rage exploded through Apollo's body, his vision washing red. "I'll kill him for what he did. Truly kill him," he growled.

River moved closer, taking his face between her palms. "I'd rather we just wash it all away. You and I, together." She kissed him with fierce intent.

The kiss ignited something primal in Apollo. His hands tangled in her silver hair, pulling her closer as need consumed him. Their mouths clashed with desperate hunger, weeks of fear and separation fueling their passion.

Apollo lifted her onto his lap, her thighs straddling him as his hands explored the curves of her body. The need to claim her, to erase any trace of Titan's touch, overwhelmed him. River matched his intensity, her arms wrapping around his neck.

They shed their clothes in a flurry of urgency. Discarded without care as they came together with raw need. River slid down on him fast and hard. Apollo's control slipped, his wolf rising to the surface as he claimed her with possessive fervor.

"You're mine," he growled, his thrusts powerful and demanding. "Say it."

"I'm yours," River gasped. "Always yours, Apollo."

They moved together with increasing urgency. Each touch reaffirming their bond. The world narrowed to just the two of them, everything else falling away as they reclaimed what had almost been lost. He needed her. Needed all of her. Every inch. Every moan. His. All his. She was his.

His climax rolled up his thighs as her body tightened around his, and she called his name, her hips slamming into his, and her mouth claiming his in a fevered clash of teeth and tongues.

Utter bliss rolled through Apollo as he filled River with his knot. His River. His mate. His everything. They sat joined, kisses hot and passionate, hands roaming overly sensitive skin, and his wolf in an utter state of complete happiness. This was his paradise. He would never want more.

LATER, AS THEY TANGLED TOGETHER BEFORE THE FIREPLACE, A WARM blanket wrapped around them, Apollo stroked River's bare shoulder. The rage that had consumed him earlier had transformed into something softer, deeper. A profound gratitude that she was in his arms.

She touched one of his new scars. Then traced another. The skin pulled beneath her fingertips.

"I'm so sorry you got these," she whispered.

Apollo kissed her head. "For you, they were worth it."

She sighed.

"Your love has changed me," he whispered. "And I am not talking about the scars. I mean my life. Who I am."

River nestled closer, kissing his chest. "It's changed us both."

Apollo's thoughts drifted to the rogues who would soon inhabit the surrounding cabins. Wolves who had been cast out, rejected, forgotten. Who had never experienced the acceptance and belonging that he now had.

"Maybe change isn't such a bad thing," he murmured, his arms tightening around River. "After all, change brought me you."

She moved his hand to her belly. "And our children."

The rogues deserved that as well. A pack, a family, young.

Suddenly, he wanted the rogues to use the cabins. Wanted them to have a place as he did. A place that made him feel secure. A home.

They lay for a long moment, and then River said, "I want our children to be born here."

Apollo smiled. "I would love that."

"We could stay here for the first couple of weeks. Just you, me, Ares, and our babies."

Apollo's ribcage tightened. "When they're old enough, I want to bring them here every month. Teach them to hunt and fish and love nature."

"I can teach them to wood sculpt. Maybe make a sculpture of all of us to put outside this cabin."

"That would be amazing. We'll need to get cradles for them."

"Maybe you could help me make them. We could use wood from the land. You can help design them."

"We should clear a bit more land and build some more cabins for the rogues. That way, we could have the three closest ones for us, my mom, dad, B, Zeke, and the other guards who want to come visit."

Apollo nodded. "That would be a good idea."

"It's not that I don't want to be close to the rogues; it's just that I don't want to disrupt their lives when we come or make them nervous. Plus, we need to build a cabin for the new Alpha and his mate as well."

Apollo sighed, thinking of the new Alpha. He and Ares had discussed it, but they still hadn't made their final decision.

"Could you get me a glass of water?" River asked.

Apollo kissed her. "Of course."

He stood and walked to the kitchen, grabbed a glass from the cabinet, and poured water from the pitcher in the fridge. He looked out the window at the woods surrounding them. If he had it his way, he and River would raise their children there, and he'd leave the whole ruling thing to Ares. Not that he didn't want Ares around. His connection and subsequent caring for his brother were a welcome addition to his life. But leading wasn't what he wanted anymore. If he'd learned one thing from the past weeks, it was that he wanted nothing more than his mate, his children, and peace.

"Apollo?"

"Coming, Kitten."

Apollo walked back and handed the glass to River. She downed half of it and then set it on the hearth.

She searched his face and sat up. "What is it?" she asked. "What can I do to help?"

Apollo shook his head. "I just wish we could stay here, but they are expecting us back tonight."

She stroked his hair and pulled his lips to hers. "Then let's make the most of the time we have."

River rolled on her back and pulled him to her. His body hardened in an instant as he claimed her mouth, and everything else floated away except for him and River.

CHAPTER FORTY-ONE

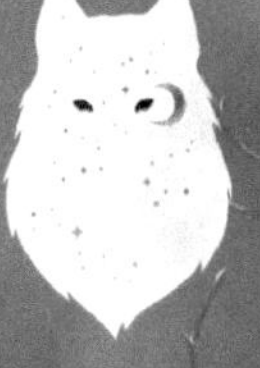

RIVER

River's leg bounced as she tried to calm her nerves, knowing what she and the others were getting ready to do.

Apollo grabbed one hand, and Ares gripped the other as the three of them sat in the same room that just a month prior had been filled with Alphas, Betas, and mates, as well as dozens of attacking rogues. On either side of them sat the council members. And sitting where they had previously, Alphas, Betas, and mates waited to hear the judgment she, Apollo, Ares, and the Council pronounced on Titan, Vanessa, Rudy, and Kane.

The audience spoke softly to themselves as they waited.

Ares kissed River's knuckles. "Don't worry, he can't hurt you."

She nodded. "I know."

"I'd be more worried about me hurting him," said Apollo.

Her wolf paced, agitated, and impatient.

River squeezed his hand. "You'll have to beat me to it." Suddenly, she felt stronger than she had in weeks.

The doors to the ballroom opened, and Zeke, Thomas, Silas,

Santiago, and Theo walked in a shackled, bloodied, and bruised Titan. Duncan and Regan brought in a cuffed, disheveled Vanessa. And Lachlan, Isaac, and Drew walked behind Kane and Rudy, who wore handcuffs but not silver ones. Only Kane had showered and wore clean clothes. River hadn't asked about him in the previous week, but it pleased her to know that he hadn't been mistreated.

Everyone turned as they entered. Most of the Alphas and Betas growled and bared their teeth as they passed. Several spit on the floor or on Titan. Words like bastard, traitor, and disgrace were thrown around like beads at Mardi Gras.

When Titan, Rudy, and Vanessa stopped at the front of the room, the guards pushed them to their knees. Titan looked up straight at River, his eyes boring into her. She wanted to look away, wanted to swallow the rock lodged in her throat, wanted to scream. She reached instinctively for the knife she had strapped at her thigh. The outline of it in its holder comforting her. She stared back at Titan like the High Luna she was.

"Bow your heads in front of your Kings and High Luna," said Osmodius.

Vanessa bowed as low as she could, but Titan continued to stare at River through his one good eye.

Santiago bashed Titan in the back of the head with the butt of his gun. "Bow."

Titan's eyes blackened, and it wasn't until River used her golden Luna gaze that he begrudgingly inclined his head.

Mercule rose to his feet, his voice commanding the attention of everyone in the chamber. "We have gathered here today to witness the trials of Vanessa, Kane, Rudy, and Titan, who stand accused of crimes against the Crown and the wolf society. Justice will be served according to our laws, tempered with the wisdom of our Kings and High Luna."

The room fell silent as all eyes turned to the prisoners kneeling before the royal family.

"We will begin with Vanessa," Mercule announced, gesturing toward the female.

Apollo stood, his golden eyes cold. "Vanessa Blackpaw, you stand accused of treason against the Crown, conspiracy to kidnap the High Luna, and aiding in the imprisonment of High Luna River Wolvenguard. You helped orchestrate the attack at our mating ceremony by shutting down cameras beforehand and weakening the exterior perimeter at the Wolvenguard estate. The resulting attack ended in the deaths of numerous Alphas, Betas, and their mates."

Vanessa's head remained bowed, her shoulders trembling slightly.

"Furthermore, you deliberately manipulated information to serve Titan's cause, knowing full well the harm it would bring to innocent wolves as well as the royal family."

"Your Majesty, please," Vanessa interrupted, lifting her tear-streaked face. "I'm sorry for what I did. I never meant for anyone to get hurt. I was just trying to-"

"Silence," Apollo commanded. "Your apologies mean nothing to the families of those who died. Your words cannot bring back the lives lost because of your actions."

Vanessa flinched as if struck, fresh tears spilling down her cheeks.

Ares stood next to his brother, commanding attention. "However, it has been noted that you eventually assisted in subduing Titan, allowing him to be captured and brought to justice. For this reason alone, you will not face the punishment of death or permanent banishment that your crimes would ordinarily warrant."

A murmur rippled through the assembled crowd.

"Do you have anything to say in your defense before we pronounce sentence?"

"Please, Highnesses, I beg you. I am so sorry-"

Apollo cut her off. "We didn't ask for your sorries. We did not ask to hear your pleadings. We asked you if you had any kind of defense against betraying your Kings and High Luna, especially when we took you in and gave you shelter, a job, and everything you could have wanted. But instead of thanking us, you stabbed us in the back and tried to take our fated mate, the High Luna of our kingdom, and give her to a man who tried to claim her without consent." Apollo's voice had risen to such an extent that River worried he might snap and slaughter Vanessa.

Just as she was going to intervene, Ares placed his hand on Apollo's shoulder. Apollo took a deep breath, and his posture relaxed a fraction.

"Instead," Ares declared, "for your crimes, you are sentenced to live out your days within the confines of your home pack, the Timber Oak Pack. You will never again leave their territory without express permission from your Alpha, your mate, and the Crown."

Vanessa's head snapped up. "No! Please, Your Majesties, anything but that! Send me to prison, banish me for a time. Anything but back there!"

"You should be grateful," Ares growled. "Your life is being spared when many here would see you executed for your crimes, me included. Be thankful for the mercy shown to you."

Vanessa collapsed forward, her forehead touching the floor as sobs wracked her body. "Please, I beg you. Don't send me back."

"Your custody will be transferred to your Alpha and Uncle, Jediah, and your soon-to-be mate, Garrick," Apollo announced, ignoring her pleas. "They have agreed to take responsibility for your rehabilitation and future conduct."

At this pronouncement, two males rose from the audience. The older one, his salt-and-pepper hair framing a stern face, neared the front with measured steps. Behind him, a younger wolf with broad shoulders and watchful eyes followed.

"Uncle Jediah, no," Vanessa whispered, her voice breaking as they reached her. "Garrick, please."

They each took one of her arms without a word to her or a

glance at her, lifting her to her feet. Vanessa struggled weakly against their grips, her eyes wild with panic as she turned toward the royal family.

"Kings, High Luna, I beg you! Don't do this to me!"

River's wolf growled. And River rose to her feet, studying Vanessa with careful consideration. "What reason do you have for not wanting to return to your pack?" she asked. "Has your uncle ever abused you?"

Vanessa hesitated, then shook her head. "No, High Luna."

"And Garrick? You know him?"

"I'm her fated mate," said Garrick, still not looking at Vanessa.

River kept her mouth from falling open. Vanessa had a fated mate, and yet she'd run from him and slept with dozens of other men, possibly more.

"Has he ever hurt you or forced himself upon you?" River asked.

Vanessa shook her head.

River approached Vanessa with graceful steps. She stopped just before the trembling female. As much as River hated Vanessa, she felt compassion for any wolf who lost their free will. But what had Vanessa done with that free will? She'd squandered it. Abused it. Used it and her sexuality to hurt people.

River's wolf sniffed the air and snarled. *No. Mercy.*

River nodded. "As neither of these two males has ever done a thing to harm you in any way, understand this. You are being given a mercy." River's voice carried through the silent chamber. "A life with a mate willing to take you back despite your unfaithfulness to him repeatedly, and an uncle willing to take responsibility for you despite you being a traitor. It is far better than you deserve."

River's gaze hardened as she continued. "If you choose not to leave with them right now, you will be branded as a traitor with a traitor's mark upon your neck, stripped of your family and pack names as well as everything you possess. You will be cast out of

North America with no money, no home, and no one will be permitted to even speak to you again on this continent. Permanently. We will also ensure that the packs in Europe, South America, Asia, and everywhere else are aware of your betrayal and the reason for your banishment. Is that what you prefer?"

Vanessa's mouth opened and closed several times before her shoulders slumped, and her resistance crumbled under the weight of River's words.

Ares stepped forward, his voice a low rumble. "Thank the High Luna for her generosity, Vanessa. If the decision had been Apollo and mine alone, you would not be leaving this room alive."

Vanessa swallowed hard, her eyes not meeting River's. "Thank you, High Luna," she whispered, the words catching in her throat. "For your mercy."

With a nod from Apollo, Jediah and Garrick dragged Vanessa toward the exit, her shackles clinking with each step. The assembled wolves watched them pass, their expressions a mix of satisfaction and lingering resentment.

As the doors closed behind them, Apollo and Ares led River back to her throne between them.

"You did well," Ares murmured into her hair.

She grabbed Apollo's hand. He looked at her, and the anger smoothed out across his face as he gave her a tight smile that told her he was hanging on, but not well. She rubbed her cheek against his knuckles and then kissed them, and his body relaxed further.

Osmodius turned his attention to the remaining prisoners. "We shall now proceed with the trial of Rudy Mountainside, former Alpha of the Northeastern pack."

Rudy didn't move or lift his head; he simply sat, head bowed, eyes on the floor.

Ares sat forward. "Rudy Mountainside. You have been found guilty of treason as well as a physical attack on a royal family member. For these crimes, you will serve out a sentence of no less than twenty years in the service of Alpha Mandla Goldmane of the Lion Pride pack in Cape Town, South Africa."

Rudy's head whipped up. "Lions? South Africa? What about my mate? My sons?"

"They were all given the option of going with you or relocating to a new pack in California. Can you guess which they chose?" asked Apollo.

Rudy growled, and his eyebrows drew together. "But-"

"No but," said Ares. "Another condition of your not being executed is that you never try to contact your mate or sons again. They have asked to have their names changed, and your mate has appealed for an annulment."

His face paled. "No. I refuse."

"It's not up to you," said Apollo. "She has petitioned us personally."

“We are not likely to make a faithful and wonderful woman be tainted for her entire life by the shame of her mate," said River. "Nor sons be shunned for the greed of their father."

Rudy looked between them, his face a tornado of emotions.

"Is there anyone who wishes to speak on Rudy's behalf?" asked Ares.

No one spoke.

Ares nodded. "Rudy Mountainside. You will proceed directly from this hearing to the airport, where representatives of the Lion Pride pack will meet and escort you to your new home. We have given Alpha Goldmane full say over your future. He may do with you as he wishes without fear of reprisal from us, as long as he keeps you in South Africa. You should also know that he has been rewarded handsomely for his help in this matter, solidifying his loyalty to the Crown. So, trying to bribe or manipulate him will be of no use."

Ares nodded to Theo and Santiago, and they pulled Rudy to his feet and pushed him toward the exit. Murmurs sounded around the room. River had never heard of wolves being sent abroad to other species, and apparently, neither had anyone in the room. But it was a good decision. It showed those in the room that death was not the only punishment for treachery.

The mood in the chamber shifted as all eyes turned back to the last two prisoners. Unlike Titan, who radiated defiance even in a kneeling position, Kane maintained quiet dignity, head bowed but shoulders straight.

"Kane," Mercule began, "you stand accused as Titan's second-in-command, complicit in his crimes against the Crown and our people. How do you plead?"

Kane raised his head, his eyes clear and unflinching as he met the Council elder's gaze. "Guilty," he said. "I will not deny my role in what happened."

Apollo's grip tightened on her hand. She glanced at him, recognizing the conflict in his eyes. This was the man who had tried to protect her during her captivity, who had wanted to help her. Yet he was also the man who had stood by Titan's side for years, enabling his rise to power.

"The sentence for your crimes could be death," Ares stated. "Do you understand?"

Kane nodded once. "I do, Your Majesty. And I accept whatever judgment you deem appropriate."

The room fell silent as all eyes turned to the royal family, waiting for their decision.

"But we have been asked to offer you a different fate," Ares continued. "The innocent survivor rogues have been given a place to live and start over."

Gasps and murmurs rippled through the room, and River glanced around, trying to make sure that tensions didn't rise. The last thing they needed was a riot.

"The innocent rogues," Apollo said. "Ones forced out not due to their actions but due to the actions of power-hungry or corrupt

Alphas. Those rogues have been given a second chance, and they have formed their own pack. The White Tail pack. But they are lacking one thing, an Alpha to lead them."

"You are an Alpha, are you not?" Ares asked.

Kane took a deep breath. "I was born an Alpha, but I have never been an Alpha."

"Then we give you a choice," said Apollo. "You may choose banishment with the same conditions we gave Rudy, or you can become the Alpha of the White Tail pack."

The crowd erupted in shouting and swearing. Even Titan roared at the prospect.

"Bastard! Traitor! I should have known you'd want everything I built for yourself. My pack. My mate. My Crown!" Titan struggled to reach Kane, but as he did, Theo kicked him in the back, making Titan fall forward on his face.

"Silence!" Apollo jumped to his feet. "You dare question your Kings? Maybe you have gone too long without a king to remember that you have no say in final judgments. That right is reserved for my brother, myself, and our mate, the High Luna. Even the Council does not pronounce judgments. They counsel us. Any of you who think you know better, come forward, and we will end this in combat. If you can best us, then you will have earned the right to pronounce judgments. For too long, we have allowed you to rule. That is the reason we are here today. If we had done more and overseen more, Titan would not have gotten so many rogues to follow him. So you are as culpable for what happened as Kane is. And believe me, in the coming weeks, every one of you who contributed to the exile of innocent wolves will kneel before us and account for what you did, just as these wolves have. I suggest you think about that. You think these wolves aren't deserving of mercy? Then neither are you."

One by one, the Alphas and Betas sat down.

River stood and joined Apollo. "Kane saved me from being

further violated by Titan. He saved dozens of rogues whom you otherwise would have murdered to protect yourselves or out of sheer vengeance. And yet, he has asked for nothing in return. Nothing. He came to us willingly. Offering to face whatever judgment we deemed fit. Would you have done the same? Or would you be on your knees, begging for forgiveness while at the same time trying to justify what you did? These are the reasons why Kane will make the best Alpha for the rogues." River's gaze fell on Kane. "But do not be mistaken. This is not just a mercy in sparing your life and allowing you to stay within the kingdom. You will work, and work hard for those rogues. And for all rogues who come to the White Tail Pack for help. You will report directly to me, and if at any time you decide you no longer want this mercy, you will be banished for the remainder of your natural life. Do you accept?"

Kane didn't speak for a long minute. "I do not deserve this mercy, my High Luna."

"No, you do not," said Ares. "But we were asked by those you saved to show you mercy, and they have made it clear that they would accept no one but you as their Alpha. As they have already been through enough, we believe this to be the best course of action. This way, you can help those you set out to help in the first place, and we can keep an eye on you at the same time."

Kane stared at the floor, and River wasn't sure he would take the offer.

"Before you decide," said River. "You need to do one last thing."

"Whatever my High Luna commands," he replied.

"You must tell King Apollo and King Ares what happened to their parents."

Titan's head whipped up. "I did it. I poisoned and then gutted them. I did it. No one else."

Ares and Apollo bared their teeth as Silas grabbed Titan from behind and put him in a headlock, choking off his air supply.

Apollo lunged forward, but River caught his arm. Titan

thrashed against Silas' grip as the silver burned into his hair and flesh, the scent filling the room.

Apollo looked at River, his eyes black, claws and teeth fully extended. She shook her head imperceptibly and then looked at Ares and did the same.

The audience looked on, bloodlust in everyone's eyes.

Holding her mates' hands, she gazed at Kane again. "Kane, is that the truth?"

His expression remained as unreadable as ever. His eyes calm but sharp, and his breathing even.

"No," he replied.

A gasp sounded around the room.

Once more, Titan reached for Kane but was unable to move. "Don't you dare. You bastard. I'll kill you. I'll rip out your lying tongue and eat your heart. If you say one word, I'll gut you and leave you for the vultures."

Kane's composure never wavered as he continued to stare at River.

"Then what happened?" Ares growled.

"Don't you dare. You f-"

River's Luna gaze fell on Titan full force. "Be Silent!"

Titan's gaze flicked to hers for only a moment, but it was enough. His mouth snapped shut, though he didn't stop struggling.

"If you cannot behave," she continued. "We can arrange for a cage and a muzzle."

Titan looked at her again, full on this time. Hate seething in his glare, she stared back at him unflinchingly. There, on his knees, beaten, dirty, and unrepentant, his hatred and madness dripping off him, she couldn't help but feel a pang of empathy for him. He'd lost everything, truly everything, and instead of realizing the extent of what he'd done, he was ready to continue, no matter the cost.

River nodded to Kane. "Please, tell us."

Kane swallowed. "Titan's mother, Deleah, killed them. She

couldn't let go of what had happened to her and Titan. The longer she lived, the worse her anger became, until it became an obsession. Then everything she did focused on getting revenge. The night the king and queen were out for dinner, she went into the kitchen of the restaurant and tampered with their meals. The humans wouldn't have noticed or been harmed by flakes of silver she put in their food, but it was enough to weaken the king and queen. When their guards ran to get the vehicle, she entered, dressed as a waitress. She told the remaining guard she was a nurse and could help. She said to make everyone back away so they could have room. As soon as he turned away, she slit both of their throats and then his before escaping into the crowd. I believe the guard she killed had a son named Bennett. King Apollo's friend, who was killed."

The room was so silent you could have heard a feather drop on a carpeted floor.

Apollo and Ares' breathing came out in short bursts. They both clutched her hands so tight she thought her fingers might break.

"Is that the truth?" Apollo whispered.

Kane lowered his head. "It is. Their deaths did nothing to soothe her, though. She'd hoped that the Council would call for Titan to come back, but they didn't. And when he spoke to them and was rejected as heir, she lost what little hope she had left and killed herself a week later."

Titan let out a pitiful whine.

Osmodius growled. "Let it be known from now on that King Jagger and my sister, Queen Genevive Wolvenguard, were murdered by Deleah Longtooth of the Meadow Moon Pack."

The entire audience sat in silence. Apollo and Ares looked at each other and then at Titan. River couldn't imagine what thoughts ran through their mind. All this time, they had believed Titan had murdered their parents, only to learn the truth- the person they wanted to punish most for the deaths of their parents was already long dead.

"Do you want to take a break?" River asked softly.

"No," said Ares. "We need to finish this."

Apollo nodded in agreement. "Kane Bravemane of the Red Moon Pack, you are hereby sentenced to live out your natural life as Alpha of the White Tail Pack and swear to take responsibility for all put in your charge. If at any time you break this sentence, you will be hunted down, marked with the traitor's mark, and banished. Do you understand?"

Kane bowed his head. "I do, my King."

Apollo nodded to Thomas and Silas, who undid Kane's cuffs and led him toward the exit. Kane stopped once to look back at Titan, but then turned and exited the room.

Silence stretched out for several moments after the doors closed, and the tension in the air grew thick with impatience.

Ares and Apollo led River back to her throne.

"Lastly," Mercule announced, "We come to the trial of Titan Longtooth."

"Wolvenguard," Titan corrected. "I am Titan Wolvenguard, son of King Jagger Wolvenguard."

Osmosdius' gaze landed on Titan. "You may have once been considered a Wolvenguard, but when you chose to follow in your mother's footsteps and become a traitor to the royal family, you ceased being a Wolvenguard."

"You cannot just take a name from someone," Titan growled. "Blood is blood."

"We have, and we do," said Ares. "You will forever be known as Titan Longtooth. You have soiled our family name. Have brought shame to our father and ancestors. Therefore, as is the law, your royal name is stripped from you."

Titan howled. "You can't do that."

"We can, actually," said Apollo. "But honestly, that is the last thing you should be worried about. You, Titan Longtooth, are charged with treason to the Crown and treason to the Wolvenguard kings by touching and kidnapping our fated mate. Causing the deaths of no less than twenty-two Alphas, Betas, and mates. And of causing the deaths of sixteen rogues at your estate."

"You also stand accused of the greatest sin a wolf can make, the marking and claiming of a female without consent. A female who happened to be an Omega, the most revered female of our species," said Ares. "Every single offense is worthy of death. Combined, they are incomprehensible. Do you have anything to say for your actions?"

"This is a farce. You have no right to punish or condemn me to anything. I am Titan Wolvenguard, eldest son of Jagger Wolvenguard and rightful King of the wolves. These laws do not apply to me."

"These rules apply to everyone," said Mercule. "Every single wolf, no matter their lineage, must be held to the same standard. You are no exception."

"So, you have nothing to say?" asked Apollo.

Titan's eyes moved from one to another of them and landed on River. "River Whitetail is mine. She will always be mine."

River refused to let him see her fear. "If you reject me now and promise to never come near me again, you may still have a chance at mercy."

Titan's eyes went black, and his fangs lengthened slightly. "As long as I live, there is not a day that will go by that I will stop planning to make her mine. Not a moment that I will not do everything in my power to find her and make her accept me as her true mate. Not a breath that I won't take that will be for the sole purpose of getting her back."

"Then you will not reject the High Luna, and give up your perverse claim upon her?" asked Mercule.

Titan spat on the floor. "Never."

"Then you leave us no choice," said Apollo. "You will be sentenced to death for the crimes you have committed. But before execution, we will give every wolf whom you have harmed a chance to confront you for what you have done to them and to voice their contempt."

Titan's eyebrows drew together.

Ares stood. "Everyone here who lost someone in this ballroom the night of our mating ceremony may take one turn to show and or tell Titan Longtooth what he did to you. However, no one is allowed to make a killing blow."

Alphas, Betas, and more stood and formed a line from the front of the ballroom, almost to the back.

The first to approach was Alpha Elena, her features twisted with grief as she stood before Titan.

"Matthias." Her voice carried through the silent chamber. "My mate of thirty years. Father of my children. The love of my life." Her eyes hardened as she leaned closer to Titan's face. "He died in my arms, choking on his own blood because of you."

Without warning, her hand flashed out, claws extended, opening four parallel gashes across Titan's cheek. Blood welled from the wounds, dripping onto his already stained shirt.

Titan didn't flinch, his one good eye staring at her with cold contempt.

Elena retreated, blood glistening on her fingertips. "May the memory of his name haunt your final moments."

Alpha Ronan came next, his body rigid. "Beta Cassius. My second, my brother in all but blood for twenty years." His voice broke before hardening again. "The most loyal wolf I've ever known."

Ronan's massive fist connected with Titan's jaw with a sickening crack. Teeth and blood sprayed across the floor as Titan's head snapped back, but still, he made no sound beyond a grunt of impact.

"He deserved better than to die for your obsession," Ronan spat before turning away.

One by one, the Alphas, Betas, and others faced Titan, telling him the names of the people he killed, and then proceeding to slash or bite, punch or kick him, for nearly an hour.

Titan lay on the floor, a bloody mess, panting, but defiant until the end.

A female Beta with a fresh scar running across her throat stepped forward, her voice raspy from what must have been a near-fatal injury.

"Emmaline," she whispered, touching the scar. "My twin sister. She pushed me out of the way when your assassin came for me."

She knelt beside Titan's bloodied form and shoved her claws into his shoulder, twisting them deep into muscle. Titan's body jerked, but his face remained impassive despite the fresh blood seeping from the wound.

An Alpha limped forward, leaning heavily on a cane. "Joseth. My son. Eighteen years old." His voice broke. "His first formal event as my heir. He was so excited to see the mating of the future King and High Luna."

The cane came down hard across Titan's back, splintering with the force of the blow. Titan's body arched, a grunt escaping his split lips.

An elderly mate of a former Alpha came forward, her graying hair pulled back in a severe bun. "My Alpha, Tomin. He sheltered me when my pack cast me out forty-five years ago." She spat in Titan's face. "You killed him for no other reason than that he was an Alpha. He never ostracized anyone. Never hurt anyone. Never did anything but help, love, and support any wolf who came to us. And you killed him." She stood over him, shaking, tears flowing from her eyes. "And if he were standing here today, he would be the first to ask for mercy on your behalf. That's the ironic thing. He would try to help you, even now, knowing everything you've done. He would ask for mercy." She swiped the tears from her eyes and took a deep breath. "Problem is, I'm not Tomin. And he's not here to save you."

With the last word, she dug her claws deep into Titan's gut. His body tensed as she twisted her claws deeper inside him. She slashed sideways and flayed him open, before digging her nails in again, tearing muscle.

Finally, Titan cried out. But the woman didn't stop. She twisted several more times, making Titan scream. Sweat broke out across his body, and he began panting.

"The king said no killing," a wolf said behind her.

"This won't kill him. It just makes him wish he were dead. Like the rest of us do."

A younger man walked to her and placed his hand on her shoulder. "Mother, it's enough."

She twisted her wrist. "It will never be enough."

The younger man knelt beside her. "No. It won't. But if you don't stop now, you will never forgive yourself later. Remember what Father always said. 'People deserve justice, but we are defined by the mercy we show them anyway.'"

A sob racked the older woman as her son lifted her to her feet and ushered her away.

A moment passed with Titan on the floor, covered in blood, before he pissed himself. The smell hit River's nose, and her stomach roiled, the room spinning.

She breathed slowly through her mouth, trying to keep from vomiting, fainting, or both.

"Are you all right?" Apollo whispered.

"I… I think I need some soda water," she managed.

"Why don't we take a break?" offered Ares. "We can get everyone something to eat."

"Please," said one of the Alphas. "Let us be done with this."

River's wolf lent her strength. *Need to see. Need to witness.*

Her wolf was right. She was High Luna. She needed to set an example.

"He's right," said River. "Let's finish this."

"Very well," Ares announced. "Let justice continue."

The remaining wolves came forward one by one, each leaving their mark on Titan's increasingly broken body. A Beta from a Southern territory drove his boot into Titan's ribs with such force that several audible cracks echoed through the room. A female whose mate had died in the attack gouged deep furrows across Titan's back, her grief transforming to rage.

With each new wound, Titan's defiance wavered, and his body convulsed. His breathing became labored, each inhale a wet, rattling sound that spoke of internal damage. Still, he refused to beg, his one remaining eye glaring with hatred even as consciousness slipped from him.

The final Alpha approached. Elkan, who had lost five wolves between the attack at the ceremony and the taking of Titan's compound. Without ceremony, he lifted Titan by his hair and delivered a series of brutal punches to his face until blood sprayed across the marble floor. When he finally released him, Titan collapsed in a heap, his body twitching once before going still.

River watched it all, her face a mask of composure despite the storm of emotions raging within her. This was justice, she told herself. Necessary. Yet the sight of such brutal vengeance, even against the wolf who had caused so much suffering, left her hollow.

Ares rose, surveying the bloodied form on the floor and the assembled wolves who stood around him, their faces flushed with both satisfaction and lingering rage.

"It is finished," he declared. "Titan Longtooth has faced the judgment of those he has wronged."

Apollo joined his brother, his posture regal despite the tension visible in his shoulders. "Titan's execution will be at dawn tomorrow. His crimes against the Crown, our mate, and our people demand nothing less than the ultimate punishment."

"Let this serve as a reminder that no wolf, regardless of bloodline or position, stands above our laws."

Apollo's gaze hardened as he addressed the Alphas directly. “Beginning next week, each territory will undergo a thorough audit of pack records and practices. Any Alpha found to have exiled wolves without just cause will be removed from their position and relocated."

Murmurs rippled through the assembly, some indignant, others nervous.

"The only exception," Ares added, "will be if the newly appointed Alpha and the rest of the pack unanimously agree that the former Alpha may remain as a regular pack member."

"This is outrageous." Alpha Larken jumped up. "You cannot-"

"We cannot what?" Apollo roared. "What is it we, the kings of the wolf world, can not do?"

Larken's mouth closed, and he lowered his eyes.

"We can and we will," Apollo continued, his voice like steel. "The days of unchecked Alpha power are over."

The room erupted in protests, several Alphas rising to their feet.

"This is an overreach!" shouted one.

"You can't dictate how we run our packs!" yelled another.

Ares slammed his fist down, cracking the wooden arm of his throne. "ENOUGH!" The word vibrated with power, silencing the room instantly. "This is not a negotiation. This is a royal decree. And this, right here, is why this is happening. How many of you would have dared to challenge our father? Or even speak back to him? In his absence, we have not done enough, and that ends now."

Apollo's eyes flashed. "For too long, we've allowed territories to operate unchecked, and look where it has led us. To rebellion. To death. To innocent wolves cast out, falling prey to those who would use them. No more. We are going back to the way things were before. We, the Kings and our High Luna, will decide justice from now on with the counsel from the elders."

"The White Tail Pack will serve as a transition point for rogues," River added. "But it's a temporary solution to a permanent problem. The real change must come from within each territory. And we are all ready to make sure this kind of thing never happens again."

"Those who oppose this decree," Ares growled, "are welcome to challenge us now or leave our society for good." His eyes swept the room, lingering on each Alpha who had voiced a protest. "Any takers?"

The silence that followed was absolute.

"Good," Apollo said coldly. "Then this is the last time we will ever allow arrogance or challenges by anyone again. We will chalk this up to what everyone is enduring due to the loss of loved ones. But next time one of you dares to call out either of us or our mate, the High Luna, it will be an automatic challenge for the throne. There will be no more warnings. No more asking if you want to challenge. It will be an implied challenge to be answered immediately."

"Council sessions will begin in two weeks. Each Alpha will present its territory records for review. There will be no exceptions," said River. "Prepare your packs as well. Let them know what is coming. If you try to change records or intimidate pack members so they don't talk, or so they lie, we will find out, and the punishment will be swift and final."

Ares looked over the group. "The trial of Titan Longtooth is now concluded."

Duncan and Zeke hauled Titan's broken body from the floor. Despite his injuries, he managed to lift his head one final time, his gaze fixing on River with such hatred that she instinctively reached for Ares and Apollo.

"This isn't over," he rasped as they dragged him toward the door, leaving a trail of blood across the marble floor. "She'll always be mine."

Apollo's growl vibrated through the chamber as he took a step forward.

"He's not worth it," River whispered. "He'll be dead soon anyway."

Her legs wobbled, but she forced herself to remain upright, her wolf strengthening her. Even so, she clutched Ares' hand.

The doors closed behind Titan with a finality that seemed to release something in the room. The tension that had held everyone began to dissipate.

"You are dismissed," Ares announced.

The wolves filed out, many casting glances at the royal family. Some nodded in reluctant acceptance, others held resentment.

When the last of them had exited, River's composure broke. Her legs gave way beneath her, and Apollo caught her.

"I've got you," he murmured, his lips brushing her temple. "It's over."

Ares' broad palm stroked her back as emotions she'd been holding in for hours burst free. Her body shook. The emotional weight of everything- the trial, the revelations, the brutal justice-crashed down on her at once.

"I thought I could handle it," she said between ragged breaths. "I thought I was strong enough."

"You were perfect," Ares assured her, his voice a soothing rumble. "More than perfect."

Apollo lifted her, carrying her to a small antechamber adjacent to the ballroom. He settled on a plush sofa with River in his lap, while Ares knelt before them, taking her hands.

"What you did today," Apollo said, "was incredible. You showed more mercy than anyone expected."

"And more strength," Ares added. "You faced him without flinching. Even when he threatened you again."

River's hands trembled. "He'll never stop. Even in death, he'll haunt me."

"No," Apollo said. "After tomorrow, he'll be nothing but ash and a fading memory. He has no power over you anymore."

The door opened, and Cherry appeared, her eyes immediately finding her daughter. Without a word, she crossed the room.

"You did good," she said. "I'm so proud of you. Of all of you. Not taking shit from any of those Alphas and Betas. Your parents would be proud."

Strider's tall frame darkened the doorway before he joined them. "We'll keep our ears open for rumors in the packs. I know shifters all over. I'll start making calls."

Apollo nodded. "Thank you."

Strider looked at her. "Are you okay, sweetheart?"

River managed a watery smile. "I will be."

Zeke and Bianca slipped in behind Strider. Bianca carried a tray with drinks and soda into the room. She gave a tight smile and walked to a nearby table.

"I thought everyone might need something to drink." She handed a drink to Ares and Apollo and then a glass of bubbly water to River.

"Thanks, B."

Bianca smiled at her.

Zeke stood by the door, his vigilant eyes softening when they landed on River or Bianca. "The building is secure," he reported. "Titan has been moved to the holding cell. Heavily guarded. Everyone else is off the premises."

River sipped the water, soothing some of the agitation in her stomach. She looked around the small gathering, feeling the weight of her exhaustion lift. These were her people- her family. They'd been through hell, yet somehow, they'd all survived.

"I couldn't have done this without every one of you," she said.

Cherry looked at her. "You've always been stronger than you realized. Even when you were little."

"Your mom's right," Strider added. "You faced the devil and didn't blink."

River leaned against Apollo, drawing comfort from his steady heartbeat. "I was terrified the whole time. I kept thinking he'd somehow break free, that he'd-"

"But he didn't," Ares interrupted. "And he never will."

Bianca knelt before River, her features softened with concern. "How are you feeling physically? The babies?"

River grabbed Bianca's hand and moved it to her stomach. "They're okay."

Bianca smiled as a flutter stirred in River's belly.

"They know their mother is a badass," Zeke commented from his position by the door.

"I'm your auntie B-," Bianca said to River's belly. "I'm going to get you the poshest baby clothes and the most expensive toys, and we're gonna play together and watch kid shows and eat junk food, and then you are good and hyper, I'm gonna give you back to your dads to take care of you while your mom and I go have girl time."

Everyone laughed, the sound breaking the last of the tension that gripped them. For a moment, they were just a family sharing a quiet moment of relief and connection.

Ares kissed River's temple. "Our children are going to have the most incredible mother. And the most overprotective uncles, aunts, and grandparents." He chuckled, glancing at Strider and Cherry.

Tears sprang to River's eyes, but this time they were born of gratitude rather than fear or exhaustion. "I love you all so much."

For several minutes, they sat together, sharing stories and memories as the horrors of the day receded. Bianca told a story about Zeke accidentally walking into a women's restroom on their first date. Strider recounted childhood adventures between River and Bianca. Apollo told everyone how Ares had ruined his favorite game out of jealousy. Ares countered that Apollo had stolen his favorite blanket. Everyone laughed as the two bickered about who had hurt who first.

Eventually, Bianca stood, stretching her back. "Well, I think it's time we let you three have some peace. It's been a long day."

"And the days won't be getting any shorter for quite a while," said Ares.

"Thank you," River said, looking at each of them in turn. "For everything."

They departed with warm embraces all around.

"I don't want to go tomorrow," River said. "I don't want to see it."

"You've seen enough, Kitten," said Apollo.

"I'll go," said Cherry.

"I will too," said Strider.

Ares nodded. "We'll meet at five thirty at the front door."

"Where is the execution going to be held?" River asked.

"At the chapel where we met with the council."

River nodded, glad it wouldn't be at the estate.

"Then we will see you before dawn," said Cherry.

Apollo nodded, and then they were alone. Just Ares, Apollo, River, and their unborn children.

They sat quietly for several minutes before Ares said, "Let's get to bed and order some takeout."

Apollo looked at River. "Burgers and fries?"

River was about to say yes when her body said otherwise. "Actually," she replied. "Do you know a good Chinese place? I am dying for some Szechuan beef, and some garlic bread, and fried chicken."

Apollo and Ares looked at each other.

"I don't think there's a Chinese place that has all that, but we can for sure get it all from different places."

River kissed Apollo's cheek. "Thank you. Oh, and a strawberry shake. I haven't had one of those since I was twelve."

Ares snorted and laughed. "I think we'd better have Lachlan get menus from all the places within a twenty-mile radius. At this rate, we will need to know them all by heart by the time the babies arrive."

River smacked him. "You're so funny."

Ares shrugged. "I aim to please."

"Then get my food, and I'll be more than pleased. I might even reward you for being a good boy if you have it here in the next thirty minutes." River winked at him.

"Hey," said Apollo. "What about me?"

River smiled and kissed Apollo. "Who do you think is going to entertain me while I wait for my food?"

Apollo stood with River in his arms and walked toward the door. He stopped as he turned the knob and looked over his shoulder. "Ares, don't feel the need to rush the food."

Ares shook his head. "The hell I won't. She makes the rules, not you. And she told me to have it here before then. And when it comes to our mate, I always do as my Luna tells me."

CHAPTER FORTY-TWO

ARES

The first light of dawn was still an hour away when Ares' eyes opened. Beside him, River slept peacefully, her silver hair spread across her pillow, one hand resting on Apollo's arm and the other on Ares' hip. On her other side, Apollo's golden eyes met his in the darkness.

"Time?" Ares mouthed.

Apollo looked at his phone. “4:35."

Ares had only gotten an hour and a half of sleep. He wondered if Apollo had gotten any at all.

With practiced stealth, Ares slipped from beneath the covers, careful not to disturb River. Apollo followed suit, both of them moving with preternatural grace as they padded silently to the door and out into the hallway.

"Do you think it's time we find a room big enough for all of us?" Apollo asked.

"It would be nice not to have to go all the way down the hall every morning to dress and shower."

Apollo nodded. "We should talk to River about it. We could take the other wing and knock down a couple of walls."

Ares nodded. "Not a bad idea. River's going to want the babies close. We could turn the room at the end into a kids' bedroom and the closer one into a nursery."

"That would leave mom and dad's room, and the room next to it, to merge."

"Definitely would be big enough for the three of us."

They stopped by Apollo's door.

"But we'd still keep our current rooms for our alone time," said Ares.

Apollo snorted. "Yeah, I'd rather not see your naked ass making love to my mate."

Ares faked indignation. "I'll have you know I have a fantastic ass. You'd be privileged to see it."

Apollo smiled and shook his head. "Well, seeing that I know what my ass looks like, I'm pretty sure I know what yours looks like, so I'm good."

Ares chuckled. "See you in ten."

Apollo nodded and headed into his room as Ares walked down the hall to his.

ARES FINISHED TYING HIS TIE AS APOLLO PULLED OPEN HIS BEDROOM door in a tailored black suit, his movements mechanical, his expression distant. The formal attire felt strangely appropriate for what they were about to witness. This wasn't just an execution; it was the final chapter of a nightmare that had nearly destroyed everything they held dear.

"You look like you're headed to your own funeral," Ares whispered, adjusting his brother's tie.

Apollo didn't answer or meet Ares' eye as Ares finished tying the knot.

"Don't worry. I'll handle this."

Apollo's jaw tightened. "I can manage it."

"I know you can," Ares replied. "I've seen you handle it. But this one is mine." He glanced back toward the bedroom where River slept. "After what he did to her... to our children... I need this."

Apollo studied his brother's face for a long moment before nodding. "You're right. You deserve your turn at him. Just save some for me if he somehow survives your wrath."

They shared a grim smile, the understanding between them running deeper than words could express.

The mansion was eerily quiet as they descended the grand staircase, their footsteps muffled by the thick carpet. Outside, the sky remained black, stars glittering coldly overhead as they neared the waiting SUV.

Cherry and Strider stood beside the vehicle. Cherry's hair piled on top of her head, her features hardened with determination. Strider's tall frame was rigid with tension, his russet hair tousled by the pre-dawn breeze.

"You don't need to come," Ares said.

"Yes, we do," Cherry replied, her voice leaving no room for argument. "He hurt my daughter. I want to see justice done. Especially if I can't do it myself."

Strider nodded in agreement. "River's mine too. I need to witness this for her sake."

"Let's go, then."

The twins slid into the back of the SUV while Cherry and Strider mounted their motorcycles.

"You good?" asked Silas.

The twins nodded.

As Theo pulled the vehicle away from the estate, Ares peered out the window at the two bikes that fell into formation behind them, their headlights cutting through the darkness.

THE DRIVE TO THE OLD CHURCH PASSED IN SILENCE, EACH OCCUPANT lost in their thoughts. As they pulled into the underground parking garage, the first hints of dawn began to lighten the eastern sky.

Ares' wolf stirred restlessly beneath his skin, clawing for release. The primal need for vengeance had been building for weeks, intensifying with each passing hour. Now, with Titan's execution mere minutes away, his wolf became nearly uncontrollable.

"You okay?" Apollo asked as they stepped out of the SUV.

Ares rolled his shoulders, trying to ease the tension. "I will be. Soon."

They made their way through the silent church, footsteps echoing off ancient stone walls. The building felt colder than Ares remembered, as if the very structure sensed what was about to occur on its grounds.

Santiago met them at the rear exit, his expression grim. "Everything's ready," he reported. "The Council is waiting."

The group walked into the pre-dawn chill. Behind the church, a small gathering had assembled on a patch of grass that sloped gently toward a line of towering maple trees. The Council members stood in a solemn semicircle, their faces impassive in the dim light.

In the center of the gathering, Titan knelt on the grass, his once-imposing frame broken and battered. Silver chains bound him, the metal hissing against what little blackened skin remained. Zeke, Regan, and Thomas stood guard around him, their faces masks of detachment.

Ares wolf surged forward with such force that he nearly shifted. Only years of iron will kept the beast contained, though his fangs and claws elongated.

Osmodius' jacket billowed in the morning breeze. "Titan Longtooth. You have been found guilty of treason against the Crown, the kidnapping and forced marking of the High Luna, and the deaths of thirty-eight wolves. For these crimes, you have been sentenced to death."

Titan lifted his head, his face a patchwork of bruises and lacerations from the previous day's vengeance. One eye remained swollen shut, but the other burned with defiance.

"Before your sentence is carried out," Osmodius continued, "do you have any final words?"

Titan's gaze swept across the gathering before landing on the twins. "Where is she?" he rasped, blood bubbling at the corner of his mouth. "Where's River?"

Apollo stepped forward, his eyes cold. "She's already forgotten you. She didn't see the point in coming to witness a dead wolf die."

Fury flashed across Titan's battered face. "She will never forget me," he snarled. "Never. You can kill me, but as long as you all live, you will know that she was mine first. She will always be mine."

Cherry made a sound of disgust from where she stood beside Strider. "You can't be that delusional." She shook her head. "My daughter was never yours."

Titan spat on the ground, blood mixed with saliva darkening the grass. He glared at them but said nothing more.

Osmodius turned to the twins, his eyes solemn. "Kings Ares and Apollo Wolvenguard, it is your right to carry out this sentence as you see fit."

Ares stepped forward, his wolf howling for blood. Every instinct in his body demanded Titan's death, every fiber craved the satisfaction of tearing out the throat of the wolf who had dared touch his mate. *His River. His Beloved.*

Without a word, Ares removed his clothing. First his jacket, then his tie, each item handed to Apollo with deliberate calm that belied the storm raging within him. As the cool morning air touched his bare skin, Ares closed his eyes, surrendering to the shift.

Bones cracked and reformed, and fur erupted across his skin. Where he stood as a man moments before, his massive black wolf now towered, blazing with primal fury.

Ares padded forward, circling Titan with predatory grace. His lips pulled back in a silent snarl, exposing gleaming fangs as he assessed his prey.

Tear. Bite. Kill.

Titan watched him, a twisted smile forming on his bloodied lips. "Do it," he taunted. "Show everyone what a monster you are. The savage twin. The one they've always feared."

Ares continued his slow circle, ignoring the provocation. His wolf wanted to savor this moment, to make Titan feel the same fear River felt when she was at his mercy.

"What are you waiting for?" Titan goaded, his voice rising. "Too weak to finish what you started? Just like your pathetic father."

Kill.

Not yet.

Ares didn't allow his wolf to strike. His eyes remained fixed on Titan, watching, waiting.

"You know," Titan continued, his voice dropping to a venomous whisper, "I can still taste her. When River kissed me at your ceremony instead of you. And when she kissed me at our home." He purred and closed his eyes, a smile playing on his lips. "When I bit her that first day... the sweetness of her blood on my tongue. The way she trembled when I touched her-"

The taunt died on his lips as Ares couldn't hold back his wolf a moment longer. He lunged forward with blinding speed. Massive jaws clamped around Titan's throat, fangs sinking deep into flesh and sinew. Titan's scream transformed into a wet gurgle as Ares tore through his windpipe with a savage wrench of his powerful head.

No touch River.

Blood sprayed across the grass in a crimson arc. His wolf held a chunk of flesh and tissue in his jaws for a moment, eyes locked on Titan's dying gaze, before dropping it contemptuously on Titan's face.

Titan's body convulsed, blood pumping from the gaping wound in rhythmic spurts that slowed with each passing second. His remaining eye widened in shock, then glazed over as death claimed him. With a final, shuddering breath, Titan Longtooth slumped forward, his blood soaking the earth beneath him.

Silence fell over the gathering, broken only by the heavy breathing of the massive wolf standing over his kill.

Dead. Finally.

Yes. Finally.

Ares remained motionless for several heartbeats, his eyes fixed on Titan's lifeless form, ensuring that the threat to his mate was eliminated.

Finally, he retreated, his muzzle and torso stained crimson. His wolf sought his brother, something almost like peace settling over him now that the bastard was dead.

Apollo joined his brother, Ares' clothes draped over his arm, his expression a mixture of satisfaction and solemn acceptance. "It's done, Brother." Apollo's hand fell on Ares' shoulder.

Ares' wolf howled in triumph.

He shifted back to human and waited for a pang of guilt. A moment of remorse for what he'd done. But as he stood naked in the growing light of dawn, blood smeared across his body, a weight lifted from his shoulders.

Theo stepped forward and handed Ares a towel. Ares took it and wiped his body down before swigging a bottle of water and spitting on the grass.

Apollo offered Ares his clothes. "It's finally done."

Cherry's eyes fixed on Titan's body. "Good riddance," she said. "Rot in hell, asshole."

Strider nodded, placing a supportive hand on Ares' shoulder. "River can heal now. You all can."

Osmodius approached, his face grave. "The sentence has been carried out according to our laws. May the goddess grant peace to those who suffered at his hands."

As Ares dressed, the Council members moved forward to

prepare Titan's body for cremation. No monument would mark his passing, and no ceremony would honor his memory. By sundown, nothing would remain of Titan Longtooth but ashes.

There was only one last thing to do. "Theo, hire a crew, raze Titan's estate. I want nothing more than dirt on that lot in less than a week."

"Of course," Theo responded.

"Do you have a preference where his ashes go?" asked Osmodius.

Ares paused.

"Down the toilet," Apollo growled.

"No," said Ares. "Hold on to them. River should decide."

Apollo nodded. "Let's go home. River will be waking soon."

Ares agreed. "But let's give it some time before we tell her about the ashes."

Osmodius bowed. "Fair enough."

Ares fastened the last button on his shirt. Despite the stink of blood that still stained his skin, he felt better than he had in weeks. The rage that had consumed him since River's kidnapping had finally been spent, leaving behind a strange sense of calm.

As they walked back toward the parking garage, the first true rays of sunlight crested the horizon, bathing the world in golden light. A new day dawned. The first of many in a world free from Titan's shadow.

Cherry fell into step beside Ares, her eyes studying his face. "You good?"

Ares considered the question before answering. "I will be. We all will be."

"River's going to need you both more than ever now," she said quietly. "The nightmares won't stop just because he's dead."

"We'll be there for her," Apollo assured her. "Every step of the way."

RIVER

River's eyes flew open at six-o-six a.m. Her wolf howled as the red ribbon burned into her leg. River breathed in deep, trying to orient herself, and then as soon as it started, the burning stopped, and the ribbon faded away. River took several deep breaths as all sensation returned to normal. Like the red ribbon connecting her to Titan never existed. River and her wolf both sighed in relief. A sigh so large that it had been as if she'd been holding it in for over four and a half years. A strange sensation raced through her, and it took her a minute to realize what it was: freedom. She was finally free. Which could only mean one thing- Titan was dead.

A sob escaped her, and then another before a laugh. Her emotions mixed together, and she couldn't process them. She was free from Titan. Free and bound only to Ares and Apollo. She didn't have to worry that he was coming for her. Didn't have to worry about him taking her babies. Didn't have to look over her shoulder every time she left the estate. Wouldn't jump in the night when something creaked or groaned. Wouldn't ever have to worry about falling asleep in her home and waking up in the makeshift prison again. Most of all, she didn't have to worry about losing Ares or Apollo to Titan Longtooth ever again.

The door to River's bedroom swung open, and Ares and Apollo entered, their faces somber, their suits immaculate except for the dark stains on Ares' white shirt, throat, and chin partially concealed by his jacket.

"River," Apollo said, concern crossing his face. "You're awake."

She nodded, muting the television. "Are you both okay?"

They approached the bed, one on each side, sitting beside her.

"We should be asking you that." Ares reached for her hand.

River met his gaze. "He's dead. I felt it. The red ribbon that's been binding my wolf to his since he bit me burned away. I woke up the moment it happened."

"Yes," Apollo confirmed softly. "It's done."

River's composure broke in a surge of relief so powerful it overwhelmed her. Even though the bond was gone and it had burned away, hearing them say the words made it real. She threw her arms around both of them, pulling them close. The scent of blood and death clung to Ares, but she didn't flinch. It was over.

"Thank you," she whispered, her voice thick with emotion. "Thank you both for keeping us safe, for ending this nightmare."

Ares' strong arms enveloped her, his lips pressing against her hair. "Always, Beloved."

"But let's be real," said Apollo. "You kept yourself safe. Yes, we would have found you, but we didn't have to because you saved you."

River nodded. She didn't want to give herself any credit for escaping. If she were to credit anyone, it was her wolf. Her wolf had saved them.

Thank you.

Her wolf chuffed. *Thank you.*

For the first time, something passed between River and her wolf. A connection that hadn't been there before. A feeling of oneness. Of being whole.

"Are you both really okay?" She pulled back to search their faces.

"We're fine," Apollo assured her, though his eyes held shadows of what they'd all been through.

River's gaze lingered on the bloodstains on Ares' shirt. She didn't ask about them and didn't need to know the details. All that mattered was that Titan was gone, and her mates had returned to her.

Ares pulled his shirt from his skin. "I should shower," he said, his voice rough.

"I'll go with you." River slid from the bed, not prepared to let either of them out of her sight, especially not Ares.

Apollo smiled, understanding in his eyes. "I'll go get breakfast for all of us. Any requests?"

"Surprise us," River said, already taking Ares' hand and guiding him toward the bathroom.

Apollo caught her other hand, pulling her back for a moment to press a kiss to her lips. "I love you," he murmured against her mouth.

"I love you, too," she whispered back before he released her.

As Apollo left, River led Ares into the spacious bathroom. Steam billowed around them as she turned on the shower, adjusting the temperature before facing him. Without a word, she undressed him.

ARES

River worked at his buttons with care, peeling back the blood-stained fabric to reveal his sculpted abs. Her gentle yet determined touch tugged the jacket from his broad shoulders, letting it fall to the floor. Next came his shirt, each button surrendering to her nimble fingers until she could push it away from his skin.

Ares stood motionless, watching her through hooded eyes as she knelt to remove his shoes and socks, then reached for his belt. The leather slid free with a soft hiss, followed by the metallic click of his zipper. She tugged his pants and underwear down in one fluid motion, helping him step free of them.

Standing before her, completely naked, vulnerable in a way only she could make him feel, River quickly slipped her nightgown down her body, where it pooled at her feet, before she kicked it aside.

Taking his hand, she guided him into the shower, the warm water cascading over them both. Steam enveloped them in a private cocoon as River reached for the soap, working it between her palms until it lathered.

Her hands moved across his skin with deliberate strokes, washing away the remnants of death and vengeance. Ares closed his eyes, surrendering to her touch as she cleansed not just his body but his spirit. Her fingers traced each muscle, each curve, removing all traces of Titan's blood.

Our River. Our mate.

Ares lowered his head, lips finding the sensitive spot where her neck met her shoulder. He kissed a path up to her ear, inhaling her scent as his hands roamed her body. His palms curved around her waist, fingers splaying across her back as he pulled her closer.

"Let me take care of you," River whispered, her hands continuing their cleansing journey down his torso.

The last pink-tinged rivulets swirled down the drain as her soapy hands moved lower, fingers wrapping around him with gentle pressure. Ares groaned against her neck, his body responding instantly.

"River," he breathed, his voice thick with need.

Her eyes met his, golden irises darkened with desire. Without warning, Ares captured her mouth in a fierce kiss, his tongue sweeping past her lips as he backed her against the tile wall. The contrast of temperatures, hot water, cool tile, and burning skin heightened every sensation.

Lifting her effortlessly, Ares pinned her between his body and the wall, her legs wrapping around his waist.

His wolf growled.

He needed her. They both needed her. Needed to feel her, claim her. Wash away Titan's last words from his mind.

Their bodies joined in one powerful thrust, drawing a gasp from River that he swallowed with another hungry kiss.

There was nothing gentle in their need for each other. It was primal, urgent, a life-affirming celebration after facing death. River's arms tightened around his neck as he drove into her again and again, the water beating against his back in a steady rhythm. The world narrowed to just the two of them, to the perfect friction of skin against skin, to the heat building between them.

"Mine," Ares growled against her mouth, the word torn from somewhere deep within him. "My mate."

The image of Titan's final moments flashed through his mind. The feel of flesh yielding beneath his fangs, the hot gush of blood, the light fading from his eyes. He had done that for her, had torn out the throat of the wolf who dared threaten what was his. Who had dared to touch her, to mark her, to claim what could never belong to him.

River's body tightened around him, her back arching as pleasure overtook her. "Ares," she cried, her voice echoing off the tiles. "Oh goddess, Ares!"

The sound of his name on her lips pushed him over the edge. His release crashed through him with staggering force, his body shuddering against hers as he buried his face in her neck, breathing in her scent. His mate, the mother of his children, his everything.

They remained joined, water cascading over them as their breathing gradually slowed. Ares lifted his head to capture her lips in a tender kiss, so different from the desperate hunger of moments before. River's fingers traced across his shoulders and up into his hair.

"I love you," she whispered against his mouth.

"I love you more than life itself," he answered, the words inadequate to express the depth of his feelings.

Eventually, Ares shut off the water and carried River from the shower, her legs still wrapped around his waist. He set her on the counter and reached for a plush towel, drying her.

He worked methodically, patting her skin dry with care. When he reached her belly, rounded with their growing children, he sank to his knees before her and pressed his lips to the taut skin.

"Hello, little ones," he murmured, his voice a deep rumble. "Your father loves you so much already."

River's fingers threaded through his damp hair.

"They're safe now," she said. "We all are. Because of you."

"Yes," he agreed, pressing another kiss to her belly. "They are safe because of all of us. You, Apollo, and I. No one will ever threaten our family again."

He continued drying her, moving down to her legs and then up her torso to her neck. When he reached the spot where Titan's bite had left its mark, now healed to a faint scar, he paused. Without hesitation, he lowered his head and licked the scar. Never again would anyone touch what belonged to him and his brother. Never again would anyone hurt his family.

Ever.

EPILOGUE

Two Months Later

RIVER

"They're being quite squirmy today," said Dr. Keller as she moved the ultrasound wand around River's enormous belly.

"You should feel it from my end," River chuckled.

The sounds of heartbeats floated across the small speaker. Apollo and Ares both squeezed her hands.

"That's them," said Apollo.

"Our little ones." Ares smiled.

"Yup. That's the first one." Dr. Keller moved around the wand, and a little face appeared, sucking their thumb."

Apollo laughed. "That one must be yours."

"Haha. Very funny," said Ares.

"How old were you when you finally stopped sucking your thumb? Twelve? Thirteen?"

Ares reached across River's stomach and punched Apollo in the shoulder. "Shut up. At least I wasn't in diapers until I was four."

"Those were not diapers," said Apollo. "They were underwear."

"Yeah, Apollo and his 'special' underwear."

River shook her head. "Be nice."

The twins mumbled about being nice and just joking before Dr. Keller moved the ultrasound around and settled on another little face, pinched up and sleeping.

"That one is definitely yours," said Ares. "He already has that pissed-off look on his face."

"She," said Dr. Keller.

River's heart quickened. "What?"

Her wolf howled.

"She. As in girl."

"We're having a girl?" River asked.

"Two girls."

Ares looked like he might faint. "Girls. We're having twin girls." His eyes stayed fixed on the screen, and he nodded as if not comprehending.

Apollo kissed River. "Of course we are. Two beautiful daughters just as strong and amazing as their mom."

River smiled at Apollo and then looked at Ares again. He still hadn't spoken.

"Are you okay?"

Ares finally looked at her, his eyes wide.

Her gut twisted. "Are… you not happy?"

"Happy? Of course I'm happy but…"

"But what?" she demanded, nervousness overtaking her.

"Do you know how many males I'm going to have to beat the shit out of to keep them away from my girls? We're going to need more security. More guards. They won't be able to go anywhere. We're gonna have to teach them to fight and be strong and-"

River cupped Ares' face. "Breathe. They will be just fine.

Remember who their grandmother is. You think anyone is going to mess with our girls when their dads are Lycan Alpha kings and their grandmother is Cherry? Trust me, we'll be lucky if any male wants to take on the challenge of being their mates."

Ares searched her face, but she saw his terror. She fought back the urge to laugh as her wolf chuffed. She'd never seen Ares scared before. The thought that he was terrified to have baby girls was almost comical.

"Breathe," said River. "Just breathe. We have a few years before we have to deal with those things, okay? We'll figure it out together, as a family."

Ares nodded but appeared no calmer about the situation.

"You're not going to freak out and be a helicopter dad, are you? Baby bumpers on all the corners, locks on all the cabinets. Plastic thingies on all the outlets. Baby gates on the stairs. Alarms on every door in the estate," Apollo chided.

"You think this is funny?" Ares asked. "What are you gonna do the first time one of our girls is electrocuted because she sticks a fork in an outlet?"

Apollo shook his head. "Pick her up, dust her off. Make sure she's okay and tell her that now she knows what happens when she does that."

"What?" he asked.

"That's what Dad did to me. I lived through it. And he was right. Once I knew what would happen, I didn't do it again."

Ares' mouth fell open.

"Okay, okay," said River. "We can discuss all this later. I'm gonna be late getting up to the cabins. I need to go."

Dr. Keller wiped off River's abdomen, and River hiked up her leggings and pulled down her dress.

She rolled to her side, and Apollo helped her sit up and get to her feet.

He hugged her and kissed the top of her head. "Don't worry. He'll calm down," Apollo whispered.

"I heard that," Ares said.

River smiled and shook her head. Never in her wildest dreams did she think that Ares would be the one to freak out about their kids. If anyone, she thought it would be her.

Dr. Keller moved the medical equipment out of the way, and River walked across their large new bedroom to the door.

"Thank you, Doc," River called.

"See you in a few weeks," Dr. Keller said. "Unless Ares has a panic attack and dies first."

Everyone burst out laughing except Ares.

"Oh, you guys are so funny. I can see I'm going to have to be the responsible one around here, like always."

River turned and winked at Ares. "If that happens, we're all screwed."

Ares' eyes blazed. "When you get back from your errand, we'll see who's screwed."

River wiggled her eyebrows. "I'm gonna hold you to that."

Ares growled.

"Okay, can you not do that until I leave, please?" Dr. Keller asked.

River smiled and turned to leave, but stopped. "Oh, and Ares, the swatches for the nursery color scheme are sitting on the changing table in there. Can you and Apollo please agree on one before I return? The workers are on schedule to complete the remodel this week, and we need to have the carpets and walls finished before they leave. I'm tired of having so many people in the house."

"Will do," said Ares.

River nodded, and Apollo walked her into the hallway and down toward the stairs.

"You're gonna ask me to let him decide the color scheme, aren't you?" Apollo asked.

River smiled up at him. "You see how he's freaking out. My goddess, he's worse than a Bridezilla about the babies. And you and I don't care what the colors are in the nursery as long as it isn't yellow or orange or brown, so let's just let him have this one."

Apollo grumbled. "Fine. But I still get to pick out the baby bedding."

"Absolutely. Just make sure it's hypoallergenic and organic; otherwise, Ares might have an aneurysm."

They both chuckled as they descended the stairs to the front door. Lachlan and Isaac stood by an SUV with a group of wolves waiting inside it for River.

She'd chosen them officially as her bodyguards because she and Lachlan knew each other the best and Isaac was as relaxed as any of the guards would get. Lachlan bowed to them, and Isaac opened the door as Apollo helped her down the front steps.

"Drive carefully," Apollo said to Lachlan. "My most precious cargo is in this vehicle."

Lachlan inclined his head. "Of course, Highness."

Apollo kissed River. "If you have any problems-"

"I won't."

"If you do, remember there's cell signal up there now. Call me if you have a problem."

"Yes, Master."

Apollo's eyes glinted. "I like the sound of that."

River smiled. "I'm sure you do. Don't let it go to your head."

"Too late. Ideas are already percolating."

"I don't doubt it."

Apollo closed the door, and River rolled down the window. "Love you."

Apollo leaned in and kissed her. "Love you too, Kitten."

He looked over her shoulder. "Ladies."

"Your Majesty," the wolves said in unison.

"Take care of my Luna."

"Of course."

"With our lives."

Apollo stepped back from the vehicle, and Isaac and the females climbed inside before Lachlan pulled the SUV away from the estate.

River blew out a breath and looked at her phone. They had a bit of a drive before they reached the cabins. Just enough time for her to take a much-needed nap.

KANE

THE EARLY AFTERNOON SUN BEAT DOWN ON KANE AS HE STOOD outside his cabin, watching the dust trail of an approaching vehicle winding its way up the forest road. He'd been expecting River's visit. She'd called ahead to let him know she was bringing some new additions to the White Tail Pack. But something in her tone had left him uneasy.

Two months had passed since his sentencing; since he'd been given a second chance he didn't deserve. In that time, the rogues had settled into their new homes, transforming the rustic cabins into a functioning community. Kane had thrown himself into his role as Alpha, working tirelessly to prove himself worthy of the trust placed in him.

"Is that them?" Austin appeared at his side. In the weeks since they'd arrived, he'd fallen into the role of his Beta, his cheerful but firm presence a balancing force to Kane's more reserved nature.

Kane nodded. "Looks like it."

The black SUV pulled into the clearing, coming to a stop near the main gathering area. Several rogues emerged from their cabins, curious about the visitors. Word had spread quickly that the High Luna was bringing new members, and excitement hummed through the pack.

Kane approached the vehicle as River's guards exited first, scanning with professional efficiency before one opened her door. River emerged, her silver hair gleaming in the sunlight, her pregnancy now clearly visible beneath her flowing dress.

"Kane," she greeted him with a warm smile. "Thank you for meeting us."

He inclined his head respectfully. "High Luna. Welcome back to the White Tail pack."

She smiled at Austin. “I’m so glad you chose to stay with the pack.”

“They’re good wolves. I can’t imagine going anywhere else.”

The rogues in attendance also bowed to her. But in true River fashion, she waved them off. In the few short months that he'd begun to work with River to help establish the White Tail Pack, he'd come to appreciate her and just how wrong he had been about her when he'd first met her.

River turned toward the SUV, saying something to the occupants inside before facing the gathered rogues. Many rushed forward to greet her, their affection for her evident in their eager faces and the wagging tails of those in wolf form.

"Everyone," River called, her voice carrying across the clearing. "I've brought some new members to join our White Tail Pack."

Kane stepped closer, unable to shake the feeling of foreboding that settled in his gut. "Who are they?" he asked, keeping his voice low enough that only River could hear.

River's eyes met his. "Wolves who, like all of you, deserve better than what they were given. The Alphas who harmed them have all been replaced. With those replacements, it allowed many wolves to get away from their controlling former Alphas, finally."

Kane's wolf stirred restlessly beneath his skin, but he couldn't focus long enough to figure out why. His wolf sniffed the air and whined.

River placed a gentle hand on his arm. "Please, everyone," she addressed the gathered pack, "welcome these newcomers and give them a chance. They're looking to start over, just as all of you were. We looked into every one of them just as we did with all of you, and we believe they belong here, at least for the time being. Besides, this is what we set up the White Tail Pack for. To give rogues a new chance."

Murmurs spread through the crowd, a jumble of excitement and wariness. Kane wasn't sure he liked where this was going, but he nodded. As Alpha, he had to set an example.

River moved to the SUV door and opened it wide. "Come out," she encouraged. "You're safe here."

A tall female with long brown hair slid hesitantly from the vehicle, her eyes scanning the crowd. Before Kane could speak, a gasp came from somewhere behind him, followed by a cry of disbelief.

"Marissa?" One of the women, Lara, who'd been with them since the beginning, pushed through the crowd, her face a mask of shock and joy. "Marissa, is that you?"

The newcomer's eyes widened. "Lara? Oh, my goddess!"

The women collided in a tearful embrace, clinging to each other as if afraid the other might disappear. Sobs wracked both of them as they whispered to each other.

"My sister," Lara managed. "My little sister. I thought I'd never see you again."

Without another word, the reunited sisters walked away, arms wrapped around each other.

Kane's wolf howled in approval.

A second female emerged from the SUV, her red hair catching the sunlight as she scanned the crowd with hopeful eyes. Again, shouts of recognition rang out as three pack members rushed forward, surrounding her with hugs and exclamations of joy.

The scene repeated with a third newcomer and then a fourth, each finding familiar faces among the White Tail Pack. Kane looked on in amazement as family members, friends, and loved ones, once thought lost forever, found each other again.

A fifth female exited, her movements anxious, her eyes downcast. Unlike the others, she didn't immediately find a welcoming face. She stood awkwardly by the vehicle, her hands twisting in front of her.

Then Kane saw him. Darius, one of the quietest members of the pack, a male who rarely spoke and mainly kept to himself, stepped from the crowd. He stared at the newcomer with an intensity that made others back away, creating a path between them.

The female looked up, her eyes finding Darius. A strangled cry escaped her as she began to weep. Darius remained frozen, his body rigid with shock or emotion, Kane couldn't tell which.

Finally, after what seemed an eternity, Darius crossed the space between them. Without a word, he wrapped his arm around the female's shoulders and led her from the gathering, his protective stance saying everything words could not.

Another female hopped out, her eyes immediately finding a male in the crowd. For a heartbeat, they simply stared at each other, the connection between them almost tangible. Then, with a cry of joy, she ran to him, launching herself into his arms. He caught her, spinning her around once before claiming her mouth in a passionate kiss that left little doubt about their relationship.

Kane turned to River, about to comment on the unexpected reunions, when movement from the SUV caught his eye. One last passenger emerged, her form silhouetted against the vehicle's interior.

She didn't move for a moment, and Kane's wolf paced and whined.

River looked back at the woman and smiled, urging her to come forward.

As she walked fully into the light, time slowed, the world narrowing to a single point of focus. Long blonde hair cascaded over slender shoulders. Delicate features arranged in a face he'd memorized years ago. Eyes, the color of a summer sky, now looked directly at him with an expression he couldn't read.

Kane's knees nearly buckled as recognition slammed into him with physical force. His wolf howled, clawing desperately toward the surface as instincts long suppressed roared back to life.

Alyssa. His fated mate. The woman who had rejected him for her pack's approval stood before him now, more beautiful than he remembered, her scent washing over him in waves that threatened to drown him. For an endless moment, neither moved, the years between them stretching like an uncrossable chasm.

"Hello, Kanan," she finally said, her voice exactly as he remembered. Soft, with a slight musical quality that had once been his favorite sound.

Kane opened his mouth, but no words emerged. His mind raced, emotions warring within him- joy, pain, anger, longing, all tangled together in a knot he couldn't unravel.

He turned to River, finding his voice at last. "Alyssa can't stay." The words emerged harsher than he intended.

River's brows drew together. "Why not?"

"She doesn't belong here. This place is for rogues who have nowhere else to go."

“Her family was removed as Alphas, and she left her pack," River countered. "She is now a rogue. She will be welcomed like the others."

Kane wanted to argue, wanted to explain that having Alyssa here would tear open wounds he'd spent over a decade trying to forget he had. But the words wouldn't come. Alyssa deserved sanctuary as much as any of them, but...

Without another word, he turned and strode to his cabin. As he passed the gathered group, they parted for him, bowing their heads as he went. His nails lengthened as his wolf tried to claw his way out to turn around. Every step required a willpower he'd never exuded before.

Finally, as he reached his cabin, the scent of Alyssa's perfume and the sounds of the pack diminished. As the door closed behind him with a soft click, Kane's composure crumbled. His legs gave way, and he sank to his knees, emotions overwhelming him in a tide he could not hold back. His wolf howled in anguish and confusion.

Alyssa. His fated mate had returned.

Kane pressed his fists against his eyes, trying to stem the flood of memories.

Their first meeting after she came of age, and the instant recognition of the mate bond. The weeks of secret meetings before her father discovered them. The ultimatum she'd been given: her pack or Kane. The devastation when she'd chosen her pack. The fight with her father and the resulting scar on his face. The utter abandonment by his family and pack after exile.

A knock at the door jolted him from his thoughts. Kane quickly wiped his face, drawing in a deep breath.

"Kane?" River called. "May I come in?"

He considered refusing, but it would only delay the inevitable. "Of course, your Highness."

He rose and moved quickly to the window, his back to the door.

River entered. "I'm sorry. I should have told you about Alyssa specifically, but she asked me not to."

Kane's shoulders tensed. Yes. She should have. "It wouldn't have changed anything."

"Perhaps not," River agreed, moving beside him. "But you deserved a warning."

Silence stretched between them, comfortable despite the circumstances.

"She asked about you," River finally said. "When she came to us seeking sanctuary. She wanted to know if you were okay. If you had found happiness."

Kane's jaw tightened. "And what did you tell her?"

"The truth. That you were alive, that you were leading this pack, that you were working to build something meaningful here." River paused. "I didn't tell her how you still carry her with you."

Kane turned sharply. "What makes you think I do?"

"Your wolf recognized her instantly. Even before she stepped into the light, I saw it in your eyes."

"It doesn't matter," he said flatly. "Whatever was between us ended years ago."

"Did it?" River challenged. "Fate doesn't make mistakes, Kane. There's a reason she's been brought back into your life."

Kane moved away, pacing the small confines of the cabin. "She made her choice. She chose her pack, her family's approval, over our bond."

River appeared to contemplate for a moment. As if choosing her words carefully. "What we see and what we think we see are often two different realities."

Kane looked at her, unsure of her meaning.

"Circumstances change. Alyssa left her pack as soon as they got a new Alpha. Not because she didn't like the new Alpha, but because she was finally free of her father's control. She deserves a second chance."

"Like the one you gave me?" Kane asked, his voice edged with bitterness.

"Yes. Exactly like that." She paused with her hand on the knob. "Just talk to her, Kane. That's all I'm asking. After that, whatever happens between you is your choice." She gave him a warm smile. "You're doing amazing up here. Everyone looks so happy. My last wish is that you find that same happiness as well."

After River left, Kane remained in the center of his cabin, torn. Part of him wanted to run, to disappear. Another part wanted to find Alyssa and demand answers. To understand why she had come.

A knock interrupted his thoughts. Before he could respond, the door opened, and Alyssa's scent washed over him. Honeysuckle and sunshine, just as he remembered. She stared at him through thick, dark lashes, hands clasped in front of her, blonde hair cascading around her like angel wings.

And in that moment, it didn't matter that she'd rejected him. Didn't matter that he'd been beaten and kicked out. Didn't matter that he'd spent years trying to forget the sound of her voice. The taste of her lips. The smell of hair. His wolf said the two words Kane had spent a decade praying for him to say about another female.

My Mate.

PROMISED AT THE MOON

WOLF RIVER BOOK ONE

Rebekah R. Ganiere

CHAPTER ONE

Natasha raced through the darkened woods south of Wolf River, heart pounding, harsh, icy breaths burning her lungs. The canary-yellow-and-black emergency bag she'd keep under the bed bounced against her spine, weighing her down. The set of keys her mom had shoved at her before pushing her out the basement window cut into her right palm.

"Keep moving." Tate from the Night Shift Relocation Services, commanding voice floated through the Bluetooth. "You're almost there."

Gunshots rang out behind her. Natasha turned. *Father!* A sharp pain pierced her bare foot. She stumbled, grabbing onto the nearest tree, and lifted her foot. A small bead of blood welled on the skin. She swiped at it. Nothing major. She had to keep going.

"You've stopped. Is something wrong?"

"I'm cut," she panted.

She scanned the familiar surroundings, her excellent night vision catching everything. The tall, slender trees looked like giant matchsticks in the dark. What was she doing? She should go to her uncle Jeremiah. Find her cousins and tell them what was happening.

A howl echoed behind her, followed by a second and then a third. *No time.*

"If you want to get to safety, keep moving," Tate urged.

Natasha took off again. The howls increased in sound and proximity. She zigzagged through the sparse foliage so fast she barely saw the individual trees. A branch caught her under the left eye, slicing into her flesh. Tears blurred her vision and stung her cheeks like tiny, wet bees. Her wolf snarled, but she kept moving.

"You're about a hundred yards from the car. Don't stop." Tate's voice buzzed in her ear through the Bluetooth like a voice inside her head.

Move! Her feet ached from trampling over the rocks, sticks and brambles that carpeted the ground like land mines.

She skidded out onto the dirt road, trying to keep her balance. The cool, late-summer wind blew against her bare arms, making them pucker with goose bumps. Her pink cami and gray yoga pants did little to keep out the chill. The scent of damp leaves filled her nostrils.

"Are you still there?" she asked.

"Yes." Tate was little comfort.

"I'm at the road."

"Go fifty yards to the left and you should see the car."

Natasha ran down the dirt access road her parents had cleared but never used. She'd always known her parents had a contingency plan for their escape if something ever happened. Most Blood Born in Wolf River did, due to the recent contentions between packs.

The windows of a dark Honda glinted the closer she got. "There it is!"

Moving quicker than humanly possible, she aimed the key remote at the car and slammed her thumb down on the button. A scent hit her nose, stopping her short. A cry escaped her lips as her heartbeat faltered.

Out of the shadows to her left a large male appeared. An involuntary squeak escaped her lips.

"Are you at the car?" asked Tate.

Natasha's stomach twisted like a wet rope. She sucked air into her lungs, trying to catch her breath. The tall male advanced on her, blocking her means of escape.

"Hello, Nat."

"Daniel." Her pulse thundered in her ears.

"Going somewhere?" He dragged a long nail down the side of the car. She winced at the shrill, grating sound. "I came for you, but you weren't home. You know tonight's the deadline, sweetheart."

"Get to the car," said Tate.

"I already gave you my decision. I won't be your mate."

Daniel sighed. "We've talked about this before. We're meant for each other. The merging of our packs is needed for the good of both. You made a promise."

How did he still not get it? She'd broken it off with him almost six months ago. "That was seven years ago. I was fifteen."

"My parents were mated at sixteen."

"Those were different times."

Natasha moved sideways around the car toward the passenger side, wishing her father were there. Her parents had prepared for this scenario. She couldn't make it all for nothing. As much as it ripped her up inside, she had to keep moving forward.

"Did you kill my parents?" she choked.

Daniel stared at her, and his eye twitched. "They're trying to keep us apart."

She stopped moving. Her rib cage caved in, ready to crush her thundering heartbeat.

"Did you kill them?" she screamed. Her wolf snarled unable to do a thing to help

"I wasn't in the house when the shots went off. I'm sure they'll be just fine if you come with me." He licked his lips, a motion she'd seen him do a million times. She used to find it sexy, until she'd realized it meant he was lying.

Tears burned behind her eyelids and her legs wobbled. Every inch of her wanted to run back and see if they were okay. If they were dead, how would she make it?

He smiled and held his hand out to her. "Come with me, Nat, and no one else needs to get hurt."

She moved around the Honda. *Think!*

He tracked her with precision. His strong, handsome face held a mixture of anger and lust. She inched toward the front of the car and he mimicked her steps with his own.

"I won't go with you." She needed a distraction. She was strong in her own right, but not as strong as Daniel.

"Can you get in the car?" asked Tate.

"You know my uncle Jeremiah will kill you for this." Natasha brushed tears from her eyes. "If you let me go, I won't tell him."

"For being the Alpha of Wolf River I don't see him or your cousins here stepping in."

Stumbling over a mound of dirt, she grabbed the car for support.

"You need to get him away from the car." Tate's flat, clinical voice sounded like a drill sergeant's.

Her gut clenched. He was right. Ever since her father and her uncle had fallen out, she'd only seen her cousins. There would be no one coming to help her. She needed to do it herself. She held the keyless entry tight in her fist. If she pushed the button again, he'd hear.

"Sweetheart, after we're mated, no one will be able to keep us apart." He moved at her fast. She gasped, pressing herself against the passenger door. "Not your parents. Not your uncle. Not even your hotheaded cousins."

His piercing blue eyes held desire. He stepped into her space, making her shiver. His body was so familiar she knew every line.

She'd seen him grow into a handsome, strong male. His musky scent hit her, no longer bringing with it a wave of desire.

He brushed her cheek with his hand, his palm lingering. When she didn't pull away, he leaned his body into hers.

"Get him close and then attack."

Natasha swallowed hard. Her head whirled. She tried to push her hair back, but it clung to her sweat-soaked face and neck. Her heart beat so loudly, it sounded like an echo in the night.

"You feel it, I know you do, Nat. The connection between us is unbreakable. No matter where you go, no matter how long it takes, I'll always find you. You're mine and I'm yours. I have been, since I first laid eyes on you." He cupped her face. "Come back with me," he whispered. His lips dipped down to hers. He lingered, not quite touching. Her body shook as adrenaline pumped through her. He pressed his lips to hers. She breathed in his breath, the taste familiar and wrong.

Her wolf bared her teeth.

A howl sounded in the distance. Daniel lifted his head and answered the call. Striking out with her knee, she caught him in the groin, doubling him over. He roared in pain and she kicked him again in the face, flipping him onto his back.

"I'll never be yours!" She slammed her foot into his gut.

"You bitch!" He gasped and rolled to his side.

"Get in the car!" Tate shouted.

Natasha raced to the driver's side, pushing on the button to unlock the car over and over, making the lights flash and the horn beep. She gripped the cold metal handle and pulled. It didn't open. She pressed the button again and still the door didn't open. Daniel banged on the trunk of the car, trying to steady himself on his feet.

Come on! Come on! What the hell is wrong with this thing?

"You're going to pay for that, Nat!" He spat blood on the ground.

Natasha looked down at the remote. Her finger was on the

damn lock button. She moved her finger to *unlock.* Daniel reached the rear wheel well, his arm outstretched. She pushed the button, and the car lights flickered and the horn beeped again. She threw the door open right as Daniel reached for her. Scrambling inside, she slammed the door, locking it. He yanked on the handle.

His bloodied face peered in the window; lips pulled into a sneer, incisors gleaming in the moonlight. He punched the window with his fist.

"Open the door!"

"Start the car," Tate ordered.

Natasha's hands shook trying to get the key in the ignition. Daniel reared back his fist and connected with the window again. The glass cracked but didn't break.

"Please!" she prayed.

Daniel punched again as the car roared to life. Natasha turned her head just in time. Shards of glass showered her hair and neck. A large, clawed hand grabbed her shoulder, grinding the shards into her flesh.

She put the car in gear and floored the pedal.

Daniel hung on tight, half running, half dragged by the car. His claws dug into her. "Let go!" She struck out, and he grabbed her wrist.

"Never!"

Natasha wrenched the wheel, pushing him with the car. He stumbled and fell. The car bumped up and down. The roars that came from behind confirmed she'd run over him. She whipped her head backward, but everything was obscured in a cloud of red tinged dirt. She should stop and make sure he was okay, but to do so was a life sentence.

She sped down the dirt road, nose running, tears streaking down her cheeks. She blinked and swiped at her face. She had to see where she was going.

"You're about a mile from the highway."

"I think... I think... I think I hurt him bad."

"That no longer matters. You're covered either way. Keep driving."

"My parents... My uncle-"

"You need to get to the highway." His voice had softened. "Head north and keep going. This is the plan your parents had for you. You need to stick to it."

"Aren't you going to stay on the phone?"

"I help people in need. You're currently out of danger. I'll text you an address on your emergency phone. You have cash and a handful of prepaid cards. I'll send you a new ID when you pick a name and get settled. Remember Razor Edge. That's who will meet you in Seattle."

"But-"

"I have to go. I have another caller." His voice held a hint of compassion that had her on the verge of tears. "Oh, and Natasha?"

"Yes?"

"Take the battery out of your phone and throw them both out of the car so you can't be tracked."

Natasha's Bluetooth beeped off. She reached the highway and stopped to glance both ways. The adrenaline tapered off and her limbs shook. She hugged herself tightly and bowed her head. She had to do this. Her parents had raised her to be strong. She threw the Bluetooth onto the seat next to her and grabbed her phone. She fished out the battery and held it out her window. She stared at it for several seconds before setting it back on the passenger seat.

Gulping down a tremendous breath, she gripped the wheel, turned left and headed north.

An hour later, Natasha pulled into a deserted rest stop. She gazed at the cement restroom. Her ragged breath coursed in and out. She stretched to relieve the ache in her back and realized she still wore her backpack. Reaching to remove the pack, she winced when pain shot through her arm. She tilted the rearview mirror at herself. The cut below her eye had already sealed shut but four pieces of glass protruded from her shoulder and collarbone. With trembling fingers, she pried them free. Small cuts covered her chest and neck. Glass blanketed her lap like party confetti and sprinkled her legs. Natasha stepped out onto the cold asphalt, spilling the shards to the ground. The seat, floor mats and every surface of the car were littered with the small fragments.

After removing her backpack, she set it on the ground and then unzipped it. She pulled out her hoodie and threw it over her bloodied cami. Next, she fished out her sneakers and slipped them on. The rest of the bag contained wads of cash, a wallet, and keys to several safety deposit boxes.

She stared at the pieces of colored plastic that now represented the wealth her family had amassed. This was all that she had left. A mournful cry escaped her lips. Never again would she hear her dad call her his *bebe*. Never again would she change at the full moon, her mother on her left and her father out in front, always protecting and keeping watch for danger. Never again would she smell his after-shave or be tickled by his whiskers or watch sappy old Cary Grant movies with her mom or-

She stopped herself, refusing to crumple to the ground and die of a broken heart.

It was possible her parents were still alive. Maybe they'd gotten out of the house.

In the front pocket of her bag were two prepaid cell phones. Her hand trembled as she dialed her father's emergency cell number. It went straight to an automated message, and her hope plummeted.

"Please call me." She sucked in a large breath. "I think I might have killed Daniel. Or at least hurt him pretty bad. I love you. I love Mom." She choked back a sob and blew out a low breath.

She had to keep it together. They would expect her to. "Please call."

She turned off the phone and closed her eyes, setting it against her forehead. She needed to get ahold of herself. Her parents had raised her better. In a werewolf community there was always the threat of violence in one form or another and since her father and Uncle Jeremiah had fallen out her parents' relationship had been strained with the pack.

With the thread that held the peace between the Wolf River pack and Daniel's getting thinner, fights had broken out over territory. Two had almost resulted in death. With the money he and his father had spread around, she didn't know who in her Wolf River she could still trust. Some of the Wolf River pack members had even joined Daniel's father's pack.

She shoved the phone in her bag and pulled down the sleeves of her hoodie. Her bracelet! She searched the ground and the floor of the car. Her palms scratched against the pins of glass as she searched under the seats. There was nothing there. Where was it? Her wolfsbane bracelet was the only thing that kept her from shifting into her wolf form. She'd not shifted in over a month, without her bracelet her wolf would tear through her and get out sometime in the next forty-eight hours- and who knew where Natasha would be when it happened.

Natasha lifted her head and howled into the night. She slapped her hands over her mouth and whirled around to see if anyone had heard. No one knew of their existence, and to show yourself to a human could have dire consequences. To howl in public was reckless at best.

Like the rest of her Blood Born werewolf pack they could change at will but with her parents keeping her locked up for the last two months, due to Daniel's threat, she'd not been able to shift and go running. Bitten shifters were relegated to only changing during the full moon. Sometimes she envied that.

She needed her bracelet. Without it to hold off her dual nature, the shift would be worse than ever, and she didn't know where she was going or where to run or… or… or-

Drained, she gathered her things, picked up her backpack and used it to wipe as much glass as possible from her seat before getting back in. She leaned forward and rested her head on the steering wheel. Giant heaves wracked her body. The wind whipped through the broken window, bringing with it the scent of the public bathroom.

The need to reach out to her cousins Logan, Caleb and Griffin for support all but consumed her. But the dread of not knowing who had betrayed her parents and told Daniel where they'd been hiding, kept her from calling anyone. There was no way Daniel had gotten in without help.

Her pack would be divided by her father's death; between those who had sided with them during his split from her uncle, and those that had sided with her uncle Jeremiah- but no matter whose side people were on, she would be used as a pawn by those wanting a war.

She wiped her face on her sleeve and breathed deeply several times. All she had was the cash in her bag and a shifter named Razor Edge, to get her to safety. Natasha only hoped she could trust him.

Read More Now!
Promised at the Moon
Wolf River - Book One

Dear Reader,
Thank you for taking the time to read *Alpha Queen.* This was challenging to write because I wanted to ensure I captured every aspect the best I could. From the settings to the character voices to everything else in between. I hope you enjoyed River, Apollo, and Ares Wolvenguard's Story as much as I do.

If you enjoyed the book, please take a moment to leave a review on your favorite retailer. Your reviews make all the difference to an author and the success of books.
Feel free to take a moment and email me and let me know what you liked about the book or who your favorite character was and why. I love hearing from readers. It makes writing so much more fun when I hear from my readers.
VampWereZombie@Gmail.com

To find out more about me and my Upcoming Releases, Please Join my Street Team for Swag and Freebies.

I also love connecting with readers! Stalk me everywhere!
I look forward to hearing from you!
Rebekah R. Ganiere - BOOKS WITH A BITE

USA Today Bestselling Author

Rebekah R. Ganiere

Dead Awakenings

Kissed by the Reaper

Fairelle Series

Red the Were Hunter - Book One

Yanti's Choice - Free Fairelle Short Story

Snow the Vampire Slayer - Book Two

Jamen's Yuletide Bride - Book Three

Zelle and the Tower - Book Four

Cinder the Fae - Book Five

Belle and the Beast - Book Six

Gerall's Festivus Bride - Book Seven

Jak the Giant Healer - Book Eight

Olivia and the Giant - Book Nine (April 2026)

Eric's Wayward Bride - Book Ten (Coming Soon)

Wolf River

PROMISED at the Moon

CURSED by the Moon

RECLAIMED from the Moon

TAMED under the Moon

UNLEASHED with the Moon

FATED despite the Moon

FOUND because of the Moon

ROCKED (2027)

The Society Series

Reign of the Vampires

Rise of the Fae

Vengeance of the Demons

Lycan King Wars

Alpha Marked

Alpha Claimed

Alpha Queen

Alpha King (2026)

Alpha Rogue (2026)

Tharnaxian Chronicles

The First

The Many (2027)

The Last (2027)

The Otherworlder Series

Kidnapped at Christmas

Vigilante at Valentine

Massacre at Mardi Gras

Hoodwinked at Halloween

Nightmare at New Year (2026)

Of Gods and Monsters

Thor's Feiry Mate (2026)

Loki's Warrior Mate (2026)

Fenrir Innocent Mate(2026)

Tyr Celestial Mate (2026)

Freya's Eternal Mates (2027)

Nocturne Bloodlines

Queen of the Night (2026)

Protector of the Night (2026)

Son of the Night (2027)

Immortal Monsters

Dracula's Bride

Frankenstein's Bride (Coming Soon)

Happy Holiday Romances

Rekindling Christmas

Christmas Lodge

NEWSLETTER

To claim your Two FREE Books and find out more about Rebekah R. Ganiere and her other Upcoming Releases
You can Go Here:
www.RebekahGaniere.com/Newsletter

www.ingramcontent.com/pod-product-compliance
Lightning Source LLC
LaVergne TN
LVHW041056080826
845145LV00007B/1588

* 9 7 8 1 6 3 3 0 0 0 9 2 6 *